M000011610

THE RADIUS

BOOK 2: LIVING IN THE RADIUS

D.M. MUGA

Edited by CHEREE CASTELLANOS
Art by TRAVIS LUCKHURST
Cover by NICOLE BUDD
Formatted by CARL SINCLAIR

COPYRIGHT

This book is a work of fiction. This book is intended for Mature Audiences Only. It contains graphic violence, vulgar and crude language, sexual content, and scenes of explicit violence and gore. Whereas, there are real places and a great deal of research was put into creating this story into a reality, it is still a fictional story. Unless it is indicated otherwise, all of the characters, names, businesses, places, events, and incidents are fictional. That is to say that they are products of the author's imagination and/or used in a fictitious manner. Whereas, the research completed to create this fictional story is designed to entertain and educate on basic survival skills, any resemblance to actual persons, living or dead, or actual events is purely coincidental. All Rights Are Reserved. No part of this book may be used, reproduced, and/or distributed in any manner whatsoever without written permission from the author.

Printed in the United States of America

© D.M. Muga, 2021

ACKNOWLEDGMENTS

First and foremost, I want to thank you for coming back for Book 2. I'm truly appreciative. As stated previously, writers without readers would make for very saddening stories and a very sorry world... worse than any post-apocalyptic or dystopian future that we could imagine. Again, thank you for taking the time to read my work of fiction. I'm glad that you have returned to the world of the Radius and I hope you enjoy the continuing story.

A special thanks for all of the help, feedback, and guidance to several special folks. Stephanie, Robert, Rick, & Cate... and of course, Lilly Mae. Thanks for being patient with this novice writer, and taking the time to help me continue forth with this series. Thanks to Jeremy for making sure that I didn't overlook anything, once again.

Thank you Cheree Castellanos (https://www.facebook.com/ForLoveBooks4Editing for your guidance and support.

Thank you Travis Luckhurst (@axiomtattoos) for your awesome cover art.

Thanks to Carl Sinclair for your clean formatting skills.

Also, thank you to Nichole Budd for the amazing cover design.

Alright, let's get this story rolling. Cheers and remember to think for yourself. Thank you for continuing on with the next installment in the story of *The Radius Series.*

THE RADIUS

BOOK 2: LIVING IN THE RADIUS

A Post-Apocalyptic Sci-Fi Thriller
By D.M. Muga

1

BENJAMIN REILLY

IT HAD BEEN ALMOST two months since the start of this whole Blue Hole Radius mess and the world that it left for Ben and the others. It had been seven weeks since Ben was at Ontario Airport in sunny Southern California. It had been a normal Friday and he was enjoying his life, feeling fulfilled. Everything had changed at 1301 on May 19th, 2023 when Alexander Mathis, his newfound friend, and his group of SXS Program scientists, over at CalTech (California Institute of Technology), created a micro black hole that resulted in a new type of hole that humanity did not yet know about, a Blue Hole, and the *Blue Hole Radius*.

This *Blue Hole Radius* created what Ben could only describe as a time warp, resulting in everyone within the *Radius* to be trapped for 1,410 years while the rest of the world moved on. The rest of the world moved on to the degree that humanity left for the stars in 3110.

Apparently, their successors left for the stars to avoid extinction from another Pandemic in the year of 3020. The Pandemic of 3020 involved a superbug called MRSA-TB that wiped out 96% of the human race that inhabited Earth One and the Colony on the Moon. Ben always found this part interesting, the aspect of Earth One and a colonized moon, partly because he liked to watch Sci-Fi movies and shows in his spare time. Ben found it ironic that he was now part of a Sci-Fi adventure. Only this time, there's no script and no one knows the ending.

On more than several occasions, Ben found himself asking Alexander questions about Earth Two, always expecting a different answer from his newfound and dear friend. Ben was always disappointed with the same answer from Alexander, "The information that we have from the SuperNet and archives left behind only goes up to the departure of humanity from Earth One."

This part Ben thought to be enormously interesting, but very concerning at the same time. There was a large number of people, to which they had no clue as to how many, that were 1,410 years further into the future than Ben and the rest of the survivors of the *Blue Hole Radius*. That's 1,410 years of technology, advancements, growth, and more of human nature.

Ben knew they were very fortunate to have survived thus far after the *Blue Hole Radius* came down and time was restored to normal transition. Nonetheless, the messages displayed that there was a lot that they did not know about the people from Earth Two, and there was something strange going on, according to Alexander.

On several occasions after they had received the second transmission that had some contradictions to the first one, Alexander expressed major concerns that there may be trouble coming their way. He even went so far as to explain that if it came to blows "it would be like nuclear weapons versus sticks and stones," with the survivors of the *Radius* having the sticks and stones. This concern is on his mind's forefront while he's driving through Crestline.

It's July 6th, 3433 and Ben's driving to the Lake Drive Marketplace, which was once a line of shops, businesses, and restaurants along Lake Drive leading to and around Lake Gregory. He had heard that Lake Arrowhead Village had been transformed into something similar.

He's been back to driving on a regular basis now that his arm and hand are healed well enough, thanks to Eileen, who sat to his right in the passenger seat. She was, and still is, a nurse and had saved his life just under seven weeks ago. Since that time, they had grown very close.

Ben smiles at the beautiful, light-skinned brunette sitting next to him, with those bright green eyes. It had been seven weeks since they had met at the start of all of this *Blue Hole Radius* madness. Sure... she had tried to kill him when they first met. But could he blame her? No. She had just lost her father to some greedy P.O.S.'s, and two of her friends to rapists P.O.S.'s. He could not blame her in the least.

He had found her, or she had found him, on his drive up to the mountain town of Crestline with his newfound friend, Alexander. Alexander and Ben were en route to stay with his Uncle Steven. It was Ben's best option, and only really viable one, since it was high ground and Uncle Steven was the only family that he had left.

Thinking about this sad reality still pained Ben. He had lost his mom and dad, as well as his brother, his wife, and their children. Ben found some solace in the fact that they moved on after the *Blue Hole Radius* incident. It had taken some time, but they had moved on to lead full lives. He was able to find out what happened to his family thanks to the massive amount of archives on the SuperNet.

Ben was pretty excited to find out that his family line lasted through the conflicts and problems that faced the world after they were trapped in the *Blue Hole Radius*. Unfortunately, after further digging, he found out that the descendants of his brother, his family, had died out during the Pandemic of 3020.

Regardless of never knowing these family members, he felt for them and hoped their end was swift and painless. He knew the evidence of the MSRA-TB virus said to the contrary, but he chose to ignore that fact and push those thoughts out of his mind.

He also always ended up rationalizing the situation of the people from the past, from his future, up until what was left, and those that left for the stars and Earth Two.

It is what it is. Tended to be the end of his line of thoughts on this path of thinking.

Everyone outside of the *Radius* was long gone, after 1,410 years passing the world by, passing them by. So many survivors within the

Blue Hole Radius had lost friends and families that were outside of the *Radius* at 1301 on May 19th, 2023. Hell, many of those people lost their family and loved ones in much more horrific ways than he. The way he saw it, he had little room to complain.

While navigating the neighborhood roads toward Lake Drive Marketplace, Ben reflects on the last seven weeks and how much the world has changed.

He keeps on returning to the messages that his Uncle's old HAM radio had received, which his Uncle referred to as Ol' Betsy. In truth, it was a main point of conversation in the cabin that the four of them now lived in, Ben, Eileen, Uncle Steven, and Alexander, to which his gracious Uncle offered without a second thought.

Ben could recite both messages word for word. In all actuality, all four of them could recite the messages word for word. Before the first message had stopped, Alexander had the foresight to write it down. The second message comes on daily at the same time.

As Ben and Eileen get closer to the Lake Drive Marketplace, he dwells on those two messages, knowing they mean something important and that there's nothing they can do about it for the time being.

::Transmission Sent from Earth Two, May 37 of 3433:: This is Commander Thomas Yang of the Icarus. Harris's Blue Hole Radius outcome was the reset button for Earth One. Those that have survived the *Blue Hole's Radius* are likely aware that your Earth is very different now, and it is.

By our calculations, you should be awake by now. If you come into contact with a deactivated *Sleeper*, do not activate it. I repeat, DO NOT activate it. Leave it where it lies, and we shall dispose of it when the time comes.

It is our hope that you are utilizing the additional technology and information that we provided to alleviate any strain that you are experiencing during this transition. Your starting population of the *Blue Hole Radius* was 8,916,237 people, and a great deal of other living creatures, both on land and in the sea. Probability and logic proposes that the best-case scenario is that roughly half of that number will survive the first few months until winter.

The Icarus, with life-sustaining and disaster relief crews, will be in Earth One's orbit within two to three months. I apologize that we cannot be there sooner. Current situations on Earth Two dictate that the earliest that we can arrive to aid and assist you will be between two and three months, on Earth One's time.

Make logical and good choices and prepare for the winter and worse. Do not make the same mistakes our ancestors did. Rely on each other and utilize virtue ethics. Commander Yang of the Icarus, Out. ::Message Received on Earth One, May 20 of 3433::

The same questions continue to come to mind whenever he thought of the first transmission from Earth Two.

What the crap is Earth Two? What have they been doing all this time? Who's Commander Yang? What the crap is a Sleeper? What does he mean about preparing for the winter and worse? What do they know that we don't yet?

There were two questions they were able to answer, with the help of the SuperNet and Alexander's research. In regards to the winter problem, the climate had shifted over roughly 1,100 years, up to the point that their successors left for Earth Two. The six satellites that were still above Earth and in orbital rotation told the story of the following 300 some odd plus years.

Alexander always made it a point to draw attention to the fact that there were ten satellites when they had left for Earth Two, and we only needed two to have the SuperNet running for our technology to work. Alexander often reminded them that they had about 300 more years for people on Earth One to be concerned with how many satellites were left. It was his hope, all of theirs, that they would have a lot more figured out by then and their future generations would not have to struggle as much as they have had to, with the survivors of the *Radius* re-establishing society and pushing past all of this anarchy.

Unfortunately, Commander Yang was accurate to warn them of

the upcoming winters. It would appear that Earth One was cycling back to another small Ice Age. As Ben had understood it from how Alexander explained it to him, several times, the Earth had gone through several Large Ice Ages and many Small Ice Ages, also called Glacials. In fact, when the survivors of the *Radius* were originally trapped, the world was still coming out of a Large Ice Age, hence the large polar ice caps.

Despite the fact that Glacials are a normal occurrence on the Earth, the combination of a Small Ice Age and lack of human beings to slow down the process of global cooling over the last 300 years, their winter was about to become starkly cold.

In fact, according to Alexander's research, winter would not only be much more frigid, but also a great deal longer than in 2023. Alexander was surprised that winter would be in full swing by October and last until March.

This was one of the main reasons Ben wanted to go to the Lake Drive Marketplace this weekend. There was a great deal more of trading and bartering going on over the weekends, compared to the weekdays. And Ben saw it necessary to begin preparing for the winter months, now rather than later.

Gone were the days where Ben hesitated on preparing for a certain situation because it might happen and he didn't want to look like a full-blown prepper. To the contrary, his paranoia and prepared-ness helped keep him and his friends alive. That and his Uncle, Alexander, and Eileen saving his ass.

Ben was certainly concerned about this new shift in their worldly climate and thought back to the days of people worrying about global warming. Ben thought it to be ironic, how humanity was so wrong on that accord, but also, so very right, but in a different sense.

The second question that Alexander was able to partly answer was that of the *Sleepers*. Most of the information about the specificity of the *Sleepers* were scrubbed from the SuperNet. Ben wasn't sure if this was some form of control from their successors over their history. However, Alexander explained that there was still some history there... and whatever the *Sleepers* were, they killed indiscriminately.

Alexander found articles and many pictures of the dead left from the *Sleepers*. In short, what they did know was terrifying. Anything with a heartbeat would die if a Sleeper was activated. They still were not sure what *activates* meant, that information was expunged from the SuperNet. There was also no video footage of the *Sleepers* in action, only pictures after the fact. That information was erased from the archives, along with how to create *Sleepers*.

When they first found this out, Alexander had pointed out that it was likely so that we don't hurt ourselves with this technology. Ben remembers countering with his perspective, "Sure, they may not want us to hurt ourselves. But I guarantee that they sure as hell don't want us to be able to hurt them."

That last thought continued to circle back to Ben's brain, time and time again. *Why are they returning and what do they want from us?*

Which always shifted his focus to the second message they had received, only a couple days after the first. Whereas, the first message proposed so many questions, it was the second message that truly had Ben and the other survivors concerned.

::Transmission Sent from Earth Two, June 1 of 3433:: This is Captain Abraham Jackson of the Leviathan.

We are en route with surveying and risk analysis teams. Earth One will be within range for two-way communication within two months, which is roughly 60 days, on Earth One's calendar.

As the previous message stated, if you come into contact with any deactivated *Sleepers*, do not activate it. Leave the devices alone and we will handle them upon our arrival.

My apologies if Commander Yang thoroughly scared the people of Earth One. The Leviathan is en route to alleviate the pain and suffering that you are dealing with.

I will send another message in two months' time with our designated landing zone, and further instructions and orders.

This message will repeat again, shortly. Thank you for your cooperation in advance.

Captain Jackson, of the Leviathan, Out. ::Message Received on Earth One, May 21 of 3433::

To Ben and the other survivors in the mountain communities, the second message seemed to hold a grueling warning to their way of life. The directness of the message, lack of compassion, and any true words of hope, displayed a rigid feeling of the authoritarian variety.

Ben understood that people were naturally scared of change and anything new is usually met with fear and overreaction. Nonetheless, he thought this situation to be different. Despite the instance that there were no real threats in the second transmission, it still seemed threatening. Ben's thoughts over the last seven weeks and their path ahead were cut off by Eileen.

She points out the window. "There's a parking spot open right there, Ben."

Ben looks over at the beautiful woman sitting next to him in his black Dodge 2500 truck, with her bright green eyes.

Well, I suppose it most certainly could be worse. He thinks to himself as he looks Eileen over on this warm day in July.

He pulls into the spot between Lake Drive ACE Hardware and Lake Drive Camping, Fishing, & Hunting.

"Perfect. Nice parking spot find, Eileen. Everything we need, right next to each other."

Eileen opens up her door and hops down. "Did you expect anything less than perfection from me, Benjamin?" She smiles at him, winks, and slams the door shut, walking to the front of the ACE Hardware store.

Ben laughs at her as he exits the truck, grabbing the pack from the back-cab and slinging it over his shoulder. "A little high and mighty, aren't we today." he walks around the truck and meets her in front of the storefronts.

She smiles at him. "I'm not sure if it's the sunny weather returning to us after a week of straight rain, or maybe it's reminiscing on saving your butt at the MS13 battle."

He grins at her, looking her up and down. It was warmer than it had been outside. Mostly due to the constant rain for the last week. She stood next to him in hiking boots, jeans, a black t-shirt, one of his, with her M&P Shield on her right hip. Ben could not help but be thankful for what he had gained since the *Radius*, despite the adversities they had faced and will likely have to face soon.

"You're not going to let me live that down, are you?" He replies.

She looks to the storefronts, "Not a chance in hell, good looking. It's my hope that if I keep bringing it up... you won't be so reckless next time."

Next time... So, she feels it too. Like there's something coming, something big that we have to face again.

Ben scratches the back of his head and grins. "You may have a point there. Look at you, still looking out for me."

He chuckles at his own joke and she gives him a look. He adverts his stare to his right, toward the post office.

"Looks like they caught another one stealing or something else that chops up to a petty crime." Ben points toward the parking lot of the post office, to the young man in a set of stockades that was set up with two other sets in the post office parking lot.

Eileen shakes her head. "What an idiot... I'm sure whatever it was that he wanted, he could have asked someone and they would have helped him out."

Ben's still looking at the young man in the middle set of stockades, remembering when they were put up about three weeks ago. He recalls the first guy having to be chained to the flagpole for a full 24 hours. The next day, Sheriff Patterson had three sets of stockades cemented into the parking lot of the local post office. He had given a big speech about it and told those around to pass on the word.

The big man had bellowed his voice, but he had sounded pained at having to resort to such laws. *"We don't have the time, man-power, or room to be housing people that break the laws. Therefore, punishments will change, effective immediately. Small crimes will be met with the stockades. Serious crimes will be met with a bullet. And before you all ask... murder, rape, and mayhem are serious crimes in my book. In short, if you play stupid games, you'll win stupid prizes."*

Eileen brings him out of his memory. "I get why we have to do these things, especially after what happened just before the rain started... But it just seems so barbaric, don't you think?" She asks him.

He looks over at her. "Yeah, that was a real shitshow, with those teenagers and that poor girl and her mother."

He pauses thinking about the two young men, no older than 19 years old, that saw it fit to rape a young girl, who Ben had found out was 14. The poor girl's mom came in during the rancid act, distracting the boys and allowing the young girl to escape. In haste and fear of being caught, the young men killed the mother with a gun they had brought with them. The young girl made her way to a neighbor's house and the boys were cornered back in her house. One was killed in the confrontation and the other one gave up, only to be swiftly executed by Sheriff Patterson. Ben had heard the story from Todd, who was his childhood friend and a Deputy as well.

Eileen continues. "No, yeah... I get it, with those monsters. But that poor guy looks like he has been there since yesterday."

Ben's still staring at her, thinking of Todd and how he had lost his twin brother, Jim, during the MS13 Battle.

"Earth to Ben. Correction, Earth One to Ben!" She blurts out at him, and he snaps out of his own mind.

He chuckles at her joke. "Yeah, sorry about that. I was thinking about Todd and Jim."

She pauses and sighs heavily. "Yeah. I was talking to his wife the other day on the phone. Jamie says that he's distant but seems like he's getting better. He goes and visits Amanda and Jim's daughter a lot. To check in on them."

Ben nods. "That's good of him. I haven't talked to him much in the last couple of weeks."

Ben looks over at the young man in stockades. "I get it's barbaric, but what are our other options? Apparently, people have thought twice before rape and murder since those two dipshits. We have had multiple people in stockades... what like seven? But they'll get the hint, eventually."

He looks back at her and she replies. "Yeah, I suppose you're right... this time."

Ben smiles back at her.

"Alright!" She blurts out. "Enough doom and gloom on this very nice and warm day!" She claps her hands together. "Hardware store or camping store first?"

Ben shrugs. "You're call, beautiful. I'll follow you anywhere." He says the last part with a prominent hint of sarcasm.

She gives him a stern look. "With that kind of rude attitude, you may just get cut off, Benjamin."

Ben puts his hands up and smiles. "What?! I was being sincere."

She grins. "Uh huh..." She looks at the camping store. "Let's go in there first. I really need some clothes that are my own."

"So, you're saying you don't like wearing my shirts and re-wearing your only two pairs of jeans that you have up here?" Ben says to her.

"You're pushing it Ben. I'm warning you... cut off." She faces him and crosses her arms over her chest.

He can't help but laugh at her. "Alright then. Let's go shopping. And find you something pretty to wear."

She laughs at him. "You're such an ass sometimes... I swear."

He laughs at her and shrugs.

Eileen shakes her head and they wander into the camping store on Lake Drive Marketplace.

Entering the store, they are greeted by a man with a revolver on his hip. Ben didn't even think twice when seeing that the man carried. He was likely the owner and everyone was armed these days. Gone were the days when people concealed their weapons or thought that guns were not needed.

The man waves at them as they cross the threshold from halfway through the store. "Good morning! Welcome to The Camping Store. Name's Dave Stine. You all let me know if you need any help!"

"Good morning!" Ben replies. "My name's Ben Reilly, and this here is Ms. Eileen Rivera... We have silver, ammunition, and gold to trade with. Is that sufficient?"

Dave Stine replies. "Yes, sir. That will be good by me. Nice to meet the both of you!"

Ben nods to the man and Eileen asks, "Which area has the women's clothing, Mr. Stine?"

Dave Stine nods. He points off to his left. "That area over there should have a good selection for you, miss."

"Thank you." She replies and turns to Ben. "I'll be over there. You go grab that cold weather stuff you wanted to grab for you and the guys. I'll grab some extra clothes. What's our budget?"

Ben points his thumb to the pack on his back. "With how heavy this thing is, I'm not too worried about it. Grab what you need, Eileen. You sure you don't want me to come over there with you?"

She gives him a smile. "Ben, it's literally thirty feet away and you can see me. I think I'll be fine... Plus, shouldn't I be the one to come with you, to make sure you're alright?"

Ben chuckles. "Hey, just trying to be gentlemanlike."

She leans in close to him, kissing him on the lips quickly, but firmly. "I know you were. We're in line of sight, so we should be good. I'll be quick though." She backs away and heads in the direction of the women's clothing.

Ben watches her go, and then heads over to the men's section.

He looks through the shelves and racks for five or ten minutes, deciding on what exactly he should get. He finds three cold weather jackets, six pairs of cold weather socks, four beanies, four sets of snow gloves, and four face shields.

He's wandering over toward Eileen, looking through the shelves and racks along the way. He passes by a shelf of snow pants and pauses.

They would be useful. I mean, once denim's wet... it stays wet, and cold.

Already having a pile stacked on top of his arms, he tries to grab some of the snow pants and ends up dropping everything. He hears Eileen laughing from behind him, right behind him.

"I knew I should have come with you. Why didn't you grab a basket?" Eileen asks, still chuckling.

Ben looks down at her basket in her left hand. She had found a snow jacket, some gloves, a couple pairs of jeans, several shirts, and even some snow pants.

Ben scratched the back of his head. "Didn't think about it, I guess."

She shakes her head and walks off toward the front of the store, returning with another shopping basket. "Here. Put the smaller items in here... so you aren't dropping everything constantly."

Ben starts doing as she says, holding the larger items over his other arm. "What would I do without you, Eileen?"

She grins at him. "Oh, you know... probably just fail at life in general."

She laughs lightly, and then looks over her basket. "I'm good, if you are."

He smiles at her. "Yeah, I think for now. If there's more we need, we can come back another day."

She nods and they head to the counter at the center of the store where Dave Stine's waiting for them. He sees what's in their baskets. "You two do know that summer's just around the corner, right?"

Ben nods. "Yes, sir. Does that cut us any kind of deals, since its off-season?"

The man looks him over. "Depends on what the offer is?"

Ben nods. "Looking at what we have here, I'm guessing we have close to 10 Gold $5 American Eagle coins worth here. I have that many on me, at 1/10 ounce each."

The man behind the counter whistles. "Well! With that kind of offer and considering the season and all... I'll throw in a few of my winter sleeping bags."

Ben replies, "Would four of them be asking too much, Mr. Stine?"

The man extends his hand. "It's a deal, good sir!"

Ben shakes the man's hand. "Alright, let me bag that up for you. Then I'll grab the sleeping bags from in the back."

Eileen and Ben hand over the clothing and Eileen looks over at him with a questioning look.

As he takes his pack off his shoulder and pulls out a small cloth pouch. He then pulls out a tube of coins. He opens it and counts out 10 Gold American Eagle Coins, then places the small coins, each in their own protective plastic case, into her hands.

"Each one of these is a tenth of an ounce of gold. Depending on the market, they are worth anywhere from $140 to $260, each... and that's when the market was around." Ben explains.

"Well then... are we getting the bad side of this deal?" Eileen questions.

Ben shakes his head pointing to their baskets. "Although the stuff that we want is out of season, it's expensive. Ten of these for all of this and cold weather sleeping bags is a good deal, for sure... Especially if it makes the difference of us freezing to death this winter or not."

Eileen looks at the coins in her hand and then at Ben. "Hmmm, that's pretty darn useful of you Ben. Freezing to death does not sound like very much fun."

Ben smiles and shrugs. "Eh, I do what I can."

Eileen looks at his pack. "But you said it was heavy. That small tube of coins doesn't seem too heavy."

Ben grins at her. "We have more... and the silver is heavier than the smaller gold coins, and they look like the actual coins you are used to. Plus, ammo is much heavier. I'd just rather not trade ammo if I don't have to. Gold and silver we can find more of in the years to come. We can melt it down and measure it out. But one of the things I never got around to learning was how to reload and make my own ammunition."

Eileen replies. "Well... maybe, we'll just have to learn.'

Ben nods. "Yeah. We could. But I hear it's best to learn from those that already know. Coming across someone like that, in times like this... may prove difficult."

"You Uncle doesn't know that sort of thing? He seems like the type." Eileen asks.

"No, yeah. He does seem like the type. But he doesn't either. He said he always steered clear of it after hearing some horror stories of some yahoos injuring themselves pretty badly."

Eileen nods. "Yeah, that makes sense, with gun powder and all."

Ben responds. "Right! That kind of put me off on it, too. Not going to lie."

Dave Stine returns with their sleeping bags and his eyes go to Eileen's hands with the coins. Eileen catches on, and hands them over to the owner of the camping store. "Here you are, Mr. Stine."

The man takes them gratefully. "Pleasure doing business with the two of you. I look forward to seeing you in the future."

Ben nods. "I'm sure we'll be back. Have a good one!"

Ben and Eileen acquire their new belongings and head out of the store and to the truck to drop off their cold weather gear and Eileen's extra sets of clothes. After they're done, Eileen turns to Ben.

"So, what else do we need?" She asks him. "Oh, and thanks for getting me something pretty. Aren't you just the sweetest..." She says this last part with a hint of sarcasm and a smile.

He chuckles. "Least I can do for my guardian angel."

She smiles and Ben stares at her in the midday sunlight, with her light-skinned complexion, brunette hair, and bright green eyes.

"What are you staring at, mister?" Eileen asks, squinting her eyes.

"You." Ben responds and watches her blush.

"Alright McDreamy... What else do we need? I was thinking we could stop by Todd and Jamie's place on the way back home."

Ben nods. "Sounds like a fine idea. We just need some lumber, nails, some Gorilla Tape, and few extra propane tanks would be good too. That and swing by a butcher on the way back for some more meat."

"What's the wood and tape for?" Eileen asks.

"For the windows, if it comes to that. We may need to board and tape them up." Ben replies.

This gets a look from Eileen, and Ben adds, "It's just in case. I'd rather have the supplies to fortify and not need them, then need and not have them.

She eyes him. "I guess so... You are the crazy prepper guy." She grins at him.

"Hey!" Ben tries to look hurt. "This crazy prepper guy has got us this far, hasn't he?... and I'm not even a full-blown prepper."

She responds, "Uh huh. Whatever you say Benjamin." She laughs at him as they go into the ACE Hardware Store and spend the rest of their morning shopping at the Lake Drive Marketplace.

2

ALEXANDER MATHIS

IT WAS SATURDAY, July 6th, 3433, and Alexander was sitting shotgun in Steven Reilly's Chevy Blazer, driving along the 18 Highway heading east toward Lake Arrowhead Village. It had been roughly seven weeks since the onset of the *Blue Hole Radius*, which Alexander had a hand in creating. Seven long weeks since he lost his family and everyone else that he had known. 1,410 years had passed by, along with those years, his family had lived on and eventually passed away.

While Steven Reilly is driving the old highway that overlooks the valley, Alexander remembers what he found out about his family that he had left behind.

Alexander had put off looking up his wife and daughters on the SuperNet as long as he could. The second message from Earth Two was an excellent distractor in the first couple of weeks. Nonetheless, around the middle of June, Alexander could not hold back his curiosity and sense of guilt any longer.

Steven, Eileen, and Alexander took turns standing watch at night ever since the MS13 Battle. Whereas, it had been relatively quiet since the MS13 Battle, the small group was not taking any chances with the security of the future. Alexander still had dreams and nightmares of that night's events.

During one of his nightly watches, Alexander searched up his wife on the SuperNet, Michelle Mathis, on his iPhone and in the cold dark night. He was able to find out some information, but she dropped off of the SuperNet and social media by the middle of 2024.

After frantically worrying if something horrible had happened to his wife and two daughters, Aliyah and Sydney, the thought occurred to him to use her maiden name. Having searched up Michelle Wyatt, he was able to regain access to her life and what had occurred to his family 1,410 years ago.

Alexander still feels guilt and a sting of pain upon remembering her changing her name back to her maiden name.

She must have done so to avoid attention and blame through association. I'm quite positive that the media spin on the Blue Hole Radius was far from positive. It must have been incredibly difficult on you and the girls, Michelle. I'm so very sorry.

He delved deeper into the archives to find out about his family. Michelle had changed her name and the names of the girls. She moved the girls back to her home state of Illinois. She did go back to work as a nurse at a local hospital and seemed to be back on track by the end of 2024.

From what he gathered on social media references and everything on the SuperNet, she never remarried and as far as he could tell, never dated either. She seemed to be completely devoted to their children, it was apparent through social media posts from her, the girls, and Michelle's parents. Every now and again, he saw pictures of his parents with the girls. He was saddened to find out that his parents passed away in a car accident in 2032. Whereas, they lived long lives, both of them in their late sixties, it still seemed too soon for them.

That same year, Aliyah, having been 22 years old at the time, had just graduated college and was getting very close to her dream of becoming a nurse, like her mother. Also, during that same year,

Sydney had graduated from High School and enlisted in the United States Air Force. Alexander recalls being taken aback by that choice of Sydney's, recalling how much that she wanted to be a scientist when he left her, when she was nine years old.

After further searching into his family's progress through life without him, in the cold night air of the mountains, Alexander was grief stricken to find out his wife had passed away in 2036 of cancer. It had been caught too late and she had a deteriorating and rough last six months of her life.

Alexander was overcome with anguish, having to put away his iPhone for the rest of that night, with the thoughts of his beloved wife passing away after he had abandoned her.

He had the feeling of being alone in a great abyss, looking out into the darkness of the San Bernardino County Mountains. The world was so quiet now and he was utterly alone, and by his own doing.

She must have felt so helpless and so alone. I'm so very sorry Michelle. You deserved so much more than that.

It was not until his next nights' watch shift that he had built up the courage to continue his research about his daughters. He had already lost his parents to a car accident and his wife to cancer. Alexander was not sure if he could handle any more tragic ends, especially to his darling little Aliyah and Sydney. Alexander came to find out that they were not young anymore, as he continued his research.

By the time of his wife's passing, Aliyah was married and had two kids of her own, a son and daughter. Alexander found himself happy at the thought that he had grandchildren, despite the fact that he would never see Trent and Leah. Regardless, Alexander found it comforting that Aliyah thrived, aside from the adversities that she had been forced to face in her life. With the predominant obstacle for her and many others when a war that broke out that was referred to as the Rh Factor War.

Nonetheless, she turned out to be a lifelong nurse. She had a lifetime marriage to her husband, Daniel, passing before her husband at the old age of 84 years old. Whereas, Alexander was sad about her passing, she truly seemed to have had a great life. Her life was very well-rounded, and Alexander's grandchildren had gone on to do great things and were successful people, leading their own lives and raising their own families.

After he noticed a few social media posts from Aliyah with Sydney in the pictures as an adult, he shifted to research on his youngest daughter. She was slightly more difficult to research. She had not gotten on to social media throughout her entire adult life. However, he did find remnants of her through her sister's digital footprints on the SuperNet.

He knew that she had joined the Air Force, but it took some digging to find more. It had taken Alexander the rest of his night watch and most of the next day trying to find out more information about his youngest daughter, Sydney Wyatt.

Toward the later afternoon hours, he finally stumbled upon an article about his daughter, *Major Sydney Wyatt of the Space Corps of Engineers: Daughter of Alexander Mathis of the SXS Project and the creators of the Blue Hole Radius.*

The article was written in 2054. Alexander did the quick math, concluding that his Sydney had been 40 years old when the article was written, making her only a few years younger than he was now. Alexander could barely contain his shock and amazement over what the article explained about his very secretive daughter. Sydney did join the Air Force out of high school. However, after her first enlistment, she was accepted and enlisted to an officer program for a new division of the Air Force, known as the Space Force. After graduating from college with a degree in mechanical engineering, and finishing Basic Officer Training, she was assigned to the Space Corps of Engineers by the age of 27. Over the next fifteen years, she rose in her field and contributed to the foundation and groundwork that catapulted the United States ahead of the rest of the world. By the time of the article, she was a Major in the Space Force, and leading the Space Corps of Engineers aboard the U.S. Orbital Space Force Military Installation Station (OSFMIS).

After finding out why he had so much difficulty finding her on social media, he dug into military records of his daughter. Alexander could not help but feel pride with his youngest daughter. She may not have turned into a scientist, but she was an astronaut and a very important person. He found multiple records on her various awards over the years.

After retiring from the Space Force, several years after the article was written, she moved back to Illinois and lived a quiet life. Alexander found himself saddened to not find any record of her marrying or having children. He did find her death certificate from 2077, when she had passed away due to cancer. She had survived the Rh Factor War of her time, and ended up dying of cancer some years afterward. It was the same cancer that had taken her mother almost five decades previously.

Alexander found himself scrolling through Aliyah's social media until he found several posts talking about how her sister had passed. The sisters had been talking but weren't necessarily close.

As it turns out, Sydney liked to keep to herself. Alexander could not help but blame that characteristic on himself, having abandoned his daughter at such a young age, when she idolized him. Alexander felt pained with guilt and sorrow, thinking about how accomplished Sydney had been, but how lonely she ended up being.

I could have been there to make sure she was not alone. There is no doubt that my contribution to the Blue Hole Radius and abandoning them resulted in her being alone nearly all of her life.

Many days since that day, he found himself reminiscing on how the lives of his wife and daughters had turned out. He always circled back to the thought of his wife Michelle and daughter Sydney, dying alone and scared. Whereas, Aliyah lived a great and full life and Sydney had an amazing military career, he could not help but miss his two little girls. They were thirteen and nine years old when he had left them... when he had abandoned them.

Alexander looks out to the road and out onto the valley below them as Steven drives along the 18 Highway, turning into Lake

Arrowhead. He's lost in thoughts of his pride of his children and happiness, along with his feelings of guilt, sorrow, and pain.

If only I had known to stop worrying about what could be... and worried more about what I already had.

After a few moments, the Lake Arrowhead Village is within view and Alexander is brought out of his memoires.

Steven pulls into the upper parking lot, with the old Stater Brothers Market, the Post Office, the burnt down California Bank Trust, and various other shops, mostly closed up now, on the upper level of the Village. Alexander looks toward the Post Office to see if it's set up the same way as back in Crestline. Sure enough, Sheriff Patterson put in three stockades at the Lake Arrowhead Village Marketplace as well.

Steven follows Alexander's gaze over to the stockades, with a young man and woman in two of the three stockades. "Huh. I wonder what they did..." Steven says aloud.

Alexander gets out of the Blazer. "Not sure... but it certainly must have not been that serious. Or they would have wound up like those two teenagers the other week."

Steven nods as he exits the Blazer. "Yeah, I suppose you're right, Alexander. But I'm damn curious as to what landed them there."

Alexander shrugs. "I suppose you could ask them."

Steven nods, shuts his door, and strides over to the two young people in the stockades. Alexander smiles and jogs to catch up to him. "Of course you want to ask them."

Steven looks over at Alexander. "Why wouldn't I? I want to know what sort of "crimes" gets you thrown into these things. We all know what happens with rape and murder... but what's the good Sheriff considering to be small crimes?"

Alexander ponders the question, as they get nearer to the two young people in the stockades.

"Hey! You two! What'd you all do to wind up in those stockades?" Steven shouts out at the two as they get a few feet away from them.

Alexander notices that the young woman, likely in her late teens or early twenties, begins to sob. The young man, roughly the same age, opens his mouth and speaks, straining to see who's standing in front of them.

"Please just leave us alone. We've already been through enough. We didn't mean any harm. We were just hungry." The young man pleads.

Alexander looks to the two young people, noticing that they are covered in dirt, drenched, and there are even some small rocks around them.

Had they been out here all night? Had people been throwing rocks at them?

"Calm down son. We aren't here to hurt you. My friend and I are just curious on what lands you into this sort of punishment." Steven says.

The young man twists his head to look at Steven and Alexander in the late morning sunlight of the day. Alexander taps Steven's shoulder and points to the rocks on the ground around the two young people. "I think people were throwing rocks at them earlier, Steven."

Steven's face scrunches. "Hmm. Well that's no good. Where's the guard that's supposed to be looking over you two? How long have you two been here?"

"Why all the questions, mister? Please just leave us alone." The young man replies.

The girl stops sobbing and tries to look up to Steven and Alexander. Alexander notices that her eyes are bloodshot, her face is stricken with tears and dirt, and there's blood on her lips, with a bruise forming around her left eye.

"Miss, are you alright?" Alexander asks of the young woman.

Steven looks over to the woman. "Well that's no good, either." He pulls a rag out of his back pockets and walks toward the young woman. She flinches as Steven gets closer. "Calm down, ma'am. Just trying to wipe off your face."

The young man comes to life. "Leave her alone old man! Or I swear I'll!..."

"You'll what, son?!" Steven snaps at the young man. "Looks to me like you two did something real stupid to land yourself in these here stockades. It also looks to me like the young lady's face is pretty beaten up. All the while, yours looks less for the wear."

This shuts up the young man. "It's not his fault. It's mine." The young woman says.

Steven gently wipes the dirt away from the young woman's eyes and tries to clean off her face. She doesn't struggle and when he's done, Alexander can see that the young man is enraged, but knows that he's trapped.

"My friend here is right. We are not here to hurt you. He was simply curious as to what your crime was. My name's Alexander, and this is Steven." Alexander replies.

The young woman tries to force a smile. "My name's Briana, and this is my boyfriend Christian. You two are the first kind people we have come across within the last day."

Alexander looks to Briana and then to Christian. "So, you two have been here for a day?"

The young man is still silent, but Briana answers. "I think so... It feels like forever. What day is it?"

"It's Saturday, young lady." Steven responds.

The young woman tries to nod, with her head in between the two pieces of wood, her hands in two more holes, trapped between the two pieces of wood.

"Then yes... it's been about a day. Yesterday we came to the market to try and get some food. We offered to trade work for some food with several of the people in the market. Most of them said they didn't need any workers right now. One guy suggested that I could work in his bedroom for food." The young woman explains.

She pauses and Alexander can see the young man, Christian getting angry. "That piece of shit!"

"Calm down Christian. Our day is almost up. Do either one of you know what time it is?" Briana questions.

Alexander looks to his watch. "It's 10:11 AM, miss."

Her eyes begin to water. "Okay then. See Christian. It's almost been a full day. We are almost done here, and we can go back home."

Steven looks at her. "Young lady. How'd you get that shiner and bloody lip?"

Tears well up in the girl's eyes, as she answers. "The bloody lip came from the guy in the Supermarket, selling potatoes and pork... the eye came from a couple teenagers throwing rocks earlier this morning. Just after the Deputy that was watching us left."

"Fucking little assholes!" Christian sneers.

Steven puts his arms across his chest. "So, I think I have a good idea of what happened, but could you tell me in your own words, young lady?"

Briana begins to cry lightly. "After he offered me to work in his bedroom, in a very vulgar way, I spit in his face. He hit me... then Christian tackled him to the ground. The man pulled out a gun, threatening to shoot us. We backed up and he looked scared. He threw a bunch of his potatoes at us and started to yell, *thieves*."

Steven's eyes narrow. "And just like that, they throw you two in here?"

Brianna begins to sob again, and her boyfriend answers. "We tried to explain. But it looked bad. We had no money or anything to trade on us and we have a bunch of potatoes at our feet. So that dipshit Deputy put us in here."

Alexander replies. "And where's the Deputy that's supposed to be watching you?"

"That son of bitch left us here once the sun came up." Christian sneered. "It was the same one who put us in these fucking stockades. The same one that didn't believe us. He said he'd be back at noon to let us go and he better not see us in the market again."

"Oh, did he now?!" Steven begins to laugh, and the two young people go silent, not sure how to react to a man laughing at their story. "Yeah... screw all that noise."

Steven looks to Alexander. "Alexander. Would you mind looking after these two young folks, and I'll be back shortly?"

Alexander looks at Steven, not sure what to make of the situation. "Sure, but what are you up to?"

Steven smiles at him. "I'm going to get to the bottom of this horse-shit, is what I'm going to do." Steven looks at the two young people. "Now everything you said here is true, right? Because I will find out."

Both of their heads nod quickly, even against the strain of the stockades.

"Alright then. You said it was the man selling the potatoes and pork in the old Stater Brothers Market?" Steven questions.

Christian replies. "Yeah, but that was yesterday... he may not be there today."

Steven smiles. "Oh... it's Saturday, one of the biggest trading days of the week. He'll be there."

Alexander nods to Steven. "Not a problem. I'll watch over them and wait for you to return. What if the Deputy comes back?"

Steven begins to stride off toward the supermarket. He turns to look at Alexander. "Don't let that inapt jerkoff give you any crap and get his name while you are at it, too. I'm sure Sheriff Patterson will be interested in one of his Deputies abandoning his post."

And just like that, Steven is off toward the Supermarket. Alexander smiles and looks back to the two young people. "I would sure hate to be the gentleman selling potatoes and pork, today."

The young woman stops sobbing entirely. "What's he going to do?"

Alexander crosses his arms. "I'm not entirely sure. But I'm intrigued to find out."

"What's it going to matter? We'll still be hungry and still not allowed to come back to the market." Christian responds.

Alexander looks at the cold, wet, and dirty young man in front of him. "I understand how the world can seem like it has turned its back on you, young man. Trust me... I understand. Nonetheless, you are still alive, and you still have someone that cares about you." Alexander looks over to the young woman.

"That's easy for you to say, when you're not in one of these fucking things." Christian replies.

"Christian! Shut up! These nice men are trying to help us. Don't be such an ass!" Briana snaps at him and Christian shuts his mouth.

"Do you two live close to here?" Alexander questions.

"We live in a rental not too far from here. Before all of this, Christian was a cook and I was a bartender in this very same Village Square." Briana replies.

Alexander nods. "Ah, I see. Well I'm inclined to think that the rental is no longer a rental and it's your home to keep these days."

"Now that you mention it. We haven't heard anything from the owners. I think they lived over in Palm Springs." Briana states.

"Then it's certainly your home now. Palm Springs is outside of the *Radius* and long gone after 1,410 years." Alexander replies to the young woman.

"Yeah, so. What good is it... if we can't eat?" Christian responds.

"Well, young man... you are certainly persistent in being negative. Look at the positives for a moment, would you? You have running water still. Electricity is still up and running, thanks to those workers at Southern California Edison up in the High Desert and just around the corner from here, at the substation."

The young man stays silent. "Seems to me the only things you need to figure out is what to do for work and you two need to find some food." Alexander finishes as he hears a shout from near the front entrance of the Supermarket.

He looks across the parking lot to see a man in plaid holding the side of his head with Steven Reilly walking behind him, with his gun drawn. Alexander smiles and shakes his head as the two men make their way to the stockades. When they reach the stockades, Steven puts his right foot into the back of the man's left leg, forcing him to the ground.

"Looks like their story checks out and this piece of shit got these two thrown into the stockades to cover his own ass." Steven blurts out.

Alexander hears more shouts from the Supermarket and turns to see two Deputies running over toward them.

"Steven." Alexander says and points. "Looks like we have company."

"Let them come, Alexander. We'll get this whole thing sorted out." Steven replies as the two Deputies come within ten feet of them and draw their service weapons.

"Put down your weapons!" A Deputy yells.

Steven looks over to the Deputies, smiling at them, then holsters his sidearm. "Deputy Bradley! Could I have a moment of your time, please?!"

"Mr. Reilly?! What exactly is going on here?!" Todd Bradley responds and holsters his service weapon and gestures for his partner to do the same. "Gomez, you remember Steven Reilly from the MS13 battle, right?"

His partner, Joseph Gomez nods. "Yup, sure do. What's going on here Mr. Reilly? And Alexander, right?"

Alexander nods to the Deputy. "Yes, officer. Nice to see you again."

With all of their weapons away and the man that sells potatoes and pork on the ground, Steven opens his mouth. "Deputies. It seems that we have a wrongful punishment going on here."

"Is that so?" Todd Bradley asks.

Alexander nods. "Yes, Officer Bradley. The two young people were looking for work to trade for food. This gentleman on the ground made some vulgar insinuations to the young lady, Briana, there. He then proceeded to hit her, which elicited Christian here to tackle the man." Alexander gestures to Christian. "He had a gun and they didn't. He also accused them of being thieves and threw some of his food at their feet to solidify his claims."

"That fucking bitch spit in my face!" The man on the floor yelled.

Without pause, Steven pulls his revolver from his hip, flips it around and pistol whips the man.

The man yelps in pain and then goes silent. Alexander sees Deputy Todd Bradley and Joseph Gomez just shake their heads and grin slightly.

Alexander continues. "One of your fellow Deputies didn't do his due diligence... which led to these two being in the stockades for the last day, with yesterday still being one of our more rainy ones."

Todd looks around. "Now that you mention it... where's Lisandro? He's supposed to be keeping watch on these two."

"He left at sunrise." Christian blurts out.

Steven nods. "That's right, Todd... I mean Deputy Bradley. If Lisandro's one of yours, he left his post which ended up with this young lady getting bruised up from people throwing rocks at these two."

Todd looks to the man on the ground and then to Christian and Briana. "Is this true?"

"I ain't saying shit. I want a fucking lawyer!" The man on the ground blurts out.

Todd chuckles. "Never mind. That confirms it." Todd reaches down for his radio. "Deputy Ramirez. This is Bradley. Come in. Over."

After a short silence, the radio crackles to life. "Uh, this is Ramirez. Over."

Todd speaks into the radio. "Deputy Ramirez, I advise reporting to your post immediately. Over."

Todd pulls a ring of keys from his hip. "While we wait for Ramirez, why don't we get this situation sorted out." Todd walks over to the stockades and begins to unlock the young man and woman.

Once Christian and Brianna are out of the stockades, Briana hobbles over to Steven and wraps him in a hug. "Thank you so very much!" She pecks him on the cheek and before Alexander realizes it, he's wrapped up in a hug from the young woman. "Thank you too! So very much!" She pecks him on the cheek, too.

Christian walks wearily up to Steven and extends his hand. "Thank you, sir."

Steven shakes his hand and smiles. "Name's Steven Reilly, young man."

Christian nods and walks over to Alexander and shakes his hand too. "Thank you. Sorry for being an ass."

"Not a problem, Christian. I understand completely." Alexander shakes his hand and responds.

Alexander looks at the man on the ground. "What about him, Deputy Bradley."

Todd turns to Alexander "Wrongful accusations can often be worse than the actual crimes. Wrongful accusations and downright lying about good people have ruined people's lives in the past." Todd looks at the man and walks over to him. "So, he'll be taking their place and will be there for the 24 hours."

"What!? Fuck that shit!" The man yells and goes to get up.

But Steven is too quick for him, pistol whipping him once again. Steven then grabs him by the collar and forces him into one of the recently opened stockades, closing it over his neck and wrists.

"Todd..." Steven smiles. "Officer Bradley, I mean. Would you be so kind?"

"Sure thing Steven... I mean Mr. Reilly." Todd smiles and walks over to secure the lock on the stockade.

Todd turns to the two young people. "Now, so that you two don't get the itch for retribution. How about you go take what you want from this liar's stand. Gomez, would you mind walking them over there, so that there's no incident."

"What!? No! That's my food! You can't just take it from me!" The man in the stockade yells.

Todd laughs at him. "You are lucky that's all I do to you. Pull that shit again and I'll execute you myself. Not only did you try to get this young woman to have sex with you in trade for food, you lied and got them put into stockades. Hell, I'm still thinking of putting a bullet in your brain, right now!"

The man goes silent and Alexander sees a puddle begin to drip down from his pant leg. Alexander turns to Todd, but before Alexander can protest the escalation of the situation, Todd winks at him.

Alexander nods, understanding Todd was simply trying to scare the crap out of the man, only being successful in scaring the piss out of him.

"Gomez, you good?" Todd asks his partner.

"Good to go. We'll be back in a few... Come on you two, let's get you two some food." Gomez guides the two toward the Supermarket. Halfway there, the young woman stops and turns. "Thanks again!" She nudges her reluctant boyfriend and then he shouts. "Thank you!"

Once the three of them are in the Supermarket, a patrol car comes racing into the parking lot. It stops about twenty feet from the stockades, and a Deputy exits the car, striding over to the four men.

He stops within a few feet of Todd. "Just what the fuck is going on here, Todd?!"

In a swift motion, Todd strikes the Deputy in the nose, sending him to the ground. Deputy Ramirez reaches for his service weapon, but Todd already has his drawn.

Alexander instinctively reaches for his but decides to leave it on his hip. He looks over to Steven and he's at the same stance.

"So, let me get this straight, Ramirez..." Todd says as he looks down at the other Deputy that he's holding at gunpoint.

The man looks stunned and very confused, with his nose bleeding all over his face.

"You locked up two innocent people, without getting their stories straight. Then you abandoned your post, which led to rocks getting thrown at them. Then you come back, as if you didn't do shit wrong. Did I get that about right?!" Todd snaps at the man on the ground.

"Shit, Todd! I think you broke my nose!" Deputy Ramirez whines. "How was I supposed to fucking know? And I only left for a little while!"

"A little while! It's 10:45 and you left at sunrise! You are fucking lucky your dumbass isn't in there next to that piece of shit! And it's your damn job to find out what's going on! That's what we do!" Todd yells at his fellow Deputy.

"What the fuck ever, Todd! Fuck them and fuck you!" Deputy Ramirez yells at him.

Alexander watches as it's now Todd that pistol whips someone, with that someone being Deputy Ramirez.

I'm pretty sure I know where this is going... Alexander thinks to himself.

Todd then reaches for the man's gun and tosses it to the side. He grabs him by his collar and shoves him forward, toward the stockades. The man tries to resist, but Alexander and Steven come to his aid, each of them grabbing an arm.

After a little bit of a struggle, Deputy Ramirez is in a stockade, with it locked and secured.

"You can't fucking do this! I'm a fucking Deputy Sheriff." Ramirez yells.

"We'll just have to see what Sheriff Patterson has to say about all of this." Todd replies. He pulls out his radio. "Sheriff Patterson, this is Deputy Bradley. Come in. Over."

After a short pause, the radio crackles back to life. "Go for Sheriff Patterson, Bradley. Over."

"Sheriff. We have an issue that needs your attention, up by the Post Office at the Lake Arrowhead Village Marketplace. Over." Todd responds into the radio.

The Sheriff replies. "Roger that. I'm down in the lower section of the same Marketplace, talking to a bunch of the locals and some of the newer residents. I'm on my way up to you. Over."

"Copy." Todd replies back.

Todd puts his radio away and looks at Steven and himself. "Thanks for all of the help with this matter, Mr. Reilly and Alexander.

The two of them nod in sync. "Not a problem. Deputy Bradley." Alexander replies.

"I'll handle the rest. You two go about what you all came out here to do." Todd answers.

Before Alexander can offer to stick around, Steven interrupts. "Sure thing, Deputy Bradley. If you need anything, we'll be at the old Bank of America... I've been wanting to take a look, since it's now a gun shop and a bank... Come on Alexander. Let's let the fine Deputy handle his official business."

Steven starts to walk toward the lower part of the Village where the Bank/Gun Store is.

Alexander looks to Todd before following him. "Have a good day."

Todd smiles at him. "You too, Alexander. Tell Ben and Eileen I said hello, please."

Alexander nods. "Will do." Alexander strides off to catch up with Steven.

Once he does, Steven looks over to him. "That's some in-house shit that we do not want to be a part of. Best to let them handle their own." Steven says to Alexander.

"If you say so, Steven... then it's likely the case." Alexander responds as they head down toward the Bank/Gun Store that was once a Bank of America branch in the Lake Arrowhead Village Marketplace.

As they are walking across the parking lot, the ground begins to tremble. "Another one?" Steven asks.

After the Earth stops shaking, Alexander looks over to Steven. "It would seem so, and with more likely to come..."

3

EILEEN RIVERA

AFTER SPENDING the morning shopping in the Lake Drive Market-place, Eileen and Ben traveled to the home of Todd and Jamie in the early afternoon. Eileen had noticed how disappointed Ben was when he found Todd to be at work. Jamie had explained that he was patrolling the Lake Arrowhead Village Marketplace for the day.

As it turns out, Lake Arrowhead had set up a much larger Marketplace than they had in the town of Crestline. Lake Arrowhead had turned into the hub of the mountain region, with a good portion of Big Bear being cut off by the *Blue Hole Radius*.

This was the main discussion over lunch at the Bradley Home between Jamie, Eileen, Ben, and even Jamie's daughter Claire, who was only six years old. The four of them had sat down to eat sandwiches and fruit for lunch on this warm Saturday.

Eileen found herself smiling at Ben, making jokes with the little girl, while their discussions encompassed their new world and what had changed since they had "woken" up.

"Claire? What did the fish say when he swam into a wall?" Ben asked the little girl.

"Ouch?" The little girl questions.

Ben smiles. "Close Claire. He said Dam."

"I don't get it." Claire replies.

Ben erupts into laughter at his own joke. "It's because he swam into a dam, sweetie."

Really!? Dad jokes?!

"Benjamin!" Eileen snaps at him. "don't teach that sweet little girl such words! I'm sorry, Jamie." She apologizes to Jamie and laughs.

Jamie laughs. "Oh no need to apologize. She hears far worse from her father and many more dad jokes than that. That's the first time I heard that one though, Ben. I'll have to pass it on to Todd."

Ben smiles. "My brother and I bought a whole book of dad jokes for our father. We liked it so much that we each bought our own copy. I still remember quite a few of them."

"You would, Ben... wouldn't you. Dad jokes... really?" Eileen smiles and shakes her head.

"Uncle Ben?" Claire chimes in.

"Yes, little Claire?" Ben responds.

"Did you feel the earthquake this morning?" She asks him.

"Yes, Claire. We did. We were in the hardware store when it happened. It was just a little one though." Ben replies.

"It may have been a little one, but it feels like we have been having quite a few in the last couple of months. Since all of this started actually." Jamie responds.

"Mommy? Are there going to be more of them? I don't like those earthquakes..." Claire asks her mother.

"I'm not sure dear." Jamie replies, obviously worried about the trend of small earthquakes over the last couple of months.

"Claire, my very good friend says there'll be more and that it's normal... given our circumstances. You never know, we may wind up with beachfront property in this new world of ours." Ben smiles at the little girl. "Have you ever seen the beach, little Claire?"

The girl's eyes light up, but Eileen interrupts before she can respond. "Ben! Don't go scaring little girls." She turns her attention to Claire. "Don't worry about the quakes, kiddo. And don't let your mean Uncle Ben scare you. Our good and very smart friend, Alexander, says it should eventually go back to normal."

Kiddo? Did I just say kiddo? Eileen thinks to herself and is instantly brought back to the memory of her father.

He used to call her kiddo, even when she was an adult.

Eileen feels pain with the memory of her father dying because of greedy people. He had protected her, as fathers should do... but had paid the ultimate price in the process. Despite it being close to two months ago, it still felt like it was yesterday. Some days were harder than others, but this was a good memory mixed in the sorrow of her loss.

Kiddo.

She smiles lightly at the thought of her father, and the world before the *Blue Hole Radius* 1,410 years ago, now.

She's brought back to the present, by the little girl gleaming with excitement. "I want to go to the beach! Mommy! Can we go to the beach!?" The little girl shouts.

Jamie looks over at Ben. "Look what you started, Ben... thanks."

Ben chuckles and pats the little girl on the head. "I'll talk to your mom and dad, little Claire. Maybe soon we can spend a day at the lake."

"Okay! Thanks Uncle Ben!" Claire replies.

Eileen catches Jamie narrow her eyes toward Ben. "You better make it happen, Ben. She has a sharp memory, and she'll never let me hear the end of it."

Ben puts his hands in the air in self-defense. "Hey! I think it would be a great idea to spend a day at the lake once it gets warmer. I think it'd be good for all of us."

Eileen looks at Ben, sitting across from her. *He's really good with kids. And a day at the lake does sound nice. Aside from the business with that teenage girl a couple weeks ago, and the few robberies... it has been pretty quiet.*

"I think it's supposed to be warming up for a while now. The rain may be behind us for some time now. It's June, for goodness sake." Eileen adds.

Ben nods. "I can get Alexander's opinion on the weather situation. Considering how much has changed with our weather and everything."

Jamie thinks about it then replies. "It does sound nice. Maybe we can go tomorrow or Monday. The more that I think about it, the better it sounds."

"Oh Mommy! Can we go to the Bear Lake!?" Claire asks her mother.

"You mean Big Bear Lake, sweetie... and no we can't." Jamie responds with a frown of concern.

"Why not, Mommy!? That's the one we usually go to!" Claire asks.

Eileen notices Jamie pauses, not sure of what to say.

Eileen interjects. "Claire"

The little girl focuses her attention on her. Eileen can see those deep brown eyes, wanting to know everything about everything, but not knowing where to start, she smiles at the little girl.

"Well sometimes, lakes dry up over time. And since the last time you and your parents went to that lake... it got a big crack in the lake and the water went away." She explains to the little girl.

The little girl frowns.

"Don't worry though, there are still plenty of other lakes up here. In fact, there's Lake Gregory right down the way from here!" She adds.

The little girl brightens up, forgetting about Big Bear Lake. "Oh yeah! I remember!"

The adults at the table grew quiet, likely all of them thinking about the drained lake in Big Bear.

After the *Blue Hole Radius* had caught up with the rest of the world's time, the Earth had changed. Alexander had explained that it had to do with the tectonic plates and the buildup of the last 1,410 years. A good part of California resides on a tectonic plate boundary, between the Pacific Plate and the North American Plate.

With the *Blue Hole Radius* reaching a depth of six miles, it was not deep enough to go below the plate boundaries. However, it was enough to create issues along the fault lines, both minor and major fault lines.

Alexander had explained to the group that because of the friction between the transform plates and the *Blue Hole Radius*, multiple minor fault lines emerged and another major fault line. The new major fault line was named the Bear Ridge Fault, named after the mountain that it cut through.

In the year 2801, the pressure beneath the Earth's surface was released along the fault lines, creating Bear Ridge Fault and multiple minor fault lines. The end result was similar to that of the 1906 San Francisco earthquake. Whereas the earthquake in 1906 was a 7.8, the earthquake in 2801 was an 8.4. The end result was several newly created ridges in the region, surrounding the *Blue Hole Radius*.

The death toll of the earthquake was relatively low, mostly due to people migrating away from the *Blue Hole Radius* over the last 780 years. The change to landscape was much more severe.

The elevation of Crestline in 2023 was 4,613 feet. The elevation of Big Bear started at 6,752 feet. The elevation of Crestline now, in 3043, is 5,093 feet, with Big Bear Valley now beginning at 7,232. After the earthquake of 2801, a new ridgeline was formed along the northeast edge of the *Blue Hole Radius*.

In a very over complicated way, Alexander had explained to the group that the Bear Ridge went on for close to forty miles and raised the *Blue Hole Radius* and a good amount of the surrounding area on the Pacific Plate, close to five-hundred feet in elevation.

After several tries, Eileen and the others finally got the gist of it. The *Blue Hole Radius* was higher than when this whole mess had started. Big Bear Lake was drained off of the side of the Bear Ridge, down into the mountain side 480 feet below once the barrier of the *Blue Hole Radius* dissolved and time went back to normal.

It was all very concerning and confusing to Eileen. She had been used to earthquakes, but this was different. She was waiting for the "big one" all of her life, along with every other Californian. Now she had found out that it had already happened, which begged the question of when the next "big one" would be?

Despite Alexander telling them that there would be many little quakes and likely no major ones, she was still worried. Alexander had told them the small quakes were just the earth that was trapped in the *Blue Hole Radius* resettling.

Although she had the fear that the ground would give out beneath her feet, he assured her that this was not the case, not with that much intact earth being held together for so long, with its deepest depth of six miles.

She always circled back to the thought that the man telling her not to worry was part of the reason why the *Blue Hole Radius* came into existence in the first place.

"Mommy! I'm finished eating! Can I go play in my room?" Claire asks.

Jamie looks over to their daughter. "Yes, sweetie. Put your plate in the sink. And please fill your cup back up with water and take it into your room. You need to stay hydrated, sweetie."

"Okay, mommy." The little girl says, as she puts her plate into the sink, fills her cup, and leaves the room, trying to be careful not to spill her cup of water.

With Claire out of the room, Jamie speaks more freely. "I sure hope that your friend Alexander is as smart as you say he is. I hope even more that he's right about the earthquakes... they are really starting to worry me."

"Me too, Jamie... me too." Eileen responds.

Ben replies, "Alexander has been doing a lot of research in the last seven weeks. If anyone has a good grasp of what's happening... it's that guy." Ben smiles to comfort her, taking a sip of his water.

"I even hear that they are trying to build a dam in the lakebed of Big Bear Lake. If they do that... the lake will return in time." Ben adds, trying to make the conversation more positive.

"And, if we ever get back to some sort of normalcy and we want to hit the slopes, what remains of the Ski Resort is close to 500 feet higher." He smiles at this last part.

"Oh, and you know how to ski, Ben?" Eileen asks.

"Actually, no. I have only gone snowboarding. I'm okay... not great." Ben replies.

"Really? Me too. I didn't know that..." Eileen responds. Even after spending the last seven weeks together and getting very close, there was still a good deal that she did not know about him.

"But remember, we are close to 500 feet higher too, Ben." She adds.

Ben nods, thinking. He then turns his attention to Jamie. "Jamie, how are you guys on cold weather gear?"

Jamie looks at him. "Good, I suppose. Why?"

Ben continues. "I don't mean to scare you anymore than you already are, with all of this earthquake and weather talk, but Alexander also told us that this winter is going to be different from what we are used to."

Jamie frowns, and looks toward the hallway, likely thinking of her young daughter playing in her room. "Well, that's just great... isn't it? I was hoping we would start getting better news after this rain let up."

Eileen watches as Ben reaches into his pack that he had brought in with him. "Oh, I hear the weather is supposed to be nice for a while. It's our summertime, after all. But I just want to make sure that your family has what it needs for the winter coming in. Alexander tells me that it's going to be colder and longer than what we are used to."

"Of course it is..." Jamie responds.

"Here." Ben pulls out the pouch that he had at the Marketplace. "Take this for you, Todd, and Claire. There's enough in there for you all to go get some more supplies for the winter. There should be enough in there for Jim's wife and daughter too. There's more silver in there than gold, mind you, but each silver coin is worth at least $50 in these times and each gold coin is worth at least five times that.

Don't let the small size of the gold coins fool you and don't let anyone take advantage of you all. "

Eileen's stunned at his generosity. She knew there had to be a small fortune in that small little pouch, based on what they had spent earlier.

"Oh, Ben... I couldn't. I'm sure that we will be fine." Jamie responds.

"Jamie. I insist. I highly doubt that Todd would take this from me, out of pride. But that would be a mistake. We have what we need and there's no reason to be greedy about it. Take the money and go see Mr. Dave Stine at the camping store. He'll set you guys up real nice. Let him know that you know Eileen and me." Ben tells her.

"Ben, I don't know what to say." Jamie responds.

"Well you don't have to say anything, but I'm not taking no for an answer. If not for you and yours... for Jim's family. Please" Ben asks of her.

Eileen's still silent, thinking of the man sitting across from her. Yes, he was bull-headed and brazen. But he was also kind and generous. Most people would not give away what he's giving away now. To the contrary, she had seen, firsthand, people kill for much less.

Jamie replies, sounding a little choked up by Ben's generosity. "Okay, Ben. But you must at least take home a pie with you. I've been baking like crazy with all of this rain. I have apple and cherry pies."

Ben smiles. "Sounds like a deal. I'm a sucker for a cherry pie." He puts the pouch into her hands.

She smiles, wiping a tear from her eye. "I'll make it two, Ben." She takes the pouch and rises to go get the pies.

Ben looks to Eileen as she leaves the table. "What do you say? Want to go to the lake tomorrow or the day after?"

And just like that... he gives away an unknown amount of gold and silver and then wants to go to the lake for the day.

"Well that was very nice of you, Ben." Eileen says, thwarting the conversation back to what just transpired.

Ben scrunches his face, obviously uncomfortable about it. "What that. That's nothing. In times like these, people need to take care of people. Not be greedy and selfish."

You really are something else, Benjamin Reilly. Eileen thinks as she just stares at him.

"So, what do you say? Lake tomorrow or the day after? I'm sure Uncle Steven would like to get some fishing in. It'd be a good excuse to get Jim's wife and daughter out of the house too." Ben asks.

Eileen smiles at him. "Sounds like a great idea, Ben. I actually planned on doing just that sort of thing, before all this *Blue Hole Radius* business went down."

Ben grins at her as Jamie enters the room with two pies. "Great minds think alike." He sees Jamie enter the room. "Oooo! Pies!"

Eileen laughs at him and so does Jamie.

After their goodbyes and hugs, Eileen and Ben leave the Bradley home and head back to Steven's cabin, now all of their cabin, in the mid-afternoon.

With Eileen in the passenger seat and Ben driving back to Steven's cabin, she turns to Ben. "I know a lot has changed. But you were just joking about the whole beachfront property stuff, right? Because that'd be one massive earthquake."

Ben laughs. "I was just quoting an old country song I remember as a kid. Something about beachfront property in Arizona, once California falls off into the ocean. And no, I don't think so. A ridgeline was created by the new Bear Ridge Fault... not a canyon or great depression into the ground. Alexander is probably the smartest man that I have ever met. If he says we shouldn't be worried... we shouldn't be."

Eileen eyes him. "Okay... but remember that Alexander was one of the people that brought this whole situation down upon our heads in the first place."

Ben nods. "Very true, very true. And I think he knows that best, between all of us. I really think he struggles with the guilt on a daily basis."

Eileen thinks about this as she looks out onto the mountain scenery around her.

"Don't you ever catch him lost in thought? I mean, he doesn't talk about his family much. But, none of us do... but we still think about them."

Eileen nods silently, knowing that this rang true with her and her thoughts about her father.

They reach the driveway of the cabin moments later. Ben pulls up next to Steven's Blazer. She can see that Steven and Alexander are unloading supplies from the back of the old vehicle.

As they get out of Ben's truck, Ben speaks. "Hey, Alexander!"

Alexander turns, with two vests in his hand. "Hello, Ben."

"Would you please tell the wonderful Eileen that we are not going to fall into the ocean because of the earthquakes?" Ben smiles at her.

Jerkface.

Eileen eyes him as Alexander begins to speak. "Ah yes. Whereas, nothing is truly impossible, that particular scenario is highly improbable. Transform plates move alongside each other and are not divergent plate boundaries. What is more, transform plates move one to two inches a year. That's about a range of 117 to 235 feet over the last 1,410 years."

Alexander turns to walk into the house to drop off the vests.

Eileen catches Ben's eye and flips him off. "Now you got him going again. Thanks, jerkface."

Ben smiles at her. "Anytime, beautiful."

He goes to the back-cab door on his side and she does the same on her side. They open the cab doors and start retrieving the cold weather gear that they had purchased earlier that day.

"He may talk a lot, but he seems to know what he's talking about. The guy is like a human Google." Ben adds.

Before Eileen can respond, Alexander steps back outside to get more of their acquired gear and continues speaking. "As I was saying... that's a lot of movement over a lot of years. Which means a lot of adjustment and shifting. You must remember, that we didn't understand plate tectonics before the *Radius* and it looks like our predecessors didn't figure out much more about them after the

Radius. Point in fact, they still haven't figured out what's actually within the Earth's core. With all of that being said, the Bear Ridge Fault is evidence to my point, that it's much more likely that mountain ranges will be created along these fault lines in our region and not shift away from each other. Therefore, not dropping California into the ocean. Does that make sense, Eileen?"

Eileen looks to Alexander. "Yes, Alexander. Thank you. I feel much better about it now."

She hears Ben chuckle. "Keep it up, Ben."

This elicits laughter from Steven as he keeps on grabbing the acquired gear from the back of the Blazer. "Sounds like you're getting yourself into trouble, Benjamin. It'd be wise to shut your mouth, nephew. I'd be willing to guess that Eileen could likely kick your ass."

Ben fakes a shocked look at his uncle. "Uncle! That really hurts."

Eileen can't help but laugh. "Your Uncle does make a good point."

Ben laughs too. "Uh huh." He turns to his Uncle and Alexander. "Looks like you found them."

Steven grins. "Sure did! We found four vests, in excellent condition."

"Found what?" Eileen asks.

Steven looks at her and smiles. "Four bullet-proof vests. Well, bullet resistant is more of an accurate term."

Eileen nods. "Oh. That's good."

"Good, that's great news!" Ben beams. "Who's the manufacturer of them?"

Steven looks back at Ben. "Three different manufacturers. Two AR500's, one Safe Life, and one Spartan. But they are all level three with the buildup coatings."

Ben whistles. "Nice find, Uncle!"

Eileen looks at Steven and then Ben. "I'm guessing that's a good thing."

Ben looks at her as they carry the cold weather gear into the cabin. "Sure is. They are not military or anything, but they are reliable manufacturers and they'll do the job."

Eileen nods. "Well that's good. But he should have gotten five." She grins at him.

Ben tilts his head. "Why five?"

"You need two, just for yourself. For the next time your dumbass runs into a firefight all alone!" She starts to laugh.

"That'll give me more time to get to you and save your butt again!" She erupts in laughter.

Ben rolls his eyes. "OH! These shenanigans, again." He begins to laugh.

"You know! You aren't a very humble guardian angel." He adds.

"Don't worry Ben... I still have a couple vests in my stash of supplies. We can turn you into a tactical bubble boy..." She says, which makes her laugh even harder.

On their way back out to the truck for another load, they calm down and Steven is walking toward them.

"Hey Uncle. What do you think about making a lake trip tomorrow or the next day? We could take the Bradley families with us and get some sunshine, with this nice weather." Ben questions.

Steven keeps walking and passes them. "Sounds like a grand idea. I could get some fishing in. I'm sure there's still a good amount of trout in Lake Gregory."

Ben nods, and they see Alexander. "Alexander? What do you think? Want to spend a day at the lake with all of us?" Eileen asks him.

"It's been a while, but I do enjoy fishing." Alexander nods and smiles.

"That settles it then. We'll go to the lake tomorrow... while things are nice and calm." Ben states.

No later than he says it does his Uncle walk past him and smack him upside the head.

"Hey? What was that for?" Ben asks.

"For saying dumb shit like that, nephew. You better not have just jinxed us!" Steven replies.

Eileen, Alexander, and Steven start to laugh at Ben.

"Alright, alright." Ben says as he knocks on the wood of the cabin wall.

The four of them finish unloading their finds from the two different marketplaces in the mountain region, heading inside to sort their newly acquired gear and lumber. Eileen makes sure to call Jamie and confirm the lake trip with the two Bradley families. After everything's sorted and put away, they sit down to a talkative dinner, discussing the events of the day.

Eileen listens in astonishment to Steven and Alexander's story at the Lake Arrowhead Village Marketplace. Hearing about the young couple that was wrongfully accused really didn't sit with her well.

"We need to do a better job of making sure we don't punish the wrong people." She responds once the story is finished.

"That's for damn sure." Is Steven's simple response.

The conversation slowly shifted to the impending lake trip and all of the fun activities that they would do. Steven and Alexander were excited to fish. Ben was very excited to go swimming, for some reason.

Eileen had a good feeling he was just excited to get to see her in a bathing suit. That's when she realized that she didn't have a bathing suit... She quickly called Jamie once more, before they got ready for bed and their night shifts.

Lucky for her, Jamie was close to her size and had an extra one for her to borrow. The men wanted to fish and swim. She was just excited to get outside in the warmth and wanted to lay out on the sandy shore of the lake underneath the warm sun. It felt like it would give her some sort of normalcy back... back from the world that she had lost seven weeks ago.

4

ALEXANDER MATHIS

ALEXANDER WAS JUST COMING off his shift of night watch. He was the third of the night this week. The group shuffled it around every week, to make it as fair as possible. Alexander had found himself going to bed closer to 8:00 PM because he had found with the third shift, from 2:00 AM to 4:00 AM, he rarely fell back asleep. After Steven relieved him for the fourth and final shift of night watch, Alexander proceeded to get a cup of hot coffee and go sit himself in front of Ol' Betsy.

Over the last seven weeks, Alexander had learned a lot from Steven Reilly on how to operate the HAM radio referred to as Ol' Betsy. He found it entertaining, enriching, and very distracting from his own personal thoughts.

With his hot cup of coffee, he scans the airwaves for news of the High Desert area and the rest of the northern part of the *Radius*. Alexander and the others in the San Bernardino National Forest region were in the far eastern region of the *Radius*.

He scans the airwaves on Ol' Betsy to listen for stories of areas other than their eastern mountain region of the *Radius*.

Alexander had heard a great deal of stories over the last seven weeks. What is more, he had done in depth research on the *Radius*, their predecessors, and the world... their Earth One. That, of course, was after he was done researching his family weeks ago. The work and purpose helped him avoid the thoughts of his wife, Michelle, passing away alone and too young. It also helped him push away thoughts of his youngest daughter, Sydney, reaching a similar fate despite having been so successful in life. Yes, his oldest, Aliyah, had a long and fulfilling life. Nonetheless, Alexander felt completely and utterly to blame for his youngest and his beloved wife's lonely demise.

If I had been there, things would have turned out differently.

Alexander knew in his logical and rational brain that there was no way to know for sure, but the thought from his heart kept on returning. One of the only things that kept his guilt and grief away, was his purpose. The purpose of finding out as much as possible to help his friends, and what was left of humanity, survive and adapt to this world after the *Blue Hole Radius*.

Most of the High Desert was in chaos, due to people fighting over food and other resources. This area was northwest of them, and relatively close.

The farmland areas to the southeast, toward Menifee, Murrieta, and Temecula, were doing considerably well. They had a set of routines and similar marketplaces of their own. It did certainly help that there was a good deal of farmland in the area and that the people were much more accustomed to the rural style of living.

Alexander had found it interesting that he had always thought of San Francisco, Hollywood, and Los Angeles when people talked about California. He was intrigued to find so many different ways of life in the very large state. Now, what was the only known civilization left of Earth One.

A few weeks back, Alexander had found out that most of Los Angeles was in ruins. It was one of the first places to become essentially devoid of human life within the *Radius*.

Hollywood had all but burned down to the ground. Between looting, people not knowing what to do, and even a few suicide cults formed within the rich and famous.

When Alexander had told the others of the news, Ben and Steven had laughed at the suicide cults put together by a few of the celebrities that had survived. "Good riddance to the lot of them. They were more useless than a screen door on a submarine." Steven had said. After the two men had a good laugh, Eileen had admonished them for taking delight in others suffering, and they had both shut up quickly. Alexander had found it rather intriguing how the four of them blended into a sort of family over the last seven weeks.

From what Alexander had heard from what was left of the news and Ol' Betsy, the mountain communities in Angeles National Forest and what was left of Los Padres National Forest were doing fairly well.

There were some coastal areas that were faring well enough. Most of them had fallen into chaos over the last seven weeks. Catalina Island was surviving exceptionally well and guarded their ports with strict scrutiny. Alexander had been in contact with a couple that was retired on the island. They had told them stories of being able to see the smoke and fire coming from Long Beach and Huntington Beach. Those major hubs of civilizations were essentially wiped off the map.

All of them were speechless when he had told them news of the major beach cities. It became evident that Californians do enjoy their beaches and didn't like hearing of their demise. Some of the only major beaches that had survived since the onset of the *Blue Hole Radius* were Dana Point down by the south rim of the *Radius*, Oxnard Shores, and the State Beach in Ventura, both by the western rim of the *Radius*.

Ben had asked Alexander the week following the MS13 Battle, "Any news on what's left of the U.S. Military?"

Alexander had not known, but he scanned the airwaves for the next week to find out. Ben was curious if there were enough of the U.S. Military left to make a positive impact and project some sort of security for the survivors. Alexander agreed but was also thinking of the military as a factor to be used as defense against the possibility of their returning predecessors from Earth Two. Alexander was still very fearful that their coming was not one of saving grace, but one of impending doom.

After reaching Edwards Air Force Base, Alexander had found the information that Ben had wanted to know. The only functional military bases still left standing were Edwards, up to the northern part of the *Radius* and the March, toward the southeast. March was inactive and more of a museum and transit base during the days prior to the *Blue Hole Radius*. Edwards Air Force Base still being around was much more encouraging to the group, since it had been the Center of the Aerospace Testing Universe.

Nonetheless, Ben was annoyed with the fact that Camp Pendleton had been just outside of the radius. "We could have really used some good Marines during all of this. Hopefully the Air Force can hack it." Ben had said, upon finding out the news of military installations.

After researching the *Radius* on the SuperNet and hearing stories on the airwaves, he had learned a great deal about their new world. Alexander had found it interesting that the closer to the epicenter of the *Radius*, the more devoid of life it had become over the last seven weeks. It was the outer areas of the *Radius* that seemed to be surviving and adapting the most efficiently and effectively.

Alexander had contributed this to several primary factors. First of which was the population density. The higher the population density of an area, the more likely that it was going to fall into chaos. Alexander had surmised that people were not used to taking care of themselves. Without a unified government to tell them what to do and provide them with a sense of security, they fell within a matter of days.

The closer that people were to the epicenter of the *Blue Hole Radius*, the worse off they were. On the other hand, the people along the edges of the *Radius* were mostly cut off from others and forced to either adapt or die off. Alexander, Steven, Eileen, and Ben had discussed these scenarios to great lengths.

The second primary factor was the dark side of human nature and how quickly some had shifted toward that side of their humanity. Without rules to govern and punishments, people did as they pleased and this often led to dire and devastating situations. This was another topic of great discussion at the dining room table during meals. In fact, Alexander had ascertained that it was likely Steven Reilly who had convinced the good Sheriff to be so strict after the MS13 Battle.

The good Sheriff Patterson had set up roadblocks and checkpoints for the mountain community and it had been relatively quiet since the MS13 battle. Nonetheless, there was this feeling of impending doom, and he knew Ben had felt it too. They had talked about it on several occasions when they were by themselves. Most of the rest of his spare time was spent with Steven and getting used to the area, his new home.

This last part was the third primary factor, impending doom. The people that were confined within the *Blue Hole Radius* for 1,410 years *woke up* to a whole new world and reality. This new world was devoid of human life, except for those that were within the *Radius*. This combined with the widespread knowledge from the SuperNet, and knowledge of *people* coming from an Earth Two, made people afraid. People often act irrationally when they are afraid of the unknown.

So, Alexander had broken it down to their primary factors: population density, adaptability of humanity, and the fear of the unknown. These factors played a large role in whether you survived or not. Alexander remembered feeling feelings of gratefulness and new beginnings after the first few days in Steven Reilly's cabin. Alexander was all but sure that he would have been one of those that didn't survive the first week if it had not been for Ben, Steven, and Eileen.

Alexander was more than grateful for Steven's hospitality and they got along famously. It was more of a formal friendship and they mostly discussed academics, government, and the varying possibilities for their future.

Eileen gave Alexander hope and showed him that people can

move on from tremendous pain and suffering. Eileen had not had it easy during the first few days of the *Radius*. That being said, she was doing relatively well two months into the *Radius*. Some might say that she was actually happy. Alexander noticed that she certainly looked happy with Ben.

Then there was Ben... Alexander had found that over the last seven weeks, Ben had become a true friend. Sure, Steven was closer to his age. But it was Ben who had brought him back from the brink. Alexander was not sure what he would have done if Ben had not found him in the airport bar and asked him to come with him. One thing was for certain, it would not have been good, and he certainly would not have lasted this long.

Alexander found himself pondering the thoughts of his newfound friends, his new home, and everything else in between. Anything that could keep his mind off his daughter and his beloved wife.

During the early hours of this Sunday morning, Alexander's focus was shifted toward the High Desert region. He was trying to discern if trouble was possibly coming their way. Alexander scans the airwaves on Ol' Betsy, focusing on frequencies that he had luck with contacting people in the High Desert in previous weeks.

As Alexander scans the frequencies, he picks up a voice. "This is Desert Eagle. Anyone on the *Radius* airwaves this morning? Over."

Alexander keys his mike on Ol' Betsy. "Good morning, Desert Eagle. This is Cornell, here. Over."

Ol' Betsy sparks to life. "Cornell! How's mountain life treating you? I thought you might be on this early in the morning. Over." The man referred to as Desert Eagle responds.

Alexander had coined the name *Cornell*, since he was previously a scientist at Cornell University, prior to the world before the *Blue Hole Radius*. His friend on the radio was a retired Senior Master Sergeant from the Air Force. Alexander had acquired a few details from his radio contact, and friend, over the last six weeks.

They had found each other the week after the *Radius* time lapse had ceased. Desert Eagle was actually his point of contact that knew a great deal about the military and what was left. As luck would have it, Desert Eagle was still in contact with some of his old friends in the Air Force. He had recently retired, having been stationed at Edwards Air Force Base. Afterwards, he moved close by to Mojave. Mojave is just over twenty miles away from the base. It was a desert town and didn't sound ideal to Alexander. However, Desert Eagle had apparently enjoyed the area enough to retire in the small town.

"Mountain life is going pretty well. The Marketplaces are working effectively, and people are getting along well enough, up here. Much better than down the hill. Over" Alexander responds.

"That's good to hear, Cornell. And yeah, that sounds about right with those big cities. I can't see how they are faring well at all. I'll keep my old ass in this small desert town. Thank you very much. Over." Desert Eagle replies.

Alexander laughs lightly. "How are things going out there, in the desert? Any new news from your old military friends? Over."

"Not sure, exactly. The whole reason I jumped on the airwaves this morning was to find out about what I saw earlier this morning. Over."

What he saw? What did he see, I wonder?

Alexander keys the mic. "What did you see, Desert Eagle? Over."

Desert Eagle continues. "It looked like a comet but then it stopped, slowly. It was in the direction of Edwards. Nothing hit the ground, because I didn't see any explosions or crashes. But it was definitely something. I got on here to see if anyone else did... and I wasn't just losing my mind. Ya know? It was there, and then it wasn't. But it was dark. Over."

A comet that doesn't hit the ground... Could it be the Leviathan, from Earth Two? No, it's too soon. Wait... It has been about two months. Not quite, but close.

He keys the mic. "Has anything else strange happened since then and how long ago did you see the ship? I mean object. Over."

Desert Eagle keys the mic with laughter. "So, I wasn't the only one thinking about it. My first thought was it had to do with those transmissions. The first one, and then the second one that comes on at 0800, every damn day. Do you think it could be the Leviathan? Over."

Alexander sits there quietly for a moment. *If it is the Leviathan, then our world's about to get much more complicated. I hope my concerns are wrong and it won't be like nuclear weapons versus sticks and stones...*

"Cornell, are you still there? Over." Desert Eagle replies.

Alexander must have been lost in thought for more than a moment. He keys the mic. "Yes, Desert Eagle, I'm still here. It's too soon to tell. You are closer to this than we are. If you could... Please touch bases with your contacts from the Air Force. I'll be back tomorrow morning, but closer to 7:00 AM and 8:00 AM. We'll say 8:00 AM, right after the daily transmission. Over."

"Thought I lost you there for a moment, Cornell." Desert Eagle replies. "Sounds like a solid plan. I'll be back on after the transmission tomorrow morning. 0800." The mic is still keyed, but Desert Eagle pauses. "Where's that high pitch sound coming from? Is that feedback or something? Hey Cornell? Are you hearing what I'm hearing? Over."

Alexander looks around to the empty communications room with Ol' Betsy in it. He can see through the window that the day is beginning to start and the night is slowly fading away, but he doesn't hear any high pitch sound.

He keys the mic on Ol' Betsy. "No high pitch sound here, Desert Eagle. What does it sound like, exactly? Over."

Alexander waits a full minute for Desert Eagle to reply, but there's not one. "Desert Eagle, are you still there? Over."

Another minute goes by without response and Alexander tries him again, with no luck. After ten minutes of trying to reach him, he stops and thinks about the situation.

Did he leave to go find out what was going on at Edwards? He did say "over" and that he would be back on tomorrow morning. Maybe he did leave. But what was that part about the high pitch sound? What if it was the Leviathan and it's related?

Alexander leans back in the chair at the desk. He takes another sip of his coffee, rethinking the conversation.

After pondering the various reasons why Desert Eagle wasn't responding, Alexander determined that he didn't have enough information to make a decision of what happened, or if anything happened at all.

It was early in the morning, and your mind has a way of playing tricks on you. Maybe I'm reading too much into this. Maybe he just went off to find out what was going on and will be back on tomorrow morning.

Alexander doesn't notice Steven entering into the communications room, and jumps when Steven asks, "Any new news?"

Alexander proceeds to spill what was left of his now cold coffee onto his lap.

Steven laughs lightly and scratches the back of his head. "Sorry Alexander. Didn't mean to scare you. I thought you would have heard me walking in. Everything okay?"

Alexander turns to Steven. "Not a problem, Steven. My fault entirely. I was lost in thought and clumsy." He stands up and looks at the coffee on his shirt. "I'd better go change before breakfast. What time is it?"

Steven replies. "It's just past 6:00 AM. You go ahead and get changed and I'll start up breakfast, before we get ready for our day at the lake and some well-needed fishing."

Alexander starts making his way out of the room. "Right. See you shortly. Fishing sounds like it's going to be a nice change of pace."

"Yes sir-ree. And you can tell us what you were lost in thought about over breakfast. Because it seems like something..." Steven adds.

"Most definitely." Alexander replies and nods. He then heads upstairs to his room. The room used to be the guest room, and Ben's whenever he would visit. Alexander had gladly taken it over, instead of sleeping on the downstairs couch, the second week of being at

Steven Reilly's cabin. Ben and Eileen had opted to share a room, which was the room on the bottom level.

Ben had said, "It's a win-win situation... you get your own room and I get an upgrade in my bedroom situation."

Alexander recalls laughing at him, when Eileen was standing next to him and wound up punching him in the arm.

"I'm just an upgrade, am I Benjamin?!" Eileen had snapped at him.

Those two are like cats and dogs... but I suppose it works for them. Alexander thought, reminiscing about the memory, as he changed out his shirt to clean up. He grabs his soiled shirt and takes it downstairs to the backyard.

He dumps it into a soap/water bucket, then proceeds to scrub it against a washboard they had found at the market a few weeks prior. Steven had explained that utilizing the washing board and hanging clothes out to dry would reduce the strain on the mountain communities water supply. They were all hoping that it would keep running. Alexander and the others saw it as a small trade off, still being allotted to have hot showers when they needed to.

So, Alexander spent a few minutes scrubbing the shirt along the washboard. He then dumps it in another bucket, filled with water and a small amount of fabric softener. Alexander shakes out the shirt and hangs it up on one of the laundry lines recently set up in the backyard of Steven's cabin.

He heads back into the cabin and smells eggs, bacon, and toasted bread. "That sure was fast, Steven."

Steven looks over and smiles. "Eggs, bacon, and toast aren't exactly the most difficult things to make, Alexander. Takes a matter of minutes."

Alexander nods and smiles. "The two lovebirds are getting up now. Your plate's already at the table, Alexander."

"Thank you, Steven. As always, it's greatly appreciated." Alexander takes a seat at the table and looks at the warm plate in front of him. "How are we doing with bacon and eggs, and bread for that matter?"

"Ah, yes... I was just looking into that, yesterday." Steven replies. "We have a good amount of the freeze-dried egg stuff to last us a while. We also still have a good amount of frozen bacon. Bread will become an issue in the near future, seeing as we have one last full loaf here I just pulled out of the big freezer out back. But as for the eggs and bacon... I've been asking around for a few chickens and also asking around for a piglet or two."

Alexander looks over at him. "Are those animals hard to come by? And how do we raise them?"

"Raising them is easy enough. You just need to keep the pigs corralled up. Same thing with the chickens. You let them out when you want to, and where you want to. And they didn't used to be hard to come by. Now between the recent re-emergence of the Newcastle Disease with the chickens and the *Radius* situation to top it off... it will take some heavy bartering." Steven explains.

"Newcastle Disease?" Alexander questions.

Steven continues. "Yeah, several years ago... the state had to euthanize a whole lot of chickens because they had this deadly disease. It took a while for that particular disease to die out and people started raising new chickens. That combined with our current situation... people are being pretty careful on what livestock they sell and get rid of."

"So, is there any hope?" Alexander asks.

"As luck would have it, there are some folks down the hill that I spoke with over Ol' Betsy yesterday. They are willing to part with four grown and producing chickens, as well as two piglets." Steven explains.

Eileen and Ben walk into the room, visibly smelling the air. "Sure smells good, Uncle." Ben admits.

"Yes, it does." Eileen adds.

"Here are your plates, you two. Have at it." Steven says, offering them two plates identical to Alexanders.

The two gladly take the breakfast plates and sit at the table with Alexander.

Ben starts eating right away and talks with food in his mouth.

"Did I hear right? Are we getting chickens and pigs?" He then proceeds to lightly choke on the food in his mouth.

Eileen chimes in. "That's what you get for talking with food in your mouth. I swear, you are a grown man-child." Eileen grins at him and the three of them laugh at Ben, while he catches his breath.

A moment later, he's able to speak again. "Wrong tube."

This elicits another round of laughter, Steven gets his own plate and makes his way to the table. "But yes, it's looking that way. We just need to make a trip down the mountain. To Yucaipa. And part with two Golden American Eagles."

"Two of them?!" Ben blurts out. "That doesn't seem like a fair deal for four chickens and two piglets!"

"Ben... it's a fair trade. Now try not to choke on your food again." Steven replies and chuckles at his nephew.

"You must remember about the times we are in, and how much food those animals will give us. It's simple supply and demand. We are lucky to have found people even willing to make a trade." Steven explains.

"What are you all huffy and puffy about, Ben? You did just give away a whole pouch of those coins." Eileen adds.

Alexander notices that Ben's eyes go directly to his Uncle. "That was different. It was for the Bradley families... and the tubes I gave them weren't even full... at least the gold one. It only had ten Gold American Eagles left in it. The other one was full with twenty Silver American Eagles." Ben admits defensively.

Steven puts up his hand. "You don't have to explain your reasoning to me, Ben. You did what you thought was right... Besides, most of that gold and silver was yours to give away. You invested way more into those coins over the years than I have."

Alexander wasn't sure how much the coins were worth, but it sounds like Ben had given the Bradley family quite a bit.

Good. They likely needed it with Jim Bradley's passing.

Alexander changes the subject, "So when are we going on the drive down the mountain?"

Ben, eager to get the subject off of him, "How about tomorrow Uncle?"

Steven smiles at his nephew. "I was thinking it'd be just me and Alexander. I don't think we should leave this place unattended for a whole day. And I'm guessing it'll take the day."

"I don't know Uncle... splitting up doesn't seem like a great idea." Ben responds.

Alexander and Eileen don't respond but wait for Steven to reply.

He nods and speaks. "It's a risk, I admit. But it's a necessary risk. I will be fine, and Alexander has shown he's capable of taking care of himself, too. It will only be for the day. We'll leave in the morning and be back by evening. If we run into trouble, we'll be back the following day, finding somewhere to hideout for the night."

"I still don't know, Uncle..." Ben adds.

"Don't worry, Benjamin. Eileen will be here to protect you and make sure you don't get yourself shot... again." Steven says, as he grins at his nephew.

"Whoa, whoa, whoa! I was worried about you!" Ben shouts out defensively. "And it was shrapnel... I wasn't even shot."

Everyone at the table bursts into a round of laughter at Ben's expense.

After the group calms down, Steven adds. "It'll work out one way or another. Simply put, this needs to be done."

This gets a round of nods from the group. "Now, Alexander. Why don't you tell us what you found out this morning on Ol' Betsy?"

All eyes turn to Alexander, and he gulps down a big bite of food. "To be honest, I'm not exactly sure what to make of it, if anything. But here's what happened..."

Alexander explains his conversation with Desert Eagle to the group. Not one of them interrupts and listens to his version of events, following with his varying theories of what could've happened and what his concerns were.

5

BENJAMIN REILLY

BEN'S FOLLOWING his Uncle's Blazer in his Dodge truck, navigating through the neighborhood. Eileen's sitting next to him in silence. The group was rather quiet after Alexander had explained his conversation with Desert Eagle on Ol' Betsy, along with his thoughts on the situation. As they drive the very short drive to Lake Gregory Regional Park for their day at the lake, Ben's mind shifts to what Alexander had said and what it meant.

Are the people from Earth Two here, already? I was hoping we had more time before we had to deal with them. Things were just starting to reach some sort of normalcy. Should we even be going to the lake today?

As Ben follows the Blazer onto a short bridge over a small portion of the west part of the lake, Eileen breaks the silence. "If the people are here from Earth Two, it doesn't sound like a good thing. Does it?"

She was thinking about it too. Of course she is. We all are...

"Yeah, I was thinking along the same lines. If it's them, up at Edwards Air Force Base... it's not a good sign. When a foreign force doesn't announce itself and goes directly to a military installation, and then communication ends with the installation, that's not a good sign at all."

Eileen looks over to him. "We don't know for sure that has happened though, and no news is good news. Right, Ben?"

Ben noticed that she sounded concerned and even scared. This made him feel unsettled. He had always known her to be strong, sometimes even a tad bit crazy, but still very strong.

"Normally, I would say yes. But there's nothing normal about our current situation Eileen." Ben turns right onto Lake Drive, heading toward the parking lot at the northwest side of the lake.

"We have lost communication with many areas since the *Blue Hole Radius* caught back up with real time. None of the news that we found out about those areas was good news at all." Ben adds.

Eileen nods. "I suppose you are right." She says as Ben pulls into the parking lot and parks the truck next to his Uncle's Blazer.

She goes to open her door and get out, but pauses and looks over to him. "Well, whatever's about to happen... let's enjoy today, even if it's only for today. We don't know when we'll get another chance to take a day like this."

Ben looks at her. *She really is something. She seems like she's scared out of her gourd, but then clicks it off... like a switch. How does she do that?*

"You have a point there, beautiful." Ben smiles at her. "Enjoying the small things is important. And I'm hoping that your bikini under those clothes gives us one of those small things I get to enjoy in the very near future." He chuckles at her.

Eileen blushes, but she turns away to open her door and hop down from the truck. "I'm sure you are, Benjamin, now stop being a perv and let's unload this truck."

She winks at him and he can't help but laugh.

The four of them unload the two vehicles and load up their picnic and fishing supplies into the two foldable wagons that they had brought from his Uncle's cabin. Ben looks around the lot and notices several other cars in the lake parking lot.

"Looks like we weren't the only ones with the fine idea of enjoying some sunshine lakeside." Ben announces.

"Yeah, but this is nothing compared to regular summer days. It looks like we'll have this part of the lake pretty much to ourselves." Steven replies.

Once they are finished, two more cars pull into the lot. The cars pull up on the other side of his Uncle's Blazer. Ben watches as Todd exits one of the vehicles with his wife, Jamie, and daughter, Claire. Jim's widow, Amanda, and her daughter, Chloe, exit the other vehicle. Ben waves at the combined Bradley family.

Ben feels heartache at the thought that one of them was missing. Ben was still very sour about Jim's passing. And if he was still sour about it, he knew that Todd was much more sour about it. Something still didn't sit right with the whole situation. Sure, they had lost people in the MS13 Battle. But something seemed different about Jim's death. He wasn't sure what, but he had a feeling. Whenever Ben went down this road of thoughts, he chalked it up to not liking that Corrections' Officer, Richard Stevens.

Before Ben can get lost down that path of thoughts again, little Claire comes running up. "Auntie Eileen!" The little girl shouts and gives Eileen a big hug around the bottom half of her body.

Ben laughs. "What am I chopped liver, Claire? Come and give me a hug, squirt."

Eileen smiles. "What can I say? I'm her favorite." Eileen grins at Ben.

Claire rushes over to Ben and gives him a hug too, and then goes straight back to Eileen.

"See. I told you." Eileen adds.

"Eileen! Eileen! Eileen! Are you going to go swimming with us?!" Claire asks. She then looks at Eileen. "Where's your bathing suit? Did you forget it?" She points to her bathing suit. "I already have mine on!"

Eileen laughs. "Me too, kiddo. It's under my clothes. You'll see once we get down to the shore."

Claire brightens up. "Good! We can go swimming then! You, me, and Chloe!"

Amanda and Chloe walk up to the group. "Chloe, you want to go swimming with me and Auntie Eileen?!"

Chloe looks at Eileen and Ben, steps back slightly and grips her mother's hand. She then looks up to her mom. "It's okay, Chloe. These are friends. You remember Ben, don't you sweetie. Ben was friends with daddy when they were kids."

Ben walks over to the timid child and kneels down in front of her. "Hey little one. It has been a while. I haven't seen you since you were a little baby. Here..." He reaches into his pack and pulls out a couple of squirt guns. "These are for you and Claire. Why don't you go give her hers?"

The little girl's face brightens quickly, then goes back to blank as she looks up to her mom. "Go ahead sweetie." Chloe's face brightens up again with a silent smile and she rushes off to Claire and begins to giggle.

He stands and gives Amanda a firm hug. "You need anything, let me know. Okay?"

She holds him for a little bit. "Thanks, Ben. Jamie told me what you did. You didn't have to do that. But thank you very much."

He steps back and sees tears begin to well up in her eyes. Jamie walks up. "Benjamin! We have been here all of two seconds and you are already making my sister-in-law cry." She punches him in the shoulder.

"Ow!" Ben says, rubbing his shoulder, exaggerating the pain.

This gets a laugh from Jamie, Amanda, and Eileen.

"What say we head on down to the shore!" Uncle Steven announces.

The group agrees and starts heading down to the lake. After about twenty minutes of setting up, Uncle Steven and Alexander make their way down the shore toward the docks, with fishing poles and tackle gear in hand.

"Wish us luck!" Steven announces.

The group waves them off as they make their way to the docks, leaving the Bradley family, Ben, and Eileen, to their secluded part of the beach. Ben notices that there are a few other families that he can see along the beach but not many people at all, and they are spread pretty far out from each other.

Ben kicks off his shoes and stuffs his socks into them, then takes off his shirt, and pulls his PX4 Storm out of his boardshorts and tucks it into the wagon. He looks over and sees Todd doing the same.

He digs his toes into the sandy shore and plops down, looking out onto the lake. He looks over at the two young girls, already playing in the water, and sees Amanda and Jamie talking, wading in the water and watching their daughters.

He stops thinking as his eyes find Eileen pulling down her pants, revealing her bikini bottom. Ben watches in amazement as she displays her light-browned body in a green bikini. After Ben looks over her body, his eyes go to her face, with her hair up in a ponytail and those bright green eyes.

From a few feet away from him, she notices him staring at her and laughs. "Stop being a creeper, Ben." She chucks her clothes at him.

"Auntie Eileen! Come swim with us!" Claire shouts. Having seen that Eileen was now in her bathing suit.

"Coming girls!" Eileen shouts back. She looks at Ben and winks, then strides off into the water to play with the two little girls.

After a few moments, Todd laughs. "Man! You have it bad don't you!"

Ben's shaken out of a daze and looks over at him. "What?"

This elicits more laughter from Todd. "Yup! You have it real bad, brother!"

Ben laughs, catching on. "Well? Can you blame me?"

Todd shakes his head. "No, sir. I cannot... I know the feeling." Todd replies as he gazes upon his wife, Jamie. "I definitely know the feeling." Jamie looks over and waves at her husband. Todd gets up. "Well... it'd be smart of us to go join them, my friend."

Todd strides over to his wife and Ben watches the scene in front of him, good people enjoying the moment.

God, I hope there are more moments like this in our future...

Ben sees Eileen wave at him, motioning for him to come in.

You don't have to tell me twice.

Ben gets up and goes to join Eileen and the others in the lake.

The group spends the rest of the morning and the early afternoon playing in the water. All the while, Alexander and Steven are fishing down by the docks. Around lunchtime, Alexander and Steven wander back to the group, having caught seven fish.

Steven puts them in a cooler that he brought along with them, promising to split the fresh fish amongst the families. Also promising to catch more after lunch.

The group have sandwiches and fruit for lunch along the shoreline of Lake Gregory. After lunch, the girls go back into the water. Alexander and Steven go back to the docks to catch more fish. Ben finds himself happy that his Uncle and Alexander were getting along so famously.

After Ben and Todd clean up the mess from lunch, he goes back into the water on this warm July day. He wades over to Eileen and wraps her in a hug.

"This is a good day." She says.

"Yes, it surely is." Ben admits. "I'm glad that I thought of it."

"A little proud of yourself, aren't we?" She smiles at him.

"Just a little bit." He replies.

She grins and then kisses him. Ben holds her in his arms in the cool water of the lake, with the sun beating down over them.

It doesn't get much better than this.

A few moments later, Ben hears Todd's voice from the shore. "Hey Ben!"

Ben and Eileen look over at Todd, putting his shirt on and starting to grab his shoes. "Now what's he doing?" Eileen asks.

"I'm not sure. But he looks like he's in a hurry." Ben replies.

Finding his shoes, he waves over at Ben. "Hey Ben! You got a minute?!" He shouts over to him.

"Well, you better go see what he wants." Eileen says.

"Yeah, I suppose you're right." Ben grudgingly admits, not wanting to leave Eileen... in a bikini, in a lake, in his arms.

She pushes himself away and turns. "I usually am." She smiles at him.

He shakes his head and wades out of the water toward Todd, who now has his shoes on and is putting his sidearm into his waistband.

Well this doesn't look good.

"Hey Todd, what's up?" Ben asks.

"Not sure, yet. But apparently I had several missed calls from Cassandra Patterson. Harold's wife." Todd explains.

"Sheriff Patterson's wife. What about?" Ben asks.

"Harold never came home last night. She said he went to make a house call because he was invited to dinner at a newcomer's home in Lake Arrowhead." Todd explains.

"Shit, that doesn't sound good. Does she know who?" Ben asks.

"Yeah, doesn't sound good at all. Even worse, he isn't answering me over the radio and no one else has heard from him since yesterday. Hell, I saw him yesterday over at the Lake Arrowhead Marketplace." Todd replies.

"Todd, do you know where he went and whose house it was?" Ben asks again.

"Yeah, that's the kicker. You remember that asshole Correctional Officer that shoved a gun into our faces the night of the MS13 Battle?" Todd asks.

"Yes...Yes, I do. Richard Stevens was his name, and something didn't feel right about that guy." Ben admits, while gritting his teeth.

"So, it wasn't just me? I thought it was a combination of adrenaline and just finding out about Jim." Todd answers.

"So, what do you want to do? Call the other Deputies and surround the place?" Ben replies.

Todd shakes his head. "The guy may be an asshole, but we don't know enough yet. And we can't go wrongfully accusing people. There could be a reasonable explanation for all of this. And I don't want another situation like yesterday." Todd explains.

"Yeah, Alexander filled us in on what happened at the stockades over there." Ben replies.

"Can you go grab your Uncle and Alexander and have them look over things while we go ask this Stevens guy some questions?" Todd asks of Ben.

"What, me? You want me to go? Why?" Ben questions.

Todd pauses. "It may be dire, it may not be. But we need to find out quickly. If I spread word that we are going to go ask this Stevens guy questions about the Sheriff, it may turn out badly. Plus, we don't know the whole story. For all we know, this Stevens guy has nothing to do with it..."

"I don't know Todd. That guy gives me a real itching to put a bullet in his brain." Ben answers.

"And here I thought you were going to be my reasonable and logical guy." Todd chuckles.

"Fine. But if anything seems hinky over there, we call in your cavalry." Ben replies.

"Sounds good. Now go get your Uncle and Alexander and meet me at your truck." Todd orders Ben.

"Will do, bud." Ben replies and goes off to get his Uncle and Alexander.

After quickly explaining to them the situation trying to locate the Sheriff, leaving out the part that they were going to see Richard Stevens and that he didn't like the Stevens guy, not even a little bit, he sees Eileen back at the cooler and blankets.

"What's going on, Ben?" She questions.

"I'm not sure, but Todd needs my help for a little bit. We'll be back before you know it. We just need to find the Sheriff real quick." Ben replies.

"What are you not telling me Ben?" She asks.

Ben shakes his head.

She'll flip if she knows that Richard Stevens guy might be involved. She got the creeps from him too.

"Nothing. We just need to find the Sheriff. His wife's worried that he was in an accident or something." He replies.

Eileen eyes him, and then gives him a quick kiss on the lips. "Okay, Benjamin. Be quick and be safe."

Ben smiles at her. "You know me."

She kisses him again, "That's what I worry about."

He grins at her. "It'll be fine. I'll be back soon. You just stay in that bikini until I get back."

She laughs. "Get out of here, you perv. Go help your friend."

Ben laughs, quickly shoving on his shoes and grabbing his PX4 Storm and starts to walk off toward his truck.

He meets Todd at the vehicles. Todd's already back into jeans, a polo, boots, and has his sidearm on his hip. He was grabbing his bulletproof vest out of his SUV as Ben came up.

"Do we really need vests?" Ben asks.

"You were the one that said to surround the place... Plus, I always wear one around town now." Todd answers and Ben just looks at him. "It's different times now, Ben. And remember. Jim was shot in the chest. If he had been wearing his vest, he may have survived."

Ben doesn't answer, understanding the message.

Todd asks, "Do you have a vest in your truck?"

Ben shakes his head. "What I have is on me now. I have a couple spare magazines for my Beretta in the truck center console, but that's it."

Todd squints his eyes at him for a second. Then he goes to the back of his SUV, pulling out another bulletproof vest with Sheriff on a huge patch across it. "He tosses it to Ben. Better safe than sorry. He walks around the passenger side of the truck. "You drive and I'll navigate."

"Sounds good." Ben gets into his truck and starts the engine. "Where to?"

"Head toward the Lake Arrowhead Village Marketplace. We're heading to John Muir Road, over near the Orchard Creek part of the lake." Todd explains.

Ben pulls out of the parking lot, leaving the rest of their group in search for the good Sheriff. While navigating out of Crestline and toward Lake Arrowhead, Todd says, "I'm serious about times being different now, Ben. You've been to war and you know how it goes."

"War? Are we in a time of war now, Todd?" Ben asks.

"No, not now. But we are in a time of chaos and those times are very similar." Todd explains.

"I suppose you have a good point, Todd." Ben admits.

Todd continues. "That's not my point, Ben... My point is that you need to treat every day like that. Yes, we're having a nice day at the lake. But we need to be ready at all times. Our family, our friends, and our community depend on it."

Ben nods his head. *He has a point. But wow, Todd has gotten deep and much darker since Jim died.*

"So next time you leave the house... every time you leave the house... be prepared as though you may not return to that house." Todd says.

They drive in silence as they near Lake Arrowhead. Once they reach the village, Todd says, "Turn right and then turn left once we hit John Muir Road. Just follow the lake around and it's a few houses down on our left." Todd was looking down at his phone, having punched in the address Cassandra Patterson had given him.

Turning left onto John Muir Road, Todd adds, "I don't mean to sound so doom and gloom, but I don't want Jamie and Claire to end up like Amanda and Chloe. You know?"

Ben nods, "Yeah, I get it."

"Plus, I'd hate to see you get hurt too, Ben. We've already lost enough good people. I know we'll lose more... in time. Doesn't mean we can't curb that loss to lower numbers with smart decisions." Todd explains.

Ben follows the road around the first bend and pulls into a driveway that is like a bridge, stopping in front of a white house that overlooks the lake with a Tan Toyota Tacoma in the driveway.

"This it?" He questions.

"That's what the map says." Todd replies and shuts off his phone and puts it back into his pocket.

Ben pulls into the driveway and shuts off the engine. He exits the vehicles as Todd gets out on his side. "How do you want to handle this?" Ben asks.

Todd nods to Ben. "Let me do all of the talking. Remember... we are just here to ask the man some questions."

Ben nods, "Lead the way Deputy Bradley."

Todd shakes his head and smiles and walks up to the front door.

Before Todd can ring the doorbell, the two men hear a thud coming from upstairs. Todd looks at Ben as he rings the doorbell.

"What the hell was that?" Ben asks.

"Not sure... but the plan is the same. Just keep your eyes and ears open." Todd says.

After a few moments, Todd rings the doorbell again. The two men wait at the door for a few more moments, and Todd rings the bell a third time, instantly the door opens up wide.

"Good afternoon Deputies! How can I help you this fine day?!" Richard Stevens blurts out as he opens the door. The two men instinctively put their hands on their sidearms on their hips.

"Whoa, whoa, whoa, cowboys! Didn't mean to startle you two!" Richard says.

Ben and Todd relax slightly. "Good afternoon, Mr. Stevens. You caught us off guard there for a moment."

Richard grins. "I get that a lot." He steps aside, and gestures them in. "Why don't you two come on in, out of that heat."

Ben looks to Todd to know what to do. Todd looks to him and nods, heading inside. Ben follows and Richard closes the door behind them. Richard gestures to them to move into the front living room. "So, what can I do for you gents?"

Todd replies, "Yes. We heard that Sheriff Patterson came over here for dinner last night and were wondering if you had seen him? His wife's worried about him."

Richard smiles wide. "Ah yes! Sheriff Patterson. He did come by for dinner."

"About what time was he here and when did he leave? Did he say where he was going?" Todd asks Richard.

Richard scratches his chin and then puts his hands on his hips, his right hand just above a revolver on his hip. Ben glances at it but thinks nothing of it, since everyone is carrying sidearms these days. He looks over to Todd and notices that his eyes linger on the gun for a little longer than maybe they should.

Richard takes notice and looks down at the revolver on his hip and smiles, then looking back up at Todd. "You like it? It's a classic. It was my father's and his father's before him."

Todd doesn't say a word but looks Richard directly in the eyes. Richard doesn't seem to waiver and continues. "But yeah, Sheriff Patterson came by for dinner around sunset. I want to say he left around 11:00 PM or so. To be honest, it's a tad bit fuzzy. We had a few beers with dinner and sat on the back porch for a while."

Todd smiles. "Sounds like the good old Sheriff. That's a very nice HD500 Ruger 357 you got there. And it's nice to keep it in your family over the years."

HD500 Ruger 357? What the hell's that, Todd?

Richard smiles widely again, reminding Ben of the *Cheshire Cat* from *Alice and Wonderland*.

"Thanks, Deputy Bradley. I sure think so. It's Bradley, right? Jim Bradley's twin?" Richard then turns to Ben. "And I believe you are Ben Reilly, correct? I didn't think you were a cop though. Deputized recently then, I take it?" Richard laughs lightly.

Before Ben can answer with a snide remark, Todd answers quickly. "Yes, on all accounts, Officer Stevens. Thanks for the info on the Sheriff. He's probably sleeping it off in the Marketplace parking lot or somewhere nearby. Thank you for your time."

Todd eyes Ben, but Ben's still confused.

Why does he want to leave and what the hell was that about an HD500 Ruger 357?

Richard looks at the both of them, grinning. "No problem at all gents. Before you all go though, why don't you have a cup of iced tea. My beautiful fiancé made it fresh, just earlier today."

There's an awkward silence as Todd's staring at Ben, trying to get a message across, but Ben can't grasp it.

"Everything alright, gents." Richard asks, smiling.

Todd diverts his attention to Richard. "Yes, sir. Tea would be nice. Thank you."

"Sounds good. I'll be right back." Richard says and heads into the kitchen.

Once Richard's out of the room, Ben asks, "What's going on,

Todd? And what the hell's an HD500 Ruger 357? Because I haven't ever heard of it."

Todd looks at him. "That's exactly the point. This guy is not who he says he is, and something's way off. The Sheriff does not drink that much. Only a beer here and there. And I'm pretty damn sure that the Ruger GP100 357 is Sheriff Patterson's... His story is bullshit for sure."

"So, let's arrest him." Ben says.

"The plan was to get information and come back with the cavalry if we had to. Now we know we need to come back with the cavalry. We need to play this smart, Ben. No reason for more loss of life." Todd explains.

"Fine..." Ben replies. "Let's go then."

"Tea, first. As not to let him catch on. Then we'll leave." Todd answers.

Ben sees Richard come around the corner of the hallway out of the corner of his eye. "You fucktards need to learn how to fucking whisper better!" Richard laughs and raises a side-by-side shotgun, pointing it at Todd.

Before Ben and Todd can react, Richard pulls the trigger.

::Boom::

The shot hits Todd dead center. The force sends Todd flying through the air, hitting the couch behind him and bouncing him back forward onto the ground face down.

"Brother number two down for the count! Look at me! Two for two!" Richard shouts and laughs. Richard then aims the shotgun at Ben. "Buh-bye Ben!"

Ben dives to the right, in front of the stairs as Richard pulls the trigger.

::Boom::

Ben blinks, trying to get the ringing out of his ears from the shotgun blasts. He reaches for his PX4 Storm and brings it up while he's crouched in front of the stairs. Down the hallway, toward the kitchen, he hears a clunking sound. Then Richard speaks. "You still alive, Ben?"

Ben sticks his head out to get a peek at Richard and a bullet whizzes by his head.

::Crack::

"Yup, guess so!" Richard laughs as he sends another two rounds down the hallway.

::Crack::Crack::

Ben ducks back and sends a few rounds through the banister of the stairs, trying to hit near Richard.

::Crack::Crack::Crack::

Richard returns fire, toward Ben.

::Crack::Crack::

Ben ducks back, under the cover of the staircase. He darts a glance toward Todd, seeing him starting to move.

He's alive!

"Oh, it looks like I didn't kill brother number two after all!" Richard exclaims. "Well, time to fix that!"

Shit! Ben thinks.

And without another thought, he dives out sideways, toward Todd's unconscious body. He sends three rounds down the hallway and hears one in return.

::Crack::Crack::Crack::

::Crack::

Landing in front of Todd, Ben feels like he was just punched in the gut, having the wind knocked out of him. His vision is blurry for a second, but he thinks he can see Richard grabbing his right shoulder.

He hears Richard yell out in pain. "OW! You shitfuck! You actually shot me!"

Ben feels a searing pain in his chest and looks down.

Was I shot, too?! No Blood! That's a good sign! Oh Thank God!... But it hurts like a mother!

Ben then hears a door slam open and he looks back down the hallway to see the backdoor open and Richard gone.

Fucking shit! Eileen's going to be pissed. Hopefully Todd can explain this situation better than I can.

Todd!

Ben pushes away his pain and returns to Todd. He rolls his body over and looks at his chest.

He sees a large slug in the center of his vest and reaches under the vest to see if it went through. He feels Todd wince in pain.

"Holy shit that hurts." Todd says with a winced voice.

Ben pulls his hand out.

No blood. That's good, but the plate is definitely warped...

"I'm sure it does buddy. You probably have at least one broken rib. You were hit with a slug." Ben says to him.

Todd's eyes start to open up. "Where's he at? Did you get him?"

"He took off. I wounded him... I think. But he also got me in the chest too. Great thinking with these vests, Todd. Real life savers..." Ben replies.

"Are you sure he's gone, Ben?" Todd asks.

Ben then hears footsteps from behind him and feels the warm barrel of a gun pushed against his head.

"Ben Reilly, you son of a bitch!" Richard shouts.

"Shit!" Ben blurts out.

Richard smiles. "I knew I should have killed you that night on the road. You are just like the late Sheriff. You just can't let things be. It got him killed and looks like it did the same thing to you."

Richard chuckles lightly. "With the Sheriff's gun, I might add."

Ben shuts his eyes, thinking this is the end.

Not like this... he thinks as an image of Eileen pops into his mind.

6

RICHARD CLARK

IT HAD BEEN ALMOST two months since Richard had escaped Chino. To him, it felt like a lifetime ago. Everything had fallen into place for him and Richard found he was enjoying himself for the first time in his life. Sure, he had fun before, a lot of fun. But he was actually enjoying himself playing house with Holly Clark.

Richard thought about how much had transpired over the last seven weeks as he drank his coffee on the back porch, overlooking the lake. Richard looks over to where he knows Sheriff Patterson to be buried, knowing because he buried him the night before.

He smiles, thinking of the events of the previous night, the look on Sheriff Harold Patterson's face when he realized that he was about to die, the enjoyment gained from burying the dumb bastard, and what he did to Holly Clark afterward.

Oh, Holly Clark, you are most certainly a keeper. Let's just hope that you are not pregnant. Because then we'll have to resort to plan A, and if that doesn't work... plan B. If we get to plan C, I guess you weren't a keeper after all.

Richard laughs lightly as he takes another sip of his coffee.

I don't think you'll like any of these plans, Holly. But then again, it's not really up to you... is it.

He looks down at his empty coffee mug then back out onto the lake.

Might as well go inside and get our story straight. No doubt someone will come looking for the good Sheriff. Pushing his car off the side of the mountain was a good choice on my part. If they find the car, they will never find the body and have to assume that animals got to him.

Richard heads back into his luxurious home, taken from the family that lived there prior to his arrival. In fact, they were buried in close proximity to the Sheriff.

Richard had figured they were certainly rich and may have even been famous, but he never even bothered with finding out who they were. In all honesty, Richard didn't care. Even when they had begged for their lives.

One by one they were shot, the son, the wife, and the father. The way Richard saw it... it was their own fault for not protecting what they had. He even told them as much, prior to their deaths. *"Good job protecting your family dipshit. You didn't even try."*

The important part to Richard was that he had found a *home* for himself and his newfound fiancé.

As he walks back inside, he hears the water running upstairs. "Holly must be up and showering." He says aloud.

After I'm done with here, she's going to need another shower.

He chuckles at his own joke and heads upstairs toward his master bedroom, with his fiancé in the shower. He proceeds to the shower, forcing her out and onto the bed, not even allowing her to dry off.

After so many times of this, Holly has stopped fighting back and allows Richard to have his way with her and rape her. Richard grins at her submissiveness.

Definitely a keeper. He thinks.

After he's done with her, he spits on her and laughs. "Best go take another shower, sweet thing... Then come downstairs, because we need to have a talk." He laughs as he pulls up his pants and heads downstairs to find himself some lunch.

He makes his way back downstairs to the kitchen and makes himself a sandwich. He searches through the cupboard.

"I know I still saw a few bags left..." He says as he searches through the cupboard of food.

"Ah! There they are." He says as he pulls out a small bag of Doritos from the cupboard. "No sandwich is complete without chips inside of it."

Afterward, he goes to the refrigerator and pulls out the jug of tea that Holly had made the previous day, pouring himself a glass.

Pleased with himself and his lunch, he sits down at the dining room table and goes to eat. He begins to think of his fiancé in the shower and why she had to take a second shower.

He laughs and spits out some of his food. "She may just have to take another shower before the day's over."

While eating his lunch, his mind shifts to the beginning of the *Blue Hole Radius* and how he got to where he was.

Blue Hole Radius... he laughs. *What a stupid fucking name. They could have come up with a better name than that. What about 'time trap' or 'time sphere' or even 'the radius prison.'*

Richard smiles as he eats his lunch, making fun of the people *from the future* and everything that got him here, to *his* new world.

Richard may not have known what was going on after 1301 on May 19th, 2023. However, he knew that it was his opportunity to make a new life for himself, and eventually a new name.

Seven weeks earlier, Richard Clark was in "Chino" or CIM (Chino California Institution for Men). He was sentenced in 2020 and was only his third-year in out of a twenty-five-year sentence. He was put away on the distribution of illicit drugs and weapons trafficking charges. If they had nailed him for all of his attributes, he would surely be serving at least double that sentence.

During the middle of the night, after the *Blue Hole Radius* had been lifted and the world had turned to chaos, Richard Clark seized his opportunity. First, he killed his overweight and annoying cell-mate, Freddie, in their cell. He followed this up with calling over one of the few guards remaining to *help* his cellmate, who was no longer breathing.

The Correctional Officer, Sergeant Roger Stevens, took the bait and allowed Richard to gain the upper hand. After smashing the guard's head into the wall, he donned the guard's clothes and proceeded to exit the cellblock. He tricked the other guard into letting him out, with him thinking he was his fellow guard in the darkness of night, only to be shot point blank in the face by Richard. The next guard Richard had allowed to live, and even set a prison riot into motion. Which gave him the distraction he needed to find his way to Roger Stevens' locker and eventually out of Chino.

Richard was even able to acquire the late Sergeant Stevens' tan Toyota truck and headed for the man's home, after seeing a picture of his fiancé.

After Richard reached Roger Stevens' home, he took his fiancé, Holly Clark, for his own... under force for the first of many times. He also saw it fitting to take over his identity, since the world was in such disarray, shifting over to becoming Corrections Officer Richard Stevens.

Richard does remember being extremely irate that the snitch that had sent him to prison was already dead by the time he had gotten to him. Nonetheless, he was able to take his frustration out on Ms. Holly Clark.

It was then that he decided to head for the luxury homes of Lake Arrowhead, with the intention of taking one for his own and newly acquired fiancé. He did have a run-in with local wannabe gangsters, under the MS13 gang. Richard had dealt with them swiftly and found his way to the home he was now living in.

Having *evicted* the previous tenants, he was quite happy with his new home. He had even made a few friends with some firefighters, after having helped them with their MS13 gangster problem. It was slightly a problem of his own, too. Since he wanted to keep the new life that he had earned as Richard Stevens, with his beautiful and somewhat young fiancé, 25 years old, and a few years older than he liked, Holly Clark.

So, help these simple townsfolk he did. He even found a way to kill a nosy cop in the process, Jim Bradley. Richard found excitement in how easy it was to blame the nosy Deputy's death on the MS13 gang.

He found himself even having a few beers with those firefighters over the last seven weeks. They had become somewhat *okay* friends through the process. John, Mike, and Tom had come over on several occasions and Richard did find it nice to have acquired friends in his newfound life, as well as people to stick up for him, if anyone else didn't entirely trust Richard Stevens.

He was aware that not everyone trusted him as quickly as the firefighters did. There was the Deputy's twin, who was also a Deputy in town. That encounter had given Richard a shock when seeing him for the first time, but he had a good laugh later on. There was also the Deputy's friend Ben Reilly and that pretty light-skinned girl, Eileen something. They had almost posed a real problem for Richard that night... There was also the expired Sheriff, but he was no longer an issue.

Richard was very happy with himself for the events that transpired over the last seven weeks. As he saw it, his death toll had to be close to, and even over, twenty. There had been around twenty dead MS13 gangster wannabes on the night of the MS13 Battle, and Richard clearly remembered taking out at least half of them.

So, Richard figured his count to be closer to thirty, so far, post *Blue Hole Radius*. Richard knew that he had only killed a handful of people prior to his time in Chino. And if a certain nosy twin brother and his friends came poking around, he would gladly push up that number to at least twenty-nine, and still counting.

He figured if they came looking for the expired Sheriff, he'll deal with them in the same manner. He would even be nice enough to bury them in close quarters to the departed sheriff and previous tenants of *his* home. This was *his* new world, and no one was going to take that away from him.

Recollecting on his past experiences, he knows there's a pressing matter to address today... which is Holly likely being pregnant.

Richard thinks about this last part as he finishes his lunch and sees Holly walk into the kitchen.

"Hello there, pretty lady." Richard says, grinning at her.

"I see you got all cleaned up again. Good job." Richard smirks.

"Thank you, Richard." She replies. "I just came down here for some food. Then I was going to take a nap."

"Not feeling well, are we?" Richard asks. "Why don't you hold off on lunch. Take a seat and let's have ourselves a chat about your sickness."

Holly looks at him with eyes of fear.

She hasn't had those eyes of fear in a long while. She's definitely pregnant and doesn't want to give it up.

She hesitates and freezes close to the refrigerator.

"I said! Sit down Holly!" Richard bellows.

She flinches and then walks over to the dining room table.

"We have avoided the elephant in the room long enough. Or should I say the baby in the womb..." Richard quips.

Holly looks away from him and diverts her eyes to the table, looking down in front of her. "I don't know what you're talking about, Richard. I just have a stomach bug. I'll be fine in a few days..."

"Bull-fucking-shit, Holly." Richard exclaims. "You are pregnant, and you know how I feel about that."

Holly shakes her head. "No!"

Richard nods his head. "Yes, Holly... you are."

Richard watches as she starts to sob, and her lip quivers. After a few moments she looks up at him with tears running down her face.

"So that's it then. You're going to kill me now?" She says, crying softly.

Richard laughs and then smiles, which shuts her up and she goes silent. "Of course not pretty lady. You are a keeper... it's just that baby that needs to go!"

Richard watches as Holly's eyes go wide. "What?! No!"

He nods, trying to calm her down. "Yes, Holly. It'll be simple. We'll just have to starve you for a week, and you should miscarry. If that little baby has nothing to eat, it will just wither away." He smiles at her.

Her eyes go wider. "What?! NO! I won't let you!"

He laughs at her. "You! You won't let me!? That's rich, bitch! I'll chain you to the fucking bed if I have to! Feed you water and nothing else! Well... maybe I'll feed you something else." He laughs at his own joke.

Holly's eyes begin to fill up with tears. "NO! I won't let you Richard! You've taken everything else! You won't take my baby!" Richard watches as she bolts from the chair and starts to run upstairs.

Richard laughs as she runs upstairs to their bedroom. "Where the fuck do you think you are going, Holly?!" He laughs. "You try to run away and run your dumbass upstairs!" He laughs again. "Looks to me like you want to get chained up to the bed right fucking now!"

Richard stands and follows her upstairs, finding her standing next to the bed with a kitchen knife in her hands.

"Just what the fuck are you going to do with that!?" He snaps at her.

Holly looks like she's in a frantic fury. "You stay right there, Richard! Don't come any closer! I won't let you hurt my baby!"

Richard laughs and steps in closer to her. He back hands the knife out of her hands and it goes flying across the room, onto the bed. He then smacks her across the face. "I'm starting to think that maybe you aren't a keeper, Holly."

Holly's eyes go wide as he grabs her by the throat and slams her against the wall.

::Ding Dong::

Richard freezes, registering that someone's at the front door. With Holly's throat in his grip, he steps to the side and moves the curtains of the second-floor window. He sees a black Dodge truck in his driveway, next to *his* tan Toyota Tundra.

"Just who the fuck is that?" Richard asks the gasping Holly in his grip. "Looks like you're saved by the bell, Holly. I almost just did something that you would have regretted."

He releases his grip around her throat, and she drops to her knees gasping for air.

"Stay the fuck here, Holly... and think about our conversation. Don't make a fucking sound and you better be in a better mood when I get back. Or we'll pick up where we left off..." Richard says as he scowls at her trying to catch her breath below him.

Without hearing her response, he strides out of the room and slams the door shut.

Stupid bitch better come to her senses by the time I come back.

::Ding Dong::

"I'm coming, asshole. Whoever the fuck you are." Richard says as he makes his way to the front door.

As he comes to the door, he double checks his holster on his right hip.

We may just have to use your gun Sheriff... I mean my new gun.

::Ding Dong::

He grins at the revolver at his hip, and unlocks the front door and opens it wide.

"Good afternoon Deputies! How can I help you this fine day?!" Richard blurts out as he opens the door. The two men instinctively put their hands on their sidearms on their hips.

"Whoa, whoa, whoa, cowboys! Didn't mean to startle you two!" Richard says.

The twin brother and his buddy Ben. Interesting turn of events.

Ben and Todd relax slightly. "Good afternoon, Mr. Stevens. You caught us off guard there for a moment."

Richard grins. "I get that a lot." He steps aside, and gestures them in. "Why don't you two come on in out of that heat."

Richard watches as the two men look at each other, trying to figure out what to do next.

Fucking Idiots.

After several moments, the two men wander inside and he closes the door behind them. He then gestures to them to move into the front living room.

"So, what can I do for you gents?" He asks.

Deputy Bradley replies, "Yes. We heard that Sheriff Patterson came over here for dinner last night and were wondering if you had seen him? His wife's worried about him."

Richard smiles wide.

That was pretty damn fast of them to put together. No matter...

"Ah yes! Sheriff Patterson. He did come by for dinner." He replies.

Deputy Bradley then asks, "About what time was he here and when did he leave? Did he say where he was going?"

Richard scratches his chin and then puts his hands on his hips, his right hand just above the revolver on his hip. He notices Ben glance at it, then look away. He then notices that Deputy Bradley's looking a little too close at his new gun.

He looks down at the revolver on his hip and smiles, then back up at the twin brother.

"You like it? It's a classic. It was my father's and his father's before him." He explains.

The twin brother doesn't say a word but looks Richard directly in the eyes.

What? Do you want to end up like your twin, asshole?

After an awkward moment of silence, he continues. "But yeah, Sheriff Patterson came by for dinner around sunset. I want to say he left around 11:00 PM or so. To be honest, it's a tad bit fuzzy. We had a few beers with dinner and sat on the back porch for a while."

The Deputy smiles. "Sounds like the good old Sheriff. That's a very nice HD500 Ruger 357 you got there. And it's nice to keep it in your family over the years."

Richard smiles widely again.

What's this guy getting at?

"Thanks, Deputy Bradley. I sure think so. It's Bradley, right? Jim Bradley's twin?" He then turns to Ben. "And I believe you are Ben Reilly, correct? I didn't think you were a cop though. Deputized recently then, I take it?" Richard laughs lightly.

He is awaiting a response from the buddy Ben, but the Deputy snaps a quick response. "Yes, on all accounts, Officer Stevens. Thanks for the info on the Sheriff. He's probably sleeping it off in the Marketplace parking lot or somewhere nearby. Thanks for your time."

He then watches as the two men look at each other with that dumbfounded look again.

Something's up... the twin knows something. Is it the fucking gun?

Richard looks at the both of them, grinning. "No problem at all gents. Before you all go though, why don't you have a cup of iced tea. My beautiful fiancé made it fresh, just earlier today."

Yeah, something's up, for sure. Best to catch them off guard. I still have that side-by-side stashed in the kitchen.

"Everything alright, gents." He asks, smiling.

After a moment, the twin answers. "Yes, sir. Tea would be nice. Thank you."

"Sounds good. I'll be right back." Richard says as he heads into the kitchen.

Once he's out of the room, he grabs the shotgun and waits near the hallway, listening to his guests.

He hears Ben ask, "What's going on, Todd? And what the hell is an HD500 Ruger 357? Because I haven't ever heard of it."

He then hears the Deputy reply, "That's exactly the point. This guy is not who he says he is and something's way off. The Sheriff does not drink that much. Only a beer here and there. And I'm pretty damn sure that the Ruger GP100 357 is Sheriff's Patterson's. His story is bullshit for sure."

Ben responds, "So, let's arrest him."

The Deputy replies, "The plan was to get information and come back with the cavalry if we had to. Now we know we need to come back with the cavalry. We need to play this smart, Ben. No reason for more loss of life." Todd explains.

"Fine..." Ben replies. Let's go then."

"Tea, first. As not to let him catch on. Then we'll leave." The Deputy replies.

Richard grins as he listens to the men conversing on how they are going to "take him down."

Not only are they dumb as fuck, they are loud as fuck.

He grins as he pulls out from around the corner of the kitchen, aiming the shotgun down the hallway, toward his two guests wanting to arrest him.

"You fucktards need to learn how to fucking whisper better!" Richard laughs and pulls the trigger on the side-by-side.

::Boom::

The shot hits the Deputy dead center, and he watches as the force sends him flying through the air, hitting the couch behind him, bouncing him back forward onto the ground face down.

"Brother number two down for the count! Look at me! Two for two!" He shouts and laughs. He then aims the shotgun at Ben. "Buh-bye Ben!"

Ben dives to the right in front of the stairs as he pulls the trigger.

::Boom::

Fucking shit! Did I miss the dumb bastard? He thinks to himself.

He shrugs. *Only one way to find out.*

"You still alive, Ben?" He shouts.

He tosses his empty shotgun to the ground and pulls out his revolver, awaiting an answer. After a moment, he sees a head poke out past the stairs.

::Crack::

"Yup, guess so!" He laughs.

::Crack::Crack::

He grins as he sends two more rounds down toward the buddy Ben. He then looks over to the downed Deputy.

::Crack::Crack::Crack::

He flinches when the wall next to him explodes, sending drywall and plaster into his face.

Son of bitch almost shot me!

He returns fire with Ben.

::Crack::Crack::

Hopefully that took care of that dumbfuck!

He glances back over at the downed Deputy and sees him start to move a little.

"Oh, it looks like I didn't kill brother number two after all!" He exclaims. "Well, time to fix that!"

Richard points his revolver at the Deputy and goes to pull the trigger. He watches Ben dive out from the stairs, trying to shield his friend.

Really, guy? He thinks as he pulls the trigger.

::Crack::Crack::Crack::

::Crack::

He feels a burning pain in his right shoulder and yells out, "OW! You shitfuck! You actually shot me!"

Fucking little shit actually shot me! Son of a bitch. I need to think smarter than these dumbfucks. He thinks to himself looking around the hallway.

Seeing the door to the back porch, he thinks of a quick plan then slams open the back-porch door and jumps into the kitchen.

I'll get you, you little fuckshit. Make your dumbass think that I ran away... while I come into the den through the kitchen. Richard grins, as he holds his right shoulder. *I'll make you fucking pay for shooting me, you sack of shit.*

He creeps around, through the kitchen, and into the den that's on the other side of the stairs, and opposite of the living room that the Deputy and Ben Reilly are in. Once he's next to the stairs, he listens to the two men blabbering about how they think Richard ran away.

These guys really are fucking idiots.

He then walks back into the living room and puts the barrel of his revolver to Ben's head.

"Ben Reilly, you son of a bitch!" He shouts at the man on the floor.

"Shit!" Ben blurts out.

He smiles and replies. "I knew I should have killed you that night on the road. You are just like the late Sheriff. You just can't let things be. It got him killed and looks like it did the same thing to you."

He chuckles lightly at how things kept turning in his favor. "With the Sheriff's gun, I might add."

Richard grins, and squeezes the grip on the 357 revolver.

This is my new world... not yours.

Richard pulls the trigger.

::Click::

Shit! How many shots was that earlier!? Shit!

Before he can think to reload, his vision goes blurry. He feels a sudden burst of warmth on his chest and begins to feel very cold. He tries to speak but cannot.

His vision begins to fade, and he begins to notice a thick taste of copper in his mouth.

The next thing he knows, he's looking at Ben Reilly and his fallen Deputy friend from a side angle.

Am I laying down? Why's it so cold? What the fuck happened? What did I fucking miss?

Richard tries to turn these thoughts into words, but all that comes are gargles and inaudible sounds.

He blinks once, and his vision becomes so blurry he can barely make out the figures in front of him. He blinks again and the blurry world around him goes white, a blinding white.

7

HOLLY CLARK

HOLLY AWAKENS in her very large bed and looks to her side, finding herself alone in the bed and the bedroom.

Good, he's not here. Which means he's already up and about. He'll probably be back later for more. He always wants more...

Holly tries to brush the thoughts of last night away from her mind and decides to take a shower. No matter how many showers she has taken since the start of this new world, she can never seem to feel clean. Nonetheless, she walks across the room and heads to the bathroom.

Once the water's heated up, she steps into the shower to try and find a moment of peace in her new reality. Unfortunately, as it is with most people, her mind starts to wander while she's trying to rinse herself clean. Her mind wanders to what her life was and what it now has become.

Holly Clark had it all, and everything was working in her favor, that was until May 19th, 2023. She didn't realize how much her life had changed because of the *Blue Hole Radius* until the following day, when Richard Clark arrived.

Prior to the *Blue Hole Radius*, she was going to school for Business Administration, while her fiancé, Roger Stevens, was working at Chino, as a Corrections Officer. Roger and Holly had been together for close to four years now, and he had just proposed earlier this year. Their plan was a late summer wedding at the beach. But all of those plans were gone now. Along with their plans to go to Yosemite National Park for her Birthday, which was yesterday.

Instead, she spent her 26th birthday shopping in a dystopian future at a makeshift marketplace, because of some *Blue Hole Radius*, with her capturer masquerading as her fiancé. Her big day was topped off with another murder, by Richard... followed up with his daily rape of her.

Falling asleep last night, she cried, for the first time in a couple weeks, and thought to herself, *happy birthday Holly... this may be your last one.*

Richard Clark had taken so much from her. She was not sure anymore on what to think of him exactly. In the beginning she hated him but was too afraid to do anything. Roger was gone and the whole world was gone along with him. No one was coming to protect her. No one was coming to save her.

It took a few days... after that morning that Richard showed up in her bedroom, her and Roger's bedroom, in Roger's uniform and proceeded to rape her. It took a few days... of him forcing her to travel with and having his way with her, daily. It took a few days... for her to come to the realization that this may be her life now. It took her close to a week to start to see Richard Clark, Richard Stevens as he referred to himself, as her capturer, her rapist, and her protector.

Over time, she learned how to better talk to him, and not be in tears. She learned how to make sure that he didn't get angry with her, as to not make matters worse. Each time he had his way with her, she became a little more numb. She had learned how to push her mind and thoughts somewhere else, while her body suffered his wrath.

Sure, she was disgusted with herself for going along with him, and slowly stopping to fight back. But what was she supposed to do? The world was in chaos and he killed anything that displeased him or didn't fit into *his* new world, as he would refer to it.

She had been there for seven of his murders, and he boasted about countless others. Holly was unsure of when she started to see him as both evil and her protector. Nonetheless, she had found that's how she viewed him now.

That was until she started to think she was pregnant and found out what he thought about that situation. These were the main concerns she had now. There was no denying it. She knew in her gut that she was pregnant. The morning sickness was a key indicator and there were other big signs as well. Like her missing her period last month, and her breasts feeling very tender and swollen.

She was pregnant and was no longer just thinking about her own survival. Now there was her unborn baby to think about.

She also felt in her gut that Richard would never let her baby live. Her baby didn't fit into *his* new world, whether it was his baby or not. She knew in her saddened heart that it was most likely Richard's and not Roger's baby. They had talked about starting to try, and she had just gone off her birth control, but the timeline wouldn't match up for it being Roger's baby.

To add to the evidence that it was Richard's, was the sheer numbers... the massive amount of times that he had raped her. The odds of the baby being Roger's didn't fit the timeline or the amount of sex that was had. The baby was Richard's and he surely still would not want her baby to be a part of *his* new world.

She was unsure if she could go on living like this. He had taken away so much from her. How could she let him take her baby too? She had begun to entertain the idea of suicide in the last few days.

I would at least take those things away from him... my body and his ability to kill me. She thinks to herself in the hot water of the shower.

Holly sobs lightly in the shower, realizing just how many times that he had raped her, how many times that she had *let* him rape her.

She begins to think of different ways to end her life, to end her suffering. She thought of poison, but if Richard found out, he might have thought she was trying to poison him. Plus, she really didn't have a clue on how to effectively poison herself, and all of the house-held chemicals sounded extremely painful. She had heard that the wrists only hurt for a minute and then it was over.

Before she can contemplate it anymore, the shower curtain is ripped open and she's startled to see Richard standing there grinning at her.

Before she can react, she's ripped from the shower and he doesn't even allow her to dry off.

She knows exactly what he wants. She doesn't fight back, and allows herself to be thrown onto the bed.

While Richard forces himself onto her, she drifts away in her mind.

She thinks of a lake, similar to the one they were at yesterday. She imagines that her baby has grown into a toddler and that she's walking him along the shore of the lake. She's not sure why she automatically thinks that her baby is a boy, but it feels right.

She smiles inside of her head, thinking about how beautiful her baby boy is. She thinks of all the things she will teach him, and all of the things that she won't. Richard isn't there in her imagined lakeside walk with her son. It's simply her and her son, whom she will raise to be a much better person than his father, and a much stronger person than his mother.

Her dreamlike illusional escape starts to drift away as she notices that Richard's no longer atop of her. She feels him spit on her and say, "Best go take another shower, sweet thing... then come downstairs, because we need to have a talk."

She hears him laugh and her vision starts to come fully back to the bedroom that she was just raped in, once again. She notices him walk out of the room, and she just lies there for a moment, remembering the dreamlike escape that her subconscious had allowed her to go to.

Maybe I can reason with him. I've been able to before. Maybe he'll listen this time. Maybe he'll change his mind... Maybe I can change his mind. Because I don't think I can go on without this baby. I don't think I can go on without my son, even if HE is the father.

With her newfound goal and resolution, she heads back to the shower, which was still running. She proceeds to rinse herself off, not truly feeling clean, and then she gets dressed for the day.

I'm sure of it. I can change his mind. I mean... I have to... she thinks to herself as she walks downstairs and into the kitchen.

"Hello there, pretty lady." Richard says, grinning at her.

"I see, you got all cleaned up again. Good job." Richard smirks at her.

"Thank you, Richard." She replies to him. "I just came down here for some food. Then I was going to take a nap."

Now is not the time. He seems too sharp, right now. Like he's the Wolf and I'm Little Red Riding Hood. I have to catch him off guard... when he wants me again.

"Not feeling well are we?" Richard asks her.

"Why don't you hold off on lunch. Take a seat and let's have ourselves a chat about your sickness." He adds, as she nears the refrigerator.

She looks at him, fearful of his tone.

What's he thinking? He sounds too calm. Even for him...

She hesitates and freezes, stopping on her path to the refrigerator.

"I said! Sit down Holly!" Richard bellows at her.

She flinches.

Oh no... he wants to talk about the baby now.

She slowly walks over to the dining room table.

"We have avoided the elephant in the room long enough. Or should I say the baby in the womb..." Richard quips at her.

She looks away from him and diverts her eyes to the table, looking down in front of her. "I don't know what you're talking about, Richard. I just have a stomach bug. I'll be fine in a few days..."

"Bull-fucking-shit, Holly." Richard exclaims. "You are pregnant, and you know how I feel about that."

She shakes her head. "No!"

Richard nods his head. "Yes, Holly... you are."

She begins to sob lightly. After a few moments she looks up at him with tears running down her face. "So that's it then. You're going to kill me now?" She says, crying softly.

Richard laughs and then smiles, which shuts her up and she goes silent. "Of course not pretty lady. You are a keeper... it's just that baby that needs to go!"

Her eyes go wide. "What?! No!"

He nods, "Yes, Holly. It'll be simple. We'll just have to starve you for a week, and you should miscarry. If that little baby has nothing to eat, it will just wither away." He smiles at her.

Her eyes go wider. "What?! NO! I won't let you!"

He can't do this! I won't let him! He can't take my baby! She thinks loudly in her head.

She hears him laugh at her. "You! You won't let me!? That's rich, bitch! I'll chain you to the fucking bed if I have to! Feed you water and nothing else! Well... maybe I'll feed you something else."

Her eyes begin to fill up with tears, but they don't feel like tears of fear to her, more like tears of anger.

"NO! I won't let you Richard! You've taken everything else! You won't take my baby!" She shouts at him.

I have that knife upstairs, for my wrists! Go Holly! Go now! She thinks, as she bolts out of her seat and up toward the master bedroom.

She hears him behind her, "Where the fuck do you think you are going, Holly?!" He then laughs. "You try to run away and run your dumbass upstairs!"

He then shouts at her, "Looks to me like you want to get chained up to the bed right fucking now!"

She rushes to the room and grabs the kitchen knife from in

between the mattress and the box spring.

I won't let you Richard! Not this time!

He walks into the room and sees her holding the knife toward him. "Just what the fuck are you going to do with that!?"

Her mind starts to panic, but she holds her ground.

"You stay right there, Richard! Don't come any closer! I won't let you hurt my baby!" She shouts at him.

He laughs at her and before she knows it, the knife's knocked from her hand.

What?! What happened?! Why couldn't I move!? Why couldn't I do it?!

She then feels the crisp hot feeling of him smacking her across her face.

She can vaguely hear him laugh as her vision blurs.

"I'm starting to think that maybe you aren't a keeper, Holly." He snickers at her.

Her eyes go wide as he grabs her by the slams and throws her against the wall.

Oh no! I missed my chance! She thinks in panic.

::Ding Dong::

With her vision going blurry, again, and her breath gone, she can hear him say something but can't make out what it is. The next thing she knows, she's on her knees gasping for air. Her mind races in hazy confusion, not registering that someone's at the front door.

She hears his distant voice say "Stay the fuck here, Holly... and think about our conversation. Don't make a fucking sound and you better be in a better mood when I get back. Or we'll pick up where we left off..."

What's going on?! My throat's on fire! I can't breathe without it hurting.

She sees a blurry vision of Richard leave the bedroom.

She then hears the doorbell ring.

::*Ding Dong*::

"*Is someone here? Help me! Help me, please!*" She tries to shout, but nothing comes out.

My throat's still on fire. He was really going to kill me. That was it!

After a few moments, she can start to feel her legs again, and she pulls herself up with the assistance of the nearby dresser. She then stumbles over to the bed, searching for the knife.

::Ding Dong::

There it is! She thinks, as she grabs it and stumbles to the doorway of the master bedroom.

She peeks her head outside the doorway and doesn't see anyone. But she can hear voices coming from down the hall and down the stairs.

"Help me!" She tries to yell, but still no words are coming out of her mouth.

No one's coming to save you, Holly. No one has come yet, and no one will ever come. Once he's done talking to or killing whoever is downstairs, he will come back to finish you off... Holly thinks to herself.

She tries to steady herself, listening to what's going on downstairs, to decide how much time she actually has.

She hears Richard's voice. "But yeah, Sheriff Patterson came by for dinner around sunset. I want to say he left around 11:00 PM or so. To be honest, it's a tad bit fuzzy. We had a few beers with dinner and sat on the back porch for a while."

She then hears another voice respond to Richard. "Sounds like the good old Sheriff. That is a very nice HD500 Ruger 357 you got there. And it's nice to keep it in your family over the years."

What are they talking about? Are they looking for the Sheriff that Richard killed last night? The Sheriff that he killed, and I helped clean up? Holly thinks to herself.

Not right now, Holly... Focus! They may be able to help you. They are looking for the Sheriff and they obviously figured out to come here. Maybe I will be able to escape this hell. Holly begins to hope as she thinks and listens to the conversation going on downstairs.

Richard replies to the other voice. "Thanks, Deputy Bradley. I sure think so. It's Deputy Bradley, right? Jim Bradley's twin?" Then Richard adds, "And I believe you are Ben Reilly, correct? I didn't think you were a cop though. Deputized recently then, I take it?" Richard laughs lightly.

She hears mumbling, so she walks into the upstairs hallway, closer to the edge of the stairs, to get a better listen.

She then hears the other voice say, "That's exactly the point. This guy is not who he says he is, and something's way off. The Sheriff does not drink that much. Only a beer here and there. And I'm pretty damn sure that the Ruger GP100 357 is Sheriff's Patterson's. His story is bullshit for sure."

What's he talking about and is he talking to Richard? She questions.

She hears another voice respond, "So, let's arrest him."

Her eyes go wide.

Yes! This is my chance! Arrest his crazy ass! She thinks loudly in her head, but still cannot manage words.

She then hears the other voice reply, "The plan was to get information and come back with the cavalry if we had to. Now we know we need to come back with the cavalry. We need to play this smart, Ben. No reason for more loss of life."

"Fine..." The second voice says. "Let's go then." He adds.

"Oh no! Don't leave! I will likely be dead by the time you come back!" She tries to shout, but nothing comes out.

"Tea first. As not to let him catch on. Then we'll leave." The first voice responds.

Oh! Thank God! They aren't leaving yet! I still have a chance! She thinks and sighs in relief.

She then hears Richard shout, "You fucktards need to learn how to fucking whisper better!" Followed with his laughter, his sinister laughter.

::Boom::

The deafening boom of a shotgun makes her flinch and duck down next to the stairs. She hears Richard yell out something but cannot discern what. She starts to rise to her feet.

::Boom::

She ducks back down to the second deafening shotgun blast.

::Crack::

She hears a much lighter sounding gun go off.

"Yup, guess so!" She hears, followed by Richard's laughter.

::Crack::Crack::

::Crack::Crack::Crack::

::Crack::Crack::

What the hell is going on down there!? World War Three?! I'm never making it out of here alive! Am I!? Holly thinks as she starts to panic listening to all of the gunfire.

She then hears Richard shouting, "Oh it looks like I didn't kill brother number two after all! Well, time to fix that!"

::Crack::Crack::Crack::

::Crack::

She hears Richard yell out, "OW! You shitfuck! You actually shot me!"

She freezes, too scared to move. After a few moments, she begins to rise to her feet.

Is it over? Is he dead or are they dead? He sounded hurt... but was it enough? She questions herself.

She hears a door slam and flinches. Then there is silence. She begins to peek her head around the corner of the hallway to look downstairs.

After a few moments of silence, she hears a voice. "Holy shit that hurts."

Then the second voice replies. "I'm sure it does buddy. You probably have at least one broken rib. You were hit with a slug."

They're alive! Does that mean he's finally dead!? She thinks as a smile starts to spread across her face.

The first voice asks the questions she was thinking. "Where's he at? Did you get him?"

The second voice replies. "He took off. I wounded him I think. But he also got me in the chest too. Great thinking with these vests, Todd. Real life savers..."

Good! I hope he's dying painfully somewhere! Right fucking now! You sick piece of shit! You sick twisted, rapist piece of shit! She thinks to herself.

Feeling better and like a weight has been lifted from her soul, she begins to walk down the stairs. About halfway down, she can see the two men on the floor in the living room. One of the men says to the other, "Are you sure he's gone, Ben?"

Holly freezes in her tracks as she sees Richard walk from the other room passing the stairs, into the living room where the two men on the ground are. She tries to scream, but no words come out.

She watches in horror as Richard puts a gun to one of the men's heads, the man sitting up halfway.

Nooooooo! Why won't you just die!? You rapist fuck! She screams in her head.

"Ben Reilly, you son of a bitch!" She hears Richard shout.

"Shit!" She hears the second voice reply.

He hasn't seen me yet and he's distracted! I can just run out the front door. She thinks as she looks to the front door, only feet away.

But he would surely catch me after he was done with these two guys. She argues with herself.

She looks to Richard and then back to the door, deciding what to do.

She hears Richard give a speech to the men on the ground. "I knew I should have killed you that night on the road. You are just like the late Sheriff. You just can't let things be. It got him killed and looks like it did the same thing to you."

It's now or never Holly... she thinks to herself, as she begins to tip-toe down the rest of the stairs.

She's at the bottom of the stairs and freezes as she hears Richard laugh.

"With the Sheriff's gun, I might add." He says.

She looks to the three men to her right, with none of them seeing her. She then looks at the door a couple feet away from her, then back to Richard, with his back to her. She looks down at the knife, still in her hand.

She takes two steps toward Richard and hears a trigger being pulled.

::Click::

She flinches and shuts her eyes, waiting for the sound of a gun going off, but nothing happens. She opens her eyes to see Richard's back right in front of her.

She doesn't think about what she's about to do, she just simply raises the knife high above her head and is staring at the back of his head. She thrusts with all of her might and shuts her eyes.

A second later she feels the knife connect with something soft, and the blade goes through it swiftly. She then feels a warm liquid cover her hands and spray against her face. She instinctively steps back and blinks.

As her eyes open, she sees Richard's back still to her, but he has the knife that was just in her hands in the back-right side of his neck roughly halfway through.

Her hand goes up to cover her mouth. *Oh my gosh!* She thinks.

She watches as he just stands there, and then tips over onto the ground with a loud thud. So loud, that she jumps and steps back a few more steps. She's too afraid to run.

Oh no! If he isn't dead, he's going to kill me for sure! She thinks as she starts to panic.

She then looks down at her hands and tries to scream but nothing comes out.

After a few moments, she tries to calm down her breathing after she sees that Richard is not moving.

The man that was halfway sitting up is now standing and looking at her, saying something that she cannot hear or understand. Her mind is no longer here. Her subconscious takes over to protect her.

Her mind instead goes to her baby and their future. *I think he's finally gone now... he can't hurt you now. He can't hurt me anymore...* Her mind drifts away to the dreamscape of the day at the lake with her son as a toddler. She begins to smile. *This is nice...*

She's shocked back to reality with the man that was on the ground, now standing in front of her with his arms on her shoulders, holding her firmly.

"I said! Are you alright, miss!?" The second voice of the two men shouts at her.

"*What?*" She tries to reply, but her voice is still not working.

8

EILEEN RIVERA

THEY HAVE BEEN GONE for some time now. I hope that everything's alright. Eileen thinks to herself, as she sits on the shore of the lake, checking the time on her iPhone.

It displays 5:37 PM, and the sun's beginning to set.

It has only been a couple hours, getting closer to three hours. But still... what are they doing?

Eileen looks over to Alexander and Steven, still fishing along the docks down the way. She then looks to Jamie and Amanda playing with their daughters, Chloe and Claire. She was happy that Chloe had opened up to her and was much more vibrant... once she got into the water.

Poor little girl... I lost my father in all of this too, but I'm a grown woman. You are a small six-year-old little girl. I could not imagine what's going on inside your head. Well... I can imagine, I'm actually living it. But it would seem so much scarier at your age... Poor little girl.

As she is lost in thought, looking onto the lake, she hears the engine of a vehicle approaching behind her. She looks over her shoulder and sees Ben's black truck pull into the parking lot. She smiles and gets up, beginning to walk toward the parking lot.

Reaching the end of the shore and the beginning of the parking lot, she waves as the truck parks and the car doors open. She notices three doors open, the two front doors and one of the back-cab doors. She then watches Ben and Todd exit the truck, with a blonde woman following behind them.

She stops in mid-stride and tilts her head.

Just picking up random women along the roadside, are we? She thinks to herself as she grins.

She dismisses the thought and continues to walk toward them. As she reaches the trio, she smiles at Ben and he smiles back, but she notices it looks forced.

"Hi Ben. Hi Todd. Welcome back. I was starting to get worried about you two." She states.

Ben and Todd don't say a word and look at each other.

"Who's your friend?" She asks, looking at the petite, blonde woman a few feet behind Ben and Todd.

Ben steps to the side, allowing her to see the woman, full view.

"This is Holly Clark. Holly Clark, this is Eileen Rivera... my um, girlfriend." Ben says, introducing the two women.

My UM girlfriend huh? I know we didn't actually talk about labels, but geez. At least sound excited about it. She thinks as she takes another glance at the petite woman named Holly Clark.

Before she can respond, she sees several Sheriff patrol cars enter the parking lot, followed by several more. Ben and Todd look back at the incoming vehicles. They park in the row behind Ben's truck and Todd begins to walk toward them. It was then that she notices that Todd is holding his chest, as if he's hurt. She looks back to Ben.

"What's going on Ben?" She questions.

Ben sighs, and replies, "Sheriff Patterson's dead..."

"What?!" Eileen blurts out.

Ben nods, "And Todd and I would have been dead too, if not for Ms. Clark here." Ben says and he gestures to the young and petite, blonde woman.

Eileen looks at the woman, who meets her gaze but does not speak and then she darts her eyes back to Ben.

"Wait! What?! What the hell happened Ben!?" She's now becoming frantic.

Before she can go ballistic, Ben walks up to her directly and embraces her in a strong hug.

"It's alright, Eileen. I'm alright, I swear. I didn't think I would be, for a second there... but I'm still here..." He says and trails off, as he just holds her for several moments.

After what feels like a very long embrace, he steps back, and she thinks she sees him wince. His hands are on her shoulder and he is looking into her eyes with those bright blue eyes of his.

"I'll explain everything, but it's easier to only explain it once. Let's go back down to the shore. Todd will handle the other Deputies and I can fill in the others." Ben says to her.

She's caught in his gaze and his calmness. "Okay..."

He nods and starts walking to the shore where the rest of the group had gathered looking at the display of Sheriff Deputies in the parking lot. Ben stops, and turns back to the other woman named Holly Clark.

"Holly, you can follow us down there if you'd like, or you can wait here. It's up to you. After I get them caught up to speed, we'll sort out a living arrangement for you. Okay?" Ben says to the woman.

The woman nods and replies, "Okay. Thank you. I'll walk down there with you, if that's alright."

"Of course." Ben replies.

The three of them walk toward the rest of their group on the shore of the lake. While they are walking toward them, Eileen thinks about what is happening and what was said.

The Sheriff is dead? The woman Holly Clark apparently saved Ben and Todd. She needs a place to stay. Just what the hell happened while they were gone?

As they reach the rest of the group, Steven steps forward. "Everything alright, Ben?"

Ben sighs. "Yes and no, Uncle." He then looks to Jamie and Amanda. "You may not want the girls to hear what I'm about to say, ladies."

The two sisters-in-law look at each other, and then at their daughters. "Why don't you two go back into the lake, only up to your knees though, girls." Jamie says to the girls.

"Okay!" The girls shout in unison.

As the girls are running off, Amanda yells after them. "Not too far and not too deep, girls!"

"Okay!" The girls shout in unison again.

Once the girls are far enough away, Eileen looks at Ben. "Alright, Ben. Spill it. What's going on? What happened?"

Ben looks around the group. "Alright... Where do I start?"

"Start anywhere, start somewhere..." Eileen replies.

Ben nods and sighs. "Alright, first off... Sheriff Patterson's dead."

This elicits gasps and questions from the group. Ben calms them down after a moment and begins again.

"The man that was masquerading as her fiancé killed him." Ben says, gesturing to Holly Clark.

At this point Holly steps back with the attention on her.

Before anyone can ask any questions, Ben continues. "His name was Richard Clark. No relation to Holly Clark. Pure coincidence... Anyways, he was a prisoner at Chino. Holly didn't know what for, but assumed it was for really bad reasons."

Ben pauses and the group stays silent. "He broke out of prison when the *Blue Hole Radius* let up and killed her real fiancé, Roger Stevens."

Wait a second... she thinks.

"You mean that creep that we ran into the first couple of nights here!?" Eileen asks.

Ben nods in confirmation. "The one and the same... Turns out, he was a real piece of work. Holly tells me that he killed several people on the way up here and the family that lived in the house that he was living in. The house that they were living in."

Ben then looks at Amanda, "Amanda, he was also the one who killed Jim... it wasn't the MS13. It was this guy Richard Clark. He told Holly about the whole thing."

Amanda looks at Ben and then drops to her knees and begins to cry. Jamie kneels down beside her and tries to console her.

Eileen looks to Ben and then to the woman, Holly Clark. "So... You're telling me that she knew all of this and is just now telling us? Why tell us everything now and not before?"

Ben steps in front of her, blocking her view of Holly Clark. He puts his hands up in a slowdown motion. "She was his captive, Eileen... he killed her fiancé and came to her home, raped her and kidnapped her."

Eileen's eyes go wide and the whole group is now staring at Holly Clark.

After a moment of silence, Eileen side-steps Ben and looks directly at Holly. "Oh my gosh... I'm so sorry, sweetie. I had no idea."

Holly shakes her head and looks down to the ground. "No. It's okay. I understand why you may be upset with me. Especially you." She says, picking her head up and looking toward Amanda on the ground crying.

"I've been with that monster for two months now... I don't know why I didn't run or scream for help. I don't know..." She says, as if trying to figure everything out right there.

Eileen watches as the woman begins to shed tears. She wasn't sobbing, but tears were coming out of her eyes.

"Like I said." Ben interrupts. "She was his captive this whole time and watched him do horrible things. She actually saved our asses. That guy, Richard had the drop on us. Luckily for us, after he shot the both of us, Holly here..."

"Wait! You were shot!? Again!?" Eileen blurts out.

Ben sighs and puts his hands up. "I'm fine, Eileen. Maybe some bruised ribs, but I'll live. Todd may have some broken ribs, but he'll live too. We both had vests on, thank goodness... Now please calm down and let me finish. Then you can yell at me all you want."

She shut her mouth but was fuming inside. *Oh, you can finish Benjamin. And then I will yell at you! I cannot believe you ran off and got shot again. What are you! Some kind of bullet magnet?!*

Ben can surely tell she's pissed, but he continues on. "She had found out she was pregnant and Richard was going to kill the baby, but try not to kill her. That's when she stepped in and saved our asses."

This gets several gasps before the group and the sobbing Amanda on the floor looks up to Ben, and then to Holly. She slowly stops sobbing and just stares at the woman.

Eileen looks back to the woman. *Oh my gosh! How sad! Raped constantly, threatened, likely beaten, and then to think your baby was going to be ripped from you...*

She cannot help but feel sorry for her, but then a thought crosses her mind. *Wait? So... if you weren't pregnant, you would have let that rapist creep kill Ben and Todd? Kill my Ben?!*

Holly might be a mind-reader, because her eyes went from Eileen, straight down the floor.

"So, the quick points are that Sheriff Patterson's dead, she has been held captive for the last seven weeks, and you two idiots almost got killed again?" Steven steps in and asks Ben.

Ben reluctantly nods. "Sounds about right, Uncle. Holly really came through in a clutch for us, and now... after Todd explains the situation to the rest of the Deputies, we plan on finding her a place to stay. So she doesn't have to go back to that house."

He then turns to Amanda. "I'm so sorry, Amanda. This has to be so much for you to process..."

Amanda sniffles and comes to her feet and nods. "I'm just glad that the piece of shit that killed my husband is dead."

This gets Holly to look up at Amanda. "Thank you, sweetie." Amanda says to Holly and she does not reply, only stands there and looks stunned.

Amanda looks at Ben. "You said she has nowhere to go?"

Ben shakes his head. "Not anymore. The valley is chaotic, and her family was from San Diego, outside of the *Blue Hole Radius*."

Amanda strides up to Holly and stares her directly in the eyes, "You can stay with me sweetie. We have an extra room and you can stay as long as you need. It's just me and Chloe, now." She then gives the young, petite blonde a firm hug, holding her tight.

After a moment, Eileen watches Holly's arms raise and return the hug. She can see tears running down the woman's face as Holly speaks softly. "Thank you and I'm so sorry..."

Amanda steps back, wiping more tears from her face. "Alright... now let's stop crying and look on the bright-side. You said you were pregnant?! How exciting! Come on! Let's go get you some food in that pregnant belly of yours!"

Before Holly can respond, Amanda grabs her by the hand and leads her off toward their cooler with snacks and food.

Jamie shrugs, "I guess we are eating now." She says and follows the other two.

Eileen looks to Ben and he can apparently tell he's about to get yelled at. Before she can, Steven interrupts her. "Just what in the hell were you thinking!? You going off to arrest some crazed killer rapist maniac all on your own?!"

Ben steps back. "In my defense, Uncle... I told Todd we should surround the place."

His Uncle steps into him. "Oh, you did, did you? Then why in the hell did it turn out this way? In fact, why the hell did Sheriff Patterson go over there in the first place?"

"Holly said it seemed like the Sheriff was on to Richard and was trying to figure out what was going on." Ben answers.

"Bullshit! What the shit is going on?! The world has gone to hell in a handbasket, and what the hell are we doing? We are locking up innocent people, trusting bad people, not trusting our guts, and not asking for help. This lone wolf shit needs to stop! This tip-toeing snowflake shit needs to stop! That shit does not work!" Steven exclaims.

Eileen watches as Ben is silent. She looks at Alexander and he simply shrugs at her with a *he's right* kind of look. She then sees Steven's attention shift toward the Deputies in the parking lot.

"Enough of this shit! These backwards ass Deputies need to be told how to handle emergency situations, because that's what we are in and it ain't going away anytime soon, dammit!" Steven exclaims and strides off toward the group of Sheriff Deputies.

The three of them watch him storm off. "Wow... and I thought I was pissed." Eileen blurts out.

Ben scratches the back of his head and looks at her. "Yeah, him and Sheriff Patterson didn't always see eye to eye, but they went way back. Back before Uncle Steven was on the search and rescue team with the San Bernardino County Sheriffs."

"Yeah, that's super sad about the Sheriff. He seemed like a good guy. And that's even sadder about Amanda's husband, Jim... That's insane!" Eileen states.

"Most certainly a sad turn of events." Alexander adds.

"For sure. I just feel really bad for that Holly Clark girl. To be having to live like that for the last seven weeks. That's just horrible." Ben replies.

"Yeah, and she would have kept on living like that, if she didn't get pregnant... and you would be dead." She says to him with her arms across her chest, ready to dig into him.

Ben takes another step back. "Now that's not fair Eileen... you weren't there and I couldn't imagine being in her shoes."

"Oh yeah, and you two cowboys go off, guns blazing, trying to arrest some maniac killer!" She can feel the blood boiling inside of her, thinking of almost losing Ben.

"Hey! Wait just a minute. We were leaving to go get back up and then he unloaded on us."

Ben explains and this keeps her quiet for a minute.

Alexander chimes in, "I'm going to let you two talk this out and go check on the others, by the shore."

Ben nods to Alexander as he walks off, then Ben continues. "I know you are mad that I almost died, again. But honestly, I'm just glad I get to see you again. When I thought *this was it*, my mind went to you, Eileen. I just wanted to see you again.

"And who cares why she saved our asses. The only thing that matters is that she did. I could not imagine what her life has been like for the last seven weeks. I'm sure she was scared to death, but she still stepped in... Better late than never, right?" He adds.

Eileen is speechless as he looks into her eyes, with his bright blue eyes.

He thought he was going to die, and he was thinking of me?... He was thinking of me.

She smiles and jumps at him, feeling her skin press against his clothed body, and feeling the anger flowing out of her body, replaced with his warm embrace.

He winces and says, "Ow. You do remember I was shot in the chest, right?"

"If you don't want to get punched in the chest, you better shut up and kiss me." She says and grins at him.

He leans in and they embrace and their lips meet, there on the shore of the lake in the fading daylight.

After a few moments, she steps back and grabs his hand. "Alright you lucky ass dumb dumb, let's go closer to the others and take that shirt off... to check out those bruised ribs of yours."

"Whatever you say, Eileen." Ben replies.

"Yup, and it better stay that way." She grins at him and he laughs.

The two walk back toward the rest of the group, now with an added member, Holly Clark.

As they reach the group, she eyes Holly and Holly looks at her.

Be nice, Eileen. She did save Ben... and he's right. She's likely been through hell and back. She did save them in the end.

She softens her looks and walks up to the group with her eyes still on Holly.

"Holly, thank you for saving Ben and Todd. I know I'm grateful, and I'm sure that Jamie is too." She says to her.

"Yeah I am! But I'm sure as hell going to have a talk with my husband about being more careful." Jamie remarks.

Before Holly can respond, Eileen hears footsteps and chatter behind them. She turns to see Steven and Todd walking their way.

"And it looks like we'll be having that talk in the very near future." Jamie says as she stands and locks eyes with her husband.

As Todd and Steven reach Eileen and the rest of the group, Jamie speaks directly to Todd. "You and I need to have some words... over there, oh husband of mine." She finishes as she points off into a direction for them to speak privately.

Todd looks to the rest of the group and then to his wife and sighs. "Alright..."

"Good luck, brother." Ben says as he chuckles.

Eileen shoots him a look. "Don't press your luck, genius. Geez, you need practice on when to keep that big mouth shut..."

Ben shuts his mouth and looks the other direction, seeing his Uncle. "So, what's the word Uncle? Did you straighten them out over there?"

Steven looks at his nephew. "I suppose you could say that..." Steven scratches the back of his head like Ben always does. "You're looking at the Sheriff of Crestline, nephew." He adds.

Eileen and the others look at Steven Reilly in disbelief.

Ben's the first one to speak. "Get the hell out of here! They gave you Sheriff Patterson's position? How the hell did that happen... and why?"

"Not exactly his position. Much smaller than that. They saw it fit to pull me out of retirement from my volunteer Sheriff position on the search and rescue team and make me the Sheriff of Crestline." Steven explains.

"What exactly does that mean, Steven?" Eileen asks.

"What it means, is that we are dividing up our resources amongst the mountain towns. Each town will have a head Sheriff and we will all focus on our own areas. With what happened to Sheriff Patterson, we can't have us being caught with our tail between our legs and just have one leader. Circumstances have changed and we have to think on a much smaller level." Steven answers.

"So more of a cellular base, instead of hierarchical, then?" Ben asks.

"Exactly like that. We all stay in contact, but in these small towns, they need someone to take care of their own, from their own. The Deputies are each staying in their respective towns and deputizing people that they see fit, since there are no more real Sheriff Academies anymore." Steven explains.

"I suppose that makes sense, for the time being. Having small communities focus on themselves and coming together when they need to. It actually reminds me of the original colonies." Alexander replies.

Steven chuckles. "I suppose it does, Alexander. Only this time they are towns. Crestline, Twin Peaks, Skyforest, Lake Arrowhead, Rim Forest, Running Springs, Green Valley Lake, Fawnskin, and what's left of Big Bear and Minnelusa.

Steven pauses, likely thinking if he forgot any of the towns. "Yup, I believe those are all of them that are up here. There are those mountain towns that are lower, but we haven't heard much from them in a while. But whoever goes down the mountain to get those chickens can check in on them on their way."

"What's this about chickens?" Eileen asks.

"The trip down to Yucaipa... to pick up chickens to raise. But someone else may end up taking my spot on the chicken run, since I'm the new Sheriff of Crestline." Steven adds.

"Oh yeah, that's right... the chickens..." Eileen, says, remembering the conversation from earlier.

"Whoa, whoa, whoa. You guys figured that all out in the fifteen minutes you guys were chatting? No freaking way!" Ben replies.

"Not exactly. Todd apparently was coming up with the idea since he had almost got himself killed, along with you. So, I guess over a few hours. He laid out his plan to the others and they all thought it was a good idea. They all felt stretched pretty thin and were concerned with always being so far away from their families. And quite simply, it makes sense to steer away from centralized authority and avoid a power struggle." Steven explains.

"And... Todd isn't going to be the Sheriff of Crestline? Why?" Ben asks.

"I asked him the same question. Deputy Todd Bradley said I was better suited for the job, since I reminded him a lot of Sheriff Patterson and how I handled the situation yesterday at the marketplace." Steven responds.

"I guess that makes sense, especially since he had already lost his brother. He's looking out for his family and for his brother's family. And, no offense Uncle... but all you have are us." Ben replies.

"Benjamin!" Eileen blurts out at him and his unneeded comment.

Steven laughs. "It's alright Eileen. I'm used to his smartass bullshit... even when he doesn't mean to be a smartass." He laughs a little more and then adds, "You're right, nephew. All I have is you all. That's why as the Sheriff of Crestline, I'm deputizing you, here and now."

"Wait, what? You can't do that. I didn't even ask to be a lawman." Ben replies.

"Tough shit, nephew. It is what it is. Your community needs you, Deputy Reilly. And think of it more of a militia." Steven adds.

"I don't know Steven. Ben has a tendency to get himself into trouble..." Eileen interjects.

"Don't I know I know it. That's why you two, along with myself and the other Deputies will be looking out for him and everyone else in our community." Steven responds.

"What exactly do you mean?" Eileen questions.

"Yes, Steven. What do you mean? Are you inferring...?" Alexander begins to question.

Steven interrupts them both. "Yes, lady and gents. When I said I'm deputizing you, I meant the lot of you. Consider yourselves deputized and to be the three newest Deputies of Crestline. But like I said, it's much more along the lines of a militia. Defend and keep the peace, and what have you." Steven explains.

It was now Eileen's turn to be confused. "Wait, what now?"

"Yes, Deputy Rivera. You heard me right. Hell, you may very well be the top of the class." Steven says as he grins at her.

"And Deputy Mathis, you are not half bad yourself. If we are lucky, the three of us can keep Ben alive." Steven says.

"Hey!" Ben responds, acting emotionally hurt.

Steven continues, "And if we are extremely lucky, we all can keep this community together and alive during the months and years to come." Steven says with a wide smile.

This old man has lost his damn mind. Me? A Deputy of Crestline? Me? Part of a militia? What's going on? Eileen thinks, trying to take in all of this new information.

What the hell happened to a relaxing day at the lake? She questions herself.

9

BENJAMIN REILLY

BEN OPENS his eyes slowly and sits up and looks around the bedroom. He looks to his side and sees that Eileen's still asleep. Being on the bottom floor, he cannot tell if there's daylight outside yet or not. So, he grabs his iPhone off of his nightstand next to his PX4 Storm to check the time.

0537 on Monday, July 8th... 3433. It's been over seven weeks now, and it's still weird looking at the year. I wonder if that will ever get normal. Ben thinks as he stretches and quietly gets out of bed.

He decides it's best to let Eileen sleep a little longer. It had been a long day yesterday. After the whole Richard Clark debacle, along with the news of Sheriff Patterson and Jim Bradley, a lot had to be done... and they weren't even close to being done.

Since his wonderful Uncle had deputized him and his friends, they also had to make sure everything was running smoothly in the small town of Crestline.

Ben recollects on the later events of yesterday afternoon and evening as he quietly gets dressed in the dark bedroom.

I cannot believe, for the life of me, why the hell he thought it best to go off and make us Deputies or the Militia or what the hell ever you want to call it. Seriously, what was he thinking?

Well, you know what he was thinking, Ben. It does make sense. Delegate and distribute power, instead of leaving a power vacuum. Power vacuums often lead to power struggles, which leads to more conflict.

He could have at least asked first, instead of just being like... Ben, you are a Deputy and part of the Militia now. It is what it is and that is what you are. I mean, I would have said yes if he asked... I think...

After the news and formalities were out of the way, the four of them had split up, along with the other Deputies that lived in Crestline. Since the other Deputies went back to their own mountain communities, it was up to them to police the small town of Crestline.

To make matters more difficult for the group, there were only eight Deputies/members of the Crestline Militia at this current moment, and half of them were brand new, including Steven Reilly, Ben Reilly, Alexander Mathis, and Eileen Rivera. Well, his Uncle was out of retirement, so there was that... Three of the other four Ben had met on the night of the MS13 battle, Joseph Gomez, Jose Rodriguez, and Janice Fuller. The last of the eight was Todd Bradley.

Luckily for the small group that was trying to keep the peace and order in the small mountain town, it was a small mountain town. With the population starting at just over 9,000 people in Crestline prior to the *Blue Hole Radius*, it was estimated that there were still close to 7,000 people left in the small mountain community.

Some people had left to find families and friends. Some people had died in the first few days for various reasons. Some had died since then, whether due to illness, crime, or pure accident. Accidents were certainly on the rise with the lack of warning signs and other labels telling people that dangerous things are dangerous. Gone were the days of public safety reminders and warning labels on just about everything. No, these were the days people either learned quickly or they were maimed or even dead.

Nonetheless, 7,000 people is a huge amount of people to cover for a small group of eight. Ben's Uncle had assured the group that their numbers would grow and that's why he was looking at making it more of a militia with some that are full-time members, the Deputized ones, and the others being called upon when and if they are needed, everyone else in the militia.

Ben chuckles to himself as he walks up the stairs to make himself a cup of coffee.

I cannot believe they made Uncle the frigging Sheriff. That's insane. What is more insane is that the other three of us are now Deputies. Like we didn't have enough to worry about.

On the bright side, it took the heat off of me from Eileen... with the whole getting shot thing and almost dying, again.

"What are we giggling about, nephew?" Steven says to him, as he walks into the kitchen.

Ben smiles at his Uncle. "Just thinking how crazy you are for dragging us into this whole law enforcement and militia situation."

"Yeah! Crazy smart, you mean!" Uncle Steven replies. "You saw how they were handling things, and I'm pretty damn sure you know that there would have been some major power struggles if we didn't divide the power. Someone had to step up... why not us?"

Ben shakes his head as he grabs his cup of coffee. "I suppose you have a point, Uncle."

"You're damn right, I do!" Uncle Steven responds. "And don't you stress too much about our numbers. I'm going to fix that today."

"How so?" Ben asks.

"Well, yesterday was just about spreading the word and making sure no one was resorting to anarchy again. Today we have that meeting at the Lake Drive Marketplace, in a few hours. That's where we'll increase our numbers." Uncle Steven explains.

"So, now we are conscripting people? Not sure how they are going to feel about being drafted into our militia, Uncle." Ben replies.

He laughs at him. "Draft? Yeah, like that would fly. Nope... we are taking volunteers, and I'm sure we will get plenty. People feel like they don't have control and a say-so in what is going on in this new world. If we give them purpose and opportunity, we'll get volunteers."

"You sure about that Uncle? These people you speak of have done some pretty terrible things since the *Blue Hole Radius*. Need I remind you that we have stockades now and have had several executions for some seriously heinous crimes." Ben responds.

Alexander walks into the room from outside of the cabin. "Good morning, gentleman. Do we still have hot coffee left?"

Ben looks to his friend Alexander. "We sure do."

Ben grabs his mug from his hand and fills it up with coffee, handing it back to Alexander.

"Thank you, Ben." Alexander replies.

"No worries." Ben responds.

His Uncle looks to Alexander. "Good morning, again. Alexander, Ben, here... thinks that people won't volunteer for our little militia and help support our community."

Alexander looks to Ben, as he sips his coffee.

Uncle Steven looks back to him. "What you don't seem to realize is that those are effective punishments and are working. We just need to make sure that we are fair and don't get power hungry, is all. I believe it was Lincoln that said something along the lines of... *Nearly all men can stand adversity. But if you want to test a man's character, give him power*... And it's best that folks like us do it, instead of the people that really want the power. Hell, I didn't ask for this and neither did you."

Ben chuckles. "Well, you got that part about right."

Uncle Steven continues. "And what you don't seem to remember is that this community is filled with Americans, nephew. They want the stability that they had a few months ago. They want structure and they have seen how quickly the world can turn into chaos. I have no doubt that we will have a strong force to protect us, when the time comes. What is more, we will have a select few out of that militia that are just enough and dedicated enough to help us police our own."

"Oh, yeah? And who gets to decide that, Uncle?" Ben asks.

His Uncle smiles and looks at Alexander. "Alexander, want to help me out here?"

Alexander nods and turns to Ben. "We will Ben, and so will they. The eight of us will decide with whomever is left of Crestline's Village Council. We will look at the volunteers. All will be accepted for the militia basis, but we will look more closely for the deputizing part of the process. There is no room for bad apples or corruption in these times. We need to make sure that we vet them, and they understand the consequences for corruption and abuse of power."

Ben nods, lightly. "Alright, I'm with you so far..."

"Don't you see, Ben. We have a chance to improve what we had before. We can start over, without really starting over. We can make sure that we have a collective of people making decisions, not the masses and not just one person. And with swift justice and consequences, we avoid long term corruption and the greed that plagued our politics and judicial system, before all of this." Ben's Uncle explains.

"Okay... let's say this works. What if one of us becomes part of this problem of greed and corruption. What will you say then?" Ben asks.

His Uncle laughs again. "Well, if I ever become corrupt and try to steal from these people... then I would rather be dead than let myself go further down that road." He chuckles some more. "I don't really see that happening, Ben, but if those in power... like us... abuse that power, we should be dealt with swiftly."

Ben nods, starting to buy into the whole idea of this modified small republic. "Okay... who gets to be the judge and jury?"

"Ah, you are starting to see it then..." Uncle Steven replies. "We will be the judge and jury for the militia and the civilians. We, being the Deputies and the Council Members. And the people will be our judge and jury... if any one of us gets out of line, we will be arrested and tried."

"What if we all get out of line?" Ben questions further.

"You really are a paranoid one. If I recall correctly, you didn't have the greatest trust in our previous government either, nephew?" Uncle Steven replies.

Ben shrugs. "These will be questions that the people have, too."

"And the people are the answer, Ben. If all of the Council members have survived up to this point, with our combined Deputies, that's 14 people making the major decisions. If by some chance that all of us get out of line and become corrupt, it's 14 versus close to 7,000. How long do you think we will last?" Uncle Steven responds.

Ben thinks about this for a moment. *14 versus 7,000... that's pretty damn scary. I guess it's in our best interest to not be greedy or corrupt.*

Ben smiles. "I suppose that might work. Is that what this whole meeting is for?"

"Yeppum. But you won't be there." Uncle Steven replies.

Ben looks confused. "What? Why? What will I be doing?"

Uncle Steven nods to Alexander. "You and Alexander are heading down the mountain to pick up some livestock. You two and Deputy Joseph Gomez."

Ben thinks about the Deputy that he met by the fire of burning MS13 bodies during the first few days after the *Blue Hole Radius*. He also remembers how sore he still is from getting shot yesterday.

It may have hit the vest, but it still hurts like a mother...

"Why us, exactly?" Ben asks.

"Well, no offense... but you and Alexander are new to this whole Deputy thing. So, Joseph is going to sort of show you the ropes and give you some insights. Plus, he has a box trailer for the livestock." His Uncle explains.

"Okay. Fair enough. But do we really need a box trailer for four chickens and two piglets?" Ben asks.

Alexander chimes in. "Well, the numbers are larger now. Your Uncle and I have been bartering deals between last night and earlier this morning. Last I knew we were up to five stops between here and close to Temecula, totaling up to twenty-four chickens, three roosters, five piglets, and even three sheep."

Ben is amazed. "Oh wow... nice! How much is that going to set us back?"

"Eighteen Gold American Eagles..." Uncle Steven Replies. "But now it's six stops and three more piglets. I was able to make another deal this morning, after my watch shift."

"Well, son of a biscuit! That's a lot of coin, but that's also a lot of food." Ben replies.

"Damn right it is! And if we play our cards right, it'll turn into much more food over time." Uncle Steven replies.

"Just how long is this trip going to take and do you think it's a good idea to send Ben off, out on his own? Shouldn't I tag along, just in case he needs saving again?" Eileen says, as she walks into the kitchen to grab a cup of coffee.

Ben and the others look to Eileen. "Good morning!" Ben says.

"Good morning, Eileen." Alexander adds.

"Good morning!" Uncle Steven responds. "And I would rather have you with me, Eileen, at the meeting. Having you and Deputy Janice Fuller there with the rest of us may help our numbers of female volunteers. I want to get enough of both sexes to show community strength."

Ben sees Eileen nod and she replies. "Fair point, Steven. But I'm not sure how I feel about sending Ben out on his own. Have you seen his track record for getting himself into trouble?"

This gets a laugh from Alexander and his Uncle and a "Hey!" from Ben.

"Ms. Eileen. He'll have myself and Deputy Joseph Gomez. Additionally, with the six stops and distance from here, it should take us only the day. By my estimation, it should take anywhere from five to ten hours. It's a wide gap of time because we don't know all of the variables." Alexander explains.

"Alexander is right, Eileen. Ben should be back by dinner time, if they get going soon. And they have the seasoned Deputy Gomez to stop Ben from making any rash decisions." Uncle Steven adds.

"Hey! What about Alexander? He's new to this whole Deputy thing, too!" Ben says defensively.

"Yes, honey." Eileen replies. "But... you are the one that keeps getting shot and almost dying. You are starting to turn out to be a disaster magnet."

This gets a round of laughter from the group, even Ben.

"I suppose it's a good idea, though. Especially if it's for that much livestock and food." Eileen says. "But, Alexander, please... please watch over my Ben."

"Not a problem Ms. Eileen. I have grown quite fond of him, too. I'll make sure he returns to you safely." Alexander promises her.

"Thank you." Eileen replies.

"Hey Uncle. That seems like more food than we need though. Are you sure we need all of that for just us?" Ben questions.

"Ben, you're still missing the bigger picture... it's not all for us. We can divide up the livestock between us and the Bradley families in the beginning. And as time moves forward, and more chickens, pigs and sheep are born, we can start giving them out to other families, then they can raise them and do the same in return. The goal is for all of us to be able to sustain ourselves down the road." His Uncle explains.

"Wow, Uncle. That's a pretty grand plan and is going to take some time and planning to figure out who gets what and when..." Ben replies.

"Yeah." His Uncle scratches the back of his head "We are still figuring out all of the logistics, but we have the time."

We have the time... what a funny way of putting it. Ben thinks.

"I think it sounds like a great idea, Steven and Alexander. It sounds like it will give people hope. I think we should even mention this at the meeting today, to help give them hope." Eileen adds.

"And see... that's why you are coming along with me to the meeting, Eileen." Uncle Steven says to her. "We need that sort of compassion and understanding and from who better than a nurse that is now one of our Deputies."

Ben watches Eileen blush and takes another sip of her coffee. "Thank you, Steven... So, when's the big town meeting?"

Uncle Steven nods. "It's at noon. But we need you boys to get some food in you and start heading over to go pick up Deputy Gomez. You all are already burning daylight."

The group agrees to get ready and get started for the day. After they all make breakfast, they sit down at the dining table and discuss the possibilities for the meeting and the upcoming months, and the routes to take to pick up the livestock along the eastern border of the *Blue Hole Radius*.

After about an hour, Alexander and Ben are ready to leave to go pick up Deputy Joseph Gomez and head down the mountain to pick up the chickens, roosters, pigs, and sheep. They made sure to pack two day-packs, put on their vests, along with their sidearms. Alexander opted for a Springfield 5.56 SAINT AR, which he was obviously getting used to. Ben opted for another 5.56 SAINT AR, to keep the ammunition the same, just in case they ran into trouble. Both men loaded themselves up with five spare magazines and one loaded into the rifles.

Eileen reminded them to pack extra food and water, just in case their trip had to take a detour. So, Ben did, all the while trying to assure her that everything would be alright.

He could tell that she was worried, but she wasn't the type of worried that was frantic and crying about him leaving. She understood the need for this trip and why she wasn't on it.

She really is tough as nails, that woman. He thinks to himself.

As they load up Ben's truck for the day trip, he looks to her. "And if you get stressed out or worried, we still have our phones. Call me and I'll call you guys to check in with each stop we make."

"Sounds like a plan, cowboy. Just don't go running off into anymore firefights." She says smiling.

"Don't worry, Eileen. I'll get him back home to you." Alexander replies.

"I know you will, Alexander. Thanks, and I want you all to come home safe... for the record." Eileen replies.

"Yes, all three of you get your asses back here safe. You hear me?" Uncle Steven adds.

"Sure thing, Uncle. Good luck with your big town meeting." Ben replies.

They all say their goodbyes, and Ben pulls out of the driveway, heading toward Deputy Gomez's home.

"And away we go, Alexander.' Ben says as he navigates through the small town of Crestline.

After about ten minutes of driving, Ben stops in front of a cabin that's on the north end of Lake Gregory. Before Ben can honk his horn. Deputy Joseph Gomez comes walking out of the cabin with his pack, a vest on, a sidearm on his hip, and rifle slung over his right shoulder.

He opens up the door behind Alexander and throws his gear into the back-cab. "Good morning, gents. Let's get this trailer hooked up so we can get this show on the road."

After they get the box trailer hooked up to Ben's tow hitch, the three men pull away from the cabin and start making their way back toward the main highway and back to the 330 Highway.

Making their way down the mountain, the drive is relatively smooth down the 330.

"So far, so good. Where's our first stop, Alexander?" Ben says.

"Well, that depends if you want to start outward and work our ways back or pick them up as we go along." Alexander replies.

"We should pick them up as we go, just in case we hit trouble and need to turn around quickly." Deputy Joseph Gomez answers.

"Good thinking, Deputy Gomez." Ben replies.

"Just call me Joseph, Ben. You are a Deputy now, too." He says and grins from the backseat.

"I suppose you're right... Joseph." Ben says. "Alright, Alexander. Where are we going?"

Alexander nods. "We have six stops in total. One in Yucaipa and one in Calimesa. Then we'll jump on the 60 West to connect with the 215 South. We then have two stops in Perris and two more in Menifee."

"Sounds good. Just let me know when we get close to each stop." Ben replies.

"Will do, Ben." Alexander answers.

Ben looks at the clock on the dashboard. It reads 0740.

"Alright, let's do this. Smooth and steady." Ben says as he heads to the first stop for livestock.

The trio make their way to their first stop in a small city called Yucaipa. The family that they meet is very nice and everything goes smoothly. They traded two Gold American Eagles for four chickens, and two piglets. The second stop is at the bordering small city of Calimesa. There, they find another friendly family and a successful trade. They traded seven Gold American Eagles for eight chickens, a rooster, and four piglets.

After the first two stops, they guide back to the freeways and jump on the 60 West. Aside from going around crashed, burned, and broken-down vehicles, the 60 West Freeway is a smooth drive. Pulling on the 215 South Freeway, the trio has to pull over to the shoulder of the road while another earthquake lasts about three full minutes.

The earthquake was the only real concern on the trip to Perris, aside from driving around stalled vehicles. Ben enjoyed the country scenery, driving through the area. There was a great deal of wide-open land, and the three talked about what was left after the *Blue Hole Radius*.

They had arrived in the city of Perris by 1130 and were at the third stop. Their third and fourth stops were much like the first two. Ben and the others were excited to see some other people doing "okay" during these times. The third stop was to an old couple's home. They traded three Gold American Eagles for four chickens, two roosters, and one piglet. The fourth stop was to an old man's home. They traded two Gold American Eagles for four chickens, and one piglet.

Afterward, the trio was back on the 215 South, navigating around the broken-down vehicles and heading toward the last two stops. The group had only seen two other cars out on the roads the entire day.

Ben and the others had discussed how many people that they thought were left and how many would actually be able to keep on going. There were obviously people in these small towns and cities, but people were not traveling much, yet. Ben and the others agreed that this was likely out of fear from raiders and thieves. It appeared that many of the people out this way were simply keeping to themselves.

The trio reached the small city of Menifee by 1300, pulling up to their fifth stop, which was another older couple. They traded one Gold American Eagle for four chickens. As they were saying their goodbyes, the older man warned them to stay off of the 215 and the 15 freeways.

Ben asked why and the man responded. "Well, you all should be fine... since there's no women in your group, but better safe than sorry." The older man went back into the house and the three men talked about it on their way to the sixth and final stop.

"What do you suppose that was about, Joseph?" Ben asks.

"If I had to take a guess, it sounds like a group of men may be rounding up women. Just because it's a new world, doesn't mean that sex trafficking won't still be alive and well." Joseph replies.

"Sex trafficking, here?" Alexander questions.

"Yes, sir. Sex trafficking was a major issue in the United States prior to all of this *Blue Hole Radius* bullshit. In fact, it's been a problem with humanity since the dawn of humanity. There's no reason to think it won't be a problem in the future." Joseph explains.

"Makes sense, but sure as hell doesn't make it right." Ben replies.

"Couldn't agree more, brother." Joseph replies.

Ben pulls into the driveway of the last stop and sees a man with a shotgun, pointed directly at them.

"Shit!" Ben says.

"Quick! Backup and just go!" Joseph states.

Ben looks into his sideview mirrors to try and back out and sees two ATV's pull alongside them, one on each side and each with a passenger pointing a rifle at them.

"Double shit!" Ben blurts out.

"Gentleman, I do believe we are boxed in. I see another truck coming up behind us." Alexander adds.

"Get the fuck out of the truck, with your hands up! This shit ends now you fucking scumbags! Give us back our wives and our daughters!" The man in front of them yells.

"What did he just say? Wives and daughters?" Ben asks.

"Best to get out with our hands up, gents. Then you can ask him that, Ben." Joseph replies.

"I think he has a point, Ben." Alexander adds.

"I don't think we really have a choice in the matter, now do we?" Ben sighs.

"Let's go figure out what the crap is going on now..." Ben says as he shuts off the engine and exits his truck with his hands in the air.

10

EILEEN RIVERA

Eileen looks upon the crowd in front of them. She was standing in front of a truck bed, with Steven Reilly behind her in the truck bed. There was another truck parked next to them with the remaining council members in the back of that truck bed.

To her concern, as well as Steven's, only three council members had survived. Jeffery Dobbs, Sheryl Nobles, and Colt Fowler. One was out on holiday when everything started. One went to go check on their family members down the mountain, and never returned. The last one, opted for suicide instead of trying to survive in this new world.

That meant that they may have to fill three seats on the council. Steven, the Deputies, and the remaining council members had discussed this stipulation to great extent. They had all agreed that elections could be tricky during a time like this. However, they had also all agreed that they were necessary to maintain their way of life.

"The right way is not usually the easiest way." Steven had said.

Standing in a line in front of the truck bed with the other deputies, Eileen was still trying to wrap her head around the fact that she was a Deputy now. It seemed so surreal. Nonetheless, she trusted Steven Reilly and his instincts.

There was a ten-foot gap between the Deputies and the new Sheriff, as well as the council members. The crowd kept their distance of close to ten feet away from Eileen and the other Deputies, Jose, Janice, and Todd. She was standing next to Todd, in front of Steven, Jose and Janice were in front of the council members.

They were three Deputies shorthanded, due to Ben and the others going down the mountain for livestock. Livestock that would help their survival, and hopefully the town's survival.

I can't tell how big this crowd is, but if they get unruly, that could mean some major trouble for us. What if they don't like what Steven has to say? She thinks as she surveys the growing crowd of people outside the former grocery store across from the lake of the small town of Crestline.

Eileen hears a megaphone spark to life behind her, somewhat startling her out of her train of thought. Her focus shifts to the crowd, watching and waiting to see what their reaction will be.

"Good afternoon, ladies and gents! For those of you that don't know who I am, I'm Steven Reilly and the newly appointed Sheriff of our small town." Steven says over the megaphone.

Eileen can hear murmurs throughout the crowd, but no one yells or speaks up.

After a short pause, Steven continues. "Your Council Members and your Deputies asked for this meeting to address our small town, together. As some of you may likely have already heard, the good Sheriff Patterson was murdered recently."

This gets some gasps and "*I told you so's*" from the crowd, but no one steps forward to address Steven directly.

News travels fast in small towns. I guess some things never change.

"Whereas, it was a great tragedy and I'm sure that you all have a great deal of questions, rest assured, the murderer has been apprehended and executed. However, this has left us with more complex problems to think about." Steven explains.

"How do you know you got the right guy!?" A voice from the crowd asks.

"Good question, sir! We know we have the right guy, because he

admitted it to two Deputies and we also have a witness to the crime."
Steven answers.

This response gets some hushed murmurs.

Steven continues. "This tragedy has shown us some major flaws in the current ways we are doing things. We are following the old ways of the world, before the *Blue Hole Radius*. That should no longer be the case. Your mountain communities have divided up and delegated leaders of the separate towns to run the day-to-day operations. Currently we have eight Deputies and three Council Members for Crestline to make the major decisions."

"So, we're just supposed to listen to you now?! Just like that?!" Another voice shouts from the crowd.

"I see your concern, my fellow American, and I understand it completely. The quick answer is both yes and no. We are still talking about how to find three more elected council members to fill the empty spots and we are certainly looking for more Deputies to fill our ranks. So yes, you are supposed to listen to law enforcement and your elected officials. On the other hand, if you all feel it fit to do so, you have the power to remove us." Steven pauses and no one interrupts him. So, he continues on, "There are only 11 of us at the moment and there looks to be several hundred of you here today. By our estimation, there are still close to 7,000 souls left in our small town. If we do a crap job and treat you unfairly, you have more than enough manpower to remove us."

This gets some nods and more hushed murmurs from the crowd.

"That being said, we don't think it'll come to that. We plan on being as fair as possible and as swift as possible with punishments. It's a strange and dangerous new world that we live in. It's in all of our best interests to come together so that we can survive and begin to rebuild everything that we have lost. That's why we are here today." Steven says and pauses.

You wouldn't know it by looking at him, but he sure has a way with words. They seem to be staying relatively calm. She thinks to herself.

"So why are you here?!" Another voice shouts and this gets some questioning *"yeahs."*

Steven answers the crowd. "We are here to start up that process again for us. We are here to start a defensive force for our small town, a type of militia. The other towns are doing the same, and we believe it will assist all of us with fighting any more groups of people that intend to do us harm. We were lucky with the MS13 battle. Next time, that may not be the case. Therefore, we are here to ask for volunteers for our defensive force. Some of those volunteers may even have the opportunity to become deputized, to help with the day-to-day."

Steven says and then pauses gesturing over to the council members. "We are also here to find out who's interested in filling the three empty positions upon the Crestline Council."

"Does this have to do with those transmissions and this so-called Leviathan showing up soon?!" A voice yells from the crowd.

This catches Eileen's attention and she looks back to Steven to see what his reply is going to be. She knows he's worried about it and so is she.

It definitely does... but what will he tell the masses?

"Great question! The truth is, we don't know. We don't know if this Leviathan and this Captain Abraham Jackson are coming or not. If they do, we certainly don't know their intentions. But what we do know... what I know... is that we need to be prepared for the future. We need to plan long-term, and this is a good start down that path." Steven explains.

He waits for a few moments for the crowd to calm down and talk about the new information provided and their proposals. "Alright then. That's about all we have for you all. If you are interested in the defensive force and/or becoming deputized, step over to your left and see me. If you are interested in running for one of the empty seats on the council, step off to the right and see your council members. Please don't rush and push. We'll be here as long as you all need us to be. Thank you for coming out... and stay safe out there, ladies and gents."

Once Steven is done talking, Eileen sees the crowd simply stay put for a few moments. There are some hushed *"was that it?"* and *"I came all the way out here for that?"*

After a few awkward minutes, the crowd begins to disperse, and they go about their daily lives. That's when Eileen sees men and women start to make their way to the trucks.

Without the megaphone, Steven speaks again. "Alright, please form nice and orderly lines, so we can get your information."

"Deputy Bradley and Rivera... here." Steven says.

The two of them turn and they each take a notepad and pen.

"Write down their names and send them over to me afterwards." Steven explains.

"Will do." Todd replies.

"All of them, Steven? What if there are a lot?" Eileen asks.

Steven points toward the direction of the line forming. "My guess is that there's only going to be twenty, tops, for starters."

She looks back, astonished. She then looks back at Steven. "Is that it? I thought there would be a lot more. Didn't you say we had close to 7,000 people in this town?"

Steven grins. "Yup, roughly. But we only had around two hundred here today, and we should consider ourselves lucky if we get at least 20 from that. People always talk a big game about wanting to *join up*. But when the opportunity presents itself, many are hesitant."

"Oh..." She looks back to the line that had finished forming, noticing to be filled with right around twenty men and women. "That doesn't seem like a lot for a real defensive force, Steven."

"More, will come. News travels fast in this small town and more will show up. I'm sure of it." Steven replies.

Todd chimes in. "He has a point, Eileen. Let people think it over and more will come out to lend their support."

She looks back to the line and the dispersed crowd behind the line. She then glances over at the line for the council members and sees only two people, a man and a woman.

"If you two say so..." She says, as she begins to take down the information of the people in line and send them off toward Steven.

Eileen and Todd make quick time with the short line of volunteers. They write down their names, date of births, addresses, and their previous careers and/or skills. After about 40 minutes, the line of 18 men and women are standing over by Steven, with 12 men and six women. She was surprised and even excited to see a good percentage of them being women. She hadn't said anything yet, but she was worried that it was just her and Janice with badges.

Well actually, I don't even have an actual badge yet... Do I need one? I'll have to ask Steven when he's done. She thinks, as she stares at the small crowd formed around Steven Reilly, now Sheriff Reilly of Crestline.

"Alright, ladies and gents. All volunteers are accepted into our defensive force of Crestline. The goal is for our defensive force to be ready and easily assembled in the case of an attack or any sort of disaster that we may need help with. We can start up with simple tactics and some training in two days. I have a good feeling we may have some more volunteers by then. As for the deputizing, we're going to have to do some background checks and interviews, to start off with." Steven explains.

One of the younger men chime in. "Hey, Sheriff Reilly? What do we call ourselves?"

"Hmmm, that's a good question." Steven replies and scratches the back of his head.

"Hey, Sheriff..." Todd interrupts. "You already have a good name for the defensive force, the Defensive Force of Crestline or DFC, for short."

Steven laughs. "Well I'll be damned. Good point Deputy Bradley." He then looks to the others. "Well there you have it. The DFC. Now go spread the word and we'll see you all back here in two days, at noon. Any questions?"

"Do we need to bring anything?" The same young man asks.

"Good question, young man." Steven says, smiling. "Bring your *go to* weapon, some water, and some lunch to snack on. If you don't have or own a firearm, raise your hand, please."

Eileen watches as seven of the men and women raise a hand.

Wow, there are still people without guns? That seems crazy, and rather foolish in this new world of ours.

"Fair enough. I'll see what I can round up for you guys and gals. No promises, but I'll see what we can do for you." Steven replies.

This gets some nods and thanks from the small and newly founded DFC, some of which are apparently unarmed.

"Any other questions?" Steven asks and gets no responses. "Alright, our new DFC members, have a great rest of your day and we'll see you back here in two days."

The group chats for a moment and then is gone within a few minutes. After they are all gone, leaving just Steven, Todd, and her, she asks, "How have they gotten this far without guns, Steven?"

Steven scratches the back of his head. "Likely with being very careful and a lot of luck, to be quite honest."

Todd whistles, "You can say that again. Sheesh! And you know they aren't the only ones that are without."

"You are likely right, Todd. But I think we can rectify a good amount of those that are without. That murdering POS Richard Clark had a good amount of firepower with him. We can likely get those seven of our newly formed DFC armed up with those weapons." Steven explains.

"What about the rest?" Eileen asks.

"Yeah... our best and first bet would be the Sheriff Station, over in Twin Peaks. After that, we'll just have to see what we can spare and give up." Steven adds.

"Steven, we are just supposed to give up our weapons to others. That seems a tad bit unfair." Eileen interjects.

She didn't feel comfortable giving up the guns that her father had acquired over the years.

He may be gone now, but they were his... because he prepared for this kind of crap.

Steven puts up his hands in a *clam down* type of motion. "Eileen, you don't have to give up anything that you don't want to. I completely understand and agree with you. However, if we have... say over a dozen guns to each of us... can we even carry that many guns at once?"

"Well, no... but." Eileen starts and then stops to think about it.

"I'm not saying all of them or even most of them. All I'm saying is that we may be able to spare a few to help people defend themselves. I know that I can't carry 10 or 12 guns at once. Hell, it's hard enough carrying a sidearm and rifle." Steven explains.

"Maybe... but I don't know Steven. What if we need those guns? Ben did already get one of his destroyed." Eileen replies.

This gets a chuckle from Steven. "He sure did, didn't he? We'll just see how things play out with the Sheriff's Department over in Twin Peaks."

"Alright then... did you want me to head over to the Sheriff's Station and see what they have?" Eileen asks.

"I was going to head over there now and check it out before too many other Sheriff's get the same idea that I just had. You are more than welcome to tag along." Steven replies.

"Sounds good." Eileen says and the two of them start walking to his Blazer.

"Uh, Sheriff... maybe I should follow you guys out there as well, so that they know you two are the real deal. You guys may be deputized but have no badges or identification to back it up." Todd says to Steven and then looks at Eileen.

"Another good point, Todd!" Steven laughs. "Would you mind following us out that way? If I remember correctly it's only about 10 to 20 minutes away from here."

"Sounds about right, Sheriff Reilly. I'll follow you guys out there and then head back here to keep an eye on the marketplace. We are still spread pretty thin, until Joseph, Ben, and Alexander return." Todd replies.

Ben... She pulls out her phone, seeing it read 1:10 PM. *I hope that they are alright. They should... hopefully... be on their way back home pretty soon. But they haven't checked in for a good while.*

"Good thinking, Todd. And when nobody else is around, Steven is just fine." Steven says as he winks to him.

"Maybe so, Sheriff... but you may as well get used to it sooner or later. Plus, it helps with chain of command. If others see us calling you Steven, it kind of portrays favoritism and even fraternization." Todd explains.

"I suppose you are right... Deputy Bradley. It's going to take some getting used to this whole formality thing." Steven replies.

"Eh, I bet it only takes a couple days or so. You get used to it real quick and it becomes second nature." Todd responds.

"Fair enough. Well... let's get to the Sheriff's Station before they run out of badges and guns." Steven says as he laughs at his own joke.

Eileen smiles and shakes her head at the man, following him to his Blazer.

The drive out to the Sheriff's Station is uneventful. Once reaching the station, Todd talks to one of the other Deputies. After some discussion, Todd's able to acquire a dozen extra Sheriff's badges for Steven, Eileen, Ben, Alexander, and any other future Deputies.

Once Steven and Eileen are introduced, the two thank Todd and he leaves and goes to head back toward the Lake Drive Marketplace in Crestline.

"Now all that's left is to see if we can't try to acquire more firearms for our little community." Steven says to Eileen.

Steven heads back over to the Deputy, talking to him and a couple other Deputies at the station.

After a few minutes of discussion, Eileen's amazed that Steven is able to procure five sidearms and three rifles from the Sheriff's Station.

"How the hell did you manage that, Steven... I mean Sheriff Reilly?" She asks him.

"When it's just our small group, Steven is always fine, Eileen... and I just used logic and patience with them. They were actually rather understanding about people needing to protect their own. It also probably helps that I wasn't greedy. I only asked for a few and they turned out to be more generous." Steven explains to her.

"Generous... I'll say." Eileen replies.

He definitely has a way with words and a way with people. It's almost like he was made for this Sheriff thing, and possibly for this new world of ours. Eileen thinks to herself as she loads up the firearms into the back of the Blazer.

She places some blankets under them and on top of them.

After a few moments, Steven returns carrying multiple boxes of ammunition to go along with the recently procured firearms.

"You sure do have a way with people, Sheriff Reilly." She says, smiling at him.

"It sure appears that way, Deputy Rivera." He says in return and laughs lightly.

Eileen and Steven finish loading everything into the back of the Blazer and head back to the front, opening the doors, they both climb back into the vehicle.

"We headed back home or to the Lake Drive Marketplace, Steven?" Eileen asks.

Steven doesn't respond and simply stares out of the windshield, up toward the sky.

"Steven? Are you alright?" She asks him.

He nods, and slowly says. "Yeah."

"So where are we headed to next? Home or the marketplace?" She asks him again.

With his eyes still on the sky, "Neither, Eileen..."

"Okaaay. Where to then, Sheriff Reilly?" She says grinning.

"Welp... I think it's in our best interest to follow that thing and see where it's going." He says, as he follows something in the sky.

"What thing?" She leans forward, toward the windshield to look to the sky. "What the hell is that?!"

Steven turns on the ignition, roaring the old Blazer to life and pulls back onto the highway, but heading further away from Crestline, further away from home.

"The Leviathan..." The words come out of her mouth, but sound foreign to her.

"It sure appears to be that and the same." Steven says as he guides them along the windy road.

"Are we following it? Following them?" She asks.

"I think it's in our best interest to see where these guys are headed and see what they want." Steven answers.

"Do you think we should though? Especially after what we heard out of Edwards. Or better put, what we didn't hear out of that area." She adds.

"We'll do our best to keep a safe distance, but I think it's important to see who they are and if we should be worried." Steven says to her as he guides them back onto the old 18 Highway, heading east.

Wow, it's actually happening. People from Earth Two are actually here. And wow! Is that Leviathan ship huge! It's like a small town of its own, up there... in the sky.

"Where do you think it's going? Where do you think they are going?" She asks Steven.

"Not sure... but it looks further than Lake Arrowhead." Steven replies. "Hey, didn't Alexander say something about Big Bear Lake being dried up, since the *Blue Hole Radius* opened back up?"

"Huh?" Eileen says in a daze, following the large spaceship in the sky, heading eastward. "Yeah, I think so... why?"

"Because that may be a good spot for something that large to land out here in the mountains." Steven replies. "Unless they plan on going outside of the *Radius* and landing out there."

"Out there?" Eileen asks.

She hadn't really thought about what was now outside of the *Blue Hole Radius*. The way that Alexander had explained it, there wasn't much out there at all, aside from the vast amount of nature that has retaken the world.

"Never mind." Steven says. "Looks like they are going to use the dried-up lakebed as a landing zone. Let's see if we can't get there in time to see these futuristic humans from Earth Two.

Futuristic humans from Earth Two... Does that make them aliens? Eileen wonders.

"Hold on, Eileen." Steven says as he presses the accelerator, resulting in the old Blazer speeding down the windy old Highway 18, toward the spaceship called Leviathan, landing in the dried-up lakebed of Big Bear Lake.

11

ABRAHAM JACKSON

ABRAHAM STOOD at the bridge of the Leviathan, his ship, awaiting to take the transport to the top of the ship to address the humans from Earth One. Or as he referred to them, the *cretins* and *barbarians* of E1. His predecessors from the Einsteinian Paradigm were of no comparison to him and his evolved human species, both physically and cognitively.

Abraham thinks of what he has planned to say to the *cretins*, to ensure that they don't pose a threat to his plan, his plan for the future of Earth One, and his followers known as the Federalists.

It had been over two months, in Earth Two's time, since Captain Abraham Jackson had left his home planet for their species' first planet. In Earth One's time, it had been nearly two months since they exited their slumber from the first *Blue Hole Radius*.

Abraham and his fellow humans from Earth Two had come to call their home E2, for short since there were now three Earths claimed by the human species. Earth One is located in the Sol Solar System, and where the *Blue Hole Radius* survivors are the last of the known humanity on the planet. Earth Two, formerly known as Kepler 452B, is located in the Kepler 452 Solar System, which is roughly 1,402 lighter years away from Earth One.

Earth Two's similar to Earth One in several ways. Both planets have a similar star. Both Planets have similar temperatures. More importantly, both planets can sustain human life. It had taken years for Abraham's predecessors to locate planets that actually were able to sustain human life.

Kepler 452B was discovered during the time of *cretins* and *barbarians* in 2015, prior to the *Harris Paradigm*. Not to Abraham's surprise, it took close to a century to find out any real details about the exoplanet, his home, and others similar to Earth Two... hence Earth Three or E3.

The human-occupied interstellar spacecrafts, also known as the Exodus crafts, that had left Earth One in 3110, and survived the journey through the stars and 1,402 light years, arrived on Earth Two in 3118. With one million souls able to travel on each interstellar spacecraft, only one-hundred-thirteen Exodus ships successfully reached Earth Two... with two-hundred-twenty Exodus ships having left Earth One.

Some of the Exodus ships' fates were known, whether it was a malfunction, rogue asteroid, or even simply human error. On the other hand, there were still a great deal of Exodus ships that were unaccounted for during the voyage, and that of which Abraham and his people still didn't know what happened to those people aboard those interstellar spacecrafts.

From an early age, Abraham was taught that space was a dark and dangerous place, and not be taken lightly. Having lost his companion ship, the Renaissance and it's full 107 souls, Abraham knew this truth all too well.

Luckily for Abraham and his crew of 101 souls, now 92 souls, the Leviathan made it to Earth One, relatively unscathed.

Whereas, there are distinct similarities between Earth One and earth Two, there are also distinct differences. For starters, Earth Two was much larger in size and in mass, relating to their orbit and affecting their yearly calendar. This forced the people of Earth Two to modify their calendar to stay on the same years as Earth One.

The people of Earth Three were instructed to do the same, but Abraham was not sure if they ever followed those orders. He doubted it, considering that they were a planet filled with *deviants* and had become wayward from the way of life that Abraham and the other people of Earth Two had become accustomed to. Hence why they were exiled to Earth 3.

Secondly, in distinct differences between E1 and E2, the sun of Earth Two, Kepler 452, had to be modified to produce less illumination, and therefore, heat, based on its age compared to Earth One's Sol. Once this technology was developed and perfected in 3030, probes were sent to Kepler 452, to prepare Kepler 452b for inhabitation. By the time the first settlers of Earth Two had arrived, the temperatures had been normalized and the planet had regained a good amount of the liquid water on the planet's surface.

The Pandemic of 3020, with the mutated strand of MRSA-TB, combined with panic, war, and other pandemic related variables, had resulted in the drastic decrease in human population of Earth One by 21,780,000,000 people, or 99% of the human species at the time. This forced the remaining 220 million humans to look to the stars to survive.

The third major distinct between Earth One and Earth Two was the comparison in gravity. The first humans on Earth Two had to discover the heavy way just how much the difference in gravity actually was. Scientists had predicted that the gravitational force would essentially double your weight on Earth Two, compared to Earth One... and those scientists were extremely close to accurate.

The change in mass and weight was adapted over time and over a few generations, alongside scientific breakthroughs with anti-aging and tissue rebuilding technology. To better assist the humans of Earth Two to adapt and survive the harshened gravitational increase, humanity relooked at the scientific breakthrough and the black hole paradox, leading to the time stalling *Blue Hole Radius*. After several experiments, some of them being horrible failures, mankind found methods to extend the human lifespan through tissue regeneration, which had a side effect of slowing the natural aging process of humans.

The average lifespan of humanity, prior to their discovery, was 70 to 80 years old. It may not have been his generation's discovery, but it was in the generation of his grandparents being born that it had occurred, those who were considered the first generation of natural born citizens of Earth Two, roughly 300 hundred years ago. Therefore, it was his birthright, and a foundation of pride for his people.

The new and improved lifespan of the human species could reach upwards of three times the previous lifespan. Abraham's grandparents, on both sides, had lived well into the 230's. Abraham could still remember them vividly throughout his childhood years, and even into his early academia years. His parents had expired roughly two months ago, when he had left Earth Two to rebuild Earth One... as it should be rebuilt.

His father had expired at 155 years old and his mother had expired at 153 years old. Abraham was their sole child and felt pain and guilt for their early expiration. However, he had known that all wars have casualties, and mostly blamed their naivety and nostalgia for their early expirations.

Captain Abraham Jackson was rather proud of himself, having reached Earth One, and having successfully defeated his opposition to his cause and his vision for the future of humanity.

In all actuality, Abraham had ascended quickly in his Global Defense career. At the young age of 73 years old, he was a Captain of his very own interstellar spacecraft, the Leviathan. He certainly utilized these accomplishments in his recent years leading up to the Grand Global War.

He had found the obvious flaws in the Utopian ways and sought out to make them not the ways of his new world, on Earth One. He was a third-generation citizen of Earth Two and it had become apparent that the first generations had lost sight of true progress. The Utopians were more focused on ensuring the survival of everyone, regardless of their moral elasticity and wayward tendencies.

Whereas, the near-extinction level event that occurred two months ago had also nearly claimed his own life and aspirations, he was sure that he could rebuild both E1 and E2 in a better, more sufficient and satisfactory image. He was unsure as to how many of his opposition had survived back on Earth Two, but he had figured it to be extremely minimal. If their casualties were a mirror image of the Federalists' casualties of the Grand Global War, then there were likely no survivors from the Utopian Union's side.

As far as Abraham knew, the 92 souls, 74 men and 18 women, aboard the Leviathan were the only survivors from Earth Two. Whereas, he felt it to be unfortunate that he had to execute six females and three males on the trip to Earth One, he knew it was a necessity that had to transpire. This was mainly due to insubordination and plausible mutiny, because they had second thoughts about what happened on Earth Two.

He was no stranger to thinning the herd and the casualties of war. Just a few months ago, Earth Two had a population of over 800 million citizens. Now, Abraham thought it likely that E2 had a population of zero or very close to it. But at least the great Commander Yang was destroyed along with the Icarus.

Despite the considerable setbacks, and current minimal number of *sleepers* left in his arsenal... Abraham was still very optimistic and self-assured of himself that his plan would come to fruition. The Leviathan only had one *sleeper* left in its arsenal, having used 28 of them back on Earth Two, and one already on the first landing on Earth One.

Despite the Leviathan only having one *sleeper* left, with a spread radius of 500 miles, the Leviathan still had plenty of dozers... with the interstellar spacecraft variety (CSDs), the STARUs with their SSDs, and of the handheld variety (IMDs on the MECCUs). He also had a great deal of ammunition for all of them. There was also the likelihood of viable and operational *sleepers* still left to be found here on Earth One, along with long-lost ancient weapons.

His numbers may be greatly reduced, and his plan may not have gone as it should have, but he still had the upper hand, both literally and figuratively. In Abraham's mind, these *cretins* and *barbarians* were no match for him and his Federalists.

Even if they still have the starting amount of close to 9 million souls, here on Earth One, they still don't stand a chance. Abraham thinks to himself as he ascends onto the platform atop of his Leviathan.

"Lieutenant Meads. Is everything prepared for my address to these barbarians?" Abraham asks the man to his right.

"Yes, Captain. Everything is prepared. However, you may want to refrain from calling them barbarians in your speech." The Lieutenant answers.

"Yes, rather good point, Lieutenant Meads. Does it say that in my speech?" Abraham asks the Lieutenant.

"No, sir. I made sure to edit out any vulgarity in your speech. Especially with what happened at the first landing point of Earth One." The Lieutenant replies.

"Right. Good for you, Lieutenant. It's greatly appreciated, and rightly so." Abraham responds.

The Lieutenant nods in acknowledgement and Abraham shifts his attention to the man to his right. "Staff Sergeant, is the barrier up and running to full capacity this time? We would not want another debacle like we had to deal with on the morrow of yesterday."

The Staff Sergeant quickly nods. "No, of course not, sir. The barrier is up and running. You will be as safe as humanly possible, sir."

"I should hope so, Staff Sergeant. Considering that I'm your commanding officer, the Captain of the Leviathan, leader of the Federalists, and soon to be Supreme Commander of Earth One." Abraham lectures the man to his left.

"Right. Once again. My sincerest apologies for the first landing point on Earth One, Captain Jackson. I had not thought these primitive humans to be a threat to us." The Staff Sergeant replies.

"Understood, Staff Sergeant. If I'm being honest, I did not think of them as a threat much either. Nonetheless, we know better now. They may be primitive humans, dating back to the Einsteinian Paradigm. However, we must not underestimate these *cretins* and *barbarians* again." Abraham admits and explains to his subordinate.

He then addresses both men on the platform that's rising through the opening on top of the Levitation. "Remember, gentleman, we need the *cretins* and *barbarians* to ensure our survival. In all actuality, we really only need about half of them. The half of them that can reproduce our future generations of Federalists, and the ones that we can reeducate."

"Yes, sir." The Lieutenant replies.

"Right, sir. We'll follow you to the end, sir." The Staff Sergeant replies.

The dome of the Leviathan opens enough to allow the levitating platform to rise above the Leviathan by roughly 50 feet. Abraham Jackson, Lieutenant Meads, and Staff Sergeant Lee are suspended in the air above the interstellar spacecraft, looking down on the *cretins* and b*arbarians* of Earth One.

Abraham can see the *barbarians* and *cretins* beginning to crowd and assemble alongside the edge of the dried-up lakebed.

Look at them down there, milling about like animals. It truly is a shame that I need them. That we need them to ensure the survival of our species. This would have been so much easier if only Commander Yang and the rest of the Utopians saw reason and logic. To think that he wanted to simply give these barbarians our technology... just like that. To infer that they somehow deserved it, simply because it existed and they are humans.

Abraham chuckles to himself at this thought.

Humans... barely. Without us, most of them will be dead long before they reach my age. And from what I know from my studies, the timeframe that these humans came from were asinine times. This very region nearly destroyed themselves, according to my memory bank. He thinks as he searches his recall memory banks.

He does a full circle, scanning the area while his memory registers his prepared speech that he had read earlier this morning. As he sees it form in his mind's eye, he looks it over to ensure that there won't be a repeat of the first landing.

I only have one sleeper at this current moment and time. Whereas, that can be rectified, if I end up using it, all that will be left is my remaining Federalists... and we need many more than 74 men and 18 women to repopulate E1, and eventually E2. He reminds himself.

Since the first landing, Abraham had taken the advice of Staff Sergeant Lee... who had advised him with speaking from the heart and minds approach. Staff Sergeant Lee had reminded him that these people from this time period were easily misled and did well with promises of grandiose, no matter how far-fetched they were.

When Staff Sergeant Lee had mentioned this, Abraham had double checked his recall memory bank, and confirmed that these primitive humans thought themselves to be highly intelligent but were guided by fear and false hope.

"Instead of saying that you are going to *fix* them, sir... why don't you simply say you are here to *help* them? Our medical advancements and technology must seem relatively similar to fiction to them. If we show them what we have to offer, and if they join us... it's likely that there will be much less loss of life and we may even be able to re-educate some of the adult males." Staff Sergeant Lee had politely pleaded with him earlier this morning.

Abraham remembers this conversation now, to help with his deliverance of his words.

Adult males? He laughs to himself.

Their adult males are like our children back home. They know nothing of sacrifice and determination. We were not considered to be adults until we were of 50 years of age. Up to that point, it was mostly academia and civil service to the common good of E2. Then, once we finally attained the status of adulthood, we began again, in our careers... from the bottom, each and every one of us.

He grins, remembering his youth and all of the hard work and dedication that led him up to this point.

Yes, you primitive cretins and barbarians. There's hope for you still. Whereas, my original outcome for your kind was a swift demise. It appears as though I need to salvage as many of you as possible... thanks to the Grand Global War and the shortsightedness of Commander Yang.

Abraham shrugs. *Just as our forefathers and foremothers used to say with best laid plans, and all... The best-laid plans of mice and men often go awry. No matter how carefully a strategy is outlined and is planned, something may still go wrong with it.*

It appears as though many of you will be allowed to live in our new world. You will just need to be re-taught and re-educated, which should not pose as too much of an obstacle. Our forefathers and foremothers did so upon reaching E2, and we will do so upon reaching E1. Remaking and rebuilding it into something more sufficient and of aggrandized excellence than the human species has ever seen.

He surveys the growing crowd around him, and he vaguely hears Lieutenant Meads advise him that he has confirmed that many of the primitive humans are armed.

Hearing the distant voice of his Lieutenant, he's brought away from his recall memory banks and brought back to the present.

"Yes, Lieutenant. Thank you for the update. I don't see it as a complication. If anything, it will display our superiority if they attempt to utilize their ancient weapons." Abraham replies.

"Very good, sir. Are you prepared to speak publicly? Should I activate the external comms and the visual projectors?" Lieutenant Meads asks.

"Yes, and that is accurate Lieutenant. Activate the external comms and projectors now if you could. Thank you." Abraham responds, as he clears his throat.

Lieutenant Meads nods and lifts his right arm, using his right hand to confirm the activation of the external comms on his MECCU (Mobile Extremity Communications and Control Unit).

Abraham smiles as he watches the crowd of *barbarian* humans flinch at the sound of the external communications coming on.

You are wise to be fearful of us, you cretins and barbarians. And you're even wiser as to not attempt an altercation with myself and my Federalists. He thinks to himself.

"Greetings, humans on Earth One, survivors of the Blue Hole

Radius! My name is Captain Abraham Jackson and myself and my crew come from Earth Two. We come here to provide aid and support, to help usher your kind into this brave new world of ours!" Abraham speaks, as the comms unit blares out his message to the humans below him.

He pauses and watches them grow tense as he starts to speak, and then he can visibly see several of them begin to talk to one another.

Abraham continues. "My words will be short with you on this midday of this wonderful day on Earth One. For we have many other settlements to visit and assist! We are indeed here to help our species survive and progress forward, together!"

He pauses for effect and to allow their meek and slow minds to process this new information.

Their feeble brains must be hurting trying to process this much information. We must appear to be divine creatures compared to them. Considering the circumstance, we are relatively close to being divine creatures compared to them. He smiles at this thought.

"To begin to show you that we are here to help, we have the means to aid your sick and wounded. We have technology well past your current capabilities. Whereas, your generation led to the creation of the Harris Paradigm, we have made drastic improvements since your time. For example, I'm 74 years old and have a full life expectancy of close to 240 years of life. The gentlemen I'm standing next to are in their 70's as well and have the same expectancy. In reference to your age, I'm a 74-year-old male human with the body of a mid-twenties human being from your timeframe." Abraham explains to them.

This gets some visible shocks and awes from the crowds down below them.

He continues. "Yes, I know. I know. It must sound unfathomable to your kind. But that is only a small portion of what we have to offer to your kind. I understand that all of you must have so many questions. We will be leaving two of our crew members behind with your kind while we go to spread our message to the other surviving settlements here on Earth One. My two crew members will be somewhat of ambassadors of sorts. providing aid, care, and beginning to provide you with our past since your time."

Staff Sergeant Lee really had an excellent idea with this approach. They seem much more manageable when provided with promises of hope and long-lasting lifespans. I really should have tried this approach with the first group of barbarians, instead of the direct approach.

He nods to himself.

Oh well though. We still have plenty of these cretins and barbarians to rebuild.

"We look forward to rebuilding Earth One side by side with your kind. Together we can usher in a new era of strength and abundance for the human species. The Leviathan will return in several days, once we have contacted all surviving settlements from the Blue Hole Radius. Your time and attention are greatly appreciated. Thank you, and I look forward to seeing you all again very soon." Abraham says as he completes his speech and turns to Lieutenant Meads nodding.

Lieutenant Meads brings up his right arm again, with his MECCU, and turns off the external comms.

"External comms and the projectors are deactivated sir. And might I say... that went rather well, Captain Jackson. Your words were clear, precise, and came across as hopeful and helpful." Lieutenant Meads says.

"Yes, sir. I would have to agree with Lieutenant Meads. This situation played out much more effectively than the previous situation over the military installation in that desert region." Staff Sergeant Lee adds.

"Yes, I noticed the distinct differences between this engagement and the last engagement. It went rather well, especially considering that we did not have to exterminate this population of cretins and barbarians." Abraham says as the levitating platform begins to lower back within the confines of Leviathan.

"Sir, who did you have in mind to be the two ambassadors from E2?" Lieutenant Meads asks him.

"I was thinking of Staff Sergeant Mahoney and Sergeant Burke. I have already notified them after my discussion with Staff Sergeant Lee on how to handle these barbarians." Abraham replies.

"Excellent choices, sir. Having a strong male and female counterpart should help portray our strength, as well as the aid and support that you are attempting to portray." Lieutenant Meads responds.

Abraham looks at the Lieutenant. "Thank you, Lieutenant Meads. And it's best you change your verbiage with barbarians. We are not portraying aid and support. We are providing aid and support to assist with their steps to accepting re-education to conform to our ways, voluntarily."

"Right, sir. My apologies but... I should add that you may want to avoid calling them cretins and barbarians from this point forward, as to not have slips of tongue and miscommunicate our intentions... once again." Lieutenant Meads replies.

Abraham nods and then replies, "That's a fair point you have there, Lieutenant Meads. Thank you for the reminder. Now please make sure that Mahoney and Burke have the supplies they require and are ready to be deployed. We should be on our way to the next major settlement."

As the levitating platform reaches the bridge level of the Leviathan, Abraham begins to walk to the bridge of the interstellar spacecraft. He stops and turns back to his subordinates.

"Where's the next major settlement that we are going to?" Abraham asks.

Lieutenant Meads lifts his right arm and looks at his MECCU. "A place called Yucaipa, Sir. It's not too far from our current location."

Abraham nods. "Very good then. Make me aware of when we are ready to depart. And please remind Mahoney and Burke to go with the hearts and minds approach. Make sure they conceal the true abilities of their MECCUs, and only use them if they are in extreme peril."

"Yes, Sir. I will advise them, once again, of our current tactics with the people of E1." Lieutenant Meads replies and strides off to ensure that his orders are followed.

"Very good, Lieutenant Meads. That'll be all." Abraham responds.

He then walks to the bridge and retakes his normal place on the bridge, looking over the Command Central Control aboard the Leviathan.

12

BENJAMIN REILLY

STEPPING OUT OF HIS TRUCK, he nods in a calm fashion to the two men on the ATV, with the passenger still pointing a rifle at him. His hands are in the air and he steps out to the front of the truck where Alexander meets him to his right... also with his hands in the air. Joseph comes up next to Alexander, with the three of them standing in front of Ben's truck.

Ben focuses his attention at the man in front of him, pointing the shotgun at himself, Joseph, and Alexander. "Gents, I think you may have mistaken us for some other folks."

"Shut the fuck up! Keep your hands up!" The man shouts at him, clearly agitated and clearly nervous.

"Our hands are up and you have us surrounded. Before anyone does anything accidentally, just who do you think we are?" Ben presses, hoping that the man doesn't have a knee-jerk reaction to pull the trigger.

"Real cute, asshole! You come here in a black truck yesterday, with a similar box trailer... and steal his wife and daughters. Then you claim to be someone else. You must think we are real fucking stupid!" The man to his left says, in the driver's seat of the ATV.

"Yeah! Where the fuck is my family, asshole!" The man in front of him yells.

Shit. This can really turn out badly if we don't calm this guy down, and soon...

"Gentlemen, I'm a Deputy with the Sheriff's department. These other two men are deputized as well. We simply came down here to barter for livestock. There are no women in our trailer... only animals." Joseph says calmly.

"Livestock?! Bullshit!" The man in front of them shouts.

"No bullshit. Go ahead and check for yourselves. Did one of you guys happen to talk to my Uncle in the last few days, over the radio? He would have gone by *The Falcon* or maybe even Steven Reilly..." Ben tries to explain as the man in front of him is clearly becoming more anxious.

"Bull-fucking-shit! You're just trying to trick me! You must have heard our conversation over the radio!" The man shouts.

"So, you did talk to my Uncle? See... we are simply here to barter for sheep. Nothing more. This is just a really messed up case of mistaken identity..." Ben replies, calmly.

"We can clear this up if one of your men simply go check the back of our trailer. You will find twenty-four chickens, three roosters, eight piglets, and no women or children. We are only here for three sheep... that's all." Joseph explains in a calm manner.

The man in front of them stares for a moment, apparently thinking about the situation. He turns to the men to Ben's left. "Hector, Manny! Go check their trailer!"

The two men nod, exiting the ATV and head out to the back of the trailer.

"If you all are lying... we are going to make you fucking pay!" The man with the shotgun says to them.

"I assure you sir... we are not lying. You'll see." Ben replies.

The man narrows his gaze at him, and they are interrupted by the two men, Hector and Manny, shouting from the back of their trailer. "Looks like they ain't full of shit, after all!"

"Yeah, all that's back here are chickens and pigs!" Another voice shouts.

The man in front of them looks visibly disappointed.

He really wanted us to be them...

"Can we lower our hands, now?" Alexander asks the man.

The man looks over to Alexander, pauses, and then nods, relaxing his hold on his shotgun.

Ben, Alexander, and Joseph all sigh with relief as they lower their hands.

One of the men walks back up toward the front of the truck and looks at Ben and the others. "Sorry guys. We really thought you were those assholes that have been stealing women and children from the area." The man says.

"Oh wow! That's horrible." Ben replies.

The man extends his hand out. "Name's Hector. That's my brother, Manny, closing back up your trailer. The man with the shotgun is Daniel. The guy in the truck behind you is Carl. And over on the other side of you all is Curtis and Brett."

Ben shakes Hector's hand. "I'm Ben, this is Alexander, and that's Joseph. We really just came out here for sheep. I'm very sorry to hear about your current situation."

"Yeah, Daniel lost his wife and two daughters yesterday. My brother lost his wife a few days before that. Curtis over there... they killed his son and took his wife and daughter as well." Hector explains.

"Dear God! That's absolutely horrible." Alexander replies.

"For sure. Is there anything we can do to help? Do you know who these guys are or anything?" Joseph asks.

Hector shakes his head. "I doubt it. They could be long gone by now... all we know is that there are about six of them, they drive a black truck with a box trailer, and there are three guys on motorcycles. Besides that, we don't know jack shit."

All of them look down at the ground as it begins to rumble.

"Another one?" Hector says, as the earth shakes below their feet.

They all wait as the earthquake comes and goes, riling up the livestock in the trailer.

"Yeah, and according to our very smart friend here..." Ben says, gesturing to Alexander. "We will likely have many more small quakes, as the land settles back in."

"There may also be a few larger ones too. I must add." Alexander replies.

"Well, we are pretty used to them, living in California and all." Hector replies.

"You all sure there's nothing we can do to help out?" Ben asks again.

"Likely not." Daniel says as he walks up. "Sorry for almost putting a shitload of buckshot into you guys. I thought for sure you guys were them..."

Ben scratches the back of his head. "It's alright, I get it. It's a tough situation to be in. I couldn't imagine."

"Yeah... we really don't have much information about those assholes. The only reason we know what they drive is because of Curtis. Before they knocked him out, he got a look at them. When he woke up. His son was dead, and his wife and daughter were gone. They hit my house when I was out yesterday. Same with Manny, over there." Daniel explains.

Ben looks to Alexander and Joseph, none of them really knowing what to say.

"You all still want those sheep? I'll bring them around up front and you guys can be on your way." Daniel adds.

"Daniel, it's not that big of a deal. You have much more to worry about." Ben replies.

"Nonsense. It's not like I need them now at all. Besides. I could use your coins to go buy supplies to hunt these bastards down." Daniel responds.

Ben nods, thinking over. "Fair enough. Sure, we'll still take them."

Daniel nods and turns to go get the three sheep to complete their trailer load of livestock.

"Good God, Ben. Is there anything we can do to help these guys out?" Alexander asks.

"I'm not sure what we can do..." Ben replies.

"He's right. We really don't have information to go off of." Joseph adds.

A few moments later, Daniel returns with three sheep tied off to some rope.

"Here you are. Sorry again, about the mix up..." Daniel says, handing over the sheep.

Joseph takes the ropes and walks them to the back of the trailer.

"Thank you, Daniel. And I hope that you find your family. All of your families." Ben replies.

"Thanks. I guess this is just the world that we live in now." Daniel responds.

"Yeah, but it doesn't have to be that way..." Ben says as he hands the man five Gold American Eagles for the sheep.

Daniel takes the payment and looks at the amount. "We only agreed on three gold coins over the radio."

"Maybe so, but the extra coin could help with supplies for finding your guys' families." Ben replies.

Daniel's face turns solemn and thoughtful. "Thank you. And sorry again for the whole mix up."

"Thanks for hearing us out and not shooting first... asking questions later." Ben replies and extends his hand to Daniel. "Good luck, Daniel."

"Thanks. Safe travels to you and your friends." Daniel replies.

Ben, Alexander, and Joseph wave goodbye to the six men and climb back into Ben's truck. The man named Carl, driving the truck, moves out of their way so Ben can back up and pull back on the main road.

"Well, that was a close call and an all-around sad situation." Joseph says.

Alexander and Ben don't answer, only nod. After a few moments of silence, they make their way back to the 215 Freeway and begin to head North on their return trip back home.

Reaching the city limits of Perris, Ben says, "I really hope that they find their families safe and sound."

"Ben..." Joseph starts.

"I know, Joseph... the chances of that happening are slim to none." Ben replies. "But I can still hope..."

Joseph nods and doesn't reply.

"Hey, Alexander... can you text Eileen and my Uncle, to let them know that we are on our return trip?" Ben asks.

"Will do, Ben." Alexander replies, pulling out his phone and starting to text.

"There... sent." Alexander adds.

"Thanks. Wouldn't want them to get worried. And can we just leave the part out about us getting ambushed..." Ben asks.

Alexander and Joseph start to chuckle.

"No really, guys. She already thinks that I'm a magnet for trouble." Ben explains.

"Maybe she has a point." Joseph replies, which gets a good laugh from all of them.

While they are all laughing, at Ben's expense, the road begins to shake and sway.

Shit, another one? And we are on an overpass. Just great! Ben thinks to himself.

Joseph and Alexander stop laughing, and Alexander asks, "Ben, should we pull over until this passes?"

"My thoughts exactly. Just let me clear this overpass and make it back to more solid ground." Ben replies.

"Right, makes sense." Alexander replies.

After another few stressful moments, Ben pulls the truck and trailer off to the side of the freeway, just past the edge of the overpass, and puts the truck into park. He can hear the livestock going crazy back in the trailer.

The three of them wait in silence, as they can hear and see the earth shaking beneath their feet.

Oh man! This one feels like a good one. Stronger than the others. I wonder how much longer it's going to last? Ben thinks to himself.

Before he can make his concerns vocal, the earth stops shaking and the world goes silent.

"Whew-wee! That was a good one." Joseph says and then he whistles.

"Yes, that was much stronger than the previous ones." Alexander says with anxiety in his voice.

"Yeah, it was. That might be the strongest one I felt in all my life... and it was a long one." Ben admits.

"I don't know how you Californians get used to the ground just shaking beneath your feet all of the time." Alexander replies, still a little shaken by the large and long earthquake.

"To be honest, you get kind of used to them... but that was a doozy." Ben replies.

"Yeah it was." Joseph says.

"I would not doubt that one caused some damage. It felt strong enough to do some damage." Ben adds.

Before anyone else can chime in, Ben hears engines approaching from the North and all three of them focus their attention on the oncoming vehicles.

Squinting in the mid-afternoon sun, Ben can see a vehicle start to form on the horizon.

As they get closer, Ben starts to make out their shapes a little more closely.

No... it couldn't be. Are those motorcycles and a...? Ben thinks to himself.

"Sure as shit is... that's a couple of motorcycles and black truck with a box trailer..." Ben says aloud.

"And that truck and trailer look very similar to ours, Ben." Alexander adds.

"Those have to be those creeps that Daniel and the others were talking about." Joseph replies.

"My thoughts exactly!" Ben exclaims.

"Any objections to following those scumbags and seeing where they're going?" Ben adds.

"None, here." Joseph replies.

"No, but we should likely trail them from a distance, Benjamin." Alexander replies.

"Right... I'll let them get a little ways past us and then turn around and follow those POS's." Ben explains.

The three men wait for the motorcycles and the truck with a box trailer to go past them. Ben eagerly watches as the two front bikes pass them, followed by the truck and then the bike in the rear.

"Looks like they were right. There can't be more than six of them. If we find out where they are going, we can get Daniel and the others to help take them out." Ben explains.

"Take them out? I thought we were just going to follow them?" Alexander questions.

"Alexander, these POS's are taking women and children. We cannot just sit by and do nothing." Ben explains.

"No, you are right, Ben. It just seems like a rather large risk... considering our numbers and theirs." Alexander replies.

"Maybe so, but that's the world that we live in now. We cannot just let people keep on doing these horrible things to good people." Ben answers. "Joseph, what do you think?"

"You had me at scumbags... I'm in." Joseph replies.

Ben smiles, as he watches the vehicles pass his truck and start to go over the overpass. "Alexander, you good?"

"Yes, Ben. I'm good." Alexander replies.

Ben looks over to Alexander. "It'll be alright, Alexander. We got this. And it's the right thing to do."

Before Alexander can reply, Ben hears crashing sounds and screeching of tires. He turns back to see the vehicles to his left. He can't see them, so he checks his side view mirror. He sees one bike down, crashed, and the second one crashing, with the driver being launched from the bike into the air. The screeching tires sound was coming from the truck as it was trying to break before hitting the bikes, or so Ben thinks.

The truck takes flight, with the box trailer in tow, and lands on its side skidding a good distance before it comes to a stop. The only vehicle that didn't crash was the last bike, who had stopped in time before hitting whatever the other vehicles had, and had also avoided running into the back of the trailer.

Without thinking, Ben shuts off his engines and jumps out of his truck. He opens up his back-cab door, grabbing his 5.56 SAINT AR.

He looks over at Joseph and Alexander, "What are you guys waiting for?! If it's them, we have them by surprise! If it's not, they need help! Let's go!"

Before they can answer, Ben bolts for the accident site and straight toward the man standing next to his motorcycle with his hands on top of his head yelling obscenities.

Once Ben reaches within ten feet of the man, he stops and brings up his AR, clicking off the safety.

If these are those scumbags and he's the only one left alive, we need him...

"Keep your hands up and don't move! Or I will shoot you!" Ben shouts at the man.

The man flinches and then freezes, not moving as Ben instructed.

"Now slowly turn around... Slowly! If I even think you are going for your gun, I will drop you!" Ben shouts at him.

The man slowly turns around. He has long black hair tied up into a ponytail. He looks to have a few inches on Ben, but also looks on the slow and pudgy side of the spectrum. His clothes tell Ben that he looks the part of a scumbag... but looks aren't everything. When he's facing Ben, he can tell that the man is sizing him up, just as Ben was doing to him.

Thinking quickly, Ben asks. "How many women and children do you have in the back of that trailer?!"

The man grins at him and starts to put his hands down. "What the fuck is it to you?! If you are going to do something, fucking do it! If not, you'd best start running, bitch..." The man starts to chuckle.

Not "what?" or "who are you?" or "why the hell would I have women and children in a box-enclosed trailer?" ... Nope, this POS said, "what the fuck is it to me?"

::Crack::

The man screams out in pain.

::Crack::

The man screams out in pain again and is now lying on the road ten feet away from Ben, trying to hold both of his legs at once. Ben had shot him first in his left leg, and then quickly again in his right leg.

We may need him alive, but we don't necessarily need him being able to walk or run. Ben thinks to himself.

"Where's your gun!?" Ben shouts at the man.

The man doesn't grin or chuckle this time and is obviously in pain and angry. "It's on my hip and I have another on my bike!" The man says through his teeth.

"Slowly take your gun and throw it away from you! If I even think you are raising it toward me and my friends, next round goes in your chest!" Ben shouts at the man.

The man doesn't reply but slowly reaches to his right hip with his hand that's now covered in blood. He grabs his sidearm with two fingers and tosses it away from him.

With his bike a good six feet away from him, Ben's confident that he can't reach it faster than he can pull the trigger.

"Now let's try this again, scumbag! How many women and children do you have in that trailer that just crashed?" Ben asks the bleeding man on the ground.

"I don't fucking know. Maybe twenty... if they're still alive." The man replies, now gripping his legs where he was shot. "I hope they're all fucking dead." The man says as he grits the words through his teeth.

"You better hope they aren't! They're the only reason you're still alive... Now! How many of you are there?!" Ben shouts at the man.

"Why don't you go and find out, hero?" The man replies, staring daggers at Ben.

Ben sights in at the man's right foot.

"No! Wait! Don't!" The man shouts.

::Crack::

The man screams out in pain once again.

"Holy Hell, Ben! Just what the hell are you doing?!" Joseph says as he catches up to him, along with Alexander.

Ben turns to Joseph. "These are the guys. He said as much. There's about 20 girls in that trailer and I'm trying to figure how many bad guys there are..."

"Holy shit! 20 of them?!" Joseph shouts. He then raises his rifle to the man on the ground who's screaming in pain.

"No!" Ben shouts at Joseph.

Joseph pauses and looks over at Ben. "What?! You said it yourself! He's one of them!"

"Yes! But... We may still need him. There may be more women stashed away somewhere nearby" Ben replies.

"Oh shit! I didn't think about that." Joseph answers.

"Hey! Big tough badass that kidnaps women!" Ben shouts at the man on the ground.

The man looks up at him, with pain and anger still in his eyes.

"Tell me how many there are of your kind or say goodbye to your other foot!" Ben shouts at the man.

"There's fucking six of us! At least there fucking was!" The man blurts out as tears are running down his face and stares at Ben with an intense mixture of pain and rage.

"See. That wasn't so hard. Way to make it harder for yourself, you dipshit." Ben says to the man.

He then turns to Alexander. "Alexander, stay here with this POS. Joseph and I will move forward. If you hear us yell for you, put a round in this shitbag and come help us up front."

Alexander pauses and doesn't answer.

"Alexander, you can't leave him by himself and we need to go check for survivors. He has a gun on his bike and another one tossed over there. He's part of a group of men that kidnap women and young girls. I don't think I have to explain to you what their intentions were." Ben explains.

Alexander nods. "Right. You are absolutely right, Ben. Go ahead, and I'll stay here... with him."

Ben pats him on the shoulder. "It'll be alright, buddy. Just don't overthink it."

Before Alexander can respond, Ben looks to Joseph. "Come on Joseph, let's go."

"Alright! But let me lead. You two are still new to this whole tactical thing." Joseph replies.

"Lead the way, Joe." Ben replies.

Joseph starts jogging toward the trailer. Once they reach it, Ben stops but Joseph keeps going.

"Joseph, what about the women and children?!" Ben asks.

"Ben, we need to deal with the threat first... then check for survivors. Now come on!" Joseph yells at him.

Ben nods, and follows Joseph to the crashed truck on its side. Joseph stops at the hood of the car right before the windshield, and so does Ben.

"Alright. Now don't shoot blindly. There may be a hostage in there with them. I'll run around the front to the underside of the truck to draw their attention. You come in seconds after to take out the threats. I'll climb up on top to get a better vantage point." Joseph says in a hushed tone.

"Got it." Ben replies.

Joseph runs around the front of the crashed truck on its side, to the undercarriage of the vehicle.

One, Two, Three...

Ben steps out with his rifle aimed at the windshield and scanning for movement. He holds his breath with his finger on the trigger.

I can't see shit through that shattered windshield.

He holds for a few more seconds, and then ducks back to the side of the truck with the hood, fearful that they can see him and he cannot see them.

"They're all dead in the truck, Ben. Three men, no movement." Joseph says, from atop of the downed vehicle.

::Crack::Crack::Crack::

"Oh shit!" Joseph yells. "It's coming from the two bikes up front!"

Ben then hears Joseph dive off of the truck with a loud audible thud.

::Crack::Crack::Crack::

They're still focused on him... Sounds like it's coming from up front to the right...

Ben readies his rifle, aiming down his sights and steps out from the side of the truck to get a better view of their aggressors.

Breathe, exhale, gently squeeze, repeat.

He steps out and sees a man with a helmet on, firing off to Ben's right, likely toward Joseph.

::Crack::Crack::Crack::

The man drops to the ground and doesn't move. Ben quickly shifts his attention to the other down motorcycle, stepping toward it with his rifle aimed at the rider that's down on the ground. He gets close enough to touch the downed rider but thinks twice about turning him over since he's face down on the road.

I've seen too many damn movies where this sort of asshole is still alive and shoots the other guy. Screw that crap. Ben thinks of himself.

::Crack::Crack::Crack::

Ben puts three rounds into the man's back and watches as his lifeless body takes the impact of the rounds and then goes back to being deathly still.

Oh well, better safe than sorry. Ben thinks and he shrugs.

He turns to walk off toward the first rider that he shot, to find him face up, still with his helmet on, but with two bullet holes in his chest and a blood pool beneath his body.

Eh, two out of three shots ain't bad. Ben thinks.

He then turns to try and find Joseph. "Joseph?! You alright over there?!"

"Yeah!" Ben hears Joseph yell back.

"That son of bitch had me pinned down by the front axle." Joseph says as he stands up dusting himself off and walks over to Ben.

He stands next to Ben. "Was the other guy alive too?"

Ben shakes his head. "I don't think so, but I figured better safe than sorry. You sure those guys in the truck are goners? I couldn't see a damn thing through that shattered windshield."

Joseph nods. "They are most definitely goners. It's pretty gross in there. If I had to take a guess it was a combination of their fingers on their triggers for some odd reason and not wearing seat belts, because someone shot someone, and it wasn't us... Actually, that could have been the reason for the accident."

Ben points to the ground that's just past the trailer behind them, which has chunks of concrete from the overpass upturned in the middle of the road.

"I think that may have been the reason for the accident." He replies.

"Wow... yeah... that must have been one hell of an earthquake to do that. That's some huge damage to this overpass." Joseph.

Ben nods. "Agreed and all the more reason we should check for survivors in the trailer and get the hell off this overpass."

"Good point." Joseph replies.

The two men make their way to the back of the box trailer, which is on its side as well, just like the truck. They have some trouble but are able to pull open the drop-down gate, which is working more as a barely swinging open door.

When they open the door, Ben's saddened to see the box trailer floor riddled with bodies.

"Can anyone hear me?!" Joseph says

Ben's heart sinks as no one answers and several moments pass.

After a few seconds, Ben shouts, "Is anyone alive in there?!"

A few more seconds of silence pass, until Ben and Joseph see a small hand raise through the bodies, and then another larger hand raises, followed by another small hand. Ben then begins to hear weakened voices asking for help and sobbing.

Oh, thank God, there are survivors... But the question is how many? That POS back there said there were nearly twenty women and children in here. Ben thinks to himself.

"Where do we even start?" Joseph asks, looking into the trailer.

"I don't know... I suppose we start taking them out one by one, from the back of the trailer forward. I guess we lay them on the road and try to see which ones we can help." Ben replies in a solemn voice.

Joseph nods in silent agreement.

"Alright, you grab this one's legs and I'll grab her shoulders." Ben adds, stepping toward the closest person, which appears to be a teenager.

"Yeah... alright." Joseph says, with a sort of sadness in his voice.

Ben could definitely relate. This was a real crap situation, and a real sad turn of events. He truly hoped that there were more survivors than then several hands he saw raised and the multiple voices and sobs he had heard. More importantly, he hoped that they were able to help those survivors.

One foot in front of the other, Ben. Don't think about it, just get the job done... think about it after it's all said and done. Ben reminds himself as he and Joseph begin to pull bodies from the wreckage of the box trailer.

13

EILEEN RIVERA

E<small>ILEEN AND</small> S<small>TEVEN</small> had reached the dried-up lakebed of Big Bear Lake just in time to see the massive spaceship with a platform that was elevated high above the Leviathan. By the time they had reached their destination, a very large screen appeared in thin air. The screen was circular and seemed almost holographic in nature.

Upon the screen was one man's face. He looked young, close to her own age. He had a stoic and stern look about him, and very military-like.

As Eileen and Steven come to a stop, close to some large rocks and a small park area, they both exit the Blazer, with both of them reaching back into the Blazer to grab their rifles.

"Greetings, humans on Earth One, survivors of the Blue Hole Radius! My name is Captain Abraham Jackson and myself and my crew come from Earth Two. We come here to provide aid and support, to help usher your kind into this brave new world of ours!" The man known now as Captain Abraham Jackson says, with a booming voice over some sort of speaker system.

Eileen looks around and sees that everyone is mesmerized by the massive spaceship in front of them and the person speaking above the ship.

Not having to push forward, due to the massiveness of the projection or holographic screen, or whatever it was... the two of them stand in front of Steven's Blazer and look back to the sky.

Earth Two? That seems like an insane idea to entertain. But here's the proof... People from Earth Two. Eileen thinks to herself.

"My words will be short with you this midday of this wonderful day on Earth One. For we have many other settlements to visit and assist! We are indeed here to help our species survive and progress forward, together!" The very large image of Captain Abraham Jackson says.

He must be the guy in the middle of those two other guys... up on that platform way up there? Is that thing just floating up there? Eileen thinks, as she strains to see the platform through the massive circular projection/hologram.

She watches as Captain Abraham Jackson smiles.

That's not a sly smile at all... He appears to think very highly of himself. Eileen thinks as she watches Captain Abraham Jackson.

Well, in his defense, he's a Captain of a gigantic spaceship.

Eileen pauses and takes a closer look at the Captain.

But still... There's something behind that smile. It's like when politicians are about to make you promises that make you think twice. Eileen thinks as she watches the Captain's mouth open again, preparing to continue on with his speech.

"To begin to show you that we are here to help, we have the means to aid your sick and wounded. We have technology well past your current capabilities. Whereas, your generation led to the creation of the Harris Paradigm, we have made drastic improvements since your time. For example, I'm 74 years old and have a full life expectancy of close to 240 years of life. The gentlemen I'm standing next to are in their 70's as well and have the same expectancy. In reference to your age, I'm a 74-year-old male human with the body of a mid-twenties human being from your timeframe." Captain Abraham Jackson explains.

"Shut the front door! This guy's 74 years old? I call bullshit." Eileen blurts out.

"Eileen... Please hold off until he's done. We need to listen to his words closely." Steven replies.

"Right. Sorry, Steven." She replies.

"Not a problem, Eileen." He says as he looks over at her. "I just don't want us to miss anything."

Shen nods in agreement and before she can apologize again, Captain Abraham Jackson continues with his speech.

"Yes, I know. I know. It must sound unfathomable to your kind. But that's only a small portion of what we have to offer to your kind. I understand that all of you must have so many questions... We will be leaving two of our crew members behind with your kind while we go to spread our message to the other surviving settlements here on Earth One. My two crew members will be somewhat of ambassadors of sorts, providing aid, care, and beginning to provide you with our past since your time."

He's leaving two people here? Interesting... I thought it would have been more, considering that he said they are here to help. She thinks as she watches the man's face on the overly large projection/hologram.

There's that sly smile again. Like he's thinking about something funny... or at least funny to him.

Captain Abraham Jackson continues, "We look forward to rebuilding Earth One, side by side with your kind. Together, we can usher in a new era of strength and abundance for the human species. The Leviathan will return in several days, once we have contacted all surviving settlements from the Blue Hole Radius. Your time and attention are greatly appreciated. Thank you, and I look forward to seeing you all again very soon."

Our kind? Aren't we the same kind? Eileen questions.

Was that the end of his speech? I didn't seem very informative...

She thinks she can see one of the men at the Captain's side raise his arm. In an instant, the massive projection/hologram is gone, and she watches as the platform descends back into the spaceship, which had landed in the dried-up lakebed.

"Wow. Well that was kind of a letdown. I thought that meeting the people from Earth Two would be much more exciting than that." Eileen says, as she sees the platform is completely out of view now.

"We should consider ourselves lucky, Eileen." Steven replies, with his eyes still on the colossal spaceship.

Eileen looks over to Steven, who's standing next to her and leaning up against the hood of his Blazer. "Lucky? Why's that Steven?"

"I have a very strong gut feeling that this could have gone sideways very quickly. I also have a good idea of what happened to *Desert Eagle* and Edwards Airforce Base yesterday morning." Steven explains.

"You really think so? And *Desert Eagle*... that guy that Alexander was talking to on the radio, up in the desert?" Eileen questions.

"Yes, ma'am. Alexander asked me to check in with him at 0800 this morning, when they were supposed to check back in with each other. There was no response." Steven says, with his focus still on the colossal spaceship.

"Now... I think I know why." Steven adds.

Eileen looks back at the Leviathan and back to Steven.

He isn't wrong often. In fact, over the short time that I've known him, he hasn't been wrong yet. She thinks as she stares at Ben's Uncle.

"Do you think that the people at Edwards reacted differently and it got them killed?" Eileen asks directly.

"Maybe..." Steven says and pauses.

"I think it may have been a two-way street." Steven adds

"How so?" Eileen asks.

"Edwards is a military installation and a huge spaceship landing there is kind of a big deal, and can be perceived as a threat. Couple that with how Captain Jackson spoke at us... I think that the interaction was very different from what we just had here." Steven explains.

Spoke at us? Did he get a weird vibe from his sly smile too?

"What do you mean, spoke at us?" Eileen asks.

"Not sure if you caught it, but he had a way about him. He's certainly the military type, but he had a certain way with words that sent up red flags. Plus, there was that unintentional smile of his. He mentioned *your kind*. Like we were different. He also acted like we could never understand that people from the future would have better technology and medicine than we do... If you ask me, that's super condescending and it tells me that he looks down on us." Steven explains.

Hmmm. Makes sense why he shushed me earlier. Eileen thinks to herself. *He was really listening to what the Captain said and how he said it.*

"So, you believe he's actually 74 years old? He looks to be close to my age." Eileen asks.

"It's believable, considering they are from the future." Steven replies. "But I'm going to need Alexander's opinion on the matter. He's the nerd of the group and he's great with these sorts of questions."

"Maybe... but I'd have to see it to believe it." Eileen replies.

"Makes sense." Steven responds.

Steven looks away from the spaceship and looks over at her. "Did you notice anything else about Captain Jackson's very short and direct speech?"

"Let's see..." She replies. "He said that they are going to other settlements. They are here to help and that they are leaving two people behind to help us. But that's strange to only leave two people with us... He also said that they'd be back in a few days."

She pauses and looks back at Steven. "Did I miss something?"

"No, the message is all there. But it was more of how he said it and his approach to us. It seemed rehearsed and very much like a political campaign speech. It didn't sound heartfelt and genuine, but he did say all the right things." Steven replies.

"It did sound rather robotic, didn't it?" Eileen says as she thinks back to his sly smile. "And what about that sly grin he kept having?"

"My thoughts exactly, Eileen. Something's off, and I think there's more to them than they are telling. To be honest, he reminds me of a fox." Steven explains.

"Well... how do we find out if they are leaving anything out and trying to hide stuff from us?" Eileen asks.

At that moment, they both look up and squint their eyes as the Leviathan lifts off the ground, high into the sky.

She watches as the colossal spaceship flies over them, with little to no sound at all, and heads away front the mountains, heading south.

"We ask the two people that they left behind." Steven answers her previous question.

She looks back to Steven, who's pointing down toward the dried-up lakebed where a small ship is with two people walking out of the side of it, a man and a woman.

The smaller ship that came from the much larger Leviathan looked to be the size of a railroad car, but slightly larger. It was rectangular in most of its shape, with cone-like ends on the front and back side of the ship. Or at least what Eileen assumed to be the front and back, since the two people were walking out of the center of the rectangle portion that faced their side of the dried-up lakebed.

On the side of the rectangular portion of the ship were two cylinders, which Eileen guessed to be thruster-like devices. She also assumed that there were two more of the same, on the opposite side of the ship, but that part of the ship was out of her view.

The man and woman walk a good ways away from their ship and stop, still in the dried-up lakebed. They then look at each other and say a few words before the woman puts her hands on her hips and the man crosses his arms against his torso. The woman then raises her hand and waves to the people on the shoreline of the dried up lakebed.

Eileen could have sworn to have seen the woman nudge the man, before he raised his own hand to wave at them and everyone else along the shoreline.

Eileen looks across the shoreline on her side, and then to what she can see across to the other side of the lakebed.

No one is moving toward them. Are they afraid? She thinks to herself.

Well... I guess, technically, they are aliens. Since they have never been to our planet before now. So, I guess, it's sort of scary.

"So, what do we do now?" Eileen asks.

"Well, we go ask them our questions, of course." Steven says, as he strides off into the dried-up lakebed.

He would... she thinks as she rushes off to catch up with Steven, who appears to be the only person actually walking up to the people from another Earth.

Catching up and striding alongside of him, she asks, "So what are you going to ask them?"

"I'm going to ask them why exactly they are here. Where's that Commander Yang guy from the first transmission? And just what the hell happened up in the desert, up at Edwards?" Steven replies in a huff, as he's walking briskly toward the people from Earth Two.

"Steven, I don't think it's smart to pick a fight with these guys. Maybe we should tone it down a couple notches." Eileen replies.

She then notices that the man and woman have taken notice of them walking toward them, turning in their direction, who are close to a hundred feet out now.

"Oh, Eileen... I don't plan on being rude about it. And I doubt that they will tell us the truth. At least not the whole truth." Steven replies.

"Well then, what's the point if you think they are going to lie to us?" Eileen asks.

"Because, my dear... It matters how they react to being questioned, and it matters in how they react to us in general." Steven answers.

"I still don't get it." Eileen says, getting frustrated slightly.

Approaching speaking distance with the man and woman, Steven glances over at her. "Just follow my lead and try not to act like you don't trust them."

Like I don't trust them? You're the one alluding to the idea that they killed everyone up at that base in the desert.

"Like I don't trust them?" She asks, sarcastically.

He doesn't reply to her but instead announces, "Good afternoon! My name's Sheriff Steven Reilly, and this is one of my Deputies, Eileen Rivera."

Oh boy... here we go. She thinks to herself as she's now a few feet away from them.

Steven steps in, extending his hand out toward the man.

The man does not instantly extend his hand, but simply stares at Steven.

"My apologies. Do people from Earth Two not shake hands anymore? My fault." Steven asks jokingly and smiles.

Eileen notices that the woman shoots the man a glance, and then looks at her and then to Steven.

"No, we still do." She smiles and steps forward, extending her hand to Steven and shakes his hand.

"I'm Sergeant Burke, and this is Staff Sergeant Mahoney, who must be a little star-stuck. It's not every day you get to meet people from the past." She says, introducing the two of them.

"Very nice to meet you Sergeant Burke." Steven replies, and releases her hand. "Nice firm handshake you have there, Sergeant."

She smiles and then steps in front of Eileen, extending her hand. "Nice to meet you as well Deputy Rivera."

"Likewise, Sergeant Burke." She says as she takes her hand and shakes it.

Holy hell! That's a firm handshake! She thinks as she feels pain in her hand from the pressure of the handshake.

As Sergeant Burke releases, she pulls her hand back and holds it in her left hand.

Was she trying to break my hand?!

"Yes, good afternoon Sheriff and Deputy. We do in fact still shake hands, but I was concerned with how that would affect your kind... here on Earth One." Staff Sergeant Mahoney says.

Eileen can see Sergeant Burke looking down at her hand, puzzled. She then looks back to Staff Sergeant Mahoney and then back to Eileen. "Oh, that's right! I must apologize. I neglected to recall the divergence in physical strength between your kind and ours. My sincerest apologies Deputy Rivera and Sheriff Reilly."

What?! Are they superhuman or something? What the hell? Eileen shouts in her head.

"I'm sure my Deputy will survive, Sergeant. But that was quite a firm handshake." Steven replies.

Steven then looks to the Staff Sergeant. "Nice to meet you as well Staff Sergeant Mahoney and thank you for your consideration. But might I ask... what's the difference between your *kind* and mine?"

The Staff Sergeant doesn't smile or flinch, but simply tilts his head, seeming to analyze his question.

"There are a great number of differences that differentiate our kinds of humans. However, if you are referring to the physical strength properties, we should acclimate in some time. I'm unsure as to how much time, since this is our first landing on Earth One. None-theless, I'm certain that our bodies will adjust to this Earth's gravity." Staff Sergeant Mahoney explains.

Eileen doesn't respond, but instead takes a closer look at this Staff Sergeant Mahoney and Sergeant Burke.

They are both of the same size, close to her size, but a little bit shorter. If she had to guess, they were around 5'6"... maybe 5'7". Both of them were lean looking and didn't look like they could crush hands with their handshakes. They did look like the athletic and military type, but not super-soldier type. Burke has blue eyes, brown hair, and light complexion with fair looking skin. Mahoney was clean-cut, with brown eyes, brown hair, and slightly darker complexion, closer to her own.

Their uniforms were not what she would expect to be from people of the future. They both wore black utility pants, with military style boots. They both had short sleeve shirts on, which were a navy-blue color. She did notice that they both had vests on, with varying compartments on them and what appeared to be their ranks in the middle of their vests. Eileen then notices their name patches on their left breast plates of their vests, with hers reading *Burke* and his reading *Mahoney*.

They don't look all futuristic to me. Where are their weapons? Wait, what's that?

She's now looking down to their arms, noticing a long bracelet-gauntlet looking device on their right arms.

After a brief moment of silence between the four of them, Steven opens his mouth before she can. "Staff Sergeant, you said there are a great number of differences. Would you be so kind as to elaborate?"

Staff Sergeant Mahoney does not reply right away, but does tilt his head again, obviously thinking.

Sergeant Burke chimes. "Excuse Staff Sergeant Mahoney with his dry tone. He can sound rather like a drone at times." She says and she smiles at them.

"As Captain Jackson had said and implied, we have a great deal to offer your kind, the people of Earth One. We are merely here to provide aid and support, in what must be an incredibly difficult ordeal that your kind has been forced to adapt to." Sergeant Burke stated.

Steven nods in agreement. "Well, we sure appreciate you guys showing up to provide us with aid and support. I'm sure there are a great amount of people that do need your help in the Radius."

"I'm sure that you are right, Sheriff. And it's unfortunate that we were not able to arrive sooner." Sergeant Burke replies.

"Yes, I suppose it is, Sergeant. We may even have whole settlements that have been wiped out before you all showed up. In fact, we had a settlement up in the desert, northwest of us, that we haven't been able to contact in the last couple days." Steven replies.

Eileen notices that Burke and Mahoney exchange a brief glance. Mahoney opens his mouth, but Burke's the one to reply the quickest. "That's incredibly unfortunate, I could not imagine what your kind has suffered in the last couple of months. But rest assured, we are here to provide aid and support for the survival of the human race."

"Ah, so you have said. That's very kind of your *kind* from Earth Two." Steven says with a smile.

This gets a strange look from Sergeant Burke.

Before she can reply, he goes on, "So I take it that you all are here with Commander Yang to help us catch up with the rest of the human race?"

Eileen then notices that Staff Sergeant Mahoney seems to sigh with frustration, which elicits a quick glance from Sergeant Burke in his direction. She then turns back to Steven and herself.

"Unfortunately, there were unforeseen circumstances... back on Earth Two, as to why Commander Yang was not able to join us here on Earth One. But again, Sheriff... I assure you, we are here to provide aid and support to ensure the self-preservation of the human species, your and my kind, alike." Sergeant Burke replies.

"Yes, ma'am... I mean, Sergeant Burke. I do believe your words sound true. And it's quite amazing to meet people from another planet. More amazing that you all are here to help. I'm sure that there are many people in need of your aid and support." Steven responds.

Unable to keep her silence any longer, "Excuse me, Sergeant Burke... what are those things on your arms?"

This receives a pause from Steven and another glance from the Staff Sergeant.

Sergeant Burke simply smiles and responds, "Very observant of you, Deputy Rivera. These are our individually issued MECCUs, which stands for Mobile Extremity Communications and Control Unit."

"Ah, I see..." Eileen replies. "What do they do?"

Sergeant Burke smiles again, politely. Eileen's unsure if she likes this woman or not. She seems kind and sincere and is answering all of their questions... sort of.

"Ah, yes. It is primarily used for communications and to perform our individual duties, in accordance with our occupations within the Federalist Legion. For instance, it assists me with my Logistics and Supply designation and assists Staff Sergeant Mahoney with his Intelligence and Reconnaissance designation. They also have certain survival capabilities."

"Very interesting." Steven replies. "So, you are Logistics and Supply and you are Intelligence and Reconnaissance?"

"Yes, Sheriff Reilly. That is an accurate assessment." Staff Sergeant Mahoney replies.

"Are there any other questions you two might have, or any aid you may be in need of?" Sergeant Burke asks.

Steven smiles at her. "No, Sergeant Burke. That about sums it all up for now. I'm sure that there are a great deal more questions, but we should be on our way home to check in on our people."

"Oh... alright then. Are you sure you don't have any other questions for us?" Sergeant Burke asks again.

Steven looks over to her and nods, trying to give her a message of some sort.

After a moment she thinks to herself. *He did say to follow his lead...*

"Like the Sheriff said. I'm sure there's a lot that we are forgetting to ask. It's just a lot to take in, is all... but before we go, do you have any questions for us?" Eileen asks.

The two of them exchange glances, which almost look confused. The Staff Sergeant discreetly shakes his head, and then Sergeant Burke turns back to them.

"No, I don't believe we do, at this moment in time. We were ordered to simply provide aid support, and answer any of your questions to the best of our capabilities." Sergeant Burke replies.

"Fair enough. Well, it was very nice to meet you two, Sergeant Burke and Staff Sergeant Mahoney." Steven says as he extends his hand out again.

This time, Sergeant Burke takes his hand, but in a much gentler fashion. Afterward, she nudges Staff Sergeant Mahoney and he does the same.

"Yes, it was very exciting to meet both of you. Thank you for being so informative. If you think of any questions by the next time we meet, ask us then and we'll do the same." Eileen says and extends her hand.

Staff Sergeant Mahoney shakes her hand gently.

"Will do, Deputy Rivera. I sure do hope that your hand is alright." Sergeant Burke replies as she shakes her hand, much more gently this time.

Eileen smiles at her. *I may not trust you, but I can't help but like you for some odd reason. You seem sincere and kind.*

"Thank you, Sergeant Burke. It's already feeling better. And you can call me Eileen if you'd like." Eileen replies.

Sergeant Burke smiles. "My first name is Alicia, Eileen. I'll try and think of some questions for you next. We are here for several days at least... until the Leviathan returns from the other settlements."

Eileen smiles and thinks she sees Staff Sergeant Mahoney shoot Sergeant Alicia Burke a look of anger, but it was hard to tell with his robotic features.

He gave her a look for sure...

"Alright, you all have a good one. I'm sure there are many more of our kind that have questions for you, since we broke the ice with you two." Steven says and begins to walk away.

Eileen turns to walk away, then turns back. "Earth One is a beautiful place, but don't trust all of our kind. Some of us don't have the best of intentions. Stay safe out there, Alicia."

Before Sergeant Burke can respond, another group of people come within speaking distance of Staff Sergeant Mahoney and Sergeant Burke. Eileen does notice that Sergeant Burke's gaze does stay with her for a moment before she greets the new group of people.

Catching up to Steven, she looks at him, "Why are we in a hurry to leave? Those are people from another planet, Steven. That's sort of a really big deal. Plus, they are being nice..."

"Yes, they are. And they answered a lot of questions and gave us a lot to think about. It's best not harassing them with a million questions, since they just got here. We found out what we wanted, and we'll make another trip out here when Alexander returns." Steven explains.

While they are walking back to the Blazer, Eileen thinks about what he said.

They didn't really answer a lot of questions. In fact, Staff Sergeant Mahoney barely spoke. Sergeant Burke, or Alicia, did most of the talking. She did answer some questions, but not a lot. It seemed like they were holding back information, actually.

"How did they answer a lot of questions?" Eileen asks Steven.

"Again, it was more of how they said their answers and with key indicator words that answered my questions. Good catch on those weapons on their arms, though." Steven replies.

"Weapons? She said it was mostly for communication and to help with their jobs." Eileen replies.

"Yes, but she also let it slip that they had survival capabilities. One plus one equals two. Simply put, those can be used as weapons. And it's important to point out that the stoic Staff Sergeant Mahoney's job in their Federalist Legion is that of Intelligence and Reconnaissance... that sounds like military special ops to me." Steven adds.

They are getting closer to Steven's Blazer.

"Huh, really?" Eileen asks.

Special ops are like the sniper guys of the military, right? Eileen questions herself.

Before she can ask this question aloud, Steven's phone rings and he pulls it out of his pocket.

"It's Alexander. They must be checking in with their current location and update." Steven says.

"Oh good, they're almost home." She replies, forgetting about her last question.

Steven answers the phone. "Hello, Alexander... everything alright down there? We got your text that you're on your way back up here."

Alexander replies, but she cannot hear the words on Steven's phone.

"Trouble? What sort of trouble? Did the Leviathan come down there too?" Steven asks.

Oh no... not again. She thinks, as she worries about Ben.

"Trouble!? Are they in trouble?!" Eileen asks as she only overhears Steven's side of the conversation.

Of course, Ben found trouble... again. I swear, that man is a magnet for trouble!

She jumps into the passenger side of the Blazer and shuts the door, anxiously looking to Steven for answers about what's going on with Ben, Alexander, and Joseph... down the mountain.

After a few moments, Steven opens up his door and climbs into the Blazer, and she catches the tail end of his sentence.

"... call us when you're all back on the road, and we'll explain what we know. Stay safe out there, Alexander." Stevens says and hangs up the phone.

"What the hell happened this time? Are they alright?!" Eileen asks, as Steven puts away his phone and turns to look at her, shaking his head.

"This is one hell of a crazy world that we inherited, Eileen..." Steven starts to explain.

"Seriously! What happened, Steven?!" Eileen asks again, interrupting him.

14

ALEXANDER MATHIS

ALEXANDER LOOKS down at the man lying on the ground... who is no longer yelling at him or moaning in pain. The man on the ground had tumbled over onto his side a few minutes after Ben and Joseph had gone up ahead. Within those few minutes, between listening to gunfire and the man yell at him, screaming that he should help him... the man had passed on.

Alexander had not rushed over to see if they needed help after hearing the gunfire, because once the man on the ground had expired, Joseph and Ben had shown up back into view, trying to open up the back of the trailer.

Now he was simply staring at the lifeless body below him, unsure what to actually think of the man.

This was indeed an evil soul, but it was still a life and it passed right in front of me. Why does this feel different from the MS13 Battle? Is it because it was slower, or that he spoke to me before he expired? Whatever the reason may be, it feels different this time. Despite myself not being the one to take his life, I still feel like an accomplice. On the other hand, this was an evil individual. I know he deserved this, but that doesn't make it any easier...

Alexander stares off toward Ben and Joseph, who had just gotten the trailer door open. He watches as they carry a body out of the trailer and places her on the ground several feet away from the trailer.

No time for wandering in my own thoughts. I should go help... he thinks to himself, with his mind now off the dead man on the ground next to him.

He strides over to Ben and Joseph, as they go for another body in the trailer.

"How can I help?" Alexander asks.

"Oh hey, Alexander. What happened to the guy I shot in the legs?" Ben asks.

"He expired a few moments ago." Alexander replies.

"Oh... I was hoping to ask him if there were more women and children somewhere else." Ben responds.

Alexander nods. "I did ask him that before he expired, but all I got out of him were obscenities and yelling at me to find help for him... But I did get the feeling that these were all of the women and children, and all of their abductors."

"I sure hope that you are right, Alexander... or at least that some of these people can give us a more concrete answer." Ben answers.

Alexander nods. "Okay, so what do you need me to do?"

Ben and Joseph lift another body out of the crashed trailer, carrying her over to lay her next to the first woman.

"This is pretty much a two-man job. But I'm guessing we are going to have trouble getting these people out of here and the help that they need. Can you call Sheriff Reilly, and see if he can't send out a radio message to folks down here to come and lend a hand and search for their loved ones?" Joseph replies.

"Deputy Gomez, that's a brilliant idea!... I'll also bring the truck around, just in case we need to transport anyone in the bed of Ben's truck." Alexander adds.

"Good thinking, Alexander... as always. The keys are still in the ignition. Also... Could you also relay to my Uncle and Eileen that we are safe and just helping out down here?" Ben asks.

"Not a problem, Ben. I'm on it!" Alexander replies as he turns and runs back over to the truck.

Once he reaches the truck, he climbs into the driver's seat and turns over the ignition. The AC from the vents hits his face, giving him a cooled sensation. He picks up his cell phone and dials Steven Reilly. After a few rings, Steven picks up.

"Hello, Alexander... everything alright down there? We got your text that you're on your way back up here." Steven says as he answers the phone.

"Hello, Steven. Yes and no. We were on our way back up, but we ran into trouble." Alexander replies.

"Trouble? What sort of trouble? Did the Leviathan come down there, too?" Steven asks.

"Trouble!? Are they in trouble?!" Eileen asks in the background.

"No, nothing like that. We are fine and we have all of the livestock. We stumbled upon an accident of sorts. Point is, we need you to send out a message for people down here to come help. We have survivors from the crash that are women and children that were kidnapped from these surrounding areas." Alexander replies.

"Good God, man! Women and children?! Right! I'll go to the nearest station to use their radio. Where should I tell them that you are?" Steven replies.

"Wait? You asked if the Leviathan had come here as well. Does that mean it made contact up there?" Alexander asks, thinking back to what Steven had said about the Leviathan.

"Never mind that for now Alexander! What's your location?!" Steven responds.

"Right! We are at the edge of Perris, along the 215 North, at the 74 juncture." Alexander replies quickly.

"Alright. We'll get the message out as soon as possible. How many survivors do you have, Alexander?" Steven responds.

"We are not sure... there were close to twenty women and children in the trailer when it crashed. Benjamin and Joseph are pulling bodies out now." Alexander answers.

"Oh, sweet baby Jesus! Alright! We're heading back to the Blazer to drive to the nearest station now. Hang tight and go help my nephew. Good luck Alexander!" Steven says.

"Right. Thank you, Steven." Alexander replies.

"Oh, and Alexander…" Steven adds.

"Yes, Steven?" Alexander responds.

"If you see a spaceship coming out your way, steer clear of it. I don't trust them. Something seems off about them." Steven answers.

"So, they did make contact? What happened? Who were they? What did they want?" The questions come pouring out of Alexander.

"Never mind that for now… deal with those women and children. Call us when you're all back on the road and we'll explain what we know. Stay safe out there, Alexander." Stevens says and before Alexander can respond, the call ends.

The Leviathan landed up there? This is incredible news? But why doesn't Steven trust them? Were my concerns accurate? Do they mean us harm?

Alexander shakes his head to clear his thoughts.

Steven said to worry about the women and children for now, which means it was not that pressing to know at this very moment. He thinks to himself.

Alexander then proceeds to turn the truck around and stops about ten feet away from the rows of bodies that Ben and Joseph had begun to lay on the road.

As he gets out of the truck he shouts over to Ben and Joseph. "Steven said he'll get the message out!"

"Good job, Alexander!" Ben shouts back.

"What do you want me to do now?!" Alexander shouts back.

Ben wipes his brow before he reaches down to pick up another body from the crashed trailer with Joseph.

"Start checking to see who's alive and who we can help?!" Ben shouts back.

"Right!" Alexander exclaims and looks down at the row of bodies. *How do I accomplish that?* He thinks.

"Hey! How do I do that?" Alexander asks.

"I don't know, Alexander! You're the doctor! Check for their pulse and see if they're breathing!" Ben shouts back.

"Right! Sorry! I'm on it!" Alexander shouts back.

He's right... I may not be a medical doctor, but I should know how to check to see if people are alive. Geez, Alexander... stay focused.

Alexander steps over to the first woman in the row of bodies, which is a young blonde woman with her eyes closed. He reaches down to check her neck for a pulse and tries to watch to see if her chest rises and falls with breaths.

He has his fingers on her neck for a good minute, without feelings of a pulse. He puts his hand by her nose, to see if he can feel her breath, since he hasn't seen her chest rise and fall yet in the last minute or so.

Damn... I think she's gone. He thinks as he shakes his head and steps over to the next body.

The next woman looks to be a middle-aged woman, with brown hair and lightly tanned skin. After spending several minutes over her body, he concludes that she's dead as well and moves to the next one.

The next body is of a small girl, who looks strikingly similar to the woman next to her. Alexander reaches down to her neck, feeling for a pulse. After a few seconds he feels a pulse.

"She's alive!" He blurts out.

He then watches eagerly to see her chest rise and fall, which her chest is doing.

"Little one! Can you hear me? Can you hear my voice?!" Alexander shouts at the small girl.

The girl moans in response. her eyes flickering.

"Alright! Little one, we are here to help!" He explains to her.

Alexander then looks the little girl over for any obvious injuries and decides that she doesn't have any that he can see.

She must be incredibly hot, having been stuck in the box trailer for lord knows how long.

Alexander picks up the small girl and proceeds to carry her to Ben's truck. With his fingertips, and the girl in his arms, he opens up one of the back-cab doors and gently lays her inside.

"Here, little one. This should help cool you down. I'll be back…" Alexander tries to explain to the unconscious girl.

Her response is another moan and her eyes flickering.

Alexander carefully closes the door to let the girl try to cool down in the AC of the truck. He then heads back over to the rows of bodies, which is now two rows of six bodies, and with one empty area where the little girl just was.

Alexander checks the next three bodies in the first row, with no luck. None of them had pulses or appeared to be breathing, and one even still had her eyes wide open, a young teenage girl.

Dammit! These girls didn't deserve this!

With tears starting to form in his eyes, he wipes them away and moves to the next row of women and children. By this point Ben and Joseph have added a third row of six more bodies.

Stay focused and logical, Alexander… these people need you. Alexander reminds himself.

Alexander steps over the first woman in the second row.

She looks familiar… Where have I seen her before? Alexander thinks as he reaches to check for a pulse.

I'm not sure, but she seems to be alive. Thank goodness! But can I carry her to the truck, like the little girl? He thinks to himself.

"Only one way to find out." He says as he leans down to pick her.

After some grunting and shifting, he's able to get the petite woman over his right shoulder and begins walking her to Ben's truck. He walks to the front passenger seat and opens the door with his free hand. He then tries to gently put her into the passenger seat.

Leaning her back into the seat, he looks at the young blonde woman lying in the front of the truck. He notices that she has bruises up and down her arms. She's wearing jeans, but Alexander guesses that there are similar bruises down there as well.

Where have I seen you before? He asks himself.

"Betsy! That's right! I was rather hungover when we met… but I'm sure that it is you!" Alexander blurts out.

Betsy's eyes flicker and she mumbles something.

Alexander had met Betsy Carter on the second day after the *Blue Hole Radius*, May 19th 3433. She had been a coworker of Ben's and he had given her a ride to her home before Alexander and Ben had made a stop at Ben's home and then began their journey up to Steven's cabin.

Alexander can recall how he had told Betsy the story of what was happening and how the world had changed over the course of sixty seconds on May 19th, 2023, turning into May 18th, 3433. He had also recalled how he had thought that Betsy didn't entirely believe his story.

Nonetheless, she was kind and polite and listened to Alexander talk for the duration of the trip to her home from the Ontario International Airport. She was supposed to meet her boyfriend, whose name Alexander could not remember at the moment, and she insisted that she would be okay by herself.

Alexander then recalls how worried Ben was about her naivety... with not understanding how much the world had changed and how she didn't *believe* in guns. Nonetheless, despite great odds, adversity, and a great amount of distance from where they had dropped her off... here she was, alive.

"Where am I?" Betsy mumbles.

"Betsy... you were in a car accident. You are safe for now? You are in Ben's truck. I'm going to let you rest here while I check for other survivors from the crash." Alexander explains.

"Car accident? But I was in a..." Betsy says and she falls back out of consciousness.

"Just stay still here and hopefully you will regain your strength, in time. I'll be back to check on you in a little while." Alexander explains to the unconscious Betsy.

Alexander carefully closes the passenger door and strides back over to the rows of bodies. When he reaches the bodies, he finds that

Ben and Joseph are done emptying the crashed trailer of women and children.

"How many do we have so far that are alive Alexander?" Ben asks.

"So far... two." Alexander replies.

Ben's mouth drops open.

"Only two alive out of twenty!?" Joseph exclaims.

Alexander puts his hands up in a *calm down* motion. "I know, but I have only checked seven bodies so far... we still have thirteen more to look over."

Ben closes his mouth and nods. "Alright, let's get to it then."

Alexander steps over the next body, next to where Betsy was. As he looks down, he notices the striking resemblance to the little girl in the back-cab of the truck and the expired middle-aged woman from the first row. This girl looks like a teenage version of the little girl. He reaches down, feeling for a pulse, and the teenage girl coughs and her eyes jolt open.

Even with her eyes open, she doesn't really look at Alexander. She seems to be in a daze and very confused. Once she's done coughing, she closes her eyes again.

"We have another live one, here!" Alexander says to Ben and Joseph.

"Well that's good news! Where have you been putting them?" Ben asks.

"I have a little girl and Betsy in your truck with the AC on." Alexander replies.

"Betsy!? From the airport?" Ben exclaims.

"The one and the same, Ben." Alexander replies.

"Wow! Crazy! She made it all the way out here..." Ben adds.

"She did indeed. Well, I'm going to carry this one to your truck and put her next to the little girl. Hopefully the cool air is helping them, since they were stuck in the stuffy and hot trailer for lord knows how long." Alexander explains.

"Good thinking, Alexander... Hopefully more people show up soon to help us with the other survivors." Ben replies.

Alexander nods and leans down, picking up the teenage girl and carrying her to the truck. Upon reaching the truck he opens the door behind where Betsy is sitting, and still sleeping. He then gently puts the teenage girls next to the little girl in the back-cab of the truck. He looks over all three of the girls.

All still unconscious, but all still seem to be breathing... I'll take small blessings, for now. Alexander thinks to himself as he closes the door softly and walks back over to the rows of bodies.

Upon reaching the bodies, Ben stands up and smiles widely. "We have three more alive, so far. We are on a roll!" He says with sincere happiness.

"That's good news, hopefully the rest are still alive..." Alexander replies.

Alexander then hears engines of vehicles approaching. He watches as Ben and Joseph reach to their hips for their guns. He does the same. He then watches as Joseph steps away from the trailer to get a better view of who's coming toward them.

After a few tense moments, Joseph waves at the newcomers.

"It looks like it's those guys from our last stop... the ones that almost killed us." He says, half laughing. He then looks back at the rows of bodies and immediately stops laughing and scratches the back of his head. "Sorry... doesn't really seem like a time for laughter."

"Thank God we have more people to help us. There's no way we could fit all of these people into your truck, Ben." Joseph adds.

"Right! And no worries, Joseph... we get it." Ben replies.

Before Alexander can chime in, he sees the men from the last stop for livestock come around the side of the trailer and stop dead in their tracks... obviously shocked by the scene they see in front of them.

The next hour or so goes by in a blur. After Alexander, Ben, and Joseph catch the newcomers up to speed, the group of men look over the bodies, trying to find the survivors of the horrible truck and trailer crash due to the raiders.

After all of the bodies are checked, it is found that there are nine survivors in varying levels of consciousness and stability, leaving eleven out of the twenty women and children in the trailer to be dead from the crash.

Among the eleven women and children that are dead are: Manny's wife, Curtis' daughter, Daniel's wife, two little girls, another teenage girl and five more young adult women.

Two out of the nine are not in very good condition, and there are a couple of the women with broken limbs.

The group of men found some saving grace in the instance that there were still nine survivors, despite their current conditions. Betsy, the two girls in the back-cab of Ben's truck, Curtis's wife, Daniel's two daughters, two more teenage girls, and one 7-year-old girl who was claimed by a family from Perris.

Over the next hour or so, people come and take their loved ones. Three are left unclaimed and there's the middle-aged woman that Alexander believes to be the mother of the two girls in the back-cab of Ben's truck.

Hector agrees to take the two unclaimed and see that they are buried properly. Alexander, Ben, and Joseph put the woman that holds a striking resemblance to the two girls in the back-cab of Ben's truck under an opened sleeping bag, and some bungee cords in the truck bed. Once Ben, Alexander, and Joseph are done loading the assumed mother into the bed of the truck, the passenger door opens and Betsy slowly steps out.

"Whoa! Betsy, take it easy! You were just in a terrible accident!" Ben says as he goes to her side.

"Yeah, I figured as much. I take it those assholes crashed the trailer and left us for dead?" Betsy replies.

"Not exactly." Ben replies.

Alexander goes to Ben's side. "Hello, Betsy. How are you feeling?"

"Ah, you are the doctor from the airport... when Ben gave me a ride home." Betsy replies.

"Yes, Betsy. I'm the one and the same." Alexander replies.

"So, what happened to those rapist assholes that put us in the godforsaken trailer in the first place?" Betsy asks.

"They are all dead, Betsy. You are safe, now." Ben replies.

Betsy looks him square in the eyes. "Am I now? Are you here to rescue me, Ben?" She says with a sarcastic tone.

"Let me guess, you are the one that killed all of those rapist pieces of shit, aren't you?" Betsy adds in the same sarcastic tone.

Ben doesn't answer, but simply steps back and scratches the back of his head.

"He didn't dispatch all of them, Betsy. Only the couple that had survived the crash. And for now, you are safe. I'm sure that we can find a home for you up in the mountains with the community that we have built up there... if you would like to come with us." Alexander explains.

"How convenient... and no thanks. If these assholes hadn't crashed and died, I was planning on killing them tonight when we stopped again." She says as she pulls a pocket knife out of her jeans pocket.

"I picked this off of one of them last night, after he fell asleep. After he was done raping me but before the next guy came in to lock me back up." She explains.

"I'm sorry that happened to you, Betsy." Ben replies, honestly.

"Nothing to be sorry about... You were right after all..." Betsy replies with a stern and matter of fact tone. "Jason, my boyfriend, never returned and I left after I ran out of food. It's been pretty much hell on earth ever since then."

"That may be so, but if you'd like, Betsy, we have a nice place up in the mountains, and I'm sure we can find an empty home for you." Alexander tries to reason with her.

"Oh, I'm sure... and thanks, but no thanks." Betsy replies.

Alexander looks over at Ben and Ben looks back at him, both of them obviously unsure of what to say to the battered woman that Alexander had met close to two months ago.

"No, heroes... I'm heading to San Diego." Betsy adds.

"But Betsy, there's nothing out there now... there hasn't been for centuries." Ben replies.

"I know what you and this scientist told me, and I know it's the way the world is now. But I need to see it for myself. The only family I had left were my parents and my little sister, and that's where they lived... I need to see it for myself." Betsy says, almost pleading with herself.

She has to see it for herself? But there are no people out there. Who knows what could be out there now... Alexander thinks to himself.

"And if anyone tries to stop me, they better fucking think twice... I've gotten pretty good with a knife." Betsy says as she flips open the pocketknife.

At that moment Hector walks up. "Everything okay over here guys?"

Ben puts his head down and shakes his head. "I don't even know anymore, to be honest."

Alexander looks to Hector. "Hector, this woman's looking to travel to San Diego... and before you say anything, do you think your men can give her a ride at least as far as you can go."

Hector pauses as Betsy turns to look at him. "As long as she puts the knife away."

Betsy smiles. "Sure thing..." and she laughs lightly.

"But now's the time to get moving. We have people that are hurt and in need of medical attention. We have some nurses and doctors back in our area." Hector adds.

"Ready when you are, Hector!" Betsy exclaims. "Just get me the hell out of here."

"Betsy, wait..." Ben says.

"What now, Ben? I don't want to go play house with you in the mountains." Betsy replies.

Alexander watches as Ben turns red and reaches into his pocket.

"No. Not that." He shakes his head and pulls out some of his Gold American Eagles and hands them to her.

"What's this Ben?" Betsy replies, shocked at the gold being put into her hand.

"Just a little something to help you with supplies on your way to San Diego, Betsy. Good luck to you and you should probably pick up a gun this time around." Ben replies.

Betsy grins. "Yeah, I had one until I ran out of bullets a while back... and aren't you just the hero of the story... thanks, Ben." She says as she turns to walk away.

She pauses and turns back around, and gives him a quick kiss on his cheek. "Really though, thanks, Ben... and until next time!"

She looks over to Alexander. "Until next time, scientist guy! Thanks for pulling me from the wreckage and everything." She says and smiles. She then turns and walks away toward the other vehicles.

"Yeah! For sure! We sure are thankful for you guys! Thanks for doing what you could!" Hector adds with sincerity.

They all say their goodbyes and the group from Menifee get into the vehicles and drive away. And just like that, it's Alexander, Ben, Joseph, the two young girls, and the dead woman, likely the mother, in the bed of Ben's truck left at the crash site.

"Well, I guess it's time for us to get going, too." Ben states.

"So, we are taking the girls back up the mountain with us?" Alexander asks.

"We don't have much of a choice... they don't have anyone else." Ben replies.

Alexander looks at Joseph. "Don't look at me... I sure as hell don't know. I'm only 28 and don't know a damn thing about kids."

"Well that settles it... they're tagging along, for now." Ben replies.

"I'll ride in the back with them. Joseph, you can ride up front." Alexander says.

Joseph nods and climbs into the passenger seat of the truck while Ben climbs into the driver's seat. Alexander opens the back-cab door and sees the teenage girl looking at him.

"Our mom's dead, isn't she?" The teenage girl says.

Ben and Joseph look back at the awake teenager and don't say a word.

"Yes, little one. I'm very sorry. You girls were in a terrible car accident." Alexander replies, not getting into the truck yet.

"Where are you men taking me and my sister?" The teenage girl asks.

"That's up to you, little one. Does your family live around here?" Alexander asks.

The girl looks at her sister then back to Alexander. "No, my dad moved us out here for work. We lived in Temecula when everything started... and they killed my dad when they took me, my sister, and mom."

Alexander shakes his head. "I'm very sorry to hear that, little one. What's your name?"

"Are you men like the other men? Are you going to hurt me and my sister?" The young girl says with no real emotion.

"Dear God... No, little one!" Alexander says and looks at Ben and Joseph.

"What's your and your sister's name?" Ben asks.

The girl looks at Ben and then back to Alexander. "I'm Mia and my little sister's name's Isabelle."

"Very nice to meet you Mia. My name's Alexander. That's Ben. And that's Joseph. We have community up in the mountains, and I'm sure that we can find a nice place for you girls to get some rest." Alexander replies.

"Will there be food?" Mia asks.

Alexander sees Ben shake his head, likely thinking about how sad this situation is.

What monsters... and to think I was having reservations about their deaths... Alexander thinks to himself.

"Yes, Mia. There will be food. We can even find some clean clothes for you and your little sister." Alexander replies.

"Okay then." Mia replies and scoots over to allow Alexander to sit in the truck.

Alexander slowly climbs in as the girl looks over at her sister, who's still sleeping but now with her head leaning up against the window.

"Can you please buckle yourself up, Mia... and your sister too?" Alexander asks.

Mia nods and gets herself and her sister buckled up.

Without another word, Ben turns the truck around and starts to head back to their home.

After a few moments, Alexander looks at Mia, who's just staring out the front windshield.

She has to have been through so much. Poor little girl, the both of them. No one deserves to be treated like they must have been treated.

"How old are you Mia?" Alexander asks.

Mia yawns and replies, "I'm 12 and Isabelle's 9... I'm tired now... can I take a nap?"

"Yes, Mia. You can." Alexander replies.

"Okay..." Mia says as she leans against her sister. She's asleep in seconds.

The truck is quiet for a long while as Ben navigates their way back home. After close to an hour, Alexander breaks the silence.

"What if we took them in, Benjamin? The four of us took them in... I mean?" he asks Ben, as the two girls are asleep in the back of the cab, the smaller one leaning against the window and the older one, now leaning on him.

Alexander can see Ben look into the rearview mirror, thinking of what to say in response.

After a moment and long sigh, he replies, "I was thinking the same thing, actually... I wonder what Eileen and Steven will think of the idea."

"Well, it would be wise to give them a heads up. I'll give them a call." Alexander replies.

He then pulls out his phone and tries to dial Steven and Eileen's phones. Both tries are met with no connection. He looks down at his iPhone and sees that he has no service. He then checks to see if he has a connection to the SuperNet... with no luck.

That's strange... We have always had a connection up to this point.

There haven't been any dead zones with our service and SuperNet yet, Alexander thinks to himself with concern.

"Hey? Are you guys able to get any phone service?" Alexander asks Joseph and Ben.

After a few moments of looking at their phones they both reply that they don't have a connection and it reads no service.

"We had service on the way down. What's changed?" Ben asks.

"I'm not sure, but it may have to do with what Steven had told me about the Leviathan landing within the *Blue Hole Radius*?" Alexander replies.

"Wait, what?!" Joseph asks.

"It did what now?!" Ben asks.

15

BENJAMIN REILLY

LEAVING the wreckage of the crash site, the rest of the drive back up the mountain was relatively uneventful. Ben had pulled over twice more when two more earthquakes occurred, neither of which were as strong as the one that caused the crash with the kidnapped women and children in the back of the box car trailer. Regardless, Ben thought it best to stop and pay close attention to the roads after the quakes had passed.

Ben was also overly curious about the news of the Leviathan touching down. But as it turned out, Alexander had little to no news other than the fact that the Leviathan did indeed land. The rest would have to wait until they returned, with the methods of communication being down at this current moment. So, Ben circled back to worrying about the day's events and the role that the earthquakes played.

The earthquakes had begun to stress Ben out and he started to wonder if these quakes over the last two months were leading up to some massive earthquake. Ben had seen too many movies about earthquakes in California. Despite the fact that many of these movies were well made and tend to have happy endings, it was the middle area that scared Ben about these scenarios. Having grown up in California, he had become accustomed to them. However, these were different times, with the times being over 1,400 years into the future.

Alexander had assured him and Joseph several times along the return trip up the mountain that the quakes would subside once the earth resettled into the areas that they were supposed to be in. Alexander had not been wrong much. In fact, Ben could not think of when Alexander had been wrong since he met the man a couple of months ago. That being said, he knew that Alexander was not all knowing, despite his high level of intelligence compared to most other people he had known in his lifespan.

"Couldn't these small quakes set off a chain reaction for a much larger one, Alexander?" Ben had asked him. With a lot of scientific explanations and rationale, Alexander explained that the probability of that happening was *minuscule*. Ben believed him, but he was still worried about the *miniscule* part. Meaning there was still a chance it could happen... no matter how small of a chance.

The topic of discussion changed once Mia had awoken from her nap. Once she was awake, Ben quickly changed the subject to what she wanted to eat once they arrived back at his Uncle's Cabin, now all of their cabin. Ben had explained that they still had a good amount of meat and eggs, placing most of the meat in his Uncle's deep freezer. Mia was mostly quiet but did admit to wanting a cheeseburger, "*if that was okay.*"

Ben had assured her that a cheeseburger would be doable, but they only had basic bread and not hamburger buns. Ben found his mind shifting to the question of how much longer they would have bread at the markets and made it a point to bring it up to his Uncle about the situation. Meat didn't seem to be much of an issue yet, and wouldn't be an issue for a while, considering what he was hauling in the box trailer behind them. But basic vegetables, fruits, breads, and other items that they would still have to barter for would not be around forever.

They would have to start thinking about how they would produce more of these items. It was still the early stages of summer, and planting season had just ended, but that was planting season from over 1,400 years ago. Ben wondered if the planting seasons were different now, which reminded him of the first transmission's warning about the upcoming winter.

There was also the question of if the area was good for raising crops, it was the mountains after all. Ben had known that California was great land for raising crops, but there were more ideal areas than others. The question came to his mind of whether or not they would eventually have to move, migrating from their home to survive. Many ancient groups of people had to do the same when faced with the harshness of Mother Nature, and Ben found it both funny and scary that they may now very well be one of those ancient groups of people. It was also a very terrifying thought about having to pick everything up and move.

Ben's mind was lost in thought about the food situation for their foreseeable future, the coming of winter and what that meant for all of them. Ben started to wonder if they could survive in the mountains. In the past, these mountains got pretty cold. It certainly snowed often during the winter months, but they had the snowplows, their heaters, and modern technology.

If we had to leave... Where would we even go if we had to move from Crestline?

Thinking about how the communication has recently gone down, Ben wondered what other technologies they would have to go without during this upcoming winter. The lack of communication and information was a major concern of Ben's, adding to his growing list of worries and concerns with their survival and foreseeable future. But he didn't want to bring it up with Mia awake and listening.

Ben noticed that she didn't talk much. She simply stared out the windows and kept an eye on her sleeping little sister, Isabelle. He couldn't blame her for not being in a talkative mood though.

Those poor girls have already been through so much. And they're still so very young.

Ben could not even imagine the horrors that they had to see and endure from those monsters. He certainly didn't want to ask them, but he would listen to them if they felt that they could talk about it.

With recalling Mia's solemn question of *"Are you men like the other men? Are you going to hurt me and my sister?"* Ben had already confirmed his worst fears that those horrible human beings had truly hurt these two little girls.

It enraged Ben to no end. He found himself wishing that he could bring them all back to life, just to be able to make them suffer in horrific ways for hurting all of those women and young girls.

Ben's mind shifts to thinking about Betsy and how much she had changed. He was glad that she had survived but was worried about who she had become. Yes, she had been naive at the beginning of the *Blue Hole Radius*. With that being said, the bitter and angry person she turned into made Ben feel sympathy for the woman. He found himself hoping that she found whatever it was that she was looking for out in San Diego, knowing that the world outside of the *Radius* had long been returned to nature. Still, he hoped that she found what she was looking for outside of the *Radius*.

Making the final few turns reaching Joseph's place, Ben looks around the cab of the truck. Everyone's rather quiet and all staring off into the distance.

Looks like everyone's just as lost in their own thoughts as I am... Man, it has been a long ass day, that's for sure.

Ben looks at the clock on the dashboard, which reads 1840, as he pulls in front of the driveway of Deputy Joseph Gomez's home. Joseph comes out of his daze as he pulls up.

"Well... that was one hell of a road trip. You guys did great, but let's not make it a habit of these road trips." Joseph says as he climbs out of the truck and grabs his gear.

"Likewise, Joseph. I'm glad you went with us, it's really appreciated." Ben replies.

"Yeah... next time we go down the mountain, we may need a

small army to go with us, to avoid some of the crap that we ran into."
Joseph answers.

"That wouldn't be a bad idea, but hopefully we don't have to go back down the mountain anytime soon." Ben responds.

"Agreed." Joseph says. "Well, alright gents... I will see you all when I see you. Which will likely be sooner rather than later." Joseph says with a forced smile.

"Have a good day Deputy Gomez." Alexander adds.

"Hey, Joseph. I can drop off your trailer later on this evening." Ben offers.

"Don't you have to make stops over at both Bradley homes and then back to your place? Don't stress it, Ben. Get it back to me when you can." Joseph says.

Ben scratches his head, remembering that his day's not over yet. "Yeah, good point. Thanks. I think I'm going to stop by the cabin first though... and get these little ones some food in them."

Ben sees Mia's face react to the idea of food. Isabelle's still sleeping. She had awoken once on the drive home, but her sister hushed her back to sleep.

"Sounds like a good idea, Ben." Joseph says and then looks at Mia in the back seat. "Goodbye, Mia. It was very nice meeting you. Ben and Alexander will take good care of you, along with Sheriff Reilly and Eileen."

"Bye." Is Mia's only response.

Joseph forces another smile at her and looks back to Ben. "Alright then, Ben and Alexander. I'll see you all later. Drive safe. Since the phone lines are down, I'll come by the Sheriff's cabin in the morning to see what the plan for the day is."

"Alright, we'll have some breakfast ready for you." Ben replies.

"Sounds good to me." Joseph says and smiles as he closes the door and walks up his driveway to his home.

Once Joseph's inside, Ben pulls the truck away from the house and makes the short drive back to their cabin. Pulling into the driveway and shutting down the engine of his truck, Ben sighs with relief of returning back to his home. He's also happy to see his Uncle's Blazer in the driveway.

Ben turns around looking at Mia. "Alright, Mia. We are here. Let me go talk to my Uncle and girlfriend really quick and we'll wake your sister up and get you girls some food. Does that sound okay?"

Mia looks at Alexander, and Alexander nods to her.

"Okay." Mia replies.

"I'll stay here with the girls while you update Steven and Eileen. I don't think they should be alone when Isabelle wakes back up." Alexander adds.

"Always a step ahead of me, Alexander." Ben says, smiling at his friend.

Alexander smiles back with a familiar look of pain in his eyes.

Makes sense considering he lost two daughters close to their ages. This must be really hard on the guy. Ben thinks as he exits the truck.

Ben's walking up the walkway to the cabin door and sees it swing open, with Eileen rushing toward and embracing him tightly. Ben returns the embrace, not realizing how much he needed a hug up until this moment.

"Steven told me everything that happened. Oh my gosh! Those poor women and children..." Eileen says, as she hugs him fiercely.

"And you!" She says as she releases him and steps back. "I heard you went and found some more trouble to get into."

Ben smiles at her, just happy to see her face again with his hands on her sides. "Well, actually the trouble found us..."

"Oh, I'm sure it did, Ben." She says as she looks around. "Wait?!" Alarm rising in her voice.

"Where are the others?" Eileen asks.

"Yeah, nephew. Where are Alexander and Joseph?" Steven says as he steps out onto the porch.

Ben takes a step back, completely releasing Eileen. "Whoa... calm down now. They are fine. We just dropped off Joseph and he'll be back in the morning to check in, since the phone lines are down."

Ben then gestures back to his truck. "Alexander's in the truck keeping Mia company, since her sister, Isabelle, is still asleep."

Ben turns to look back at Eileen and his Uncle, who both have perplexed looks upon their faces.

"We tried calling you guys, but the phones are down and so is the SuperNet... With the whole crash and hurt women and children, we were not able to save them all." Ben starts.

Eileen and Uncle Steven's confused looks are exchanged for looks of shock and sadness.

"How many survived, Ben?" His Uncle asks.

Ben sighs. "There were only nine survivors out of twenty women and children... Most of which were claimed back down at the crash site. Thanks to your message before the lines went dead." Ben says, looking at his Uncle.

"But Mia and Isabelle's mom was not one of the lucky ones." Ben adds.

"Oh no." Eileen says as she covers her mouth.

"I know... she's in the back of my truck under a sleeping bag. Mia knows, but her little sister doesn't know yet. Mia's 12 and Isabelle's 9." Ben explains and then looks back to his Uncle.

"Uncle, I was hoping..." Ben starts to ask his question of the girls staying with all of them.

"Of course, there's no question about it. They can stay as long as they need to. We can put them on the pull-out couch in the living room." Uncle Steven says, before Ben can finish his question.

"Thank you, Uncle. We didn't know where else to take them." Ben replies.

"Not a problem and enough talk of this. Those poor girls must be exhausted, filthy, and starving." Uncle Steven replies.

"Yes, where are they? So, I can take a look at them and make sure they are alright." Eileen says.

"They're in the back-cab with Alexander..." Ben says but is unable to finish his sentence. Eileen is down the walkway and into the driveway, reaching the far side of the truck and opening the back-cab door.

Ben scratches his head and smiles at Eileen's compassion for the little girls that had lost everything and had most certainly suffered horrific events. He then turns to his Uncle.

"Thanks again, Uncle." Ben says.

"Enough already, nephew. What would you have me do... turn them away? No! We take care of as many as we can and we figure out the how about it, later. Plus, we have bigger things to worry about, Ben... The Leviathan landed and I believe that they are here to stay. Regardless if we want them to or not." Uncle Steven explains.

"So, it is true!? Those people from Earth Two are here!?" Ben says excitedly.

"Yes, nephew. Captain Abraham Jackson and his crew are here. I don't know how many yet. But they are here. Eileen and I even talked to a couple of his Federalists, after the ship left. A man and woman, both military types of people. We were thinking of going back to Big Bear tomorrow with Alexander and yourself, to get your take on the two of them." Steven explains.

"What?! You talked to them?!" Ben says excitedly. "Tomorrow?! Yeah, that sounds like a good idea! You said they were military types, what branch... or nationality... I guess?

Wow! People from another planet. What a crazy world?!

He knew the concerns of the people from Earth Two, but it was all still surreal. People from a different planet are actually here. Despite all of the concerns and red flags that they had discussed in the last couple of months, it was still pretty damn exciting... at least to Ben.

"That was the plan, until just now..." Steven replies. "Now, I'm thinking we need a day to deal with our new situation."

Ben scratches the back of his head, looking back toward his truck. He sees Alexander now out of the truck and Eileen is on the other side. Both of his dear friends were talking to the young girls, but he couldn't make out what was being said with the softened voices. He could see that they were both now awake.

Poor girls. This must be all very confusing for them... and all so very tragic. I wonder if the smaller one understands what's going on. She just lost her mother, her second parent to be taken away from her... Ben thinks to himself as he tries to remember what his mind was like when he was a nine-year-old boy.

I think I would have been confused as hell, not to mention sad as hell. But I have also heard that little girls are often much quicker to the catch than young boys. Either way, it's a good thing Eileen's here. There's the whole medical field expertise, but there's also the fact that she's a woman... I'm not sure what these girls would think if they were all just men here. I wonder if they will ever trust men again...

Ben scratches his head and turns his attention back to his Uncle. "Yeah. It may not be a good idea to leave them alone at the moment, going to run off and talk to some Earth Two aliens."

Uncle Steven nods. "Let's take tomorrow to assess how bad off these girls are and try to figure out what to do from there. And there's the livestock to deal with as well."

"Right. I wanted to drop off the girls and then I'll go over to Bradley's to start dividing up the animals amongst us." Ben replies.

"Nonsense, nephew." Uncles Steven says as he shakes his head. "You've had a long enough day, and these girls have at least seen your face as someone who saved them. Stay here with Alexander and Eileen and help get the girls settled."

Ben looks back to Eileen, Alexander, and the two girls, now all standing outside the truck and within view of Ben and Steven. Eileen's kneeling next to the younger girl, Isabelle, and Alexander's standing on the other side of the older one, Mia, as she overlooks Eileen evaluating Mia's little sister and asking them both questions.

"You sure, Uncle? I can take care of it..." Ben questions.

Looking back toward his Uncle, he sees his Steven smile at him and wink. "Oh, I'm sure. It's actually an order, seeing as I'm now your Sheriff."

"Oh, I see how it is... all of a sudden, huh?" Ben replies, smiling back.

Uncle Steven shrugs, "Hey, it is what it is... but I do think you should help me get some of those animals out to put in the backyard. I emptied out the large and small sheds out back."

"Sounds good. What are we keeping here, Uncle?" Ben asks.

"We are pretty much going to split it up into thirds between the three houses. We'll unload eight chickens, a rooster, three piglets, and a sheep. The rest will be split in half between the Bradley families." Steven explains.

"Are they set up for the animals?" Ben asks.

"They were last time I checked, before the phone lines went down." Uncle Steven replies.

"Yeah, about that..." Ben adds.

"I know. It's a major obstacle now and I wanted to get Alexander's and your input on the new development. I have my ideas but wanted to see what you two think... but we'll have time for that later. Let's get this show on the road so I can get going and you can get those little ones settled in." Uncle Steven responds.

Ben nods and goes to the back of the box trailer, with his Uncle following him.

It takes just over half an hour to get the newly acquired livestock into their respective sheds, and Ben was pretty proud of themselves for not losing any of them in the shuffle, with none of them running off. It wasn't entirely easy, but the job was done, with his Uncle leaving in Ben's truck at 1925. Ben looks at the waning sunlight in the distance.

Probably another half hour or close to an hour left of light this time of year... Or at least, that's what it used to be like this time of year. Who knows now, especially with it being noticeably cooler up here during the summertime. Ben thinks to himself, circling back to his worries about the upcoming winter.

Ben shakes his head and wanders inside the cabin, noticing the warmth and smell of food drifting off from the kitchen, now just realizing how hungry he actually was.

When was the last time I ate? Ben thinks as he walks into the kitchen and seeing the pot of stew on the stove.

He sees Alexander and Eileen sitting at the table with Mia and Isabelle, with all of them having bowls of stew in front of them.

We are going to need to find a bigger dining room table. Ben thinks to himself as he smiles.

"How's the stew? Sure smells good." Ben announces.

Mia looks up at Ben, and then goes back to eating, obviously very hungry. Isabelle, the younger one who was asleep for nearly all of the trip since she was pulled from the wreckage, simply stares at Ben. She looked startled by Ben's entry into the room and was unsure of what to do.

"Isabelle, that is Ben. He helped Alexander save you and your sister, and he's my boyfriend... He's a good guy." Eileen explains to the little girl, and winks at her.

Isabelle looks over to her sister for confirmation, and Mia nods without saying anything then goes back to stuffing her face with the stew.

Good God! They must be starving... poor girls.

Ben walks over to Eileen and kisses her on the top of her head. "Thanks for vouching for me." He says as he smiles.

"Sure thing, hon." She says with a grin. "But before you eat, you should probably go rinse off."

Ben lifts his arm, smelling his musky odor.

I did do a lot of running around and heavy lifting today...

"Yeah, alright. I'll take the first shower." Ben replies.

"Make it a short one though, Ben." Eileen adds. "We need to save enough warm water for the girls and then Alexander, too. Plus, once you get out, the girls can jump in the shower and you can sit down and enjoy your dinner. Who's up first for watch tonight, again?"

Ben raises his hand. "First watch shift is mine for this week."

She nods to him. "Okay. You go get cleaned up. Then I'll get them ready to get cleaned up and get them situated to get ready for bed. Where are they sleeping?"

"The couch pulls out into a bed." Ben replies.

Eileen turns to the girls. "Mia, Isabelle... Is that okay with you, sleeping on the couch bed after you two take a shower?"

Neither of the girls answer right away, when they both look up. Isabelle looks to Mia, then Mia looks to Alexander. Alexander nods. "It's comfy. I slept there the first night I came here a couple months ago."

This gets a question out of Mia. "You didn't live here before?"

Alexander smiles at her. "No, Mia. I met Ben when all of this started, and then Eileen a couple days later. This is Ben's Uncle's home and he was kind enough to share it with us. His name's Steven, remember?"

Mia nods.

"I used to live out on the east coast with my wife, Michelle, and daughters... Sydney was your sister's age, and Aliyah was 13." Alexander explained.

"Oh, they aren't here, too?" Mia asks.

"No, Mia. They are not..." Alexander replies.

Ben can feel his heart sink thinking about Alexander's family and the grief he must still be going through.

"What happened to them?" Mia asks, just as any young child would ask without thinking of the implications.

"Well, they moved to where my wife was born, in Illinois. Do you know where that is?" Alexander asks.

"Yes, I've seen it on a map. My family moved here from Texas. We used to live in San Antonio." Mia replies.

"Very nice! I have never been but hear Texas is nice." Alexander answers and Mia nods.

Ben notices that Isabelle has stopped eating and is listening to Alexander as well. What is more, Eileen's listening too. All of them were interested to find out what happened to Alexander's family, including Ben.

"My wife went back to nursing, raising our daughters. Some years later, Aliyah became a nurse too and eventually had a family of her own, with two kids, Trent and Leah. Sydney, my youngest, went into the Air Force. She became a scientist like me, and eventually became a leader in the Space Force." Alexander explained.

Wow! Space force, huh? No shit...

"So, one turned out like her mom and the other like you? Did the one that went to the Space Force get to go into Outer Space?!" Mia asks.

"Yes, she did... several times." Alexander replies.

"Your daughter was an astronaut?!" Isabelle asks, with this being the first time Ben has heard the little one's voice.

"Yes, Isabelle. She was." Alexander replies.

"Wow." Isabelle says slowly.

"Where are they now?" Mia asks.

This question really hurt Ben's heart. *Geez, kid. Just twist the knife in, why don't you.*

Alexander smiles at the young girl. "They lived their long lives, after we were all trapped in this *Radius,* and they all passed away a long time ago."

Mia looks embarrassed for a moment. "Oh... I'm sorry, Alexander."

"It's alright Mia. It was a very long time ago." Alexander replies, "A very long time indeed."

Alexander looks up to Ben and then over at Eileen.

"I'm glad you were able to find out what happened to your family, Alexander." Eileen says, barely being able to hold back her tears, but still with her eyes glistening.

Ben scratches the back of his head. "Yeah, sounds like they turned out pretty damn awesome, Alexander."

"They did, didn't they." Alexander answers.

"I think so." Mia replies.

"Me too!" Isabelle adds.

Alexander smiles at the two girls and they both provide small smiles in return.

Well that's a good sign. Hopefully, as time goes by... they start to feel safer and start getting back to being kids. I truly hope that they have a chance to regain their childhoods and grow up, just like Alexander's kids did.

Ben sighs. "Alright, I better go clean up."

"What?" Eileen says. "You're still here? Go get cleaned up stinky!"

This gets another smile and even a light giggle from the girls.

"Alright, alright... I'm out of here." Ben says, smiling as he turns to head downstairs to get cleaned up, then get some food, then off to his watch shift.

16

EILEEN RIVERA

Taking one day to get the girls settled in and the animals situated actually ended up taking two days and a couple trips to the Lake Drive Marketplace for supplies. Eileen had begun to realize just how reliant they had been on their phones and SuperNet up to this point.

Yesterday, she was on one of the trips to the Lake Drive Marketplace and there was a good amount of the people from town that were very worried about the lack of communication. Sheriff Steven, was riddled with questions... which he had no answers to.

Whereas, the group had a good idea of why there was a recent change in their communication capabilities, with that change being the lack thereof, Steven was not ready to start a panic and get people all riled up.

He continued to assure them that he would speak with Captain Jackson and see if he couldn't help with the situation. Eileen and Ben had provided many of the same assurances during their afternoon patrol of the small town of Crestline, that Tuesday afternoon. In truth, it was Alexander and Steven's theory that Captain Abraham Jackson was behind the sudden loss of communications and the SuperNet. It didn't take much convincing for Eileen and Ben to see their reasoning and logic.

Adding more fuel to the fire of distrust between the mountain communities and the people of Earth two, the four of them were convinced that Captain Abraham Jackson and the Federalists had something to do with Edwards Air Force Base, too.

To find out more information, Steven sent Deputy Joseph Gomez along with Deputy Janice Fuller and a small group of other people from Crestline's newly formed militia, the DFC, to Edwards Air Force Base. The groups consisted of two vehicles and eight people in total. Steven wanted to avoid another situation of their people being outnumbered in another conflict along the roads.

Eileen found it interesting that two of the new members of the DFC were the young couple from the stockades, Briana and Christian, which Alexander had pointed out to her. She was happy to see such young people stepping up to help their community and protect it. She figured it made sense for the wrongfully accused young couple, not wanting what happened to them to happen to anyone else.

Regardless, the scouting group of the DFC left earlier this morning and were expected to drive back by this afternoon. Steven had sent them the back way through the mountain to the High Desert, instructing them to take the 395 up toward Edwards. They were instructed not to go in if it looked dangerous, and at the sign of trouble to high-tail it back home. In the world before the *Radius*, the trip would have only taken an hour and half. With the group leaving around 8:00 AM on this Wednesday morning, they weren't expected back until around 4:00 PM, before they would get worried about them.

Shortly after the scouting group had left, Mia and Isabelle had a ceremony to celebrate the life of their mother. Alexander and Ben had thought it best to bury her in the far back corner of the property, in the area right before it slopes down. The idea was that the girls could come visit their mother's grave when they wanted, and talk to her.

Steven agreed with the idea, but Eileen wasn't sure if it was really healthy for the girls. Alexander had reminded her that people had been doing this practice for centuries and many relatives had often been buried near their homes so they could pay their respects.

Eileen trusted Alexander's opinion and saw that he wanted nothing more than to take care of the two young girls. The younger one, Isabelle still didn't speak much, but Mia had started to talk more and more to Alexander, to herself, and even to Steven and Ben. Eileen hoped that in time, Isabelle would open up more as well.

The ceremony was short, with the girls saying goodbye to their mother over her grave, a wooden cross as her marker. Both girls cried and then Alexander ushered them back into the house to look at the new clothes that had been acquired for them at the Lake Drive Marketplace.

They had also been able to find some feed for the animals and enough studded T-posts and vinyl welded wire to help enclose and separate the animals, keeping the chickens and rooster in the smaller shed, and the sheep with the piglets in the larger shed. This is what Eileen was doing with Ben when she heard vehicles pull up in front of the house.

She looks to Ben and then Ben looks to the sky.

"If I had to guess, it's around 1400. Maybe... I don't know. It's after noon, for sure. It's really hard to tell without our phones. But it sounds like the scouting party has returned." Ben says.

"Yeah, we need to get watches next time we are in the Market. We should have thought about this earlier." Eileen replies.

Ben shrugs. "We can't always think of everything."

"I expect more from you, Ben. You are supposed to be the prepper guy." Eileen says with a sarcastic smirk.

"Yeah, whatever you say..." Ben says with a smile.

She nods. "Good, you're catching on." She says and laughs at him.

"We better go see what the news is." Ben says, putting down the tools and the last bit of the vinyl fencing.

She gets up and follows him through the side of the house, careful not to trip on the alarm system that Ben had set up when they moved in. It was made up of ropes and a lot of various items that bang against each other and make noise. She follows him through the side gate, closing it behind her, which puts them just outside the front porch of the cabin.

She can see Joseph, Janice, Briana, Christian, and the others all talking at once with a frustrated look on Steven's face and wide-eyed look on Alexander's. She and Ben walk up to the group.

"Quiet!" Steven shouts. "You all aren't making any sense!"

"Where are the girls?" Eileen asks Alexander.

"They are inside resting. They are still pretty tired from today's events and likely still recovering from everything that happened with those monsters out on the road." Alexander replies.

"Now! One at a time... Please! Joseph, why don't you start us off." Steven says loudly.

The rest of the group looks to Joseph. Joseph sighs and she can see that he's trying to calm himself down.

"Everyone's dead, Sheriff. And I mean everyone." Joseph blurts out.

What?! Everyone at the base is gone?!

"Everyone at Edwards is dead? Are you sure?" Steven asks.

"No, Sheriff... you're not understanding me. It's not just Edwards. When we got to Kramer Junction... that's when we saw the first of them." Joseph adds.

"The first of who, Joseph?" Steven asks.

"The first of the dead bodies, Sheriff... and we kept going to Edwards and saw more of the same." Joseph replies.

"How did they die, Joseph? Were they shot?" Steven asks.

"No clue, Sheriff. But we didn't see any wounds or blood anywhere. Just bodies collapsed on the ground, on the road, in houses, at the base, and it just kept going. Once we got to Mojave... where your contact was located... we finally got the idea that it may have been a virus or disease." Joseph explains.

Oh dear God! A deadly pathogen?! Eileen thinks as her eyes go wide and she looks at Ben.

"But, Joseph, you all are fine." Steven points out.

"Right! Yeah that took us a little bit to catch on to... after we were done panicking for a little bit." Joseph answers.

Eileen then sees the look of embarrassment on several of the group's faces.

"So, it's not a pathogen or a virus? How do you know?" Eileen asks.

Joseph shrugs. "We don't really know for sure, but if it was... I don't think we would have made it back at all. I mean if the bodies were carriers, there were so many of them that we would have got it too. Right?"

"Deputy Gomez. What did the bodies look like? Were there any signs of vomit or blood, or anything that was strange at all?" Alexander questions.

"Aside from all of them being dead? No... wait... just their eyes." Joseph admits.

"What was wrong with their eyes?" Steven asks.

"Nothing really, just the fact that they were all closed. Every single one of them. I didn't think much of it at first, but after what we saw on the road... with the women and children... It finally struck me as strange. A lot of their eyes were open after they died and we pulled them from that trailer of death. This was not like that. None of these bodies' eyes were open... not a single one." Joseph explains.

"Are you certain Deputy Gomez?" Alexander asks.

Eileen can see that the man's brain is working full speed and he's thinking something, for sure.

"I can't say for sure, but everybody that I saw, had their eyes closed. We went from Mojave down toward Rosemond and even Lancaster. A whole shit load of the same. Without GPS and not knowing what else was in front of us... and honestly with all of us being pretty freaked out, we turned around and went the same way back home... here."

"Smart thinking, Joseph." Steven says, scratching the back of his head. "I'm glad you all made it back here safe and sound."

"So, Deputy Joseph... if you had to describe these bodies, did they appear as though they were sleeping?" Alexander says, interrupting Steven.

Joseph looks to Janice and then to the rest of them and their heads all nod.

"Yeah, sleeping is a good way of describing what they looked like. But they were not sleeping. We checked dozens of bodies before we stopped checking." Joseph replies.

Sleeping... wait... Eileen thinks, connecting the dots for herself.

"Son of a bitch... it was the *sleepers*." Ben says it loud enough for everyone to hear, but likely just meant to think it to himself. Looking up, he realized he said it aloud.

Alexander shakes his head and sighs. "Yes. I'm afraid so. I believe this had to do with the *sleepers* that Commander Yang warned us about."

"Shit! I knew they had something to do with this! Between this and them knocking out our communications and access to the SuperNet..." Steven says aloud and angrily, likely also not realizing he was speaking his mind and not in his mind.

He looks up and sees that everyone is catching on to his train of thought. "Alright... Nobody panic, and nobody is to create panic. You hear me?! Everyone here, keeps their damn mouth shut!"

He looks around the group, to all of them. "Do you understand me?!"

This elicits a bunch of quick nods at once.

"Good! Alright. Here's what we are going to do. You all get back in your vehicles and use your bullhorns to go around town to let everyone know that there's an emergency meeting at the Post Office. don't tell them what you saw. I will tell everyone at the meeting." Steven explains.

This receives another round of nods.

"Again, don't go scaring the shit out of people. Give me a few hours to formulate a viable plan and we'll go over it at the meeting." Steven adds.

"What time is the emergency meeting, Sheriff?" Briana asks.

He looks down at his wristwatch. "We'll say in four hours, at 1800 or 6:00 PM."

Of course he thought ahead enough to have a wristwatch... or has he always had one?

The group just stands there awaiting further instruction. No one ready to move, letting the new information sink in.

"Alright ladies and gents! This is the primary reason we formed the DFC, to help us defend against aggressors and invading forces. Don't panic and keep a level head! Get the word out about the meeting and then meet me at the Post Office at 1800. Now you all get going!" Steven explains and then orders.

With the groups saying their goodbyes, the two vehicles are filled back up with the scouting party and they all head off with their orders.

Once they are gone, only the four of them remaining, standing in the driveway.

After a moment, Steven speaks again. "Son a bitch! I knew they were up to no good. With that talk of helping us but referring to us as *your kind*. Arrogant pieces of shits! They think they can just come back and invade us."

"What?! Invade us?!" Eileen asks, alarmed.

Steven looks up to her and doesn't respond.

"He's right Eileen. It's damn near a textbook invasion. You go after a region that is already in chaos. You take out their military. You take out their communications. Then you come in, offering help and salvation." Ben replies.

"We just cannot catch a break, can we?! It's enough that we have each lost people that we have loved. Then we are thrown into this whirlwind of a new world, 1,400 years into the future..." Eileen begins.

"Actually, 1,410 years into the future, Eileen..." Alexander interrupts.

"Dammit, Alexander... really? Right now? I know the exact amount of years. That's not the point. The point is that we had to have an actual battle! That's right! A freaking battle with the MS13 gang! The point is that we are now attempting to take in and raise two young girls because their parents were killed by monsters and rapists! My point is that we just got finished dealing with a psychotic maniac that has been picking us off one by one... even the late Sheriff Patterson. My point is!" Eileen continues her rant of anger and frustration with the realization that they are about to be invaded in the very near future and are going to be having to fight for their lives again.

She pauses for a second to catch her breath and collect her thoughts. Feeling her blood begin to boil. She looks around and none of them are trying to interrupt her.

"My point is that this ass-backwards of a new world really sucks! And if some arrogant pieces of shit think that we have made it this far, just to be put to *sleep* or turned into slaves, or whatever the hell they have planned for us... they have another thing coming! I won't allow them to take away what life we have left! What life the children have left, like those two girls in that cabin! My point is, I'm sick and damn tired of this shit! If they want a fight, let's give them one and kick them the hell off our planet!" Eileen says this last part as she runs out of breath.

She has so much rage and anger building up inside of her from everything that has been going on.

I just want to live my life in freaking peace! Is that too much to ask for?! She screams inside her head.

Steven pats her on her shoulder and nods to her. "I'm right there with you, Eileen..."

"Me too, babe." Ben adds and looks at everyone else. "She has a point, gents. A very angry point, but it's valid. I'm sorry hon... were you done talking? I don't want to interrupt your rage rant." He gives her a grin at this last part.

She eyes him as he puts up his hands in self-defense. "Yeah, I'm done." She replies. "For now..."

"Well, without trying to piss you off anymore, you're a hundred percent right, but I don't think you should be talking to the two Federalists posted over in Big Bear. What were their names, again?" Ben replies.

"Mahoney's the robotic intelligence and reconnaissance guy, and

Burke's the logistics and supply gal. Mahoney seems like a real stick in the mud, but Burke didn't seem half bad... aside from lying to us about Edwards and why they are actually here." Steven responds.

This focuses Eileen's mind on Sergeant Alicia Burke. She had liked the woman, but she had also felt like she was holding back information from them. She can feel herself calming down.

She sighs and adds, "Yeah, I got the same feeling about the two of them. Burke was nice, but something definitely seemed off."

"Alexander what's your take on these *sleeper* things? Robots? Jedi Ninjas? Monsters?" Ben asks of Alexander.

Before Alexander answers, he looks at her. *I did kind of bite his head off... but in my defense, he did correct me on something that really didn't matter.*

She sighs, "I'm not going to yell at you again. Sorry, Alexander. It was just bad timing for you to be correcting me."

Ben laughs. "Yeah, man. I thought you were a married man. You should know better than that..." Then Ben goes quiet, likely realizing that he just brought up his dead wife.

"Sorry, Alexander. Didn't mean to be insensitive." Ben adds.

For the first time, Eileen sees Alexander's mood change and he narrows his eyes for a split second at Ben, but then his face returns to the normal academic Alexander that they all have grown accustomed to.

Did he just get mad? Did I see that right? Makes sense for Ben to be the one to piss off the calm and poised Alexander Mathis.

The moment of slight anger was there and then it was gone as Alexander began to speak. "Well, I have given it some thought before this new information about Edwards Air Force base and the surrounding towns and cities. Whereas, it cannot be definitive, it's apparent that a *sleeper* is some sort of weapon. I don't believe it to be robotic but to be made of machinery. I definitely don't think that a *sleeper* is a monster or any other form of living creature. This is primarily because the bodies sound as if they are unharmed and untouched. In fact, they appear to be sleeping."

"So, what do you think they are?" Steven asks him.

"Currently I have two dominant theories. One is that it's some sort of viral agent released into the air. However, I recall reading something similar to that in a previous war, here on Earth One, that had to do with the Rh factor... So, whereas, that may be a possibility and they could have improved on the previous design of those biological weapons. I'm leaning more toward my second theory of a massive explosion from a modified bomb, based on technology that we didn't have yet." Alexander explains.

"I don't know Alexander. Don't bombs and explosions leave destruction and not dead people that look like they are sleeping?" Eileen asks.

"She has a point, Alexander. That's not like any other bomb or explosion I have heard of. The biological weapon theory kind of makes more sense." Ben adds.

"That's what I thought at first as well. But I was leaving one key factor out of the equation, which is the *Blue Hole Radius*... We know that the technology developed by the SXS Project and the advent of the *Blue Hole Radius* forced a paradigm shift from the Einsteinian Paradigm to the Harris Paradigm. And in our previous paradigm, the one where we came from... we had nuclear weapons that could be modified to detonate a massive electromagnetic pulse that could wipe out electrical grids in entire regions. Seeing as we showed them how to slow down time on quite a large scale, it's not too far-fetched to assume that they improved upon that science." Alexander further explains.

This time, Eileen has no response and neither do Steven or Ben.

After a short pause, Alexander continues. "This is why I think it's some sort of futuristic bomb that detonates a massive wave that doesn't wipe out electronics and destroy cities, but rather... it only wipes out humans."

Eileen's eyes go wide at the realization of what Alexander's saying and she hopes that he's not right.

If he's right... the people have the ability to wipe us out without us being able to even put up a fight. Dear God! I hope he's wrong...

"Whoa, whoa, whoa! So you saying that these people from Earth

Two created an eco-friendly nuke that just wipes out people? Seriously man, why the hell would anyone create something like that?!" Ben blurts out.

"I'm uncertain if the blast affects other creatures as well, but it's apparent that it's extremely effective against the human body, leaving everything else in the area intact." Alexander adds.

"What the crap, man! Really?!" Ben says, obviously thinking of their odds if Alexander's right.

"Alright... So, Alexander... this is what you think these *sleepers* are?" Steven asks.

"Yes, Steven. I can't say for sure. But I have put a lot of thought into it." Alexander replies.

"Well... If either of the theories that you have said are true, that's all bad news for us. But if you are right, there's a silver lining." Steven says.

"Silver lining?" Eileen interjects.

"Think about it... If they have this technology, then why haven't they used it. They used it on Edwards, but not here... That tells me that they need us for something." Steven replies.

"Or hopefully... they ran out of the damn things." Ben adds.

"Yeah, there is that... but either way, those are good things. So, either they ran out or they need us for something. If we find out why they need us... that gives us an edge." Steven responds.

"Well, how the hell do we figure that out?" Eileen asks.

"My apologies, I thought it was obvious, Eileen." Alexander replies.

"We ask them, my dear." Steven answers.

"Yeah, okay... Hey Federalist people, are you here to kill us all? I don't see them answering with a *Yeah! Good job on figuring it out!*" Eileen replies.

"Remember, it doesn't matter if they tell us the truth or not, but it does matter on how they answer our questions. Hell, if we are close to the real answer, it may trip them up enough to let something slip." Steven explains.

"Dammit! We know they are here to hurt us. I wish we could just go in guns blazing... Take out all of these Federalists assholes!" Ben says, annoyed.

"Yeah, but we don't know what kind of weapons they have and how they work. We have just seen the aftermath of one of their weapons. It's safe to say they have others." Steven replies.

The things on Burke's and Mahoney's right arms... what were they called?

"Oh Yeah! Those MECCU things on their arms!" Eileen blurts out.

"My thoughts exactly, Eileen." Steven replies. "But first thing's first... we need to figure out how we are going to explain all of this to the people and how to convince them that these Federalists are bad news."

"That should be pretty obvious, once we tell them about the *sleeper* that they used on Edwards." Ben replies.

I don't know... we were offered, well not immortality... but damn near close.

"No, Ben. Your Uncle has a point. Captain Jackson spoke about new technologies to help us. Hell, he claimed to be 74 years old and he looked my age. People would do anything for that sort of technology and medicine..." Eileen explains to her bullheaded boyfriend.

This guy! Wants to go in guns blazing when we don't have a freaking clue what we are up against! I know I'm pissed too, but really?! Come on, Ben... at least try and think out a plan! Eileen thinks as she shakes her head.

Ben must have sensed that she was becoming annoyed with him, because he looked her in the eye, then down at the ground.

"Oh right... yeah... that makes sense. Shit! This does really suck!" Ben blurts out.

"You can say that again..." Eileen replies.

"Either we can piss and moan about it or we can go figure this out. Let's head inside, check on the girls, and then try to wrap our heads around what we are going to say at the emergency meeting in town." Steven replies.

The man has a point. Whatever the hell these sleepers are, these Feder-

alists have another thing coming if they think they can just come here and screw up our world worse than it already is. I'm sick and damn tired of people thinking that they can take from others, just because they think they deserve it! Eileen thinks to herself as she follows Alexander, Ben, and Steven into the cabin to try and figure out a plan for the people of Crestline.

17

BENJAMIN REILLY

GOD, I hope that Alexander's wrong about the sleepers. What the shit?
They made freaking fracking eco-friendly nukes that only wipe out us... or
they built a biological weapon that does something very similar. Either
way you look at it, it seems like we don't stand a chance. Ben thinks, as he
navigates the winding road toward the dried-up lakebed of Big Bear
to speak with the two Federalists that Captain Jackson had left
behind, Mahoney and Burke.

I guess we'll find out soon enough... Ben thinks as the drive with
Eileen and his Uncle Steven is a silent one, with all of them likely as
deep in thought as Ben was. Alexander had opted to stay back with
the girls.

Two cars were following Ben, making a total of nine of them
going to see Staff Sergeant Mahoney and Sergeant Burke. Each
vehicle had three passengers. Ben, Eileen, and his Uncle in his truck,
Deputy Joseph Gomez was following them in his vehicle with the
young couple that had joined the DFC, Briana and Christian. Ben
was impressed that the young couple stepped up to the call for arms
and joined the DFC after everything that had transpired with the
stockades at the Lake Arrowhead Village Marketplace. Deputy Janice

Fuller was in the third vehicle with two other DFC members. Ben could not recall their names at the moment.

With being about ten minutes out from Big Bear, he checks his clock. *It's 0910... and I believe it's Thursday already. Geez, time flies.*

Ben smiles as he drives. *Yeah it does, considering it's frigging July 11th of 3433!*

Ben's mind circles back to the emergency meeting, yesterday.

The meeting had gone as well as Eileen had predicted. Ben had hoped that she was wrong and people wouldn't be blinded by promises of youth and salvation, but it turned out that he was the one that had too much faith in people's common sense.

Everyone on the DFC seemed to be on the same page, but Ben could still see several of the members of the newly formed militia contemplating the medical advancements of the people from Earth Two. He just hoped that when the time came to fight, they would choose the side of their fellow man and woman.

The town of Crestline, on the other hand, was close to a fifty/fifty split. The crowd was enormous, compared to what Eileen had told him the crowd was for the last meeting. Uncle Steven had said that this was mostly due to the lack of communication... with there being none, but word of mouth still working fine and well. It made sense to Ben. People were scared and wanted to know what was going on.

His Uncle didn't hold back any punches. After the four of them had discussed at length what to tell the town... they had all come to the decision to be as transparent as possible. They had all agreed that the old ways of holding back facts and only providing half-truths or misguiding people were the old ways and should not be followed any longer. It had been Ben that had pointed out that if they have gotten this far, they deserve the full truth and nothing less. Everyone else agreed that the people should know what they believed themselves to be up against.

Ben was confident that they would see common sense. They had to. These people from Earth Two had wiped out an entire area of people with unknown casualties. These people had also, likely, knocked out their communication.

What Ben had explained to Eileen was accurate. This was a textbook invasion strategy. Take out the military, take out communication capabilities, make promises to divide the people... all that was left was for them to strike.

That was the main part that worried Ben. He had not figured out why they had waited at all. They had the firepower.

What were they waiting for? What was stopping them?

In Ben's mind, Alexander had to be onto something with Captain Jackson needing something from them. Whereas, Ben had no idea what that was exactly, he had a good idea that it was not anything good. At least good for the people of Earth One, which was their home.

Ben had ended up being very wrong about people and common sense. He was astonished with how many of the townspeople had begun to defend the people from Earth Two... without even knowing them, really. Sure, there were those that made the trip to go meet Mahoney and Burke. As it turns out, Eileen was not the only one that thought Sergeant Alicia Burke seemed like a good person. This had ended up swaying many of the people's opinion.

There were shouts of, "How do you know it was them?" "They said they are here to help?" "They promised us our youth back!" "How do you know that the military weren't the ones that struck first and they were just defending themselves?!"

Ben was taken aback by how easily people were misled. Eileen had been right. Many of them were blinded by their technology and promises.

Ben had to admit, it did sound pretty cool being over seventy years old and looking and feeling to be only in his thirties. However, that didn't dismiss the very likely scenario that those same people that are making all of these promises committed an act of genocide. And he figured that if they were willing to do it once, they were willing to do it again.

By the end of the meeting, more people had begun to think of the promises from Captain Jackson, Staff Sergeant Mahoney, and the kind and angelic Sergeant Burke.

His Uncle had to take the stance of going to find out more information and promised to return with more accurate information. This was replied with, "Go ask Sergeant Burke! She'll explain everything!"

His Uncle promised to get more information and down to the actual truth of it. Ben was scared as hell that the people were more worried about being young again, compared to the devastation of their *sleepers* and God knows what else they had developed over 1,410 years.

It was obvious by the time the meeting was over that they had all felt somewhat defeated. The evening had been rather quiet, with the group going along with their evening dinner and then standing their respective watches.

On a positive note, Ben was happy that the girls were getting a little more talkative. Whereas, they mostly spoke with Alexander and Eileen... It was a start.

Before they all got ready for bed and their shifts, his Uncle remained adamant that he was going to get to the bottom of this and prove to *the mindless mob of sheep* that Captain Jackson and the others were here to do them all harm.

Ben was uncertain that the people would come to their senses any time soon, even with all of the facts. It had become evident to Ben, back in 2020, that people can be easily misled, and it can take a long time for the real truth to sink in. Ben truly hopes that his Uncle's right and they come back with the information needed to convince the others.

Seeing the dried-up lakebed as they enter Big Bear, Ben realizes that none of them have said much during this drive, and even this morning.

Ben sighs heavily. "Alright. So, what's our game plan? That way, we are all on the same page?"

"The game plan is to ask them the direct questions about the *sleepers* and communications. We need to be polite and courteous, but still have a plan to take those two down, if need be. We still don't know what those MECCUs actually do." Uncle Steven explains.

"Polite and courteous... sure thing, Steven. But I'm telling you that Sergeant Burke is two-faced. There's a reason why so many of the people trust her already. She's as sly as a fox." Eileen replies. "And if they do get out of hand, I'm shooting at their MECCUs, before we find out just what the hell they do. If what Alexander said was right, there's no telling what those oversized bracelets do."

Yup... she's still pissed. Ben thinks about how fiery she was yesterday.

Her mood had not changed much after the emergency meeting, unless she was around Mia and Isabelle. She always put on a smile and softer voice when they were within sight or earshot. Nonetheless, Ben knew that she was still very fired up about these Earth Two people and their likely act of genocide out toward Edwards Air Force Base.

"Polite and courteous, but still have a plan to kill those two. Sounds like an old saying from the Marines. Mad Dog Mattis, if I remember correctly." Ben says as he takes the final turn, coming out to a parking lot in front of a park and recreational area at the beginning of Big Bear.

"Remember though... We are not looking for a fight here. Just information, you two. Eileen, I'm afraid my nephew may be rubbing off on you with his rash decision-making trait." Uncle Steven says, with the second part directed toward Eileen.

"Don't worry, Steven." Eileen says as she jumps out of the truck, reaching back in to grab her rifle and slinging it over her shoulder. "I'll play nice until they stop playing nice first."

"Remind me not to make that woman mad." Ben says to his Uncle as she shuts her door and he gets out on his side.

"You just figured that out now, Nephew?" Steven says with a

smirk. "Let's go find out what Mahoney and Burke have to say. I'm curious if they will remember us from a couple of days ago. They have surely seen a lot of us... since then."

"Here we go then." Ben replies, as he confirms that his PX4 Storm's still at his hip and easy to reach. He then grabs his rifle, shutting his door behind him and follows his Uncle and Eileen into the dried-up lakebed.

Walking off the *shore* into the dried-up lakebed, Ben finds the ground to still be very moist from the water that was there a couple months ago.

Such a shame this lake went dry. It was a nice place to come up in the summertime to beat the heat. But why's it still so moist? Ben thinks and then recalls the good amount of rain they had received the weeks prior.

Duh Ben, it was raining cats and dogs for a week straight. Wow time really does fly. That trip to the Lake Drive Market place seems like a year ago... not only a few days ago.

Ben looks ahead at a group of people talking to two people, who Ben thinks to be Mahoney and Burke. He looks past them, to the craft that Eileen had described to him.

Wow... a real-life spaceship from the future. Or are we from the past? Sometimes this whole time-difference really gives me a freaking headache.

Ben looks at the spaceship that resembles a large railroad container, which had cone-like ends on both sides, making it hard for him to conclude which end is the front and which is the rear of the craft. He also took notice of the cylinders on the sides of the ship. From their angle of approach, he could tell that the same cylinders were on the other side.

Those have to be how it flies. Ben thinks. *That sure as hell is not like any aircraft I have ever seen. It looks too damn heavy to take off like a Harrier or a Helo. However it works, Eileen was pretty spot on in its description. I wonder what it looks like inside...*

Having worked on aircraft for close to the entirety of his adult life, and with being a licensed pilot on single-engine, fixed-wing aircraft... he's mesmerized by the spacecraft.

I wonder how hard it is to fly that rock. I mean, I know they are from the future, but could it really be all that different? Ben thinks quizzically.

Hell, they could have made flight easier over the years... then again, maybe not. He double guesses the difficulty as he thinks about the advancements of the weapons and the fact the 1,410 years had passed him by.

Before Ben realizes it, the three of them stop, with Fuller, Gomez, and the others having caught up with them, stopping next to him.

Realizing that he was in a daze from staring at the spaceship, he steadies himself.

Stay focused, Ben! Don't go off into la-la land and start daydreaming!

Ben notices that the man and woman are now facing them, only several feet away, and the other group that had been there had already begun to break apart and walk away.

Ben sees the two of them to be relatively short people. Not a super kind of short, but just shorter than Eileen. He finds it curious as to why the two of them are of the same size, but have different builds. The man, Mahoney, is just as his Uncle had described him. He looks stoic and robotic, but also calculating. He also has that grunt and recon look to him.

Definitely don't underestimate that one...

Ben looks at the woman, who is slightly shorter than Eileen. Alicia Burke is also exactly how his Uncle and Eileen had described her. She is lean, like Mahoney, but slender. She has a lighter complexion than Mahoney and bright blue eyes. He began to see why so many people spoke so highly of her. She was attractive and emitted confidence, as she looked up to the new group of them... armed and outnumbering the two of them. She didn't seem to be bothered by the weapons and the nine versus two odds.

Probably shouldn't underestimate her, either...

"Hello, again. Sheriff Steven Reilly and Deputy Eileen Rivera." Sergeant Burke says. "Welcome back and it's good to see that you brought friends."

Wow? Really? She didn't just remember their names, but their full names and titles. Yeah, definitely don't underestimate these two...

"Good morning, Sergeant Burke. Staff Sergeant Mahoney, nice to talk to you again too." Uncle Steven replies.

"Hello, Staff Sergeant Mahoney and Sergeant Burke." Eileen says, as her eyes linger a little longer on Burke, eyeing her suspiciously.

Sergeant Burke smiles, "Alicia is fine, still... Eileen. I did actually think of a couple questions for you. I was hoping that you would come back."

This seems to catch Eileen of guard, with her response being, "Oh, really? Okay... good."

"My apologies if we look like a daunting force, with our rifles and guns and there being nine of us. Recent events have taught us to not travel in such small numbers as we met last time. I assure you that we just came back here to conversate with you all." Uncle Steven says, as he extends his hand.

Mahoney takes his Uncle's hand, and Ben braces to see his Uncle wince in pain, having heard of their strength. Ben waits and notices no change in demeanor. After shaking his hand, he shakes Burke's hand.

"Thanks for going easy on me with the handshake this time, Alicia." Uncle Steven replies, as they release.

Alicia Burke smiles in response. "Of course. And my apologies on our last encounter. It was my first time speaking with people from this Earth. And I'm sure that your kind has been through so much, as of recent. It's bloody understandable for you to want to travel in larger numbers. That's very intelligent of you, Sheriff Reilly."

Wow! This woman's mind is like a steel trap. He thinks as he looks over to Mahoney. *I'm sure his is too, with those calculating and conniving eyes of his...*

Ben then looks at what Mahoney and Burke are wearing. Their clothing looked normal enough, just a little on the dark side with their black utility pants, military style boots, navy-blue short sleeve shirts, and body armor. Well, what at least Ben assumed was body armor, with added compartments to them.

He then looks to their right arms, which hold their MECCUs.

They only appear to be about six inches long and maybe an inch thick... Mobile Extremity Communications and Control Units. Ben thinks, as he recalls what Burke had explained to Eileen what the acronym stood for.

They don't look to be all that dangerous... but by the looks of their lack of concern with all of our guns, I'm betting that those MECCUs can do a good amount of damage.

"I'm glad that we were not misperceived as threatening. We would hate to have a confrontation over a simple misunderstanding." Uncle Steven replies.

Burke simply smiles and nods and Mahoney doesn't say a word. Ben took their silence as not really seeing *them* as a threat at all.

After an awkward moment of silence, Eileen's the first one to speak. "So, Alicia. You said you had some questions for us."

Sergeant Alicia Burke smiles and then nods. "Yes... I had two main questions. Firstly, I was curious if anyone knew if Dr. Theodore Harris survived? Based on our understanding of your *Blue Hole Radius*, we thought it unlikely... but thought it would be ideal to ask. He did reshape the world of Earth One and was the catalyst that led to the technologies that brought my people to Earth Two."

Eileen looks to Ben, and he shakes his head. "A friend of ours, Alexander Mathis, was there when everything happened, and he said only a few of them survived. He mentioned something about people turning into spaghetti before they disappeared."

Ben could see the disappointment on her face.

"Just as we expected. And yes, the phenomenon known as the *spaghettification* phenomena. We are very much aware of this scenario with modern science." Burke replies.

Modern science... it almost makes it sound like we are obsolete.

"You said, Doctor Alexander Mathis is alive, correct? He was a Theoretical Physicist on the SXS Program." Sergeant Burke asks.

Ben nods slowly. "Yes, that's our Alexander. He's back home with little orphaned girls that we found out on the road. They needed a place to stay. So we took them in, and Alexander has taken a real shine to them."

"That turn of events has sound logic to it, according to Dr.

Alexander Mathis's background previous to the *Blue Hole Radius*." Staff Sergeant Mahoney interjects.

Ben looks over at Mahoney, "I suppose it does."

How much do they know about us? Geez! They know Alexander's family background. Do they know about the rest of ours?

"Well that is a very wise decision of your group. You will have the means to repopulate the area once this situation is resolved." Staff Sergeant Mahoney adds.

This gets a quick look from Sergeant Burke.

"Just what do you mean it was a wise decision? Are you inferring that we are going to use those girls to repopulate, Mahoney?" Uncle Steven asks, sternly and directly.

Mahoney's gaze narrows. "It's Staff Sergeant Mahoney, Sheriff Reilly."

"If you say so, but I don't know many good leaders that see little girls as simply baby makers." Uncle Steven replies.

Mahoney doesn't say a word, but instead stares at his Uncle, while his Uncle stares right back at him.

"Sheriff, as I said before... Staff Sergeant Mahoney has a dry tone and can come off sounding similar to that of a drone. Please excuse his unintended offense. He surely did not mean that you use the girls to repopulate. Likely, Staff Sergeant Mahoney only meant that the girls would be beneficial in the survival of the human race, toward the future." Burke replies.

She then looks to Mahoney, "Is that an accurate statement, Brian?"

Ben watches as the man's gaze is shifted and focused toward Burke, with much more of a softness. "Yes." He says and nods back to Ben, Uncle Steven, Eileen, and the others. "I'm still getting used to how your kind speaks and expresses knowledge."

How we speak... it seemed pretty straightforward to me...

"Alicia?" Eileen says, getting everyone's attention. "You said you had two questions. What was the second?"

Burke nods and smiles. "I did have a second main question and the sunset follow question. You already aptly answered the second question. Informing me that there were several known survivors from the original SXS Program, with Dr. Alexander Mathis being one of them. Do you happen to know the other ones? And the subsidiary question was how quickly did your world change after time had ceased to be stalled for the last 1,410 years?"

Ben scratches the back of his head and the group just kind of looks at each other.

After a moment, Ben opens his mouth. "I'm not sure who the other survivors were from the SXS Project. Alexander might recall, but I'm not sure if they'd still be alive up to this point. As for our world, once time caught up with us... or we caught up with time... or whatever..."

"It was hell on Earth for a good while, Alicia. It was literally like living in the Book of Revelation. But seeing as you all are here to help us and prodigy safety, security, and salvation... I guess all is well that ends well." Eileen replies, interrupting him.

Shit... she's getting pissed, again.

"That we are, Eileen... that we are." Burke responds back.

Uncle Steven nods and smiles. "Well alright then. If that's your reasoning for coming back to Earth One, our world, then you won't mind answering a few of our questions in return."

"Of course not, Sheriff Reilly, ask away. Did you want to know more about the advancements in medicine?" Burke replies and questions.

"Actually, I was more curious as to why Captain Jackson found it necessary to shut down our communication capabilities here on Earth One. It seems that since we last met, none of us have been able to communicate through our various devices and the SuperNet is down." Uncle Steven says, without really asking a question.

Ben, as well as the others, notice the glance that Burke gives Mahoney.

"And to make matters more confusing and concerning... it seems that one of those *sleepers* that you all warned us about, may have accidentally gone off, in an area north of us, wiping out a great deal of people and not much else." Uncle Steven adds.

Burke's eyes go wide and she exhales through her nose.

Ben's Uncle doesn't wait for a response but presses forward. "We have two main ideas of what the *sleepers* are and just need to confirm which theory is right. One is that it's a viral agent, a biological weapon of sorts. The second one, which my money's on, is that a *sleeper* is a futuristic bomb that sets off an explosion that somehow only targets humans."

Ben can see that the smile is no longer on Burke's face. She looks over to Mahoney for direction, but, instead, he speaks. "That was an unfortunate event that occurred up north of here. Your kind was warned to stay away from the *sleepers*, to avoid such a detonation. Unfortunately, they did not heed our warning at the military installation upon our first arrival on Earth One. As for the communications, Captain Abraham Jackson thought it necessary to restrict your ways of communicating, to avoid misinformation and widespread panic upon our arrival."

Son of a bitch... Alexander was right! It was all them! The comms, the SuperNet, Edwards Air Force Base, the sleepers!

"So, it was you guys! Why?!" Eileen blurts out.

Before anyone can answer or step in, the Leviathan comes quickly into view and is over the dried-up lakebed in a matter of seconds.

Damn, that ship is huge. And double damn... it's fast as hell! Ben thinks as he's astonished by the massive spaceship.

"It looks like we'll get to ask the infamous Captain Jackson that ourselves, Eileen." Uncle Steven adds.

Burke's eyes go from the sky to his Uncle. "Sheriff. I highly advise that you don't instigate the Captain. He has been known to have a short temperament. You must trust that we have the human species' best intention in mind."

"Bullshit." Eileen blurts out.

"Yeah, I'm calling bullshit too. The road to hell is paved with good intentions." Ben adds.

As Ben says this, he can hear and feel the men and women behind him readying their weapons.

"You know nothing of what you speak of. You have been asleep, yourselves, for over 1,400 years! The world is not as you knew it. Humanity is not as you knew it." Burke says sharply toward them.

She turns back to the Leviathan that had just landed behind Burke and Mahoney. Ben watches as part of the ship opens up and a levitating platform exits the ship, heading toward them. Ben can see close to a dozen men on the platform, with one man in front.

That has got to be Jackson, up front. How the crap does that levitating platform work? And what's that shimmer around those men on that platform thing? Ben thinks to himself as the platform nears within fifty feet.

The platform doesn't make much noise as it lands just fifty feet away from all of them, and the smaller spacecraft. Ben does feel the gust of wind as the platform touches down on the dried-up lakebed. Once the platform is on the ground, the dozen men stand still on the platform, staring at Burke, Mahoney, and Ben's group.

In a hushed voice over her shoulder, Burke warns Ben and the others. "Don't start a fight you cannot win, Sheriff Reilly. Because your kind won't win against us. There are events that have occurred that you know nothing of."

"That may be so, Alicia. But what events we do know does not look good for your kind." Eileen snaps back, not in a hushed tone.

"Is everything alright, Staff Sergeant Mahoney and Sergeant Burke?" The man in the middle questions.

"Yes, Captain Jackson. Everything's in order here and being handled appropriately." Burke replies and Ben watches Mahoney nod in confirmation, rather quickly.

They are scared of him. It's written all over their faces and their movements. What's worse, I think he knows it and I think he likes it. Ben thinks, getting a good look at Captain Abraham Jackson.

He's about the same height as Burke and Mahoney, maybe even just as tall as Eileen. He looks to be very close to Eileen's age, a few years younger than himself.

But this guy's supposed to be 74 years old...

He wears the same style fatigues, but his short sleeve shirt is solid black, contrasting his pinkish colored skin. He has dark brown hair and bright blue eyes, similar to his own. He notices that Eileen's description was spot on, once again, with Abraham Jackson looking stoic and stern, and everything military.

Everything about this guy screams power hungry and dictatorship. Yeah, that crap ain't going to fly...

Ben steps alongside, and in between Burke and Mahoney, with a couple of feet gap between each person. Still inspecting the Captain of the Leviathan from Earth Two, Abraham Jackson.

"So, you are the great and powerful, Abraham Jackson? The man that traveled across the stars... here to save us from ourselves and show us the right way to live?" Ben asks the man in front of the other eleven men, all of which are to his sides on the platform that's encased in some sort of shimmering, translucent film.

Abraham Jackson narrows his gaze and focuses on Ben, and Ben sees him clench his jaw.

"Yes. I'm Captain Abraham Jackson and I did come here... with my fellow Federalists and the Leviathan to usher in a new era of strength and abundance for the human species." Captain Jackson replies, sternly in a matter-of-fact sort of way.

"That's a nice line, Abraham. The whole hearts and minds approach, I take it? Did you have that approach with Edwards Air Force, before you dropped a *sleeper* on them, killing hundreds of thousands?" Ben questions the Captain of the Leviathan.

Abraham Jackson tilts his head in what looks to Ben like confusion and anger.

This guy's not used to being talked to like this. He definitely doesn't like not being referred to with his title, Ben thinks as he smiles.

"Sir, they pieced together what the *sleepers* are and what happened at Edwards. They also know about the disrupted communications. They have a primary member of the SXS Program in the settlement." Staff Sergeant Mahoney explains.

"That is apparently evident, now... Staff Sergeant." Captain Jackson says sourly.

Ben hears the clicking of a hammer on a revolver and his Uncle speak. "That's about enough out of you, Mahoney. Another word or if you reach for your fancy bracelet... you're about to have a new hole in that head of yours."

Ben looks over to his Uncle, seeing that he has his revolver pointed at the back of Mahoney's head.

He then sees movement out of the corner of his eye, to his right, where Burke is.

"No, No... Alicia. Same goes for you. Don't you dare move." Eileen says to Burke, in an eerily calm and angry voice.

Ben looks to his right and sees Burke freeze, going for her MECCU, and sees Eileen with her M&P Shield pointed at the back of her head.

Well, looks like we are doing stuff today... Ben thinks as he hears multiple rifles racking and coming to the ready behind him. *And it looks like I'm at the head of it all... Well shit, I guess it's going to be one of those days...*

He looks back to Abraham Jackson. "So Abraham... It seems that you have likely committed an act of genocide here on our Earth and that you have come here under false pretenses... with promises of grandeur."

"To whom do I have the pleasure of speaking with?" Captain Abraham Jackson replies, without answering the question.

"My name's Ben Reilly. And I've got to say, it doesn't really seem like a pleasure to meet you." Ben replies, which gets another clench of Abraham Jackson's jaw.

"And who might your associates be? So that we can have more cordial communications." Captain Jackson replies.

There's silence behind Ben and then Mahoney speaks. "The one behind me is Sheriff Steven Reilly. He's the Sheriff of their settlement."

"Another word, Mahoney and I will make good on my word. Don't press your luck. You don't need to die here today..." Uncle Steven replies with a hardened sound to his voice.

"So, I take it that your avoidance of the question on genocide is confirmation that you committed the heinous crime." Ben says, pressing the question of genocide onto the Captain again.

"Is this settlement the one that you look after, Sheriff Steven Reilly?" Captain Jackson questions, gesturing toward the area of Big Bear.

This asshat is ignoring me, just to piss me off. This smug son of bitch.

"No, it's not, Captain Abraham Jackson." His Uncle replies.

"Then from which settlement do you hail from?" Captain Jackson asks.

His Uncle stays silent and Ben knows why. Giving out that sort of information can put their people's lives in jeopardy.

Unfortunately, Christian speaks up from behind Ben, "We are from Crestline! Why?!"

This gets a look from Ben over his shoulder and he hears his Uncle swear under his breath, "Shit."

Dammit Christian!... We're going to have to have a discussion on OPSEC, if and when we get out of this.

Before Ben realizes what is happening in front of him, Captain Jackson raises his right hand, and his MECCU opens up instantly, with a mechanical arm coming out to the right of it. Within a few seconds, the arm forms into a small cannon, a blue orb forms just outside of the small wrist cannon. He points it in their direction, and the blue orb is there one second and gone the next.

Ben looks to Eileen, with Burke standing in front of her and Eileen still holding a gun to her head. He then looks to his Uncle, who's holding a gun to Mahoney's head out in front of him.

Ben watches as a shock wave seems to hit Mahoney, and then he slumps down to the ground.

"My condolences, Sergeant Burke... for Staff Sergeant Mahoney and yourself. I will not have these *barbarians* speak to me in such a manner, nor will I have these *cretins* thinking they can best me."

Burke looks at her fallen fellow Federalist. "Brian! No!" She then looks back at Captain Jackson.

Ben notices she reaches her left hand over to her MECCU, tapping it several times. Eileen doesn't do anything to stop her, likely still in shock from seeing a blue orb just come out of Abraham Jackson's MECCU.

At that moment, another blue orb forms at the end of Captain Jackson's wrist cannon, extending from his MECCU. Ben also notices that several other blue orbs appear from the other Federalists' MECCUs... all pointed at Ben, Eileen, his Uncle, and the rest of them.

"Oh shit!" Ben blurts out.

He sees, out of the corner of his eye, Burke sticking out her hand in a *Stop* motion.

Ben instinctively pulls out his PX4 Storm but isn't able to raise it quick enough. Ben's eyes go wide as he sees the blue orbs flying toward his Uncle, Eileen, Burke, himself, and everyone else behind him.

He cannot look away, and time seems to slow down as the blue orbs reach them... only to stop a few feet in front of them and disperse into a radiant blue wave over and to the side of them.

He blinks, confused as to what's happening, his sidearm still only halfway raised up to shoot at Abraham Jackson and the other Federalists on the platform.

Everyone else must have been just as confused and shocked, because no one says a word, simply staring in shock and confusion.

He watches as the dispersing blue wave around them gives way to a translucent curved wall, just a few feet in front of them, looking very similar to the shimmering translucent film surrounding Abraham Jackson's platform. Only with this one starting exactly where Sergeant Alicia Burke's hand is out in a *Stop* motion.

What the shit!...

18

EILEEN RIVERA

EILEEN WATCHES as the radiant blue waves hit the translucent shied, bouncing off and dispersing into a wave all around them. She blinks a few times, registering what just happened.

We're still alive? Eileen thinks as she watches radiant blue waves hit a shimmering barrier that she can only describe as a force field.

She had truly thought they were about to die, and her heart was still beating at a rapid pace.

She looks over to Ben to make sure that he's still there. She then looks to Steven and then to the body of Mahoney that's laying on the ground. The body didn't look like it had any blood pouring from it or any wounds of any kind. In fact, Mahoney looked like he was sleeping in a very awkward position with his eyes closed.

"Is that what a *sleeper* does? I thought it was a bigger explosion..." Eileen says aloud, not even realizing she was talking.

"No, Eileen. Those are a much smaller version of what *sleepers* do. We call them dozers and those specific dozers are referred to as IMDs... Now! If you wouldn't mind, could you start shooting your antique weapons at the maniac that just killed another one of my friends?!" Alicia Burke explains quickly and then shouts at her.

"Wait, what?" Eileen pulls her M&P Shield away from Burke's

head, bringing it down to her side and looking at the translucent field in front of them with blue orbs still hitting it, dispersing bright blue waves everywhere around them, but none of the blue orbs were penetrating the shimmering shield and hitting them, turning them into sleeping dead versions of themselves.

"What about your force field or whatever it is? Won't our bullets destroy it?!" Eileen questions, worried about the shimmering shield that's currently saving their lives.

"No, Eileen. We designed Armor Enclosures for defensive measures with offensive capabilities. Things can't get in, but things and people can get out. But more importantly, we found out that your antique weapons can damage our Armor Enclosures... over time. Similar to the damage that our IMDs inflict upon our AEs. But your projectiles result in a much more hastened deterioration of our AEs. So, if you don't mind... start shooting those ancient pieces of iron at those men trying to kill your group and myself!" Alicia Burke explains in a very frustrated and louder voice than she has heard from the small woman.

IMDs? AEs? Projectiles? What on God's green Earth is this woman talking about?! And wasn't I just holding a gun up to her head? Why the hell is she helping us?! Eileen thinks and then looks back down at Mahoney's lifeless body.

::Crack::

::Crack::Crack::Crack::

::Crack::

Eileen jumps from being startled by the gunfire that's erupting right next to her. She looks to her left and sees Ben and Steven with their rifles pointed toward Captain Jackson and the rest of the men on the platform.

::Crack::

::Crack::Crack::Crack::

::Crack::

::Crack::Crack::Crack::

::Crack::Crack::Crack::

::Crack::

She watches as Ben and Steven shoot across the fifty-foot gap between themselves and the people trying to kill them. She watches as the bullets go through their side of the force field and hit the other force field, which is encasing the entire platform. After a few seconds she sees that a bright yellow line is starting to form where Ben and Steven are hitting Captain Jackson's force field.

::Crack::

::Crack::Crack::Crack::

::Crack::Crack::Crack::

::Crack::

She watches as the bright yellow line on the platform's force field becomes bigger and splinters off in different directions. She then notices more yellow lines appearing.

Those are lines... those are cracks... She thinks as she inspects bright yellow lines forming on Captain Jackson's force field, with the contrast of blue waves hitting their own force field.

"Any day Eileen... you heard Burke! Our bullets have an effect on their force fields or whatever the hell she called them!" Ben shouts at her.

She looks back over at him, as he hits his magazine release and the magazine dropping to the ground. He reaches into the pocket on the front of his vest and pulls another magazine out and slams it into his rifle, and the bolt goes home.

"Hey Burke! Did you guys figure this out about your force fields over at Edwards Air Force Base?! Is that why you guys killed them?!" Ben shouts at her over the gun fire from the others behind her, who have now stepped up next to her and are also firing at the barrier that encases Captain Jackson and the other Federalists.

"Yes, that's correct. Their reaction enraged Captain Jackson and he utilized one of our last *sleepers* on that military installation. It was rather rash and wasteful, considering why we are here." Burke says back in a loud voice.

"I fucking knew it! I knew we couldn't trust your people!" Ben shouts back.

"Deputy Reilly, you must understand that..." Burke replies.

"Screw that shit! We'll talk more about what your people are up to, once we get out of this mess! How much longer will your force field last Burke?!" Ben shouts back at her.

She watches as he raises his rifle, aiming back toward Captain Jackson and the others. He then looks back at her.

"Eileen. Wake up! We are still alive, and we are still in this! Get your rifle up and let's put some hurt into these assholes that are trying to turn us into sleeping dead people!"

She looks at him and then snaps out of her haze. She holsters her M&P shield and then unslings her rifle, clicking off the safety and aiming toward Captain Jackson, directly.

::Crack::

::Crack::Crack::Crack::

::Crack::Crack::Crack::

::Crack::

::Crack::Crack::Crack::

::Crack::Crack::Crack::

::Crack::

"Now that's more like it!" Ben shouts at her. "Hey Burke! You didn't answer my question. How long do we have until your force field goes down?!"

Looking over Burke's shoulder, she sees her tap her MECCU as she keeps her right hand extended out, holding up her force field. She then sees a small holographic screen materialize above her MECCU, with a lot of different diagrams and numbers displayed on it.

"My AE's at 63%! We have maybe five more minutes until it collapses! Likely closer to three minutes!" Burke shouts back.

::Crack::

::Crack::Crack::Crack::

::Crack::Crack::Crack::

::Crack::

"Three minutes is better than nothing! Let's hope their shield goes down before yours does!" Ben shouts out between firing his shots.

::Crack::

::Crack::Crack::Crack::

::Crack::Crack::Crack::

::Crack::

"Hey Burke! Does your spaceship have this sort of force field too!" Steven asks her.

"Yes, Sheriff Reilly! It does!" Burke replies.

"Alright then!" He shouts back over the gun fire.

Steven then stops firing and turns around to face the rest of the members of the DFC unit.

"Alright! Here's the plan. Once you need to reload, step back and let those behind you get some shots in! And while all that is happening, make sure you follow Sergeant Burke's movements as she guides us to her spaceship!"

This receives shouts and nods of understanding from the DFC unit members.

Steven then looks back to Burke. "Burke, slowly lead the way to your ship... so that we have a chance of surviving more than three minutes!"

She nods and begins a slow sidestep as Eileen and the rest of the group slowly move along with her to stay behind the protection of her force field.

::Crack::

::Crack::Crack::Crack::

::Crack::

"Alicia! How much longer until our bullets break through their force field?!" Eileen shouts at her over the gunfire.

"Likely any moment, Eileen. But remember they still have their own personal AEs from their individual MECCUs!" Burke replies back.

Shit! They have more force fields for us to get through... Eileen thinks as she looks across to Captain Jackson, who's staring fiercely at all of them, continuously firing those blue orbs at them.

She can see the frustration on his face as the blue orbs from the MECCUs turn into radiant blue waves, washing over Alicia Burke's force field. She looks to his MECCU, as another blue orb materializes and is launched at Eileen and their group.

As it hits the barrier and turns into another bright blue wave, she looks back to Captain Jackson and his MECCU.

That's it!

"Hey Alicia, if our bullets hurt your force fields, do they damage your MECCUs too!?" Eileen shouts at her over the gunfire, making sure to continue moving with Burk's pace toward her spaceship.

::Crack::Crack::Crack::

::Crack::

::Crack::Crack::Crack::

::Crack::Crack::Crack::

::Crack::

Burke turns her head to look at Eileen with a look of thought. "I'm not sure! It has not been tested against your antique weapons. But it stands up to reason that they could damage it."

Eileen nods and looks to the spiderweb of bright yellow lines forming on the force field that's protecting Captain Abraham Jackson and the rest of his small group of Federalists.

"It's worth a shot and will stop them from using more of their force fields... if they don't use them before that one goes down." Eileen replies.

"Hey Ben! Steven! Once their shield's down, aim for their MECCUs on their right arms! That may give us a chance at stopping their second set of force fields from being able to be used!" Eileen shouts at them.

Ben looks over at her and smiles. "Beauty and brains! Nice thinking Eileen!"

He then looks over his shoulder at the DFC members behind him. "You heard the woman. Start aiming for their big ass bracelets now, so when we break through, we already hit them."

Eileen looks back at Captain Abraham Jackson who has stopped firing and is looking directly at her. He then looks over his own force field, likely realizing the frailty of its current condition. He then looks down at his MECCU and Eileen can see a small screen materialize.

Upon looking at him, he shoots another glance at Eileen. He then begins to step back through his men, and other Federalists take his place at the front of the platform. She can see him make his way to the back of the group. She watches as he taps his MECCU and puts his hand out in front of him, with the same *Stop* motion that Burke had done to activate her own force field.

Shit! He either heard us or figured it out on his own. He had to have heard us over the gunfire. We are pretty damn close to each other. She thinks as she looks over the other men of the group of Federalists. She realizes that none of them are putting up their own force fields yet.

Why hasn't he given them the order to do the same? She thinks as she stares at the man in the back of the group with his own force field up, but the rest of his men are still shooting their blue orbs at herself and the others.

Did he hear us? He had to have heard us... we are literally only fifty feet apart... Is he now testing the durability of the MECCUs? That's insane!

At that moment, a piece of the force field, in the middle of the bright yellow web of cracks, disappears, right where Captain Jackson was just standing.

"Aim for their right arms!" Ben shouts.

With the Federalist only being fifty feet away, the shots are not difficult ones to make accurately.

Eileen hears one of the men scream in pain, as his MECCU shatters on his blood-soaked forearm. The man screams out in pain quickly, with the next few rounds hitting him in his vest and one hitting him in the head.

"Their vests are solid shields, but those MECCUs are not reinforced! Aim for their arms and then their heads!" Ben shouts.

::Crack::Crack::Crack::

::Crack::

::Crack::Crack::Crack::

::Crack::Crack::Crack::

::Crack::

Seeing that the entire front area of the force field is now shattered on the ground around the front of the platform, she aims at one of the men standing in front of Captain Jackson. She sees as he goes to reach for his MECCU, but a little too late.

::Crack::Crack::Crack::

The man screams out in agony as his arm is now missing his right hand and his MECCU is shattered and splintered in his forearm. The next shot puts the man out of his misery and he drops to the floor.

::Crack::

::Crack::Crack::Crack::

::Crack::

Eileen watches as the man right next to him falls, who's also blocking Captain Jackson, then the man to his left falls as well. She pauses and looks over at Ben and Steven.

They're going for Captain Jackson too, taking out the men in front of him. She thinks to herself. *If we take him out here and now maybe this madness will end... like cutting off the head of a snake.*

Captain Jackson is looking directly at her, and she thinks he can read her mind about what she's thinking.

"Lieutenant Meads! Get us out of here, now! The rest of you! Get your personal AEs up! We are done here!" Captain Abraham Jackson shouts to his men.

Two more Federalists drop before the rest of them put their hands out in front of them, with their own shimmering force fields appearing.

Eileen and the others continue firing at the remaining five Federalists on the platform, which is now rising off the ground. The platform quickly retreats back into the Leviathan, and Eileen can see yellow lines forming on their personal force fields.

"Dammit! He's getting away!" Ben shouts out as the platform recedes behind the closing gap of the Leviathan.

"Hey Burke! How much fire power does the ship have on it?!" Steven asks.

"The Leviathan only has one *sleeper* remaining in its arsenal and Captain Jackson will be reluctant to use it." Alicia replies.

"Why? And what else does he have at his disposal?!" Steven snaps at her.

"The last *sleeper* that we have…" She pauses for a moment. "The last *sleeper* that he has holds an extinction radius of 500 miles… If he uses it, our plans here are useless and our species will likely die out. However, there are a great number of CSDs onboard the Leviathan. I'm unsure as to how many." Alicia explains.

"Well, at least he won't use that *sleeper* on us like Edwards. But what the crap are CSDs Burke?!" Ben asks her.

"Carrier Stationary Dozers. They are much stronger than the IMDs or Individual MECCU Dozers." Alicia replies.

"Well, isn't that just peachy fucking perfect." Ben responds.

Eileen glances back to Alicia and then looks to the rectangular looking spaceship.

"Will your ship protect us from the blue orbs from that ship?" She asks, pointing at the Leviathan.

"Somewhat, but not long term. I would advise we get into my Security Tactical Assault and Recovery Unit and relocate to a different region." Alicia says.

"Let me guess… it's called a STARU?" Ben asks Burke in a sarcastic tone.

"Who the hell cares, Ben! Move into the damn ship now!" Eileen blurts out.

"She's right! We are sitting ducks out here against that big ass spaceship!" Steven says as he makes the small dash to the opening of the STARU.

The rest of the DFC unit members follow suit, followed by Eileen, then Ben, and then Alicia Burke. As Eileen enters the STARU, she sees that it's rather spacious inside and there are what can be described as very large windshields on both ends of the rectangular spaceship, where the coned ends are. They remind her of the viewing areas on tour ships that take you to go see underwater creatures. The sort of ones where you can see the whole ocean around you, at the bottom of the viewing area. Only these viewing areas are to each side of the spaceship.

She watches as Alicia walks over to the wall directly across for the opening of the spaceship. The panel is covered in circuits, panels, knobs, controls, and other items that she's unfamiliar with. She watches as she presses a button and she feels a *whoosh* as the opening closes behind her. She turns around to see that the opening is gone, and they were all completely inside of the spaceship.

Eileen sees a light hit the wall where the opening just was. She turns to see that the light was coming from a large screen that materialized in front of Alicia.

"Just what exactly is the plan Sergeant Burke?" Steven asks her.

"Well, firstly Sheriff Reilly... I'm disabling our locator module, so the Leviathan won't know exactly where we are going." Alicia replies.

"And just where are we going?" Ben questions.

"I cannot tell you yet..." Alicia replies.

"And just why the hell not?" Ben asks.

Eileen watches her tap on the materialized screen like it was a solid screen. After a moment she sees a red light flashing on the upper right corner of the screen and then the flash is gone.

"There... Now I can tell you. It would have defeated the purpose of disabling the locator module, just to tell them where we were going. This STARU also has a recording feature with audio, which is now also disabled." Alicia explains.

"So, they can see and hear us in here?" Eileen asks, looking around the large railroad car spaceship, with two very large viewing ports on the ends.

"Not anymore, they can't. Now take a seat please. All of you." Alicia instructs.

The group of them look around and don't see anywhere to sit down.

"Where?" Eileen asks.

Alicia looks around the spaceship. "Ah, yes... right." She says as she turns around, rotates a dial, and hits several buttons along the wall next to the transparent screen.

Eileen hears the sound of a soft hum of a machine and she looks around the spaceship to see two rows of six seats form near each viewing port at each end of the ship.

"That should be enough for everyone. Now please sit down and strap in. Captain Jackson may be able to get a few shots off prior to our retreat." Alicia says.

As if to prove her point, the spaceship rumbles and sways. Eileen looks to large viewing ports and sees a radiant blue wave disperse down the huge windshields.

Eileen and the others rush over to their seats. Eileen goes for the end seat to her right, with Ben following her. She sits down in the front row, far left. Ben sits next to her, with Steven sitting next to him. She fumbles for her seat belt, as another shock wave hits the spaceship. The rest of the DFC unit members all grab seats as well.

"That should be a sufficient hiding place for a short time." Alicia says from behind her.

Eileen twists her head to see Alicia tapping on the transparent screen that now has a map of what looks to be North America. She then turns back around to see the Leviathan directly in front of them.

She watches as several blue orbs materialize out of very large cannons in front of the massive spaceship. Eileen's eyes go wide as the orbs are released from the cannons and she grips Ben's hand tightly.

Oh my gosh! No!

She exhales in relief as their spacecraft begins rapidly moving backwards, or at least backwards from Eileen's perspective.

Their spaceship speeds away from the dried-up lakebed of Big Bear and she sees the Leviathan become small very quickly. She then gets a view of the valley below the mountains. An area where she had to pass through to get to Crestline, close to two months ago.

She looks down to the bottom part of the huge windshield and sees the highways and freeways, thinking she can see the area where Stephanie and Eddie had died a couple of months ago, at the hands of two escaped inmates from Patton State Hospital.

She strains her eyes to try and figure out which area is Redlands, where her father used to live... before he was killed by drunk thieves.

They had been his neighbors that had turned on her father on the first day of this whole *Blue Hole Radius.*

Before she can discern where her former home was, the area is gone and they are over another mountain range.

The remembrance of her lost friends and her father pains her heart. She had not thought of this too much in the last week or so. At least not in a saddening or tragic way. Most of her thoughts of her friends and family had been of fond memories over the last couple of weeks. She felt as though she was truly beginning to heal. But going over the area where they died brought back the memories of how they died, and how cruel humanity could turn so quickly.

With the immediate threat gone and the view during their voyage giving way to old memories, she gets lost in thought. *I miss you dad... I wish you were still here with me... I know you would know what to do. Everything seems so crazy and insane now. Where do we go from here?* She thinks as though she's speaking to her father in her mind. *I wish you could answer me from wherever you are now. I just wish you could tell me what to do. How to fix all of this crazy ass mess of a world we now live in.*

She looks out the viewport to see the mountain range give way to a forest that's larger than she has ever seen. She looks to her left and right, out the large viewing port, just to find more trees and more hills and mountain ranges of trees. Every now and then she sees a lake or a river.

What she does not see is any sign of civilization or human life. A realization forms into her mind and she continues to see a vast amount of nature that she's usually only accustomed to in National Parks or mountain ranges.

She turns her head to see Alicia sitting in a chair in front of the transparent screen, looking at the map on the screen.

"Are we outside of the *Radius,* Alicia?" Eileen asks her.

Alicia turns to look at Eileen. "Yes, Eileen, we are currently outside of your *Blue Hole Radius* and heading southwest."

"Oh..." Eileen replies and looks back to the large viewing port on her side of the spaceship.

"We're outside of the *Radius*? Everything looks so green... but there's no sign of human life out here. It's like we were never here." Eileen says aloud for all to hear.

"Yes, Eileen. But you must remember that Humans haven't been on this Earth for roughly 300 years... aside from those of *your kind* that were trapped within the *Blue Hole Radius*." Alicia explains.

"Oh..." Is Eileen's only response.

"So, where exactly are we going Burke?" Ben chimes in with the question that must be on all of their minds, except for Eileen's. She cannot seem to get over how much nature has retaken the Earth in a relatively short span of time.

I guess 300 years isn't all that small of a timespan. But still... no sign that we existed before this? Eileen thinks to herself.

"We're going to circle the globe and then double back to North America. The hope is to ensure that the Leviathan won't follow us, because this STARU is no match for the Leviathan."

"Is there anyone else left down there... Besides for us that were trapped within the *Radius*?" Eileen asks as she looks back to Alicia.

"No, Eileen. You are the last humans of Earth One." Alicia replies.

"Are you sure?" Eileen questions.

"Yes, Eileen. We did scans prior to landing over the military installation in one of your desert regions within the *Blue Hole Radius*." Alicia explains.

"Oh... wow." Eileen replies and goes back to staring out of the viewing port, now seeing the Pacific Ocean beneath them.

Could it really be true? We're what's left of the human race? I wonder how many of us are actually left. She ponders these questions as she looks at the ocean below the spacecraft as it begins to circle the globe.

19

ALEXANDER MATHIS

"THAT SMELLS REALLY BAD." Isabelle says to her sister and Alexander.

"Stop complaining Izzy. Are you going to complain every time we come outside to feed the animals?" Mia says to her little sister.

"I don't know... is it always going to be so stinky?" Isabelle says and sticks out her tongue at her sister.

Alexander smiles as he watches the two girls. "Well, it will always stink and then again it won't. Over time you'll get used to it... but you are right, Isabelle. The pigs' food is especially stinky."

"See! I told you!" Isabelle shouts at her sister.

"Whatever..." Mia replies.

"Do you know why it stinks more than the grass and hay we feed the sheep, or the chicken feed that we feed the chickens, girls?" Alexander asks them, as they finish dumping the food into the pigs' stall, and move toward the sheep.

Both girls shake their heads no.

"It's because it's scraps of old food. Whatever we have left over from our meals, we dump into a big pot and then we bring it out here." Alexander explains.

"So it's old food?" Mia asks.

"Yes, Mia." Alexander replies.

"That's gross. I don't like leftovers. They don't taste the same as when they're new." Isabelle replies.

"I'd have to agree with you there, Isabelle. But pigs will eat just about anything and they love the stuff we give them. Do you see how fast they eat it up?" Alexander says, pointing back to the piglets.

"Yeah! They're little piggies." Isabelle says, laughing and gets a light chuckle from Mia.

"You're stupid, Izzy." Mia says as she stops laughing.

"Mia, please don't call your sister stupid. It was a funny joke and you know it." Alexander says to her calmly and with a smile.

"Yeah, I guess so." Mia replies and then looks at her little sister. "I'm sorry, Izzy. You aren't stupid."

Isabelle smiles at her big sister. "I know."

Alexander smiles at them. "Alright, you two go check for eggs and put them in your basket. After you're done, let them out for a little while. I'll go let the sheep out to roam and check on the hay in her little area."

"Okay, Alex." Mia says. "Come on, Izzy. Try not to drop any eggs this time."

"Hey! That was an accident, Mia! Don't worry Uncle Alex... I won't drop any!" Isabelle turns back to him and assures him with a big smile.

As they walk a few feet he hears Mia say quietly to her little sister, "You know he isn't our real uncle, right?"

"Well... what else am I supposed to call him? He's a grown up! You calling him just Alex sounds rude, sissy." Isabelle responds.

Mia darts a quick look over her shoulder to see him looking at them and still smiling. Surely embarrassed because she knew he had heard the entire conversation, Mia says quickly, "Fine, whatever. Don't you know how to whisper? Why do you have to be so loud?"

"I know how to whisper!" Isabelle replies.

Alexander shakes his heads and laughs silently as he walks over to the sheep. He lets the sheep out of her side of the larger shed and checks the hay situation.

She looks to be pretty good on food. We may need to see if we can find more at one of the markets or make another trip down the mountain. I wonder if sheep can just eat the wild grass around here... I don't see why not. I'll have to ask Ben and Steven. They might know. I'm still new to this whole raising animals thing.

Alexander then walks over to the smaller shed with their eight chickens, one rooster, and where the two children are.

"So, how'd we make out girls?" Alexander asks.

"We have six eggs, Uncle Alex!" Isabelle responds.

"Yeah, we double checked and there were only six of them..." Mia adds.

Alexander looks down at the watch that Steven had given him. Apparently, Steven liked watches. It made sense to Alexander, considering his age, which wasn't that much older than himself.

"Well, it's only 9:30 in the morning girls. We pulled nine in total yesterday. So, in all honesty, that sounds like a pretty good start to the day." Alexander explains to the girls.

"If you say so, Alex." Mia says and looks at the chickens roaming around them pecking at the ground. "Are we going to have enough food for all of us, Alex? I can skip dinner if it helps Isabelle get more food."

Alexander looks at her and shakes his head and smiles at her. "Mia, you are only a child. If anyone were to miss meals, it would be us adults. But don't worry about that. We are doing pretty good in the food situation. We do need to start a vegetable garden soon though. Maybe later you girls could help me out... I've never made one, but Steven and Ben gave me some tips on how to start."

"Our mom used to have a garden before..." Isabelle starts to say and then turns around to look over the mountain ridge, obviously lost in thought of being reminded of her mom and looking toward her grave.

Poor girls have been through so much. It's a miracle they have made it this far... Alexander thinks to himself.

He watches as Mia turns around with her little sister and puts an arm over her smaller shoulder. Isabelle tilts her head to lean on her big sister.

And they made it this far for a reason. Their parents may not be around to protect them anymore. But we sure are... I sure am.

Alexander sighs, and then forces a smile. "So, you're telling me that you two can show me the ropes on how to build a garden?!"

Isabelle turns around quickly, with tears in her eyes. Her expression turns to one of excitement and she sniffles, wiping her eyes quickly with her forearm and beams a newfound smile. "Yeah! I can show you how to Uncle Alex!"

Mia turns as well and smiles at her little sister and tousles her hair. "You mean, we'll show you Uncle Alex." Mia says and then smiles at Alexander.

Alexander smiles back at them. "What say we go start thinking about some lunch?"

"But you said it's only 9:30 in the morning?" Mia questions.

"Then we'll just call it Brunch. Are you hungry or not?" Alexander says, with a smile.

Mia smiles back and nods.

"What's brunch?!" Isabelle asks.

Alexander laughs lightly. "Come on. Let's go find out."

"Okay!" Isabelle shouts and trots off toward the back of the cabin.

Alexander turns to look over the mountainside, thinking he heard something or feels a strong gust of wind. His eyes go wide as he sees a small aircraft start to fly over the valley with blue rays streaming after it... or even chasing after it.

The aircraft is there and then it's gone, making a quick turn. He looks to see where the blue rays came from, if anywhere aside from the small aircraft... unsure of what exactly they were. He looks to his left and peers, seeing nothing for a moment. Then he sees the Leviathan come into view, reaching the point where the small aircraft diverged and took off in a different direction.

Alexander watches in amazement and confusion as the massive spacecraft just sits there, as if deciding what to do.

What's going on?! Was that the small spacecraft that Sergeant Burke and Staff Sergeant Mahoney had over in Big Bear? Was the Leviathan shooting at them? If so, why would they just stop in their pursuit? And why would they shoot at their own people?

Isabelle has taken notice of what's happening by this point. "Alex? What's that up there? Are those aliens?"

Alexander sighs with the realization of the girls possibly being in imminent danger.

He turns to her with a forced smile. "No Mia. I mean, yes... Those are the people from Earth Two. The ones we have been talking about."

"That spaceship looks mean, Alex. What should we do?" Mia replies.

Alexander watches as the Leviathan stops hovering high in the sky over the mountain ridge close to the valley, shifting direction north... toward them.

"I'm not sure, little one..." Alexander replies.

This does not seem good. Not at all... Something happened. That's for certain. And whatever it was, it looks like Captain Jackson is unhappy with someone. Considering that the others left to go speak with Sergeant Burke and Staff Sergeant Mahoney, it's not a far stretch to assume that the Reilly's and the others were involved...

"Alex, it's coming this way. What do we do?" Mia says with a slight sound of panic in her voice.

Alexander looks over at her. "Go head off inside and make some sandwiches for the three of us. Make some extras for later. We may have to go on a trip."

"What?! Why?!" Mia says with obvious concern in her voice.

"Mia..." Alexander says, putting his hands on her shoulders. "I need you to try and stay calm and be strong for your little sister. I won't let anything happen to the two of you. Not while I'm still alive. I promise."

Mia looks shaken up still, but she relaxes slightly after hearing these words from him. "Okay... are you sure? What are you going to do?"

"I'll be inside in a moment. I'm just going to put away the chickens and the sheep really quick, so they don't get out and get lost if we have to go on a little trip." Alexander explains.

"Okay..." She says as she turns to walk away.

Alexander watches as she looks over her shoulder to make sure he's still there, every few feet. After she's inside the cabin, he goes back to lock up the chickens and their one sheep. After securing the livestock, he heads back to the cabin.

I wonder what happened and why the Leviathan would come here. He thinks as he looks at the sky, unable to see the massive spaceship any longer. *God, I wish we still had communication lines up and running.*

Alexander heads into the cabin to find Mia and Isabelle in the kitchen, getting out the makings for sandwiches.

"What kind of PB&J do you want, Uncle Alex? We still have the smooth and crunchy peanut butter and we have strawberries or regular jelly left." Mia asks him as he enters the kitchen.

They had run out of the sliced meats and cheeses some time ago. Luckily, they were able to barter for a good amount of peanut butter and jelly. No one seemed to complain about it and the girls seemed to like them enough as well. In these times, it was difficult to be picky with what food was still available.

Bread was beginning to become an issue and Steven and Ben were brainstorming ways to acquire more, or even make more bread, when the time came. Which the time was very near with them only having about half of a loaf left in the cabin.

Whereas, they still had a good amount of other foods to keep them going for a while, on top of the newly bought livestock in the backyard, Alexander was not looking forward to running out of bread. Which looked like that day might very well be today.

Nevertheless, Alexander knew that life was still adjusting to the new world that they had inherited. He had just hoped that things would turn out well enough for the girls to have a good rest of their childhood and never have to experience the horrors that they endured with those monsters that were rounding up women and young girls. Just thinking about those rapist monsters that they had encountered on the road made Alexander's blood boil.

"Uncle, Alex?" Mia asks.

Snapping Alexander back from out of the depths of his own brain, he looks at Mia and smiles. "Surprise me. I'm sure anything that you girls make will taste delicious."

"Okay." Mia says as she forces a smile back.

She's scared. She doesn't know why... but she knows that the Leviathan showing up around here is not good news. It's crazy how kids pick up on things that they know very little about. Like a sort of intuition... that we have when we are young, and we lose over the years of conforming to the realities of the real world.

Alexander goes to the fridge, getting the pitcher of iced tea. He pours three glasses full and sets them at the table for them. Shortly after, the girls place three plates at the table, each with a PB&J on it. They take their seats next to each other, with the third plate right across from them where he's sitting.

"We made three more like you asked and put them back into the bread bag, since it was empty. One of the sandwiches is made up of the butt bread, though." Mia explains as she takes a bite into her sandwich.

Isabelle laughs, likely at the word butt.

"Good job girls. I'll put them in a bag with some bottled water after we finish our sandwiches." Alexander replies.

"Where are we going?" Isabelle asks.

"I'm not sure yet, Isabelle. We may just go for a little hike, after our snack." Alexander replies.

"Brunch. You said it was our brunch, Uncle Alex." Isabelle replies.

"That's right, Isabelle. I did." Alexander says with a smile.

The three of them go about eating their PB&J sandwiches and drinking their iced tea. Whilst doing so, Alexander wonders what happened to Steven, Ben, Eileen, and all of the others that went with them.

If I recall, there were nine of them in total. Considering what I saw, something certainly occurred and it was an event that led the Leviathan to fire upon one of its own ships. Because I'm pretty sure that the smaller aircraft was actually the small spacecraft that Staff Sergeant Mahoney and Sergeant Burke were in possession of.

But the real question is, what could have happened to lead up to that scenario? And how would that result in the Leviathan coming to our small town? Can that massive spaceship even land anywhere around here? Our lake still has water in it and the rest of the area is pretty full of houses, shops, and mountainous areas.

After they are done eating their sandwiches, Alexander sends the girls to go get cleaned up and brush their teeth. He wasn't sure how often they had been keeping up on the regular hygiene routines and thought it highly unlikely that the monsters that had stolen them cared anything about their personal health. So, whenever he found the chance to get them to keep up on their hygiene, he encouraged them to do so.

He was happy to find that the girls didn't find it an annoying chore. However, that also concerned him, thinking that they were now excited to be able to clean up and do the simple things like brush their teeth.

It was not too long ago, at least to Alexander, when he was constantly reminding his own daughters to go clean up. Which usually resulted in eye rolls and lies of how they already did. Alexander smiles at the small memory of his kids trying to avoid showers, deodorant, and brushing their teeth.

While he was lost in thought at the sink drying the dishes he had just cleaned from their meal, he hears Ol' Betsy crack to life in the cabin's designated comms room.

"What's that?!" He says aloud, placing the last of the dishes onto the counter and walking to the comms room.

He can hear static as he enters the room.

"It's static, but it's coming from somewhere..." He begins.

Before he can think anymore, he hears a voice over Ol' Betsy, an unfamiliar voice.

:: **Hello people of Crestline. This is Lieutenant Meads, of the Federalist Legion from Earth Two. You are instructed to make your** way to your local small body of water, which appears to be a small lake. You are to be there within one hour's time, and no later than one hour. If you come willingly you will not force us to extradite you from your dwellings and detain you. Make the smart choice. Make the right choice. Captain Abraham Jackson is offering you mercy and salvation. It is 1000, by your time. Be here no later than 1100. Report to your local lake for further instructions from Captain Abraham Jackson of the Federalist Legion. This message will repeat every five minutes, until 1100. That is all, people of Crestline ::

Ol' Betsy goes back to playing static noise.

"Well that doesn't sound good for us whatsoever." Alexander says aloud.

He looks down to his watch, seeing it read 10:01 AM. Then a thought crosses his mind.

If Ol' Betsy is working, maybe our phones and the SuperNet is back up. It stands to reason, considering they are all on the same networks. Well, kind of...

He rushes out of the comms room and upstairs to his bedroom. He reaches the room and goes to his nightstand, retrieving his iPhone from the top drawer. He hits the power button and waits for it to power up. After a few anxious moments, it comes to life and he clicks to get onto the SuperNet.

"Yes!" He shouts, as he sees the SuperNet is back up and running.

Their message may have been local and only to Crestline, considering that they mentioned our town by name. But it looks like they had to unblock the entire network to even send the local message. That would make sense with how many fail-safes they had designed for the SuperNet before they left for Earth Two. Now the real question... Do any of the others have their phone on them? Because I definitely didn't have it on me.

Alexander had stopped carrying his phone on him the day prior, with his constant attention going back to checking to see if the network was still down or not. It had become so frustrating, that he thought it best to simply put it away.

He quickly scrolls to Steven Reilly's number and clicks his name.

Putting the phone to his ear, he hears his voicemail right away.

Damn... Makes sense Steven would have done the same. Hopefully Ben and Eileen are a little more attached to their phones than we are.

Alexander scrolls back up in his phone to Benjamin Reilly and clicks his name. He puts his phone to his ear and then hears it ring after a couple seconds. An exasperated sigh leaves him as he listens the phone ring.

After the fifth ring, Ben picks up. "Uh, hello... Alexander, is that you?"

Alexander smiles, and begins to walk out of his room, back downstairs. "Yes, Ben! It is! Are you guys alright?!"

"Uh, yeah. But why are the phones working again?" Ben replies and questions.

"Captain Abraham Jackson must have stopped blocking the network to get a message out to us." Alexander replies.

"Huh, what message... wait. Hold on. Let me put you on speaker so everyone in the ship can hear you. Burke, do you have Bluetooth or anything like that to have us all hear him on the ship?" Ben replies to Alexander and then is obviously talking to Sergeant Burke.

Ship? Sergeant Burke? So, they are on the smaller spacecraft...

"Thanks Burke. Okay. You're good to go, Alexander. We can all hear you now. It's all of us that left for Big Bear, plus Burke... now." Ben explains.

"Oh okay... Interesting. So, I take it that it was you guys flying away from the Leviathan not too long ago." Alexander responds.

"Yeah, Alexander, that was us. But what's this about a message from Abraham? Whatever he said, don't listen to him. He's a liar and tried to kill all of us." Ben questions and warns him.

"Actually, Alexander... The son of a bitch wants to kill most of our men and anyone that doesn't fall in line. To top it off, he wants to take our women and children! If you see that POS, shoot first!" Steven says over the phone.

"Okay. Well one of his Lieutenants just sent out a message over the radio, telling all of us to go to Lake Gregory. It was not a request but sounded like an order and warning. He gave us an hour, saying he's showing us mercy and salvation. It sounded like it was directly toward the people of Crestline, and only us." Alexander explains.

"What?!... That's crazy! Don't listen to a damn word that crazy maniac says! Stay put in the house and you should be fine, Alexander." Ben replies.

"That's not entirely accurate Deputy Reilly. I mean Ben Reilly." A woman's voice says.

"Who's that Ben? And why?" Alexander questions.

"Hold on, Alexander..." Ben replies.

A new voice comes over the phone. "Dr. Alexander Mathis. My people have the technology to scan large regions for human life. Hiding in your dwelling is not ideal. You will be located and detained."

"Okay... What should we do then? And who is this?" Alexander asks.

"My name's Alicia Burke, Dr. Alexander Mathis. Formerly part of the Federalist Legion, myself. Up until earlier this morning... If the message is only for your settlement, then retreat from your settlement, and do so quickly. Before my brothers and sisters cut off your exit points." Alicia Burke responds.

Retreat? Where? I know I have been here for close to two months, but I still don't know the area that well. I'm from the other side of the continent, for goodness sake! Alexander thinks as he begins to worry about the girls.

Reaching the bottom of the stairs, he turns around and heads back to his room to pack a bag for their immediate exit.

"Where should I go?" Alexander asks.

"Alexander." Ben says. "This is Ben, again. You said the network is back up, right? Use the SuperNet to take the 138 Highway to Silverwood Lake. It's about half an hour north and slightly west of us. But you need to go now."

Alexander nods, as though they can see him. "Right. SuperNet is working for the time being, and they gave us one hour. So, it will hopefully be up for the entire hour, since the message is to repeat every five minutes."

"Sounds good, Alexander. Now get off the phone, grab what you

can, and get you and the girls the hell out of town. Stay safe bud."
Ben replies.

"Yeah, Alexander... stay safe and watch those girls for me." Eileen
adds.

"Alexander, we are making plans to return shortly. Just get out of
Dodge and we'll figure it out." Steven adds.

"Will do. You all stay safe as well. I'm glad you guys are alright. I
was starting to worry." He replies.

"We're good, Alexander. Close call, but good. Call us when you
get to Silverwood. Now get off the phone and get going, bud." Ben
replies.

"Right... bye." Alexander says and ends the phone call.

Wait, I forgot to ask them where they were and about the spaceship.
Alexander thinks and then shakes his head. *Not important right now,
Alexander... The only thing that's important right now is getting those two
girls out of Crestline, and quickly...*

The earth begins to shake beneath his feet and Alexander braces
himself against the earthquake. After close to a minute of shaking, he
checks his surroundings to find no damage from this last quake.

*How many is that now in the last few days? I wonder if this one origi-
nated from the Bear Ridge Faultline, like most of the previous earthquakes...*
Alexander thinks to himself as he heads toward the girls, wanting to
get them out of the house within the next few minutes.

20

BENJAMIN REILLY

"REALLY? The last humans on Earth? That seems pretty damn insane if you ask me... Just how many of us are left?" Ben asks as he questions Burke's statement.

"Yes, Deputy Reilly. Your kind from the *Blue Hole Radius* are the only humans left on Earth One. We are not sure exactly of the number currently. We did perform a global scan after the incident at the military installation in one of your desert areas." Burke explains.

"You mean when you all committed genocide and killed a lot of innocent people. And cut the crap with the Deputy Reilly shit, Alicia Burke. My name's Ben Reilly. Either Ben or Reilly is fine, because I sure as shit am not calling you Sergeant Burke anymore. You all don't deserve titles after what you did! Fucking Federalists Legion my ass! In our world, your kind is executed for being traitors." Ben spits back at her.

This gives her pause and she doesn't reply for a moment. Ben takes this moment to take a look around the STARU spacecraft, seeing everyone is either listening to him or staring out the viewing glasses of the spaceship, or both...

After a moment, he looks back to Burke. "How many of us are left? Our kind and your kind?"

Burke sighs and replies, "As far as our kind, I'm not entirely sure, but the number is likely under 500... We had two interstellar crafts leave Earth Two to come here. The Renaissance was destroyed along the way through the dangers that come along with interstellar travel. The Leviathan left with 101 souls and arrived with 92 souls. After today's events, there should be 85 souls remaining from the Leviathan, including myself. I'm not sure how many of the Utopians and fellow Federalists survived the Grand Global War, back on E2."

Grand Global War?! What the hell?!

"Wait a damn minute! So, you're telling me that you guys came all the way out here, after you all demolished your planet, just to remake ours in your own image? Am I getting that right?!" Uncle Steven asks.

Burke sighs again. "That explanation is leaving out a great amount of detail and circumstance, but it's accurate for a short version, yes."

"Why, Burke?! For the love of all that is holy, why?!" Uncle Seven asks.

"Wait! You said there's under 500 human beings left alive from Earth Two, and from the sound of it... that's high balling it. How many people are left here?!" Ben interrupts with his own question.

Burke looks at him with a face of defeat. "Our numbers are not 100% accurate, with certain areas harder for us to scan, but the scan produced a number of roughly just over 2 million souls left on Earth One, aside from our kind. The actual count came out to 2,003,076 souls left after the scan following the military installation incident..."

2 million? How many did we start off with when this whole thing kicked off?

"Holy hell! Only 2 million of us left?! We started out with close to 9 million, according to Commander Yang's message!" Eileen blurts out.

"Yes, that is accurate, Eileen. And is one of the reasons why Captain Abraham Jackson holds your kind in such low regard and plans to rebuild what is left of your civilization." Burke replies.

"Well, isn't he the hypocrite! If I was a betting man, I'd have money on him being the reason why Earth Two's down to a few hundred people left, if any at all! And he thinks he can just come out here and start fresh with becoming a tyrant?!" Uncle Steven replies.

"Yeah! What exactly is his actual plan, Burke?" Ben adds.

"In reality, tensions had been brewing between the Utopian Union and Federalist Legion for the last decade. The release of your kind from the *Blue Hole Radius* escalated those tensions into a full-scale war on Earth Two. But yes, it was Captain Jackson that utilized the massive amount of *sleepers* on the population of Earth Two, when it looked like our side would soon become the losing side..." Burke explains.

"What the hell, Alicia?! You went along with this?!" Eileen asks sharply.

"Yes... in the beginning it seemed like the right thing to do. Commander Yang wanted to just give your kind our technology and let your kind decide what to do with yourselves. He did want to offer guidance but didn't want to step in with any real solutions. But over time, things began to unravel within the Federalists Legion ranks and many of us continued forth out of a mixture of fear and faith in the cause... the cause that your kind could be salvaged and incorporated into our kind." Burke says, trying to plead her case.

"Let me take a wild guess, Burke..." Ben begins to say. "Abraham said that he would provide us with the technology when we earned it and followed the ways of your kind to a tee. And when people started dying on Earth Two, shit got real and some of your Federalists had second thoughts. Then your great and glorious Abraham had to eradicate these people for your great cause and the future of humanity. In fact, he saw it fit to kill millions on Earth Two, because he was about to lose a war... Does that sound about right?"

Burke nods and sighs. "Again, you are leaving out a lot of details. However, that's incredibly accurate of what occurred on E2... but the population prior to the Grand Global War was over 800 million citizens. How did you come to your conclusion without knowing our history?"

"You've got to be shitting me Burke! Over 800 million dead on Earth Two and you still followed this asshole here?!... And I came to that conclusion because I do know your history! I know our history! Human history! History may not repeat itself, but it sure as shit rhymes! And that's how fucking asshole tyrants work! When they don't get their way, they hit the reset button, regardless of how many get hurt, in the hopes that they are left standing!" Ben yells at the woman from Earth Two.

The spaceship stays silent, as if everyone's taking in the information and not knowing what to say.

After an awkward moment, Ben opens his mouth again. "Shit Burke! Seriously?! Why are you following this asshat?! Why should we even listen to you?! Hell! Why did you even help us if you believe in his cause so damn much!"

Ben sees a tear form in her left eye and it runs down her face.

Oh, would you look at that. These all-knowing, futuristic humans still have feelings and can cry! Good! I hope I offended you, you...

"I don't know! Alright! I knew what he did on E2 was wrong! But what were we supposed to do?! Several of us spoke up against him, and I was getting ready to do so as well... He killed those people for even saying anything to him on our way here... He killed nine people, knowing the Renaissance was dead and gone, and we may be all that was left from E2!" Burke yells out and Ben can tell that she's having somewhat of a breakdown.

Ben watches as she looks to her hands, then looks back up, with more tears in hers. "I followed him because I was afraid to die. Once I realized what he was willing to do to get what he wanted, it was too late!... My family was still on E2 when it happened, and they even supported him and the Federalist ideals!... And then he killed the rest of my friends!" She shouts at Ben, at all of them.

After a short pause, she continues. "All the people that I have known for decades are gone now! And when he killed Brian, I was more scared for my own life than worried that he was gone! That's why I helped you! I didn't want to die! I know it's cowardly, even after all of my decades of training and schooling... I still grew up to be a coward!" Burke says and then she puts her face in her hands and begins to sob.

Ben feels himself feeling bad for yelling at her. *Dammit! Why the hell do I feel bad for yelling at someone that had a hand in 800 million dead! What?! Just because she's a woman and she's crying?! Shit on a stick, this is some real bullshit!*

He turns his head back around and looks out his side of the spaceship. Below them all he can see is ice. After a few moments the ice gives way to snow-capped mountains and forests. Ben finds himself lost in what he's seeing below them.

Where the hell are we? Antarctica or some shit?

After a few more moments of silence and quiet sniffling from Burke, Eileen asks the question that Ben thinks they must all be thinking. "Alicia, where exactly are we and where are we going?"

Ben hears Burke sniffle and sigh in the way that people do after crying and trying to recompose themselves. "Um..." She pauses, but Ben cannot take his eyes off of the snowy scenery below him and does not look back at the softly sobbing Burke.

"We are going over the Arctic Circle, reaching the former territory of the UNAT or the United North American Territories..." Burke says pausing again and then adding, "We should be arriving at our destination shortly."

"And where's that, Alicia?" Eileen presses.

"I located a cave system that's big enough to hide the STARU. I found a cave opening that is open enough for us to fit in and avoid the scanning process of the Leviathan. We took the long way around the globe here, to throw off Captain Jackson. I believe the caves were once called the *Upana Caves* when they were much smaller... in your time." Burke replies.

Ben hears Burke sniffle again. "It's in the lower North West Territory of the UNAT or what you knew as *British Columbia in Canada.*"

Ben watches as the snowy scenery gives way to a darker green mixture with snow-capped mountains and forests. It's difficult to see anything specific with how fast the spaceship's moving.

We went around the Earth? That quickly? How fast does this thing go? And this is Canada? I had heard that there wasn't much up here, but this is ridiculous. There's nothing up here but snow and trees...

The STARU begins to slow and Ben can begin to make out water and more trees with less snow on them, but still having some spots of snow here and there.

It's July isn't it? I heard Canada is cold, but this cold? Really? How cold does it get up here now?

He turns to ask Burke and sees her now standing, looking at him. "My apologies for losing my composure. I assure you that I'm here to help. I may have aided you for cowardly reasons, but I know now what path I must follow."

"Burke... We all fall down. We may not all be complicit to genocide, but we still all make mistakes. What really matters is what you do afterwards." Uncle Steven says, unbuckling himself and standing as well, grabbing his seat as support.

"You saving our asses back there, should really count for something... and it sure as damn does. My only question now is whether you are going to help us or are you going to have second thoughts about going against your fearless leader of a tyrant?" Uncle Steven asks.

"Captain Jackson will kill me regardless, whether I come back or help your kind. No matter what he says. He's wonderful with words, but I have seen him to be truly cruel at heart." Burke says.

Ben unbuckles himself and faces her, ready to say something. Eileen unbuckles and puts a hand on his shoulder as she rises up next to him. Ben looks over at her and she shakes her head at him.

"What? So, we are just supposed to forget and forgive the fact that she was here to rule over us with an iron fist? Or that she had a hand in killing millions back on her home planet? How can we forget something like that Eileen?" Ben asks her.

"I know, Ben. I know. But she did save us, and you know it. We were all but dead without her. She may have done it to save her own skin, but she brought us here too... alive. We should at least give her a chance, Ben." Eileen replies.

Ben looks at her with a look of confusion and then looks to his Uncle. "Uncle?"

"She's right, nephew... and you have to look at brass tacks... we are definitely screwed without Burke's help. At least with her, we have a chance against Abraham and the others. Hell, she just gave us a great amount of intel on them. We outnumber them like crazy!" Uncle Steven replies.

Ben looks at his Uncle, with confusion... processing the reality of what he has said.

Has the world gone completely batshit crazy all over again?

"Ben Reilly, if I may... I have been doing a lot of thinking while being on your planet alone with Brian Mahoney. A lot has changed in the last couple of days and I have seen that we are not all that different. If Captain Jackson... if Abraham has his way, most of your kind will die and he will pick and choose who repopulates Earth One and that will only be the beginning." Burke says to him.

"Well, I'm sure as hell glad that you see us as the same as your kind. That's great!" Ben snaps back.

"What I'm trying to say is that I think I know what one of your old idioms truly means now... *It's better to die on your feet than to live on your knees...*" Burke replies.

Son of a bitch... Ben thinks about the woman in front of him saying a quote he knows very well and to be very true. Annoyed and impressed that she even knows the saying.

Before Ben can reply with a comment that he can't think of yet, he feels a vibration in his jeans.

Huh?

The vibration happens again, and then again.

Ben reaches into his pocket and pulls out his iPhone that he still had kept charged and on him on a daily basis. Despite it not working for the last few days, it was hard for Ben to part with it. In fact, he still had not parted with his wallet yet either. Some old habits were hard to get rid of.

"My phone's ringing..." Ben says.

The phone vibrates in his hand.

"What?! Who is it?! Answer it!" Eileen shouts at him.

Ben looks at her and then back to his phone with Alexander

Mathis's name on the caller ID. Everyone on the STARU spaceship is dead silent. Ben finally picks up after the fifth ring.

"Uh, hello... Alexander, is that you?" Ben says.

"Yes, Ben. It is. Are you guys alright?" Alexander replies.

"Uh, yeah. But why are the phones working again?" Ben questions.

"Captain Abraham Jackson must have stopped blocking the network to get a message out to us." Alexander replies.

Message? There's another one?

"Huh, what message... wait. Hold on. Let me put you on speaker so everyone in the ship can hear you." Ben says to Alexander.

Ben then looks back to Burke, "Burke, do you have Bluetooth or anything like that to have us all hear him on the ship?" Ben asks her.

"Bluetooth? Do you mean like a speaker for your comm?" Burke asks.

"Yes, do you?" Ben presses.

Burke nods and hits a few buttons on the wall behind the transparent screen. "There, your comm should work for the entire STARU, now."

"Thanks Burke." Ben tells her.

"Okay. You're good to go, Alexander. We can all hear you now. It's all of us that left for Big Bear, plus Burke... now." Ben explains to Alexander.

"Oh okay... Interesting. So, I take it that it was you guys flying away from the Leviathan not too long ago." Alexander responds.

"Yeah, Alexander, that was us. But what's this about a message from Abraham? Whatever he said, don't listen to him. He's a liar and tried to kill all of us." Ben replies to him.

"Actually, Alexander... The son of a bitch wants to kill most of our men and anyone that doesn't fall in line and take our women and children! If you see that POS, shoot first!" Uncle Steven adds.

"Okay. Well one of his Lieutenants just sent out a message over the radio, telling all of us to go to Lake Gregory. It was not a request but sounded like an order and warning. He gave us an hour, saying he's showing us mercy and salvation. It sounded like it was directly toward the people of Crestline, and only us." Alexander explains.

"What?!... That's crazy! Don't listen to a damn word that crazy maniac says! Stay put in the house, and you should be fine, Alexander." Ben replies.

"That's not entirely accurate Deputy Reilly. I mean Ben Reilly." Burke adds.

Ben shoots Burke a quick look.

"Who's that Ben? And why?" Alexander questions.

"Hold on, Alexander..." Ben replies.

"Dr. Alexander Mathis. My people have the technology to scan large regions for human life. Hiding in your dwelling is not ideal. You will be located." Burke answers him.

"Okay... What should we do then? And who is this?" Alexander asks.

"My name's Alicia Burke, Dr. Alexander Mathis. Formerly part of the Federalist Legion, myself. Up until earlier this morning... If the message is only for your settlement, then retreat from your settlement, and do so quickly. Before my brothers and sisters cut off exit points." Burke explains.

Shit! They're in Crestline!

Ben looks over at the young man named Christian, and the young man instantly bows his head.

Dumbass! Telling them where we live!

"Where should I go?" Alexander asks over the speakers of the STARU.

"Alexander. This is Ben again. You said the network is back up, right? Use the SuperNet to take the 138 Highway to Silverwood Lake. It's about half an hour north and slightly west of us. But you need to go now." Ben tells his friend.

"Right. SuperNet is working for the time being, and they gave us one hour. So, it will hopefully be up for the entire hour, since the message is to repeat every five minutes." Alexander replies.

Good, but he needs to get out of there... like now!

"Sounds good, Alexander. Now get off the phone, grab what you can, and get you and the girls the hell out of town. Stay safe bud." Ben replies

"Yeah, Alexander... stay safe and watch those girls for me." Eileen adds.

"Alexander, we are making plans to return shortly. Just get out of Dodge and we'll figure it out." Uncle Steven adds.

"Will do. You all stay safe as well. I'm glad you guys are alright. I was starting to worry."

"We're good, Alexander. Close call, but good. Call us when you get to Silverwood. Now get off the phone and get going, bud." Ben replies.

"Right... bye." Alexander says and the phone call ends.

Ben looks up to Burke. "What's Abraham up to, Burke?"

"Knowing Abraham, he wants vengeance for killing some of ours, but mostly for disrespecting him the way you spoke to him during our last encounter." Burke replies.

"Yeah, that sounds like that arrogant POS. What would he do in a situation like this, Burke?" Uncle Steven asks.

Burke pauses for a moment and sighs as she seems to be concentrating. Ben notices that she looks deeper in thought than he has seen with Alexander. Alexander has seemed like he was lost in thought, but Burke seems like her mind is actually somewhere else.

Ben looks over to Eileen and she shrugs. "I don't know..."

Ben looks back at her and then she focuses on him, coming back from wherever she just was.

"Looking back at his previous engagements and training records, he's most likely going to use the people of your settlement as negotiating tools to flush us out and capture and kill us." Burke answers.

"What?!" Eileen replies.

"Oh, that's just great... he's going to use the people of Crestline as hostages and kill them if we don't give ourselves up. Just fricking-fracking-fucking great!" Ben replies.

Burke nods in confirmation. "That is the most likely scenario, given his traits and history."

Ben turns to Deputy Joseph Gomez. "Hey, Joseph... can you call

Todd and tell him to get Jamie, Claire, Chloe, Jen, and Holly out of there and up to Silverwood and meet up with Alexander?"

"Sure thing, Ben. Good thinking." Joseph replies.

Ben looks at the others. "If anyone else has friends and family back home, call them now and tell them the same. Tell them to drop what they are doing and get out now."

Janice nods her head along with the other two DFC members that Ben doesn't know or remember their names. They walk off and use their phones to call their friends and family back in Crestline.

Ben pauses and so does everyone else, noticing that the STARU has completely stopped and he looks out the viewing glass opposite of him to see trees and the opening of a cave. He then looks behind him, to see the inside of a massive cave.

"So, I take it we are here?" Uncle Steven says.

"Yes, Sheriff Reilly. The Leviathan should not be able to see where we are, for now." Burke replies.

"So, it sounds like you want to help us now, instead of kill us and rule over us with tyranny. Got any plans on how to help us stand a chance against your futuristic and sadistic tyrant?" Uncle Steven responds.

"My designation is merely logistics and supply, but I do have several years of combat training from my early service years... and I do have some supplies for you, that should assist us in reducing casualties." Burke replies as she walks to the side of the ship where the door was and starts reaching toward one of the many panels along the wall.

"Alicia, just how old are you and the rest of your people?" Eileen asks her.

Ben looks to Eileen and then back to Burke, curious of the answer.

"I'm only 57 years old, with this having been my seventh year as a full-fledged citizen of E2." Burke answers as she turns a knob and pulls a lever.

What?! She only looks to be around her early twenties, no older than

22 or 23! What's up with these people?! And citizenship at 50?! What kinds of backwards ass laws do they have?!

Ben's focus is then shifted to the panel that receded upward, revealing several large shelves lined with vests exactly like the one that Burke and the other Federalists were wearing. She then walks closer toward where Eileen and himself were standing, turns a knob and pulls another lever. This one displaying several smaller shelves lined with MECCUs.

Ben looks at the MECCUs in astonishment.

There's enough for each one of us and then some...

"This should assist us with reducing casualties and help us survive against Abraham and the others that mean to do you harm." Burke says with a solemn face.

Ben nods at the newfound weapons and defensive device. "Just who the hell are you people and what are we up against?" Ben asks her.

She looks at him and nods. "I'll explain more about us and Earth Two while I assist you with calibrating your MECCU to your individual-selves."

She walks over to Eileen first with an MECCU, "Here, Eileen. If you would allow me to install this on your right forearm."

"Actually, you may want to install that on her left arm, Burke. So, she can still use her gun." Ben advises her.

Burke looks at him in confusion. "But why would you need your antique weapons any longer, with our MECCUs?"

Ben looks at her and smiles. "After you are done telling us about your kind, I'll tell you some things your history books may have left out about our kind."

Ben sees a faint smile from Burke and then she focuses her attention back on Eileen and places the MECCU over her left forearm.

"Ow! What the hell! That hurts!" Eileen blurts out as the MECCU is placed over her left forearm.

Great, this sounds like it's going to feel lovely...

"Hey Burke... Can you open up the door on this spaceship?" Ben asks.

Burke looks up at him from placing the MECCU on Eileen's arm. "Yes, but why?"

Ben rolls his eyes. "Well, I don't see any bathrooms in this STARU, so I planned on relieving myself behind one of those rocks in this big ass cave. Is that alright with you? Does your kind from the future still have to piss and poop?"

Ben sees that she turns a light shade of red. "Yes, Benjamin Reilly. We do, actually... There is one toilet aboard each STARU, that extends out when needed. But I bloody doubt anyone is going to want to relieve themselves in front of the whole lot of you." She replies as she taps a button and turns a knob along the wall and the opening appears next to him.

"Alright then, I'll be back in a few... If anyone else needs to go, now's the time people. No stopping along the way to Crestline and sounds like we may have a fight on our hands when we get there." Ben says back into the STARU as he walks out into the Upana Caves.

He makes his way to find a secluded area of the cave and looks back to see most of the others shuffling out of the STARU.

We have enough crap to worry about as it is. I don't need to worry about pissing or having to crap myself if we end up in another big ass battle... this time against space invaders instead of thugs and gangsters. Yay for us! Ben thinks, grinning to himself.

21

EILEEN RIVERA

SHIELDED from the scanners of the Leviathan, Eileen and the others listen to Alicia Burke as she goes over a crash course on how to use the MECCUs... particularly their IMDs (Individual MECCU Dozers) and their AEs (Armored Enclosures). Despite the instance that the MECCUs hurt like hell when they are placed onto your arm, the process was relatively smooth. The pain was swift and then a cooling sensation eased the pain just as quickly as it had begun. It was painful, yes... but more shocking than anything.

"You could have warned me, Alicia!" Eileen had blurted out, since she was the first to receive a MECCU and go through the *bonding* process.

Alicia explained that the burning sensation was actually transmitters being placed into their arms to create a *bond* between the user and the MECCU, making it individually reactive to the user. Alicia went on to explain something about an additional procedure that their kind undergoes shortly after birth. It had to do something with cognitive development and also assisted with better communication and reaction time between the MECCU and the user. Alicia assured them that with practice and time, they would bridge the gap.

Eileen found the MECCUs relatively user friendly and figured that with time, she would get used to the added 32 ounces, or two pounds, to her arm. Alicia assured them that the weight would feel like close to nothing in time.

With the added weight to her left arm, she was excited to find that the vests from Earth Two were much lighter than their own bullet-proof vests. What is more, the vests from Earth Two formed with their owner and provided coverage wherever the vest was. She was amazed to find that the vest felt just like a cross between dri-fit and a winter jacket. She was more than glad to trade out her old vest, and it appeared that everyone else was as well. Brianna and Christian more so, since they didn't even have one to start off with.

Ben had questioned the integrity of the vest and Burke explained that they could withstand most projectiles from "our" antique weapons. Ben asked several other questions and seemed overall happy about the exchange. He did refer to it as an upgrade to their previous armor.

Eileen did ask why they needed them with the force fields. Burke explained that they were a last line of defense, in case "our" ancient weapons were able to penetrate "their" AEs. When asked about why they hadn't armored their MECCUs, she simply shrugged and answered that the operation and design of the MECCUs was not her designation. She did say that it was likely an oversight on their part.

"An oversight? That was one helpful oversight!" Ben had replied back and laughed. This in turn, gained laughter from everyone except Burke. It helped with lightening up the mood, despite the real concept of a looming battle.

Eileen found it interesting that people from 1,410 years into the future still made the same mistakes that they did. Oversight on certain crucial areas that could cause harm and somehow this Abraham guy had thought that being a dictator would work out in the long run. She had wondered if they taught people of Earth Two the history of "her" Earth, or if Abraham just didn't pay attention on that day or heed their warnings.

Eileen's rather happy with herself and feels confident with her new vest and MECCU, but still is curious if it will be enough to go against Abraham and the rest of the Federalists from the future.

When this doubtful thought crosses her mind, she looks to ask Ben what he thinks. Before she can ask him, the transparent screen changes from the map of North America and their location to that of the Leviathan and to the face of Captain Abraham Jackson.

"What the shit?!" Ben blurts out.

Eileen looks to Burke, with eyes of shock. "I thought he couldn't locate us, Alicia?!"

Burke shakes her head. "He can't... rest assured. This is a message sent out to all STARUs attached to the Leviathan."

"Are you sure he doesn't know where we are, Burke?" Steven asks.

"I'm sure, Sheriff Reilly."

At that moment, the giant head version of Abraham Jackson begins to speak. "Sheriff Reilly and the rest of your *barbarians*. We offered your kind our technology and medicine and you spat in our faces. It seems you want to continue to live on as *cretins*. Lucky for the rest of your kind, I will bring them salvation and the ways of the Federalist Legion. However, for your treacherous group of *barbarians*, your lives are now forfeit!"

The camera that's filming Abraham pans out, revealing a portion of the Leviathan in the background, displaying Abraham on a platform outside of the Leviathan, hovering over Lake Gregory. Alongside Abraham are five Federalists to his right, and five more Federalists to his left. In front of him are six men on their knees at the edge of the platform.

"Oh no!" Eileen says as she gasps and tries to see if she recognizes any of the men on the edge of the platform on their knees. After a quick moment she's relieved that she doesn't know any of them but is still horrified about what will likely come next.

Abraham continues speaking. "My loyal Federalists are still locating and acquiring the citizens of your small settlement, but we have attained most of them already in the last hour. For every hour that you do not return and face your executions, I will execute citizens of your settlement, and to provide validation of my word..."

Eileen watches in horror as six arms raise from the Federalists at Abraham's sides, with blue orbs forming from their IMDs. A second later, the six men on their knees are each covered in a blue flash and they fall off the edge of the platform, into the lake.

"You bastard!" Ben shouts at the screen.

"He cannot hear you, Ben Reilly..." Alicia replies.

She watches Ben look at Alicia with eyes of rage and then turns his head back to face the screen.

"He's still a fucking bastard! Dammit! I really hate this guy!" Ben shouts out.

No one else in the STARU speaks, likely from shock and being stunned with horror, just like her.

"By your time, it is 1101. You have until 1200 to surrender yourselves to your execution and this loss of life... valuable lives to sustain our survival as a species, I must add... will cease. You have my word. And to show you further validation of my word, you can even view the next group of barbarians to take your place if you are too cowardly to surrender yourselves for your crimes against the Federalist Legion." Abraham says as he looks to his right.

The camera shifts away from Abraham and his Federalists to another platform. This platform has several Federalists standing behind a group of people. The group's larger than the first, and mostly made up of men, all but two...

"Oh my gosh!" Eileen says aloud.

"Son of a fucking bitch!" Ben yells.

"Oh, sweet baby Jesus! No!" Steven adds.

The rest of the DFC members and Burke are silent as they stare at the next group of people scheduled to be executed in less than an hour if they don't turn themselves in.

On the platform, there are about a dozen people from Crestline. Eileen recognizes three of the people on the platform, and obviously Ben and Steven do as well. In the middle of the group, stand

Alexander with Mia and Isabelle in front of him, with his arms over the girls.

Eileen watches as Alexander shakes his head and mouths what she thinks is *"I'm sorry."*

The camera shifts back toward Abraham, who's now smiling.

I really hate this guy too! If he does anything to Alexander and those poor girls, I'm going to make him wish that he was fucking dead! Eileen screams inside her head.

"Whereas, it would be a great loss to our species if we lost Dr. Alexander Mathis... I believe his life and the life of your two adopted orphans will provide the incentive required for you rebel *barbarians* to surrender yourselves to your undeniable fates. Please don't force me to take away one of the greatest minds left of your kind. The choice is yours. You now have 56 minutes to return to your settlement. We are positioned upon your local lake. The STARU that you stole, along with Sergeant Burke, will be able to get here within that time frame, regardless of where you are on this Earth. Time is of the essence." Abraham finishes saying, as the video screen goes back to the map of North America, with their own location marked and the location of the Leviathan in Crestline.

"That piece of shit needs to die..." Ben says, grinding his teeth.

"Agreed..." Eileen says, meeting his gaze and nodding.

This gets a lot of agreeing *"yeahs"* and shouts from the others, except from Steven and Burke. Eileen looks over at Steven, trying to figure out what he's thinking. Once everyone's done claiming their hatred and despise for Captain Abraham Jackson, Steven turns to Alicia.

"Hey Burke." Steven says to her.

Alicia looks over to him. "How many did you say they had left? I mean of your Federalists?"

"There are 84 Federalists remaining, Sheriff Reilly." Alicia replies.

"I thought you said, there were 85 Federalists left?" Steven replies.

Alicia nods. "There were 85 left, when I was one of them. I no longer am."

That a girl!... Eileen thinks. *I knew I liked you! I trust you about as much as a politician, but it's a start, Alicia.*

"Good on you, Burke... Now, what exactly can this STARU of yours do?" Stevens asks.

"What exactly did you have in mind, Sheriff?" Alicia replies, with a tilt of her head.

"You're from the future, so I'm hoping you have some sort of cloaking technology. Like in all of our Sci-Fi movies..." Steven responds.

This gets a curious look from just about everyone inside the spacecraft.

What are you cooking up in that head of yours, Steven?

"Yes, Sheriff. The STARUs are able to avoid detection from the human eye and our radar systems. How do you propose we use this to our advantage?" Alicia replies.

"Well... I propose that we swing by my cabin real quick, undetected, and then I'm going to go ahead and surrender myself to Abraham, and only me because you all are already dead... or so I'll tell that asshole..." Steven explains.

"I don't understand, Sheriff Reilly." Alicia replies.

"What?..." What do you mean, Steven?" Eileen questions.

"Yeah?! What the crap, Uncle?!" Ben adds.

"Everybody just calm down, now... I'll explain everything on the way to my cabin. We don't have time to waste. Now get this flying freight car back into the sky and make sure no one can see us, Burke." Steven says, looking at the whole group, and then to Alicia.

Alicia sighs with confusion and nods, heading over to the transparent screen. Within a few moments, their STARU is out of the Upana Caves and back into the sky.

Eileen then turns to Steven. "Just what do you have cooked up in the head of yours, Steven?"

"Yeah, Uncle! What exactly are we doing?" Ben says, adding his question into the mix.

"Let me explain, and make sure to listen carefully... we only have time to go over this once." Steven begins...

As the STARU lands in front of their cabin, Steven finishes explaining his grand plan to the group.

"What the hell, Uncle?! What kind of plan is that? You go in there by yourself and hope for the best?!" Ben says to his Uncle, with obvious concern for his well-being.

"Yeah, Steven... I'd have to agree with Ben..." Eileen adds.

"Are you sure, Sheriff?" Joseph questions. "It's rather risky..."

"Yes, I'm sure. It's the best way to get the upper hand on this POS. And make it much more likely that we come out of this alive." Steven explains.

"Yeah, most of us may end up alive! But it doesn't sound good for you! Seriously, Uncle... I'm not okay with this plan." Ben says, trying to explain his concern for his Uncle again.

"I hear you nephew, but we are out of time, and this plan does make sense. Back me up here, Burke..." Steven says to his nephew and then turns to Burke.

"Now hold tight and I'll be right back. I just need my coat to cover up this damn brick on my arm." Steven says, as he leaves through the opening that just appeared on the side of the STARU heading into his cabin.

Eileen turns to Alicia. "Alicia, we have to have other options here. You said you know Abraham well. What other options do we have?"

"Whereas the plan is hastily developed... it's a logical approach. Captain Abraham Jackson will be caught off guard and he won't expect your kind to be smart enough to outsmart him." Alicia replies.

"So, you're saying it'll work then, and we can get them out of here and leave them stranded without the Leviathan?" Ben questions her.

"I'm inferring that it can work, not that it will. And we still need to be overly concerned with boarding the Leviathan. Again, my designation is logistics and supply. I can get you to the control center, if most of the other Federalists are outside with Abraham... like your Uncle thinks they will be. It does make logical sense, considering our... their low numbers and wanting to show a great force to your kind of this settlement. They are easily outnumbered... but I'm concerned about that part." Alicia explains.

"About what part, Alicia?" Eileen asks.

"Captain Jackson and the rest of the Federalists being outnumbered..." Alicia replies.

"That's a good thing, Burke... don't forget what Abraham tried to do to you." Ben advises.

"No, Ben Reilly. It's not that. It's the instance that Captain Jackson knows he's outnumbered. Our previous scans showed 7,101 souls living in your small settlement. Captain Jackson knows this and that's what concerns me..." Alicia explains more clearly.

"Okaaaaay. But Burke... What are the chances of my Uncle making it out of this alive?" Ben questions.

"Ben, your Uncle is not the only one going to be in harm's way. Burke needs to get Joseph and the others on the Leviathan while you and I cover Steven's approach. There's also Alexander and the girls... and everyone else in Crestline." Eileen explains to him.

She can see that he's clearly concerned about his Uncle, but they were all in danger. She was concerned that sometimes he could be so smart and other times he could be so narrow-minded.

"There is a real possibility that none of us make it out of this, Ben. If your Uncle thinks this is the best way to go, I'm with him." Eileen.

Ben scratches the back of his head. "Yeah, you're right Eileen. I'm just worried, is all."

"Hey Burke! Nice camouflage on your STARU ship! That's pretty damn impressive! All I see are you guys standing at the door and part of the inside of the ship! It's just like those Sci-Fi movies!" Steven exclaims.

Eileen turns to see Steven standing outside of the STARU looking at the spaceship, or rather the lack of it. Steven whistles and then climbs back in, not entirely sure of what to grab onto. Ben steps over and reaches out his hand to help him into the STARU.

"Thanks nephew. Alright! Let's get this show on the road." He says and looks down to his watch. "It's already 1135, so we still have just under 25 minutes... Burke let's get the lovebirds off into the tree line, next to the main parking lot for the lake trail, then off to the Leviathan for the rest of you, and I'll go have some choice words with Abraham the tyrant."

Burke nods and heads back to the transparent control screen. Within seconds the opening is closed, and they are back on their way to Lake Gregory.

"We need to come in slow, everyone. That way, we don't accidentally hit any flying wildlife and give away our position." Alicia explains and the lake comes into view.

"Oh my gosh. Wow!" Eileen blurts out and puts her hand over her mouth as the Leviathan comes into view.

"Yeah! Right!" Ben adds.

"Yup... that looks pretty damn intimidating." Steven adds.

Eileen looks over the lake. Steven had been right about Abraham providing a show of force with the Federalists. As they came in slow over the Lake Drive Marketplace, she could see people lined up along the small bridge, in the main dock parking lot, and in the parking lot next to the trail. The crowd was at least ten times the size of the emergency meeting and the town meeting that Steven had for the formation of the DFC.

Whereas Eileen was shocked to see close to the entire town in one area, she was even more amazed by the Leviathan and slew of STARUs around the massive spaceship. The Leviathan covered most of the middle area of the lake, displaying how truly massive a spaceship that it was. The colossal spaceship was hovering just above the lake by what looked to be merely inches. There were no ripples coming from underneath and the water looked to be silk-like.

Above the Leviathan were a dozen STARUs and there were another dozen around the base perimeter of the Leviathan. There were also the two platforms from the video that they had watched earlier. Abraham was on one platform with his entourage of other Federalists soldiers. The platform to Abraham's right holds Alexander, Mia, Isabelle, and the rest of the dozen people from Crestline. The Federalists guarding them are now gone.

Where'd the guards go? Are they that short-handed? I guess if they tried to run, they'd have to swim, and they wouldn't get very far.

Eileen focuses on the girls and Alexander.

Don't worry girls... We'll get you and Alexander out of there...

Eileen's startled by a STARU flying right past them, almost hitting them and knocking them out of the sky.

"Whoa! What the shit?!" Ben exclaims.

"Burke, you may want us to get out of their pathway, so this plan isn't over before it begins." Steven advises.

"Right Sheriff Reilly, my apologies. I should have been paying attention to our surroundings." Alicia replies.

Alicia guides the STARU toward the tree line at the end of the parking lot. The lot is filled with people.

"I'm going to have to drop you two off on the road a little higher and you'll have to jog down to the edge of the lake." Alicia says.

"Fair enough. Yeah, it looks crowded right here and seeing two people pop out of thin air may give us away." Ben responds.

Burke takes the STARU to the road above the southside of the lake trail and hovers down low to the road. The opening appears in front of them.

"Ben." Steven says to his nephew. "Here, swap me rifles... my .308 has a better scope on it than your SAINT and it packs a harder punch."

This gets a sideways glance from Ben. "What if you need it?"

Steven laughs. "Yeah, like I'm going to have time to pull out a bolt action rifle against a bunch of those Federalists, each with their own MECCU and all of those STARUs out there." Steven shakes his head. "I love you, Ben... but sometimes you're about as dense as water." He laughs again.

"Fine, Uncle... whatever you say, you old jerk. No need to be a dick about it." Ben says, smiling at his uncle as they exchange Ben's AR for Steven's bolt-action .308 and the magazines for each.

"Okay, you're clear, Ben Reilly and Eileen Rivera. Good luck to the both of you." Alicia says.

"Thanks. Good luck to the rest of you." Eileen replies and then looks at Steven. "Stay safe Steven, and get those girls out of there."

"Will do, Eileen." Steven replies.

"Yeah, Uncle. Stay safe you old jerk..." Ben replies with a smile.

"Likewise, nephew. Good luck." Steven replies with a returned smile.

Ben turns and jumps out of the STARU. Eileen quickly follows him, and they go straight into the tree line, she turns around quickly, just in time to see the opening close up and it looks as though nothing was ever even there.

"Wow, that really is some good camouflage. Nice." Ben states.

He then looks over to her. "Alright pretty lady... let's get going. Uncle should be showing back up over the edge of the town in about fifteen minutes without that fancy camouflage, and then the fun starts."

She gives him a look. "Fun, Ben... really? None of this screams fun to me. Actually, it screams doom and gloom."

Ben scratches the back of his head. "Yeah, I know. But it's easier to make light of crap situations like this... than dwell on the *we might all die* part."

He has a point...

"Yeah... good point. Let's go watch the fun and see what we can see." Eileen replies.

Ben smiles at her with those bright blue eyes, and she starts to believe that everything was going to turn out just fine. She knew the odds were against them but looking into his eyes gave her hope and strength.

The both of them are able to make it to the shoreline within a couple minutes, finding a large boulder to hide behind. Eileen takes the right side of the large boulder and lays down, sighting down on her rifle. Ben does the same on the left side of the boulder.

"Put up your force field, just in case we get spotted." Ben tells her.

"Smart thinking... but I believe it's called an AE." Eileen snarks back at him with a smile.

He grins back at her. "Whatever you say, beautiful."

"And don't you forget it." She says as she smiles back and read-justs to type in commands to her MECCU so she doesn't have to have her hand out in a stopping motion, which would make it really hard to support her AR.

After a few seconds, she sees the shimmering AE engulf her whole body, likely making her silhouette turn into a shimmering outline. Alicia had explained that there were different settings to the AE and the body film setting seemed the most appropriate without giving them away too much.

She looks over to see that her thoughts were confirmed, seeing Ben covered in a translucent shimmer. He's looking back at her smiling.

"Look at you, looking all sexy and shiny." Ben says.

"I was about to say the same thing to you, handsome." Eileen says, blushing.

A STARU catches her attention, coming from the north part of the town. She watches it go to the side of the Leviathan that she cannot see. After a few moments, it's back in the air and going back to the North part of town.

"What do you think they are doing?" Eileen asks.

"Look over there..." Ben says, gesturing to the back side of the massive spacecraft.

Another STARU comes over from the towns and gets very close to the Leviathan. The opening appears and a bridge forms between the STARU and the Leviathan. She watches as she sees women and children being ushered into the massive spaceship. Most of the smaller kids are crying and the women look to be extremely frightened.

"Well, that doesn't look good..." Ben says.

"No... it does not. I hope Alicia, Joseph, Janice, and the others are able to get in there and take control of that gigantic spaceship, because it looks like Abraham is up to something... for sure." Eileen says as she watches the last of the women and children enter the Leviathan and the STARU take off toward the southside of the town.

"That's for damn sure. Man, I really hate this Abraham guy..." Ben says.

Eileen nods in agreement and something catches her attention off to her left in the distance.

"Ben, look over there. I think that's your Uncle." Eileen says, gesturing to his left, to the west side of the lake where a lone STARU has appeared and just hovering about a hundred feet in the sky.

Eileen looks toward Abraham and sees that his attention is drawn to the lone STARU as well. She thinks that she can even see him smiling, as though he has already won.

Keep smiling, asshole...

"Yeah... that's got to be your Uncle. That STARU sure has Abraham's attention." Eileen adds.

22

BENJAMIN REILLY

BEN WATCHES as the lone STARU approaches the two platforms in front of the Leviathan. Ben was impressed with his Uncle being able to fly the ship. Burke had given him the quick ins and outs of the STARU navigation and its own Armored Enclosure. Despite the simplicity of the design and extremely driver friendly controls, it was still impressive to see his Uncle flying a freaking spaceship.

Way to go Uncle! Flying a spaceship from another world and you're a natural at it. Hopefully, that means that Joseph and the others can figure out how to use those big guns or CSDs or whatever Burke called them.

Ben watches as the sleek freight car looking spaceship makes an abrupt stop in front of the platform with Alexander, the girls, and the others. The opening to the STARU and a bridge is extended from the STARU to the platform.

Nice flying Uncle. You may need some work on your parking job, though. Ben thinks to himself with a smile.

Ben sees that all of the Federalists on Abraham's platform raise their MECCUs and blue orbs quickly form out of their IMDs. He then notices that the other STARUs are now converging on his Uncle's STARU, with four large cannons pointed at Alexander's platform and his Uncle's STARU.

Large blue orbs form quickly just ahead of the barrel of the cannons, with two in the *front* and two in the *rear* of the freight car looking spaceships. The blue dozer orbs from the STARUs are easily ten times the size of the blue dozer orbs from the MECCU's IMD. The cannons in the rear of the STARUs extend out further, out past the cannons in the front of the STARUs.

What the shit? Those things have those dozer cannons on them too?

"Hold, Federalists! Hold! They are outnumbered and outmatched and they know it!" Abraham bellows his orders to the men standing next to him and the dozen or so STARUs that are now surrounding his Uncle's STARU and Alexander's platform.

The dozen STARUs in the sky stay steady with their large blue orbs pointed at his Uncle, Alexander, the girls, and the others. The Federalists alongside Abraham do the same.

"Holy hell. Burke wasn't kidding. We wouldn't stand a chance with hitting them head on." Ben says, surveying the scene in front of him.

"Oh goodness, those girls have to be so scared right now." Eileen replies.

Ben looks over the small figures on the platform that are Mia and Isabelle. Ben and Eileen can see them easily enough, with lake Gregory not being a huge lake, despite it having a surface area of roughly 84 acres.

Remembering that the zoom on the scope of his Uncle's bolt-action is way better than his standard AR setup, he looks through the scope to get a better visual.

He sees that the two young girls do look very frightened. He also sees Alexander in a protective stance over the girls, holding them close to him. Ben shifts his scope on the STARU that is bridged to Alexander's platform, seeing his Uncle exit the STARU with his hands in the air. He's wearing his old hiking jacket and he can see that his Uncle has tightened the wrist snaps on the sleeves, to not let them see his MECCU.

At that moment, that huge screen projection that Eileen had told him about shows up above the Leviathan. It's insane looking to Ben.

It's all one screen but looks like you can see the images on the screen from wherever you stand. On that huge screen is his Uncle, walking down the bridge extending from the STARU to Alexander's platform.

"Oh, this asshole wants to make a spectacle of this." Eileen blurts out.

"It's worse than that... he wants to make an example of us." Ben replies.

"Where are the rest of your rebel *barbarians*, Sheriff Reilly?" Ben hears from Abraham's voice as it bellows now from some speaker system that he cannot quite see.

This is really just a big show for this douchebag... putting us on display like he has already won.

Ben looks to the STARUs in the sky, with the cannons and blue orbs at the end of each of those cannons aimed at his Uncle, his friend, the girls and everyone else on that platform.

Well, I guess from his perspective... he has already won. Come on Joseph! Don't let us down in there. And Burke, you better not betray us, dammit!

Ben then hears his Uncle's voice over the speakers that Abraham's voice was just on. "They are dead, Abraham... because of your brain-dead Federalist bootlicker! I was able to end her miserable life, but at the cost of all of my own kind!"

Ben sees Abraham smile and then his face turns stern. "It's Captain Abraham Jackson, you *cretin*. And I'm impressed and saddened by this news. Impressed that Sergeant Burke came to her senses and took out most of you. Saddened that they escaped their executions from my own hand. Where are their bodies, I must ask?"

Uncle Steven shakes his head. "You tyrant types are all the same, Abraham. You think you know everything and that the world must bend to your will. That only you have the right vision for people, and if they don't agree with you, then they are expendable. I buried my friends and family up in the snow of the Canadian mountains... and before I threw Burke's body to the sharks in our Pacific Ocean, she told me what happened back on Earth Two."

The massive projected screen pans back to Abraham.

"I don't expect your kind to fathom our ways and what transpired on E2, *barbarian.*" Abraham replies with a scowl.

Good! He's buying Uncle's story about us being dead and gone. Little do you know asshole, Eileen and I are zeroed in on your tyrannical ass. Plus, Joseph and Burke and the others are inside your big-ass spaceship, taking it over... hopefully....

The video feed above the Leviathan goes back to Uncle Steven, displaying a battle of wits that looks to have Captain Abraham Jackson on the losing end, despite their obvious might and advanced technology.

"Oh... I understand. I understand that you killed close to 800 million people back home, and that's the only reason you haven't killed all of us yet. You need us to repopulate." Uncle Steven snaps back with a grin.

The video feed on the screen, once again, shows Abraham's platform.

This gets a shocked look from Abraham. Obviously taken aback with the fact that his Uncle had figured out his plans. For the first time, he sees confusion from the great Abraham Jackson.

"Whoever's filming this for the Federalists deserves a freaking award. I doubt they meant to make themselves look bad and air out all their dirty laundry, but that's exactly what's happening." Ben says to Eileen.

"Right! What a positive side effect. Let's just hope it's enough to throw them off their game." Eileen replies.

"Whatever you think you know is wrong!" Abraham shouts at Uncle Steven.

His Uncle laughs. "Well, what I think I know is that you are taking all of our women and going to use them as breeders. I think you are going to send our children through some sort of reeducation process to indoctrinate them into your kind of folks. I think you are going to kill most of our men, if not all... because you think us to be a threat. I think you were never going to let my dear friend, Alexander, and the rest of these good people of Crestline go."

Uncle Steven pauses for effect and he looks over to the people of

Crestline along the shore of the lake. He then looks back to a stunned and fuming Abraham Jackson.

"Good. He's shaken up... Uncle's doing good at stalling that egotistical maniac." Ben states.

"Yup. That's for sure. Let's just hope that it's enough time for Joseph and the others... and none of those super soldiers out here with us get any bright ideas." Eileen responds.

"What I think is that you are tired of your *hearts and minds approach*, because that was never your goal. If you had it your way, you would have killed the lot of us. But you need us... because there's only what?... 84 of your shithead Federalists left?" Uncle Steven questions, pressing Abraham further.

The massive projector screen pans back to Abraham to find his face twisted and enraged. Ben cannot help but smile.

Keep it up, Uncle. You got this.

"What?! How do you know that?! No! Our numbers are in the millions aboard the Leviathan!" Abraham yells out, obviously angry that the truth of his numbers was figured out.

Uncle Steven laughs again. "Not so damn stoic... are you now, Abraham!? Our kind may be dispersed and in disarray, but that's partly because of you shutting down the SuperNet and our communications. If they were to find out what you planned to do here, you may not win against 2 million people on our Earth! Our home! We, *barbarians* and *cretins*, won't give it up without a fight!"

Ben's Uncle then gestures to the people along the shoreline.

"The truth is out there, Abraham. In fact! You are the one that filmed this whole damn thing for the entire town to see. And if I know people... there are a few out there that are recording this right now and uploading it to the SuperNet for the rest of our kind to see. Since you so kindly opened back up our communications to get your message out to us. Your arrogance has bested you, Abraham. And it will be your downfall. Mark my words..." Uncle Steven says, and points out to Abraham.

This gets a confused look from Abraham and then his head is spinning, looking at the thousands of people that are still on the shore of Lake Gregory. After a moment, he then focuses directly on Steven.

Oh shit... he's really pissed off now. Watch out Uncle. Ben thinks as he sights in on Abraham, specifically his rising MECCU.

"So be it! You want to act like children, you'll be treated as such! This complicates things, but we are still superior to your kind in every way! Now it's time to prove that!" Abraham shouts.

"Kill them all!" Abraham shouts.

"Oh shit... shit just got real!" Ben blurts out.

"This guy is literally insane!" Eileen adds.

Ben is surprised when he doesn't see blue orbs flying away from the cannons the very next second. On the other hand, he's overjoyed that their pause in following orders granted his Uncle enough time to tap his MECCU and bring up his AE. The Federalists must be confused from the order or are just shocked to see their leader out of his mind and irate.

"Quick! Get behind the force field and get to the STARU! I'll hold them back!" Uncle Steven yells at Alexander and the others on the platform with him.

"The what?!" Alexander questions.

"I said kill them all! This settlement is lost! Nothing but mindless *barbarians*! Kill them all now!" Abraham shouts as a blue orb leaves his own IMD and bounces off of Uncle Steven's AE, sending a radiant blue wave all around it.

Angry at not killing his Uncle, Abraham shifts his aim toward one of the people on the platform that was not behind the AE yet. A blue orb hits the man directly and he goes limp, falling into the lake.

"Get in the damn spaceship, Alexander! Now!" Uncle Steven yells again.

Alexander doesn't question this time. Instead he picks up a girl under each of his arms and runs up the small bridge and into the STARU. Another person outside of his Uncle's AE falls to another blue orb coming from Abraham's IMD.

At that moment, several blasts from the STARUs hit the platform where his Uncle is standing. Three more people go limp, with one falling into the lake and the other two falling atop of the platform. The other four people must have made it inside of the STARU, because Ben cannot see them when the blue waves disperse. What he does see is his Uncle down on one knee and his AE riddled with bright yellow cracks.

"Nooo!!! Uncle!" Ben shouts as he opens fire on Abraham with Uncle's .308.

Eileen opens up fire next to him without any words.

::Crack::

::Crack::Crack::Crack::

::Crack::Crack::Crack::

The rounds hitting Abraham's platform get his and the other Federalist's attention. Ben can see Abraham smirk and then the other Federalists start firing in their direction, with blue orbs hitting all around them and radiant blue waves going over their own AEs.

Ben sights back in on Abraham's MECCU, with his IMD now solely focused on his Uncle.

Hang in there, Uncle!

::Crack::

Ben starts to see bright yellow cracks where he is trying to hit the same place over and over again, aiming for Abraham's right arm.

::Crack::

::Crack::Crack::Crack::

::Crack::Crack::Crack::

::Crack::

A bright yellow crack forms in his field of vision, to his left. He then quickly looks over at Eileen, to see several bright yellow cracks forming on her AE as well.

Shit! We're running out of time!

Ben then hears gunfire erupt to his left from the parking lot for the trail head. He then sees muzzle flashes come from the other side of the lake, the boating ramp parking lot northwest of them hitting the shields on the STARUs above them. Some of the Federalists that were shooting at them shifted aim to the crowds in the different parking lots.

"Looks like the people of Crestline finally caught on!" Eileen yells over at him.

Ben watches in terror as several of the STARUs shift aim toward the people in the parking lots. The people panic and many of them fall to the ground, after a blue dozer orb impacts them, sending out flashes and waves of radiant blue over the people in the parking lots.

"Oh no!" Eileen shouts. "Those poor people!"

After a few seconds, Ben forces himself to tear his eyes away from the frightful scene of *sleeping* people in the parking lots, with the survivors running for their lives.

Stay focused, Ben! Focus... What about Uncle?! How are you holding up, Uncle?

Ben looks through his scope at his Uncle and doesn't see him, but rather a bright yellow wall that is his failing AE. His Uncle's AE force field is within seconds of collapsing, leaving him open to the *dozer* attackers and ending his life. Ben's mind is racing with fear and anxiety.

His Uncle may not have been his father, but Steven Reilly had always looked out for him over the years. What is more, he had been there for them, Ben, Eileen, Alexander, and now Mia and Isabelle, through all of this chaos from the *Blue Hole Radius*. Ben had thought about it many times. Aside from his own folks, he couldn't think of a better person on this Earth. He was smart, strong, honorable, compassionate, and always figured things out. The dreadful thought crosses Ben's mind.

Did he know?! Is that why this was his plan?! To give the sadistic maniac a target and distract him?!

Ben's mind races further. *You planned this! Didn't you?! You knew that if you could get Abraham off his game and show his true colors that he would drop his guard and lose his shit. Was dying part of your plan Uncle!?*

Ben tries to shake the thought of his Uncle dying from his head.

Dammit! No! Not today!

He sights back in on Abraham's MECCU.

::Crack::

He expels the spent brass and loads another into the chamber, slamming the bolt home.

::Crack::

Ben watches as a small whole is newly formed, giving Ben the ability to shoot Abraham's MECCU. The hole is close to the size of a basketball but should hopefully be all he needs to hit his mark.

"Yes!" Ben exclaims. "Finally!"

He expels the spent brass and sends the bolt back home

::Click::

Shit! Shit! Shit! Not now!

Ben fumbles for another ten-round magazine for the .308 bolt-action rifle. After what feels like an hour, he's able to release the empty magazine and insert the full one, pushing the bolt home and a round into the chamber.

He sights in on Abraham's MECCU as a blue orb is forming out of the end of the IMD. The blue orb releases and he fires.

He sees the MECCU shatter and blood splatter on Abraham's arm. Looking through the scope, he can see a screaming Abraham holding what was left of his right arm. He quickly shifts his focus over to his Uncle.

"NOOOOO!" Ben yells out! "Uncle!"

Ben looks in horror as his Uncle is lying face down on the platform, along with several others of the fallen townspeople on the platform.

"Maybe he just collapsed?! Maybe he's okay?!" Ben blurts out.

"What?! What's happening?!" Eileen yells out at him.

To thwart any hopes that Ben still had, several blasts from the STARUs in the sky release the larger blue orbs from their cannons, with each of them hitting the platform where Steven Reilly is. The platform is covered in a blue flash, followed by the disbursement of blue waves all over his Uncle.

"You son of a fucking bitch! You piece of fucking shit! I'm going to fucking kill you, Abraham!" Ben yells as he stands up and sights back in on Abraham.

Sighting in on him, he sees that he's still holding his arm. Moreover, he notices that Abraham's now missing his right hand.

"Good, motherfucker! I hope that fucking hurts!" Ben yells, as though he can hear him.

Ben's slightly stunned and thinks he can actually hear him, because he stopped screaming about his arm and his focus is pointed in his direction.

::Crack::

Ben puts a round right where Abraham's face is, producing a bright yellow crack in his AE.

::Crack::Crack::Crack::

Eileen empties her magazine and goes to reload another thirty-round magazine into her rifle.

The mixed smells of dirt, carbon, sweat, and trees fill his nose as he hears movement come from the Leviathan.

Ben then pauses as he sees even larger cannons protrude from the Leviathan, with massive blue dozer orbs forming at the end of the CSDs. These dozer orbs are the size of SUVs and small trucks.

After a quick, dreadful thought of the cannons being faced toward himself and Eileen, he looks at Eileen with wide eyes. Unable to produce words, he looks back to the Leviathan as the blue dozer orbs are released from the cannons.

Is this it? Is this really the end this time? How can we win against those kinds of weapons? Dammit! There has to be a way to beat these assholes! Abraham must pay!

Ben's shockingly amazed as he watches the blue orbs hit the STARUs in the air, and not hit them or the other people on the ground.

What's happening, right now?! Seriously, what the shit!?

"They did it! They took control of the Leviathan! Ben! They did it!" Eileen exclaims.

With the realization of what Eileen says hitting him. He looks back to the platform where his unmoving Uncle's body lay, alongside several others on the platform. Still unable to produce words, Ben raises his rifle back up and sights in on Abraham, with only one thought now on his mind.

Kill

::Crack::

The bright yellow crack spreads.

Ben expels the spent brass and chambers another round in his Uncle's .308, staying sighted in on Abraham's head. He can see his eyes, which are a bright blue color... just like his. The look on his face is a mixture of pain, anger, and confusion. It looks like Abraham's staring directly at Ben and his rifle.

Ben still only has one thought on his mind...

Kill

::Crack::

Ben's view is obstructed by something and he pulls his eye away from the scope after that last shot. He's angered to see a STARU blocking his field of vision of Abraham.

"AHHHHH! Get out of the way! You fucking flying freight car!" Ben yells at the STARU.

A few seconds later, the STARU seemed to oblige his request and takes off, heading west toward the valley. Ben sights back in to find the platform empty... no Federalists on it and certainly no Abraham. Ben's eyes go wide in disbelief.

"AHHHHHHHH! You get back here and face me you fucking coward!" Ben yells as he takes aim at the fleeing STARU.

::Crack::

::Crack::Crack::Crack::

::Crack::

His and Eileen's rounds keep on going, not knowing if they are hitting the escaping STARU with Abraham Jackson on it due to its speed. Ben watches in a fueled rage as the other STARUs follow the one with Abraham on it.

"Abraham!!!!!" Ben yells out.

Ben looks over to where the STARUs just were... now somewhere else in the *Blue Hole Radius* or the rest of the world. He then looks back to the parking lot to his left. He can see the asphalt riddled with sleeping bodies... not actually sleeping, but all dead. He looks across the lake to the other parking lot and sees the same scene of bodies on the ground in awkward positions of sleep, never to awake again.

"Ben, they are gone!" Eileen shouts out at him. "Snap out of it! We have to go check on the others. They could be hurt!"

Ben turns to Eileen with wild eyes of hurt, pain, and rage. Before he can respond, something grabs his attention from above the Leviathan. It's another massive spaceship, looking to be the same size as the Leviathan.

"Oh! What the hell! What the crap is this shit now!" Ben yells out at the massive spacecraft above the Leviathan.

"Really! Can't we catch a damn break! What now?!" Eileen yells out, alongside him.

A loud voice comes out from the gigantic spacecraft, "This is Commander Yang, aboard the Galileo! Captain Jackson, you are to surrender immediately or be fired upon and destroyed! Cease and desist or have your entire Federalist force perish!"

"Yeah! It's a little late for that! Those assholes already got away! Thanks for showing up late to the fight!" Ben yells out at the interstellar spacecraft known as the Galileo.

Ben then looks back to the fallen figure of his Uncle Steven Reilly. With his Uncle's .308 rifle now in his right hand, he grips the shoulder stock intensely, making his hand hurt. He disregards the pain and he looks at the lifeless platform, and then off into the distance... where Abraham and the other Federalist had fled. He looks back to the figure of his Uncle, an unmoving figure.

"AAAAAAHHHHHHHHHHHHHHHHH!!!!" He yells into the sky, and Eileen is at a loss for words to console his grief and loss.

Ben's vision goes bright white, and he feels like he's in the clouds. An instant later he feels like he comes crashing down, hitting something hard. Pain sears through his entire body. He tries to look around, but realizes that his eyes are closed with his eyelids feeling ridiculously heavy.

"Ugh... Ow... What the crap happened?" Ben moans.

"Ben!? Oh, thank goodness!" A woman's voice says from next

to him.

He forces his heavy eyelids open, revealing a much blurrier vision of the beautiful woman from his dream with the bright green eyes. He blinks several more times and his vision focuses a little better.

"What happened?... Where am I?" Ben says groggily.

"Why do I feel like I was hit by a truck?" He adds.

He feels as though he cannot move his limbs, and his mind is still very foggy. Half of his mind still thinking he's standing along the shore of Lake Gregory.

"Oh my gosh, Ben! I'm here! It's me, Eileen. You are safe on the Leviathan..." The woman says, and starts to sob again.

"It's been four days! You have been asleep for four days, since the surgeries. I'm so happy you're awake!" She adds.

Eileen? Four Days? Surgeries? The Leviathan? AHHHHHH!

A searing pain surges through his head and it feels as though his head is on fire and being frozen at the same time.

"AHHHHHHHHH!" He screams out in pain.

"Oh No! Alicia! Alexander! Someone get in here!" The woman shouts.

The pain continues in his head and it feels as though it's now coursing through his body.

"What happened?!" Another woman's voice says.

"I don't know! He started waking up and then he started scream-ing! He's in pain! Please do something!" The woman with the green eyes next to him says.

"AHHHHHHHHH!" He screams out in pain once again.

He then feels an ice-cold pinch in his arm which spreads through his entire body. The pain swiftly recedes, and his mind goes foggy again.

The other woman speaks again, sounding like she's on his other side, opposite of the green-eyed woman. "We've never done the procedures on a person of this age before, Eileen. At least not since the colonization of E2... It was successful, but it may take more time for his body to adjust to the..."

23

LESLIE YANG

LESLIE YANG LOOKS over the world of her ancestors from the control deck of the Galileo interstellar spacecraft. She stands next to her father, Commander Thomas Yang, and several other survivors from E2. She looks over Earth One, or E1, with amazement. It's slightly smaller than her home planet, but it looks so pure and pristine to her.

The Galileo has the viewpoint of looking down onto the North American continent and the Arctic, as well as a good amount of the South American continent.

She can see that the Arctic and the northern half of North America is covered in white, being covered in ice and snow. She can see that South America looks to be lush and green, but North America doesn't look exactly as she recalls from her memory bank of pictures of Earth One. Most of the eastern side of the continent appears to be under water now. What was once known as the Floridian Peninsula is now completely covered by the Atlantic Ocean.

What is more, she notices that an extensive desert region now exists, encompassing a majority of the eastern coastal region and of what's left of the eastern continent. The landmass connecting the two continents, Central America, is just as lush and green as South America.

Their destination, the *Blue Hole Radius*, is surrounded by what appear to be mountain ridges and more green and lush areas. The monitors indicate that there are forests that run from the *Blue Hole Radius*, all the way down to Central America.

I wonder if there are still ancient structures from their time. I wonder if any of the seven wonders that we learned of are still intact.

"Take the Galileo in closer, Lieutenant Willis. Ensure that we are not observable through the Leviathan's radar systems. The element of surprise is essential to our survival." Her father says calmly.

"Right, Sir. Will do." Lieutenant Willis replies.

Leslie looks over to her father. Seeing that he's remaining stoic and calm in these times amazes her. Nonetheless, she knows that there's a deep seed of hatred and rage beneath that calm exterior. She knows this because she feels it too... for her younger brother, for her mother, and everyone else that was lost on E2 two months ago.

"We may be incredibly outnumbered, but we still have the element of surprise on our side." He says as he turns to look at her.

"Incredibly outnumbered is an understatement, Sir. Whereas, it appears only the Leviathan successfully made the journey, it's still likely one hundred versus our twelve." Leslie replies to her father.

Being a Lieutenant in the Utopian Union, and with her father being the Commander of the Exploratory and Security Command, she knew better than to refer to him as father, especially considering recent events.

"Maybe so. Nonetheless, for the sake of our species, we must do what needs to be done. It would be favorable for Abraham Jackson to face justice for his crimes against humanity. However, the survival of the human species is much more important than our own retribution." Her father replies.

Our own retribution! Really? Mom and Calvin are dead! Along with the rest of E2! That Rotter Piece of Shit needs to suffer the worst of fates! Leslie screams inside her head.

She would rather say these words for all to hear, but knows better than to speak so harshly against her father. They had already all been through so much, and there were only twelve of them left on the Galileo and another 201 survivors back on E2, looking for other survivors and to rebuild... if they could even rebuild civilization with a mere 201 citizens of the Utopian Union and whoever else they might find.

Obviously, seeing her frustration with his wording, her father adds, "I feel your frustration and rage, my daughter. However, we must think of our future rather than our own selfish ideals. We are far past the realm of being able to be selfish, and won't return to that time anytime soon. I assure you though... my second priority, aside from ensuring the survival of the human species, is to make Abraham pay for his crimes... for his global genocide."

Leslie stares at her father for a moment, uncertain whether or not to speak. After a short silence, she pauses and then looks back to the beautiful scenery of Earth One from her orbit, high above.

Through her peripheral vision, she sees him nod in acceptance of her acknowledgement of his directives and faces forward. "Where exactly is the Leviathan and the Federalists, Lieutenant Evans?"

"Based on our surveillance, they are on the eastern edge of the *Blue Hole Radius*, Sir. Also, Sir... based on recent images... there appears to be a conflict being engaged upon in the Leviathan's vicinity." Lieutenant Evans replies.

"I see, Abraham is wasting little time with enforcing his will on these poor people. As if they have not already had enough to deal with..." Commander Yang says, and sighs heavily.

"Lieutenant Willis, take us in nice and slow. Hopefully, this engagement of Abraham's results in our favor and his folly." Commander Yang orders.

The Galileo moves out of Earth One's orbit above North America, and heads for the *Blue Hole Radius*. Specifically, for where the Leviathan has landed and is apparently in a conflict with the survivors from Earth One.

Yes... I hope it's in our favor and your folly, you Shit. Let's just hope you don't fall during your folly. A quick death is too good for you, Abraham

Jackson... you cowardly disgrace of a human being. Leslie thinks to herself, recalling what happened, just months ago back on E2.

When the Grand Global War had started, she had been stationed upon the Solace Moon Observational Colony for her first duty station, after her attainment of adulthood and citizenship. The SMOC was designed to deal with threats from outside of the Earth Two's orbit and handle them before they became a problem for the citizens on their planet.

Earth Two had a regular habit of being hit by comets. It was found that the large mass of the planet tended to pull stray space debris, providing potentially disastrous consequences for the population of Earth Two. Leslie had enjoyed her two years on the SMOC and found her work rewarding, being a protector of the people.

Leslie was a brand-new Lieutenant and only a second-year citizen of Earth Two, at the young age of 52 years old. Having her father as the Commander of the Exploratory and Security Command, she knew she could get stationed at a more comfortable duty station and less isolated from everyone else, but she didn't want others to think that she did not earn what she was given. So, she chose the isolated Solace Moon Observatory Colony.

Calling it a colony was a broad statement, considering that colonies at least had thousands of people within them. No, on SMOC, also referred to as the Solace, there were only 242 citizens of Earth Two on it.

The colony was vast, and had different bases all over the moon with tunnels connecting them, however, there were very few people. In all actuality, it did not take many people to make sure that the Solace was running effectively. With twenty-two bases connected through tunnels, each base consisted of eleven stationed citizens. Even calling them bases was a stretch in Leslie's mind.

Nonetheless, it was peaceful on the Solace, very rewarding, and she grew to know the members of her base very well over the last two years. Lewis, Willis, Evans, Smith, Jones, Taylor, Williams, Roberts, Wright, and Green. Captain Lewis was their lead officer, with herself, Willis and Evans being the two subordinate officers. Smith and the others were enlisted citizens.

Through their service training, following their twenty-five years of academic training, the citizens of Earth two were sorted between officers and enlisted. The citizens were selected for the divergent ranks, based on their completion of their academia years and their personal profiles. Enlisted could always challenge the assignment of being enlisted. However, the challenge took additional trials and testing, and usually took roughly a decade to transcend to the officer ranks.

Leslie had met the requirements to become an officer in the Exploratory and Security and Command with ease, and with additional training from her father as an academic. This was one of the primary reasons she chose the isolated duty station of the Solace. To prove to on-seers of her advancements that she was just like everyone else and earned what she had... despite who her father was.

At the onset of the Grand Global War, Leslie had formally requested to return to Earth Two to assist the Utopian Union against the Federalist Legion. She had been promptly denied her request and was ordered to stay on the Solace. She had a firm idea that it was in direction from her father, but was unsure... with every citizen on the Solace being denied their request to join the fight down on E2.

This created animosity amongst the citizens on the Solace and resulted in several defectors to the Federalist Legion. She never quite understood the romantic notion and idealism of the Federalists. The Federalist Legion was a newly declared faction or revolutionary army in their eyes. It had only been around for close to a decade and was really only a political party, up until six months prior to the demise of the Utopian Union. Up until that point she thought everything on E2 was peaceful and going well. She was deadly wrong.

She was shocked when Wright and Green defected to the Federalists, abandoning their post at the Solace with multiple others. They had stolen a STARU and headed back down to E2. She was sure that they would meet a traitor's death and felt sorry for them. She still didn't know what became of them and the others that defected from the Union, but she figured it likely that they died with the rest.

It became evident once her father explained why the Federalists went against them, that discontent and revolt had been brewing for the last decade from the self-declared leader of the Federalist Legion, Captain Abraham Jackson.

The history books, their history books... her history book... will tell the tale of the Grand Global War lasting a decade, from the beginning of the Federalist Legion faction to the global genocide of E2's 800 million souls, and how the war criminal, Abraham Jackson, fled... too afraid to see the destruction that he had created. In reality, the real fighting only lasted a few hours and calling it a fight, or a grand scale battle, would be absolutely wrong and inaccurate. It was a massacre at a whole new level of atrocity, in the wake of Abraham Jackson.

Since the end of the Grand Global War and most of the lives on E2, she had researched everything she could find out about Abraham Jackson. She wanted to know him inside and out. With the help of her father, she learned as to why this man saw it necessary to destroy human civilization on their home world... killing somewhere around 800 million souls, Federalists and Utopians alike.

Leslie had never met the man prior to seeing propaganda videos. She knew he was only two decades older than her and already a captain of his very own interstellar spacecraft. After the dust had settled, it was hard for her to understand why he hated the Union so deeply and why he committed such a horrific act of genocide.

Two months later, after the Grand Global War, Leslie knew the man to be a true coward, unable to admit defeat or that he was wrong to mislead so many people of E2. When it was apparent that his faction was losing steam and the error of their ways was being displayed for all to see, he used the massive arsenal of *sleepers* he had aboard the Leviathan and Renaissance to make sure that he was the one who wrote their history.

It had been two months since her father, Commander Thomas

Yang, brought the Galileo to the Solace to visit his daughter during those difficult times. It was during that visit, with her father only having a skeleton crew aboard the ship, that Abraham Jackson launched his deadly assault of mass genocide on E2.

Her father explained that Abraham likely thought himself to be on the planet, because his visit was not scheduled and he had recently made his movements much more discrete, with the turmoil and discontent of the Union and the Legion rising. He had even opted to come visit her on an interstellar craft that was not his own. The Galileo had originally been under Captain Brown's command.

Whereas her father survived, the Council, Congress, and Oversight Committee all perished with the rest of the population on E2.

Fortunately, depending on how you use the term, there were 201 loyal citizens still aboard the Solace, plus her father's crew of twelve. Her father ordered that there should be 22 men and 22 women remain behind on the Solace. One purpose was to continue to protect E2 and the secondary purpose was to begin repopulating. He explained that it was their duty to begin to do so, or that our species would surely perish. Whereas, the order seemed unfair to many, especially the women... they did not object, having seen the footage of what happened on the ground below. The citizens were left on Solace on a volunteer basis, with the remaining 157 survivors of the Solace and 12 members of the Galileo going back to the ground.

Her father asked for volunteers from Leslie's base unit and his own skeleton crew, to accompany him to Earth One. Leslie figured his logic to be that they'd be loyal to him and her, likely reducing the idea that there would be a mutiny on the way or when they reached Earth One. It was smart and logical, but it worried Leslie that there still may be Federalists in their midst.

As it turns out, all of them volunteered, forcing her father to handpick a skeleton crew to go after Abraham. He explained that he didn't want to lose more precious human life than necessary, should they fail in their journey for justice.

After they had returned to the ground to survey the massive scale of global genocide, Leslie knew he could not deny her the chance to find Abraham and bring him to justice. Not after having to bury her brother and her mother.

In the end, he chose eight of his original crew, as well as Willis, Evans, and Leslie. She had insisted she was accompanying him. He ordered the rest to stay on E2 to rebuild.

The citizens returning to and staying on E2 had a duty to their species that was two-fold as well. Their first objective was to search for more survivors, on the off chance that there were some who shielded from the devastation of the multitude of *sleepers*. Their second duty was to begin repopulation and await the return of Commander Yang or prepare to defeat Abraham Jackson... in the likelihood that Commander Yang failed.

It had been two months since they left 157 known souls on E2 and 44 souls left on the Solace. She had hoped desperately that they would find more survivors, but knew how effective the *sleepers* were. Despite the odds being stacked against them, she had faith in the others. Faith that they would rebuild their home and begin their civilization all over again.

They had the knowledge and the technology. Whereas, their numbers were extremely low, she had faith that they would endure. She also gained hope from the realization that there was still Earth Three...

Traveling across the stars, across 1,402 light years, to find Abraham Jackson and his Federalist followers. She had begun to ask herself why anyone would commit such terrible acts. She thought of how she would confront him and ask him when he was brought to justice.

Now, looking over Earth One, descending upon the Leviathan and the Federalists... descending upon Abraham, it didn't matter to her. She no longer thought of why or wanted to understand the ins and outs of Abraham Jackson.

She simply wanted justice. She wanted justice for her brother, Calvin Yang, who was only a decade away from becoming a full-fledged citizen. Taken away from this world at the young age of 40. She wanted justice for her mother, Amy Yang, who was a wonderful educator at one of the most prestigious academies on E2. Taken away from her passion of teaching and her family at the age of 149 years old... with close to another good century left in her natural lifespan.

Despite the concepts of revenge or idealism or other selfish traits being indoctrinated out of her over the first fifty years of her life, she knew she wanted more than simply justice. She wanted revenge for her family and all of the other families that Abraham Jackson had put to *sleep* on E2. She wanted to make him suffer for all of eternity... and regardless of the calm demeanor that her father displayed, she knew he felt the same.

Death would be too much of a mercy for you, Abraham Jackson. If... No... When I get my hands on you, you won't simply go to sleep. You will be awake through all of the pain and suffering you shall endure, you Rotter Piece of Shit!

The Galileo descends over the Leviathan, with every CSD, and newly developed CSA, pointed at the Leviathan and the surrounding STARUs. Over the small body of water, she can see a battle unfolding beneath her and the Galileo.

You better not die yet, Abraham! Not until I get my hands on you! You waste of human flesh!

24

BENJAMIN REILLY

BEN SEES his Uncle waving to him from the front porch of his cabin. He looks younger to Ben somehow. Ben looks down to his hands and his lower body. He feels younger. He doesn't have a mirror or anything to check his reflection, but he feels younger, like he's a teenager.

He has some recollection that something terrible has happened to his Uncle, but it seems like a distant memory.

That's right! I'm here for the summer! To stay with Uncle Steven! Mom and Dad just dropped me off. I wonder what the twins are doing?!

Ben looks off to his left, hearing a roar. He sees a Tyrannosaurus Rex walking down the street. Ben smiles at the enormous creature, unafraid. He sees a Stegosaurus bouncing around like a colossal bunny rabbit, and the T-Rex looks to Ben and then the other dinosaur. It roars and heads off toward the bouncing stegosaurus.

Cool! Ben thinks to himself, as he's unafraid of the massive creatures down the street.

Ben looks back to his smiling Uncle. "Hi Uncle!" He shouts at him.

Ben tilts his head in confusion as his Uncle says something, only twenty feet or so away... but he can't hear his voice. He only sees his lips moving.

Suddenly, the cabin gives way to his Uncle Steven standing on top of some sort of dark surface. He looks around him and realizes that he's on the lake. Ben feels like he's further away from his Uncle now, but he's still waving at Ben and smiling.

He looks down and sees that he's on the shore of Lake Gregory. He notices that his hands and his lower body look bigger now... he's bigger now. He also notices some sort of big bracelet looking thing on his left arm, and he sees he's holding a rifle in his right.

"What's going on?" He says in a much deeper voice. He feels older than he did a few seconds ago.

"I'm so sorry, Ben." A woman's voice says next to him.

Ben looks to his left and sees a beautiful, naturally tanned woman with bright green eyes. He feels his heart race as he sees her, but he's confused. She's crying, with tears slowly coming out of those bright green eyes.

"Are you okay?... Who are you?" Ben says to the woman.

Ben blinks and sees that he's back on the shore of Lake Gregory, looking at his Uncle smiling and waving.

What just happened?

He looks to his right again, and sees the beautiful, green-eyed woman... still crying.

"Eileen?" Ben says, remembering her name from the bright room he was just in, with that place now seeming like a dream... a very painful dream.

She simply continues to stand there looking at him, with tears flowing out of those bright green eyes.

Ben turns his attention to his Uncle on the dark surface, hovering over the shimmering lake. He notices that his Uncle is no longer smiling, waving, and looking at him. He's looking over to his left, seeing a massive spaceship in the background, with another... *platform*... hovering over the shimmering lake.

Ben sees a man standing on top of the platform, and instantly feels a burning rage enter his mind and body.

"Abraham." Ben says, as he grits his teeth.

The man smiles at him and then raises his right arm, with the same oversized bracelet thing that he has on his left arm.

MECCU... He thinks to himself.

The man stares at Ben, smiling.

Abraham Jackson! Ben thinks with pure hatred and rage, and his thought echoes around the whole lake as though he's shouting it from a megaphone.

A small blue orb appears outside of his MECCU. Ben's eyes go wide as he shifts his focus back to his Uncle. The second he does, he sees that his Uncle is covered in a radiant blue wave. Uncle Steven then closes his eyes and falls to the ground.

"NOOOOOOOOO!" Ben yells.

He instinctively raises his rifle and takes aim, sighting in on Abraham. He doesn't hear the gunshot, but he sees that Abraham is screaming without any sound coming out. He sees that he's holding his right arm.

Ben smiles with a grin when he sees that his right hand is missing.

"I hope that hurts, mother fucker!" Ben yells at him.

Abraham stops screaming and stares at Ben, dropping his injured arm to his side, letting it bleed profusely. Abraham doesn't say a word, but only stares at him. Then a large cloud flies in front of him, blocking him for a second. The cloud quickly dissipates, and Abraham is no longer there. He's gone.

"You sack of fucking shit! I will find you, Abraham!" Ben yells into the sky and he feels the whole world shake through the vibration of his voice. With his voice echoing along the lake and through the mountains.

He then feels a soft hand in his and looks to his side, seeing the beautiful green-eyed woman. Ben feels an instant wave of calmness expand over his mind, body, and soul.

"Eileen." Ben says to her. "What do I do now?"

Eileen has stopped crying now, but she doesn't answer him. She just stares at him.

"Eileen? What should I do? I don't know where to go from here..." Ben asks her.

Her lips don't move, but he hears her voice loudly. "Come back to me, Ben. Please wake up... Please wake up..."

Ben's vision goes bright white once again, and he feels like he's in the clouds. This time, he doesn't come crashing down. Instead it feels as though he floats down. His eyes don't feel as heavy as the last time he was in this bright white room. He braces for the pain that he associates with this room and the brightness, but no pain comes.

He sighs, heavily.

"Where am I?" He says as he begins to open his eyes.

With his vision clearing, he sees Eileen at his side again with those bright green eyes.

"Ben!?" Eileen shouts with panicked excitement. "Are you okay?! Do you feel any pain this time?!"

Eileen then turns her head. "Alexander! He's awake again! Alicia, please bring more of that sedative, just in case!"

"Eileen... why are you yelling?" Ben says as he smiles at her.

"Oh! I'm sorry Ben..." She says and quickly changes the volume level of her voice. "Is your head hurting again? Alicia said it was a side effect of the procedures combined with your age. She said that your brain had pretty much rewired itself, afterwards... since you already had so many memories. I guess they do this to their infants to avoid this sort of reaction. But she also said you knew the risks..."

"My head's feeling a little fuzzy, but it doesn't hurt." Ben replies.

She smiles at him. "Good, I'm glad."

Then her expression changes to one he knows well.

She's pissed...

"So, now let's talk about how you ran off without telling me, and thought it smart to have their technological advancements surgeries done... without telling me, I'll remind you again... Do you know how incredibly stupid and dangerous that was?" Eileen says in a normal tone of voice, but with a very angry pretense to it.

"Uhhh." Ben starts and then feels flashes of pictures in his head.

He raises his right hand and pinches the bridge of his nose.

He hears the tone in her voice change. "Oh no... are you okay?"

"Yeah, I think so... just give me a second really quick." Ben replies.

He focuses on the images popping up in his head, like a photo reel.

Not pictures, memories...

He stops the reel and it stops on a photo that shifts into a live memory. He's inside a bathtub with bubbles, and the water's warm. He has a toy battleship in front of him and a purple octopus. He watches as he plays with the two toys and notices that he cannot interact with the memory. Only watch it. He then hears a soft voice from his left and the live memory shifts to a very young version of his mother.

"Mommy!" A young squeaky voice yells.

Ben thinks the age is no older than three or four.

Pause. He thinks to himself.

He's surprised to see the live memory pause, freezing his mother in place at the doorway of their family home bathroom.

Wow! What the hell? When was this? Ben thinks to himself.

Next, without realizing it, he thinks Location and Time.

My family home, in Riverside. December 5th, 1992 at 1902.

The thought was his own, but felt more rigid... more precise and robotic.

What the shit?

"Ben, are you sure you are alright?" He hears Eileen ask.

He's drawn out of his memory and he's now looking at Eileen. "Yeah... I think so."

"Okay... because you said to give you a second and then your face went blank and you just stared off like a freaking zombie, Ben." She says looking at him. "Are you sure you are not in any pain? Like last time?"

"Last time?" Ben asks.

"Yeah... you woke up three days ago and started screaming in pain. Alicia had to give you one of their sedatives and you've been out ever since." Eileen explains.

"Oh... yeah" Ben says, seeing the live memory pop up in his mind... from three days ago.

"So, what? I've been out for about a week, then?" Ben asks, to confirm his live memory.

Eileen nods. "Yes, Ben. Because of your reckless decision, you have been in a comatose state for a week now."

Ben looks at her in the eyes. "And you've been here the whole time?"

"Well... most of the time. I've been staying on the Leviathan with Alexander, Alicia, Lieutenant Leslie Yang, and many of the others. It's safer on this ship than it is out there. At least until we actually locate Abraham and the rest of the Federalists." She explains.

Ben bolts upright, startling her. "Abraham! Where's that son of a bitch!" Rising so quickly, Ben feels dizzy and light-headed.

"Calm down cowboy..." Alexander says, entering the room. "You've been out for a week. Let's get some more rest and some solid foods into you before you go running off again."

"Yeah! Bullshit... You are not leaving my sight again, Ben. Not until I know you won't run off and do some more dumb crap like getting some advanced implant put into the back of your skull, plus a series of injections to steady your aging process." Eileen snaps at him.

Ben scratches the back of his head, "What day is it?"

"Don't you have an automatic calendar in that upgraded brain of yours, now? It's Friday, Ben. July 19th of 3433." Eileen lectures him.

"Yeah, Ben. Catch your breath and get caught up on what's going on. Plus, Sergeant Burke and Lieutenant Yang tell me it may take some getting used to your new advancements, and that memory bank that's still booting up in that thick head of yours." Alexander adds.

Ben grits his teeth and then looks back to Eileen, and then is softened by her eyes. "Where's my Uncle's body, Eileen?"

Eileen sighs. "He's in storage. We wanted to wait for you to wake up before we had a ceremony. Most of the other survivors already had their ceremonies for their lost loved ones."

Ben then recalls the CSDs firing upon the crowds of people and the radiant blue waves everywhere... through his live memory snapshot.

This is going to take some getting used to.

"How many casualties?" Ben asks.

Eileen turns and looks at Alexander, with him sighing. "There were 4,357 casualties on our side of the battle, Ben."

"Oh, dear God!" Ben blurts out.

"Yes, Ben." Eileen says, grabbing his attention. "That's why we are all hiding in the Leviathan until we find Abraham. The survivors are scared to death, with a lot of them being women and children."

"What? Why? Do we even have any clue as to where that POS is?!" Ben says, getting angry all over again.

"Before you guys arrived. Before Steven stepped in and saved me and the girls... Abraham had already started executing those that would not come out of their homes and to the lake. He was abducting the women and children and killing the rest. Additionally, there were those that were in the crowds that were struck down in the parking lots." Alexander explains.

"That's insane! And we have no clue where that sick piece of shit is?!" Ben asks his friend.

Burke and another young woman walk into the room. The dark-haired woman with an Asian complexion and dark eyes speaks. "It's good to see that you are recovering well, Benjamin Reilly. My name's Lieutenant Leslie Yang, of the Utopian Union."

Ben is confused by the newcomer and doesn't say a word.

Lieutenant Leslie Yang continues on. "We are searching your Earth for Abraham Jackson. Rest assured Benjamin Reilly, we will find him, in time. However, there are others of your people that need help, aid, and assistance. We have a dozen STARUs out helping other settlements, and the Galileo, under the command of Commander Yang, is out searching for Abraham. Trust me when I tell you that we want him brought to justice just as much as you do."

We'll just see about that...

"Commander Yang, huh? Any relation?" Ben asks.

"As a matter of fact, he's my father... and to be clearer, Abraham killed over 800 million people on E2. We have the same goal, Benjamin Reilly." Lieutenant Leslie Yang says.

"Yeah, we heard about that..." Ben replies.

Lieutenant Leslie Yang nods and gestures to Burke. "Sergeant Burke here will help and assist with your recovery and rehabilitation."

She then looks at Eileen. "Deputy Eileen Rivera, If Sergeant Burke does anything out of the ordinary, report her directly to me and she will be executed for her affiliation with the Federalists. Whereas, my father has given her mercy and the chance to atone, I'm not of the same mind."

Ben sees Burke visually gulp and get nervous.

Looks like she got in trouble... Ben thinks as he grins at the former Federalist.

"I look forward to working alongside yourself, Benjamin Reilly, and the rest of your people. I shall let you acclimate to your new surroundings and the improved upon status of your body." Lieutenant Leslie Yang says, and exits the room.

"Yeah, nice meeting you too..." Ben says as she leaves the room.

Ben then looks to Burke. "So, Burke... when do we start?"

He tries to move his legs off of the bed and shifts his upper body as well. His legs don't respond, and he goes tumbling off the bed onto the cold floor.

"Holy hell! Ben! Really?" Eileen blurts out as she comes to his aid.

Alexander, Burke, and Eileen help him back up into the bed.

Once he's back in his bed, with a few grunts from the others, Burke looks at him. "Firstly, we need to teach you how to use your memory bank, and you need to let your body recover from being out for a week."

"Yeah, you idiot! What were you thinking?" Eileen asks. "It's a damn good thing that you are pretty, Ben. Geez, I swear!... Are you okay?"

Ben scratches the back of his head and looks around the room, starting at Eileen, Abraham, then Burke.

"Yeah... I think so. But now that I think about it, Alexander was right... I'm pretty damn hungry. Is there anything good to eat on this spaceship?" Ben asks.

Alexander laughs and Eileen just shakes her head.

"Of course you are, Ben... Of course you are..." Eileen replies, shaking her head at him.

She then smiles at him, with those bright green eyes. "Let's see what we can find you on this massive hunk of a spaceship. They do have some pretty good food on here, that's for sure..."

"Good deal then. Let's start there and then I'll worry about putting one foot in front of the other." Ben replies, looking at Eileen.

She smiles at him. "Good! You are finally listening to some common sense. Sounds like these upgrades may have been a good thing after all."

This gets a round of laughter from Alexander and Eileen. Ben smiles back and sees Burke standing there awkwardly.

These upgrades were a good idea alright, despite the loss of a week and that searing pain. These upgrades are going to help level the playing field, so I can hunt down every single one of those murdering Federalist bastards... saving the great Abraham Jackson for last. He's going to pay dearly for what he has done... Ben thinks as he smiles at Eileen and his friend Alexander.

AFTERWORD

Thank you so very much for reading *Living in the Radius: Book 2 of The Radius Series.*

It's my hope that you enjoyed the second installation of this story of survival as much as I have enjoyed writing it.

If you enjoyed reading this book, please consider leaving a review on Amazon.com. As always, it would be greatly appreciated. You can also find D.M. Muga on social media.

Facebook: @DMMUGA

Instagram: @dmmuga

If you would like to read more by D.M. Muga, *Book 3 of The Radius Series* is scheduled to be released in the Summer of 2021.

ABOUT THE AUTHOR

D.M. Muga is a survivalist enthusiast and considers himself somewhat prepared for varying scenarios, based on the ideal that no one can truly be perfectly prepared for any given scenario. *Chance* will always be an unpredictable variable in the equation of life and survival.

D.M. Muga is a United States Marine Corps Veteran, from 2002 to 2007. He has earned several academic degrees, a B.A. in Political Science, an M.A. in National Security Studies, and another M.A. in Education with his focus in History.

D.M. Muga resides in Southern California with his wife and two daughters. He works in the field of Education. He's adamant with his hopes to live out the rest of his life in peace, but prepares for the future, *"planning for the best, but preparing for the worst."*

facebook.com/D.M.MUGA

instagram.com/dmmuga

Made in the USA
Monee, IL
01 November 2021

81168641R00194